MW00435906

THE LAST HOPE

A KATE MURPHY MYSTERY

C.C. JAMESON

The Last Hope

By C.C. Jameson

Copyright © 2018 by C.C. Jameson

All rights reserved. Reproduction in whole or in part of this publication without express written consent is strictly prohibited.

This is a work of fiction. Names, characters, businesses, places, events, and incidents are either the products of the author's imagination or used in a fictitious manner. Any resemblance to actual persons, living or dead, or actual events is purely coincidental.

WARNING: This book is intended for mature audiences and contains disturbing and potentially offensive material.

Thank you for taking the time to read this book. Please leave a review wherever you bought it or help spread the word by telling your friends about it. Thank you for your support.

Published by Creative Communication Solutions Ltd.

Previously published as *Twisting Fate* (ISBNs: 978-0-9940630-0-7, 978-0-9940630-3-8, 978-0-9940630-2-1, and 978-0-9940630-1-4)

—————

ISBN: 978-1-988639-34-5

Last updated June 18th, 2018

Editing by Marley Gibson & Claire Taylor

CHAPTER ONE

Kate Murphy
Secret Hiking Spot, Maine

WARM, salty air kissed Kate Murphy's freckled skin as she sat, perched in surroundings that embodied her emotions.

Early summer rays bombarded the ocean, forming tiny diamonds that sparkled in the distance. Mere minutes later, the same peaceful, glistening water would morph into powerful waves that crashed onto the jagged rocks one hundred feet below Kate's dangling legs, pulverizing any debris that may have been floating along for the ride. She sipped her bottle of water while soaking in her favorite scenery. The soft chirps and warbles of a few birds accompanied her thoughts.

Life was pretty good these days, even though Kate's latest attempt at becoming a detective had been rejected yet again, but at least now she was part of a different district. It meant fresh opportunities and new people. Maybe her next application would be approved.

Kate stood up, finished her drink, and then returned the empty stainless-steel bottle to her backpack. It clunked against her phone, which she dug out: it was 1:03 p.m. Five missed calls and one voicemail.

Weird.

The message must have come in during the past hour when she came into range. All she ever got around here was one bar, and it only appeared if the winds were blowing in the right direction (with no clouds on the horizon) and lucky leprechauns sprinkled their magical signal-boosting powder around her.

Crappy coverage.

She should change cell providers. Then again, there was something to be said for enjoying quiet time and being unreachable, especially when she was here.

She tapped her way to the voicemail screen. Unknown number. She pressed "play" and listened to it over speakerphone.

"Miss Murphy, I'm calling on behalf of Kenneth Murphy. My name's George Hudson, and I'm the defense attorney who's been assigned to your uncle's case. He's been arrested. He wanted me to let you know he's currently being held at the Roxbury Precinct, accused of murder. Your uncle says he's innocent, and I'll do my best to prove that he is. Sorry for leaving this important message on voicemail. I would have preferred doing it in person, but your uncle said I might have a hard time reaching you, and I didn't want to wait too long. I'll give you a call later this week with more details."

What?

Kate jumped to her feet, staring at her now-silent phone. Had she heard that right?

She listened to the message again, this time with the phone pressed against her ear.

She had to head back if she wanted to get enough cell coverage to do anything. Kate stuck her phone back in her bag, strapped it on tightly, and then ran the three miles she'd just hiked, back to her car.

When she reached her Subaru, it was already 1:45 p.m. She was starting to regret her decision to drive out-of-state on her day off. She was 170 miles away from the Roxbury station.

Kate drove fast on the winding, scenic roads, ignoring the breathtaking views she would usually savor. She far exceeded the speed limit, mastering the unpaved bends like a professional race car driver. The skills she'd honed during police training certainly made driving her Impreza even more fun than before, but this time her mind was on autopilot.

Why was Uncle Kenny accused of murder? He was the last of her living relatives, the only human being she felt connected to and loved by. He couldn't have killed anyone.

After fifteen years of psychotherapy, Kate was mostly over the gory memories of finding her own mother, father, and little brother murdered in their family home, throats slit, her mother half-naked and raped, and blood dripping down the kitchen walls.

Today was June 23rd, the twentieth anniversary of that awful day. It was why she'd requested—and had been granted—a day off.

Kenny, her dad's older brother, had taken Kate in when she was thirteen years old. He didn't have children of his own, so he and his wife, Lucy, had decided to adopt her. They'd done the best they could to protect and help her get over her horrible loss and trauma. The therapist's bills had been expensive, especially on Kenny's welder's salary. Lucy's chain-smoking had quickly ruined her health. She'd died of lung cancer when Kate was twenty-three. Tragedies seemed to occur every decade for Kate, and now, at the age of thirty-three, her uncle was in jail. And for murder? Kenny was all she had left in the world.

He couldn't have killed another person, could he? No, no way.

A white-tailed deer crossed the road two hundred feet in front of her, snapping Kate's attention away from the past and returning it to the present. She knew this part of the countryside like the back of her hand. Another two miles and she'd be on paved roads, and then it'd be five more miles to the state highway where she could get decent cell reception.

When she finally reached the end of the cellular dead zone, Kate pressed the voice command on her steering wheel.

"Call the district commander at the Roxbury police station."

Siri confirmed her request, and then Kate heard a ringing

sound, followed by Susan's British accent. "Captain Cranston's desk. How may I be of service?"

"Hi, Susan. It's Officer Murphy."

"Yes. Kate, right?"

"Yeah. I got a voicemail from a lawyer saying my uncle, Kenny Murphy, has been brought in for murder and he's being held at our station. Can I talk to the district commander and find out what's going on?"

"He's in a meeting right now, and there's a queue of people waiting to see him, but I'll let him know you called."

Kate tapped her fingers on her steering wheel and shook her head.

A message wouldn't do much to help Kenny... but that's all Susan could do.

"I'm on my way to the station. I should be there in about two hours. Do you think he'll still be around?"

"I don't know, love. Not sure how long his meeting will be, but doubtful he'll stick around after it's over and he's done seeing these other fine folks. But who knows? You might be able to catch him on his way out. I'll leave him a note to call you back ASAP."

"Thanks, Susan."

Kate returned her focus to the road, sneaking intermittent glances at the phone in her cup holder, and hoping he'd call her back. Then again, why would he? That wasn't proper. She wasn't following the chain of command. She had no right to go to him directly. As far as she knew, there was no official police handbook designating the appropriate person for police officers to talk to when their loved ones were arrested for murder. When she'd first joined the district, Capt. Cranston had told her that his door was always open. She hoped he'd meant it.

A giant billboard promoting Clark Ferguson, a handsome, brown-haired Boston mayoral candidate with a million-dollar smile, welcomed her to Massachusetts. Kate still had a solid hour of driving to get to Roxbury and traffic could be wicked bad. She checked the clock on her dash again: 3:30 p.m.

Today's Tuesday.

She might just get there in time to see Capt. Cranston before he left for the day.

∿

SEVENTY-FIVE MINUTES LATER, Kate veered into the station's lot, parked her car, and then ran three flights of stairs to the district commander's office, only to find it empty and locked.

Shit. Too late.

She wouldn't be able to hear the official word on Kenny's arrest, but she should still be able to talk to her uncle and learn what they'd told him and see if he was doing okay. The poor man was probably scared to death.

She made her way down to the detention area and found the officer on duty; his name tag read "Reynolds." She recognized his face but couldn't remember his first name.

Dave? Don? Dean? One of those "D" names.

"Hey, Reynolds."

"Hey, Murphy. What brings you here? Aren't you supposed to be taking a few days off?"

She smiled. She'd only been here a couple of weeks, but being a female officer seemed to help her male counterparts remember her name... and her schedule? Maybe it had nothing to do with being a woman in a man's world. Wasn't it always easier for any group to remember the new kid's name?

"Today was my only day off. I got a message telling me my uncle has been arrested and is being detained here. Do you have a Murphy in the cell?"

"Let me see. I'm just here for a few minutes covering for Matthews. Bad burrito," Reynolds said with a laugh. He then looked at Kate and became serious again. He returned his attention to the computer screen. "Don't know who he's got in here. Let's see... Kenneth Murphy?"

"Yeah, that's him. Can I see him?" Kate asked.

"Sure, do you need an escort?"

She shook her head. "He's my uncle, no need."

Reynolds nodded and stood to open the door. "You know the drill. Leave your stuff here."

Kate emptied her pockets and left her backpack with him. Reynolds and Kate then walked over to Kenny's holding cell, their footsteps echoing against the bare, white concrete walls. An antiseptic smell reminded her of her last hospital visit. Most cells were unoccupied, and Kate soon spotted her uncle's balding head a few feet away. He was sitting on a jail bed, staring at the floor in front of him. What was left of his hair was restless and out of place. His white mustache had seen better days.

"Kenny!"

He looked up, eyebrows raised, faint dimples appearing on his cheeks from his growing smile.

"Katie, sweetie. I'm so glad to see you."

"Mr. Murphy, please put your back against the wall," Reynolds said. After her uncle complied, Reynolds unlocked the door to let Kate in, relocked it, and then addressed her on his way out. "Holler when you're done. Fifteen minutes max. Matthews will be back shortly."

Kate hugged her uncle. He was seventy-six years old and frail, but his arms held onto her like she was a lifebuoy in a violent storm.

She sat next to him on the bed and looked into his tired, brown eyes. They seemed sadder than usual and confused.

She tapped his leg and gently squeezed his knee, "How are you holding up?"

He answered by raising his shoulders and shaking his head, his mouth forming an upside down U.

"Tell me everything," Kate asked.

"I don't know what happened. Why do they think I killed that man? That's the craziest shit I've ever heard."

"Tell me about the arrest."

"They showed up at my house this morning. Two plainclothes officers with a warrant and four or five uniformed men."

"What did they say?" Kate asked.

"They wanted to know if I was Kenneth Sam Murphy, so I

told them I was. Then, they said I was under arrest for the murder of Paul McAlester."

"Who?"

Kenny's eyes widened. "That's what I said! But one of them got ahold of my wrists and handcuffed me while they read me my rights. They said they had a warrant to search the house. I was too dumbfounded to remember anything else they said after that. Next thing I know, I'm being questioned about what I did three nights ago."

"What did you say?"

"I said I didn't remember, but I probably heated my dinner and watched a movie while drinking a scotch or two."

"You don't remember?"

Kenny shook his head, and Kate felt a black curtain of despair fall over them.

He has no alibi.

"I'm getting old. Most nights blend into one," he said. Then, he gazed at Kate's face, softening some as he smiled at her. "You don't come and visit often enough. All I have left are memories. Some good, some bad. Lately, the awful ones have been on the reel, and I drink to shut them down. Normally works for a few hours until I fall asleep."

Kate hugged her uncle again, feeling guilty for not being there for him more often. Her failed marriage had been at the forefront of her mind lately, and she had needed more alone time than usual. And then the anniversary of her family's murder... That was no excuse, though. Her uncle didn't deserve to be neglected just because she couldn't get her shit together.

"I'm so sorry. I'll make things right. I'll talk to the district commander tomorrow and see if I can find out something new that could help us."

Kenny nodded, and he scratched the back of his neck. A forced smile appeared under his mustache. Kate knew that look too well. It meant he was terrified, just like when he'd found out about his wife's cancer and how large her medical bills were going to be. Kate knew better than to tell him to voice his feelings. No way would an old, Irishman like him spill the contents of his heart.

Changing subjects was always the best option when he scratched his neck or faked a smile.

"I got a call from your lawyer," Kate said. "How did you find him?"

"You know I can't afford one, so they assigned him to me. Seems nice enough."

Kate knew how tight her uncle's finances had been, and still were. He'd been poor for the past twenty years. He ate lots of canned beans and could barely keep the heat on some months. Once again, guilt got ahold of her. She should have given him more than ten percent of her paychecks. He deserved more; especially after all he'd done for her. But she didn't make that much, and the job forced her to live in Boston, which wasn't cheap at all. Ten percent was all she could afford most months. However, she was hopeful things would change soon when she finally made homicide detective and had the chance to get murderers off the street. *Real* murderers, like the one who'd killed her family.

A cacophony of emotions stirred inside her—rage fighting against fear and sadness—but none reached the podium. She hated feeling out of control when facing a terrible situation she couldn't do anything about. Kate forced herself to take a deep breath and see the silver lining to this dark cloud. At least her uncle would be getting three square meals a day for free.

"Most of the court-appointed lawyers are good," she said. "Be honest with him. Tell him everything you can. It has to be a mistake. Did they say anything else?"

Kenny shrugged again and shook his head. "They found my blood and my DNA at the crime scene."

"What?" Kate couldn't comprehend how his genes could have made it there without him. "Did they say where the murder occurred?"

"No, but they asked if I had a car or access to one. He must live somewhere far from me."

"When was the last time you drove?"

"I told them. About thirteen years ago. I sold the car to cover some of Lucy's medical bills. I haven't driven since, not even a rental car. Remember your graduation from the police academy? I took the bus then a cab to get there. Made it in the nick of time."

Kate smiled and kissed him on the forehead. She remembered how much perspiration had been on his shirt that day. He must have run a lot as well after getting out of that cab. He had worn his best outfit: a short-sleeved beige shirt with vertical brown lines, a matching pair of brown pants, and a wide orange tie. But she also clearly remembered the smile on his face when he finally snuck his way to the family section of the reserved seats just as the guest of honor was delivering his speech. Kenny had been so proud of her.

He leaned toward her, his bony hands grabbing hers, and he said, "I'm not perfect, but I'm no murderer. I don't want to die with this label added to the Murphy name. Our lineage has had enough of a bad rap. I still want to take you to Ireland before I die, you know? You need to see the Irish coast for yourself, see how green it is, how beautifully rugged the scenery is. You have to meet your cousins. Our family is bigger than you think. You'd love it there in Cork."

They sat still, hanging onto each other's hands as Kate let their physical bond temper the harsh reality.

The sound of a key in the lock brought her back to the here and now.

"Time's up," Reynolds said.

Kate gave Kenny one last hug and looked at him, "I love you. I'll do everything I can to make this right and get you out, okay? Just be brave and patient, and we'll fix this."

He squeezed her hands, nodded, and, for the first time in the fifteen minutes she'd spent with him, she saw hope appear in her uncle's teary eyes. She had to turn away before her own started to water.

After making her way back from the cells, she grabbed her things from the front desk and then headed home.

~

KATE SAT ALONE in her apartment, realizing there wasn't anything she could do until tomorrow. Nothing but hope that Capt. Cranston would tell her what was really going on and that their evidence wasn't airtight.

In the meantime, she occupied her mind by Googling the victim's name and found two articles that mentioned his death. There was no reference to her uncle... at least not yet. But chances were, his name would be in tomorrow's headlines.

She had to find a way to prove his innocence, and fast.

CHAPTER TWO

Kate Murphy
Roxbury Police Station, Boston

KATE SAT in one of the four padded stainless steel chairs outside the district commander's office, crossing and uncrossing her legs and picking imaginary dirt from under her trimmed fingernails.

His office door was open, but he was sitting at his desk, reading. Susan had told her that he was wrapping up a case, and then he'd see her.

"Murphy, come in," his husky voice called out a few minutes later.

Kate got up and walked in. "Good morning, sir."

His oversized body amplified the power that emanated from him, yet his gray hair and blue eyes, when accompanied by the smile he was beaming at her, turned him into a teddy bear. Maybe this was what they called *innate charisma*. His open hand pointed to the chair in front of his desk, and Kate took a seat.

"Fitting in nicely with the guys here?"

"Sure. No problem there, sir."

"I got this note from Susan," he said, waving a little piece of yellow paper in the air. "Why did you want to see me?"

"My uncle, sir. He was arrested yesterday for murder."

The district commander raised his eyebrows, adding a few horizontal lines to his already streaked forehead.

"Heard about the arrest, but it didn't occur to me that one of our own could be related to him. There are so many Murphys in town."

"He's the only relative I've got. He adopted me when I was thirteen."

"I see. So, you're here because you think he's innocent?"

Kate shrugged. "I know he's innocent. I'd like to prove it, but I don't even know where to start. Maybe... I was hoping I could see the evidence we have against him." She corrected herself as soon as she heard the words leave her lips. "No, I misspoke. I don't want physical access to the evidence. I want to know what proof we have and maybe what possible motives they've come up with, that type of stuff. I know how it is, and I don't want to interfere with the investigation. But, at the same time, I can't just sit here and wait."

He nodded his head toward a file on his desk. "Well, from the brief I got, they found his DNA at the crime scene, so that's gonna be hard to refute."

Kate sat still, not knowing how to push for more.

The district commander turned his attention to Kate's file, which was sitting on his desk. He flipped through pages of notes, sometimes pausing to read entries. Probably stuff her previous supervisors had filled in, past evaluations, commendations and reprimands, or other things like that. She didn't quite know what was in her file. Kate had only been in this district for two and a half weeks. She'd requested the transfer because she thought her chances of becoming a detective would be better here. She'd already been turned down four times at her previous district, and, although she hadn't yet started the process here, she desperately wanted to. She'd aced the detective's exam last year. The interviews were a different story, though. All of that was probably in her file.

"Tell you what, Murphy," he said before leaning back in his chair, his eyes locked on Kate as if sizing her up and contemplating the consequences of what he was about to say. "I can see you really want to be a detective, and I can understand why you'd want to do everything you can to help your adoptive father. I admire that. And your last supervisor thought you could improve your teamwork skills and get more hands-on experience... So, here's what I propose: I'll let the detectives know that you'll sit in on the case as a way to gain more experience, but"—he paused and raised a hand, as if he could put a speed limit on Kate's fast-escalating hopes—"with two conditions."

He lifted his index finger. "You can only do it in your spare time. I need you patrolling the streets and answering calls. We're short-staffed as it is. If you feel like hanging around with the detectives, after or before your shift, that's fine by me. However, this isn't paid overtime. The department won't be liable, and we can't cover you should anything happen, so you're not gonna do any real investigative work with them out on the streets after your regular work hours. You can only shadow them here in the building, all right?"

Kate nodded. "And what's the second condition?"

His middle finger joined his index. "You absolutely cannot touch or come close to the evidence or be involved in changing the direction of the investigation. I don't need to lecture you on the chain of evidence. Don't go near it. If you pay attention to how the detectives talk, think, cooperate, and handle the case, you may learn a thing or two that will help you with your detective's interview next time. But don't get your hopes up for freeing your uncle. Their case is pretty tight."

"Thank you, sir."

As she moved to leave his office, he stopped her. "Hold on a sec before I forget."

He picked up the phone and hit one of the pre-programmed buttons. "Fuller, Cranston here... I've allowed one of our new officers to sit in on the McAlester murder investigation. Her name's Murphy... Yep, she's the accused's niece and adopted daughter."

Kate couldn't hear the man's exact words, but the mumbled voice that reached her ears had grown louder.

"I know, I know... but she won't be able to *do* anything, only sit in. Think of her as a piece of furniture or wallpaper. Conduct your investigation as if she weren't in the room."

The voice at the other end of the line was now so upset that Kate could clearly hear words like "protocol," "inside investigation," "improper," "irresponsible," and "emotional."

"Listen, I'm the district commander, and I've made my decision. When you talk to your team, you may want to present the idea as 'detective training.' She wants to become one anyway. I'll send her down to your desk in a minute or two. Be nice."

He hung up before lifting his head and looking her square in the eyes. "I'm doing this as a favor. I can recognize potential and passion when I see it, but these guys won't be happy to have you around. Be as invisible as possible."

"Of course." Kate understood the meeting was over and got up.

"Fuller's desk is on the second floor, on the right."

"Thanks, sir. I really appreciate your help."

"Don't thank me. Just prove you're worth it," he said. "And close the door behind you."

SMALL VICTORY.

However, Fuller certainly didn't want her there. Best get the introduction meeting over with before she lost her nerves.

She followed Capt. Cranston's directions and stopped at the door labeled "Detective Lt. Mark Fuller."

She knocked and waited.

Nothing.

Knocked again.

Nothing.

Didn't Capt. Cranston just tell him she'd be down to meet him in a couple of minutes? Where'd he go?

She slowly pushed open the door. "Detective Fuller?"

Nobody was in the office.

She closed the door and walked down the hall until she

reached a lunchroom. It was small: a fridge, kitchen sink, half a dozen cupboards, a vending machine, a coffee dispenser, and a few tables and chairs. Two boards on the wall were overflowing with colorful bulletins. An assortment of tea boxes, a container of sugar packets, and a jar of instant decaffeinated coffee occupied the small counter space. An odor of curry lingered in the air. The room was empty except for a couple of plainclothes men sitting at one of the three small round tables, stirring their coffees, a pint of milk sitting on the table between the two of them. She hadn't yet been introduced to the detectives in this district, so she wasn't sure who they were. They certainly looked like detectives in inexpensive suits.

The one in the light gray suit had matching hair, thick bushy black eyebrows, and a salt-and-pepper mustache. He appeared to be tall, reasonably slim, and probably in his early fifties. The other one seemed younger, in his late thirties or early forties, but not as fit. Seated, he looked like he had extra weight around his waist. Maybe he was just big-boned. His outdated brown suit and beige shirt had seen better days. Kate wondered if he'd slept in it. He wore black, plastic-framed glasses like Kate had seen her dad wear in his wedding pictures. The younger man had curly, dark blond hair and had a mischievous grin on his lips.

She decided to address the older man.

"I'm looking for Detective Fuller," Kate said.

"His office is down the hall," he replied, not even bothering to make eye contact with her.

He immediately returned to the one-way conversation he was having with his younger colleague.

Annoyed, Kate put on a smile and insisted, "I'm sorry, but I've just come from his office, and he's not there. Is there anyone I could leave a message with?"

The man turned to face her, shaking his head and frowning. "Detectives don't have secretaries. Just call him and leave him a message."

He returned to his story about his neighbor's lawnmower.

Really?

Kate clenched her teeth and smiled even wider. "I'm really

sorry to bother you again, sir, but would you happen to know his number or extension?"

The other guy broke his silence. "Come on. Just do it, write it down for her." His voice was surprisingly soft and velvety. He could have been a radio DJ for an after-hours jazz program.

The older man sighed, put his coffee mug down, and then retrieved a business card and pen from his breast pocket. He flipped the card over, wrote "x 679," and then handed it to Kate.

"Thank you, I appreciate it," she said, taking the card off his hand. "Have a great day. Sorry to have interrupted your coffee break."

She was glad to walk away from him and wondered if she'd ever met a bigger prick in her life. Matt, her ex-husband, immediately came to mind, so she shook the thought of him away.

Kate returned to the corridor she'd come from, flipped the card, and then stopped in her tracks. The front of the card read "Detective Lt. Mark Fuller."

Jerk!

She decided to let herself into his office. He'd probably be back any minute now. How long could it take him to finish his coffee and laugh at her behind her back with his buddy? She left the door open, sat in one of the two chairs across from his desk, and waited. She noticed a piece of lint on her uniform and flicked it off. He evidently knew who she was. Her name tag said it loud and clear.

"He's just an ass," she muttered.

A few more minutes passed, and Kate focused on her breath. That was what the therapist had shown her to do whenever bad feelings or memories crept up, which they inevitably did.

1-2-3-4-5-6 in, hold it, 1-2-3-4-5-6 out.

1-2-3-4-5-6 in, hold it, 1-2-3-4-5-6 out.

She felt calmer now.

A minute later, a voice spoke from behind her.

"So, you figured out who I was then, Murphy."

She turned around and shot him a sarcastic smile. He was

much taller than she had expected. "I did, Detective. Thank you for so kindly giving me your contact information."

He walked around his desk, sat down, and then scowled at her. "We both know you shouldn't be on this case. Plain and simple. The last thing I want around is an emotional woman crying and whining that her uncle's been wrongly accused."

Kate leaned forward and lowered her voice, just to make sure she wouldn't come across as anything close to emotional.

"I can assure you, Detective, that you won't see or hear me cry or whine. I'm a police officer, and I *will* be a detective one day. Yes, my uncle is the accused here, but I will not take anything personally. I'm good at letting go of personal attachments, believe me."

He waved his hand at her. "You can't mess with our process. You'll see we've got plenty of evidence to prove he's guilty."

"But what if his DNA had been planted by someone else? You wouldn't want to accuse the wrong guy and let the real killer run loose, would you?"

"Why the fuck would someone want to frame your uncle?"

She did her best to remain calm and professional. "What motive would my uncle have for killing a stranger? He's a frail old man who feels bad when he has to kill a fly."

Fuller sat back and stared at Kate.

"Okay, you may have some valuable information on our prime suspect. We have yet to come up with a plausible motive, but you can't speak unless we ask you a question. Capt. Cranston is forcing me here, and as he said, you'll be invisible... You'll be a fucking wallflower and nothing more, understood?"

Kate nodded. "Yep, understood."

He got up, and Kate followed him down the hall to conference room two. It was relatively small for a conference space, but probably the perfect size for a team of detectives to work on a homicide case. One wall had windows looking outside, but the other three were covered from floor to ceiling with corkboards and whiteboards. Pictures of the crime scene and a map were pinned on the corkboard. There were also pictures of her uncle and other people she'd never seen before.

Were they suspects? The whiteboard had a list of possible motives; many items like "financial gain" and "lover's triangle" had been crossed off.

Lover's triangle?

The thought of her uncle involved with a woman other than her deceased aunt made her cringe, but there was no point in thinking about it. It had been ruled out by the detectives.

Fuller turned around and made eye contact with her. "You can't touch anything, understood?"

Kate nodded again and continued moving around the room. The map had two pins on it: her uncle's house and another, which she assumed was the crime scene. File folders were piled on the table, and two computers showed the Boston PD logo floating and bouncing off the edges of their screens.

"The guys will meet this afternoon to discuss. They're wrapping up another case in court this morning," Fuller told her.

"I'm on patrol until 4 p.m. I'll come in as soon as I get back."

"Whatever, but come in plain clothes. I don't want your name tag to affect the team's judgment or behavior."

"I understand."

Kate was going to have to switch her schedule around and work evening or night shifts if she wanted to sit in and help her uncle.

Detective Fuller walked out of the room, and Kate followed.

He closed the door. "Remember to stay out of our way, Wallflower," he said, heading back to his office.

KATE RAN down the stairs two steps at a time and found her shift supervisor. He was easy to spot. At around 6'5", he was the tallest uniformed man in the precinct.

"Sergeant, any chance I could switch shifts for a while? Could I get evenings? Or night shifts?"

Sgt. Anderson had files in his hands and a confused look on his face.

"What? When?"

"I need more time for personal stuff in the day, and I was hoping to switch shifts with someone for a day or two."

"Sure, if you can find someone who's willing to switch with you. Then, run it by me again. Oh, and make sure that person's partner is fine with it, too, because they'll be working with you. I won't let anyone do their patrols alone at night, not even for one shift." He pulled a piece of paper out from one of the files he was holding. "Here's a copy of this week's roster."

"Okay. Thanks, Sergeant."

She glanced at the list of names and wondered which one of these officers would be easiest to approach. She didn't know many of them yet. In the twelve years since Kate had joined the police force, she'd never had a regular partner. She wondered why for a moment. Most cops settled in with a partner, but she'd never done that. Instead, she'd been passed around from cop to cop, partnering up on an as-needed basis with whomever needed a partner for a few days. Either that or she'd worked dayshift, where having a partner wasn't standard procedure, especially with the budget cuts the police were forced to deal with.

She and the others on patrol never had much to talk about. Kate liked to keep her personal life private and didn't want to hear about the ups, the downs, and whatever else was happening in the other cops' lives. Maybe that was why nobody wanted to partner up with her on a regular basis. Perhaps that explained the negative points on her last evaluation. Was it the "teamwork" issue she had to work on? If it had made its way into her file, then it had to be important. Could it be a significant flaw to fix or at least improve upon?

Meh.

Maybe one day she'd get around to it.

"Roll call is about to start; you better hurry," the sergeant said, pulling her back to reality.

Kate glanced at her watch. He was right. She folded the roster, placed it in her breast pocket, and then rushed to the meeting room.

~

AFTER ANSWERING four domestic disturbance calls, dealing with one breaking and entering, and issuing half a dozen speeding tickets, Kate was done with her shift.

She was returning her patrol car keys when she ran into Officer Mansbridge. She remembered his name because he was the chubbiest cop in the district and probably the most talkative as well. In just a few days, she'd heard all about his wife, his kids, his tooth problems, his back pains, his retirement dreams, his fear of heights, and... what else? Oh yeah, she couldn't forget how he had listed every single dieting fad and why they were all scams.

"Hey, Mansbridge, would you be interested in switching shifts with me for a little while? Just a few days?"

"Hey back, Murphy." He smiled at her, but it seemed forced. "I'm doing well, and how are you doing today?"

Argh.

She hated it when people wanted to make small talk. Pointless. But she needed him to do her a favor, so she played along. "Sorry, how are things?"

"Life's good, Mary's pregnant again," he said with a smile. This time, it appeared genuine.

"Congratulations!" Kate hesitated, not sure if asking a follow-up question would result in a twenty-minute conversation. She really needed to join the detectives as soon as possible. "When is Mary due?"

"She's twelve weeks, so... early January."

"That's fantastic."

Kate remained quiet, hoping Mansbridge wouldn't expand on this or other irrelevant details for too long, but she was pleasantly surprised when he continued.

"So, you want off day shift? Mary would certainly prefer to have me home in the evenings. Let me talk to Smitty, and I'll get back to you."

"I'll give you my cell number," Kate said. She scribbled it

down and then handed him a ripped page from her unofficial notebook.

"How long?"

"I don't know. Probably just a day or two."

"Okay, I'll text you later," he said, grabbing his car keys and walking away.

"Thanks, Mansbridge. Have a safe shift."

She rushed to her locker, changed out of her uniform, and then headed to conference room two where she walked into a discussion, midstream.

"But that doesn't make sense," an Asian woman said.

"Have you checked with the bank?" Detective Fuller asked.

A tall and slender brown-haired man continued, "Yes, and there wasn't any. I also ran a check across all US banks. Nothing else."

"Okay, let's look at it from a different perspective," Fuller said, and his eyes locked onto Kate as he finished.

He made quick work of the introductions, motioning to the tall, brown-haired man, then the woman, and then the chubby blond she'd met in the lunchroom with Fuller earlier, and saying, "Detectives Chainey, Wang, and Rosebud." They nodded hello and he added, "Here's our wallflower. Wallflower, these are the detectives."

The conversation picked up where it'd left off.

"Wallflower" is probably better than mentioning my last name.

However, Kate was confident they'd figure out her identity soon enough. Heck, Rosebud probably saw her name tag this morning.

Whatever.

She couldn't care less what he called her. At least she got to sit in and learn more about the case.

"What we have is DNA that matches his old sample from a decade ago. Did the lab re-test it against the fresh sample?" Fuller asked.

Old sample from a decade ago?

Kate had completely forgotten about that. Her uncle had drunk himself silly a few days after Aunt Lucy's death.

Was it the night of her funeral?

She couldn't remember the exact date, but he'd gotten into a bar fight. A one-time incident, but it had coincided with someone getting killed in an alley near the bar. An assault charge wouldn't have required a DNA sample under normal circumstances, but due to the timing and proximity of the murder, they must have tested him, and his DNA must have remained on file since then. That was how they'd matched it so fast. Kenny had since moved his drinking to the privacy of his home—no more chance of getting in a fight—but Kate knew he wasn't a violent guy. That incident had been out-of-character for him.

Rosebud replied, "Yes, LeBrun, the new guy, compared it to the old sample on file. Just to be extra-safe, I asked the lab supervisor, Luke O'Brien, to test the recent sample himself. That LeBrun kid looks so young; I didn't want to bet it all on him."

Luke O'Brien... That name... Could it be my Luko?

She hadn't thought about him since... Well, last time she'd talked to him was the day of her family's murder. She'd also seen him at the funeral, but what can kids say at such an event? They hadn't spoken in twenty years.

It may not be the same Luke O'Brien anyway. Probably isn't. What are the odds?

Then again, he was from the East Coast, always loved dissecting animals, admired police officers growing up, and Boston seems like a good option for moving up the career ladder if he followed his dreams of becoming a scientist.

Luko working at the Boston PD crime lab would be plausible. Likely? No. But possible.

She forced herself out of her head to refocus on what was important.

"Did we get a match on the rest of the fingerprints at the crime scene?" Fuller asked.

Chainey answered. "Most belonged to the victim, but there were quite a few from unknown people. No match in our database."

"Do we have family members, friends, or past girlfriends who could be matches? Could we request fingerprints from them?" Fuller asked.

"No wife or girlfriend as far as we know. The body was released, and his funeral is tomorrow. I'll attend and make note of people who may be of interest," Chainey said.

"Good. Wang, go with him and take pictures, discreetly." Fuller continued his examination of the board. "What else have we got? Have you made progress on a motive for Murphy? Did you get any new information from him?"

Chainey sat on the corner of the table and flipped through his notebook. "His not-owning a car checks out. His neighbors haven't seen him drive in years and his license has expired. They see him at the bus stop once in a while. That's how he goes to the grocery store and liquor store, normally late afternoon. They haven't heard or seen anything unusual. They usually see light from his living room TV in the evenings."

Fuller scratched his chin with his thumb and forefinger. "Okay, do you know what buses come near his house?"

Wang shook her head.

Fuller frowned. "Well, look at the routes and see if he could have reached McAlester's house by bus."

"Bicycle?" Rosebud asked.

"Didn't check," Chainey said, shaking his head. "I doubt he'd physically be able to get there without breaking a bone or having a heart attack. Steep hills, high-traffic roads, and the guy's old and out of shape."

"Check anyway," Fuller replied. He glanced at the wall behind him. It was covered with images, maps, and other information Kate couldn't read from where she stood. "Okay, we'll meet again tomorrow. I'm tracing back the victim's and suspect's previous addresses. Maybe we'll find a common link that'll point us to Murphy's motive."

The three detectives left first, with Wang nodding at Kate on her way out. Fuller approached the door, and then stopped, waving his hand from Kate to the door, "Wallflower, after you."

Kate left the room without speaking. *What's the point anyway?* They had nothing but DNA, but that would be enough to

23

prove him guilty unless she could show that he was being framed, but why and by whom?

She checked her cellphone, but nothing from Mansbridge.

Kate could go and visit her uncle, although she wasn't sure where they'd transferred him. With today's hectic schedule, she'd missed his hearing, but there was no way he was still in the holding cell at the station. Plus... what in the world was she going to tell him? She didn't have anything comforting to say, and she wasn't allowed to divulge the details of an ongoing police investigation. She wasn't willing to risk losing access to the detectives and their knowledge of the case for such an avoidable faux pas.

She looked at her watch: 3:55 p.m. She remembered reading a memo about the crime lab's operating hours: Monday to Friday, 9 a.m. to 5 p.m. She'd never stepped in the DNA lab before, but she knew the building was in Maynard. Although televised police drama series always portrayed the crime lab conveniently located down the hall from where the detectives worked, it didn't take her long to understand that it wasn't the case in real police life, at least not in Boston.

The DNA lab was about thirty miles away, so, depending on traffic, getting there before they closed was possible. She peered out the window to assess the traffic: vehicles were moving, albeit slowly.

Could she get there in under an hour and find out if the lab supervisor was indeed the Luke O'Brien she knew as a child? It was worth a shot.

What else was she going to do?

CHAPTER THREE

Kate Murphy
DNA Laboratory, Maynard, MA

KATE'S POLICE BADGE, ID, and a signature in the logbook was enough to allow her past the security desk. The officer on duty informed her that the supervisor hadn't left yet, but the lab was officially closed.

She walked to the elevator and read the department listings until she saw what she was looking for: *DNA lab - second floor*.

She got in the elevator and headed up. When she reached the correct floor, two glass doors with the Massachusetts State Police logo etched on them were all she could see. She tried pulling them open, but they were locked.

The noise from her attempt stirred movement in the dimly lit area at the back of the room. A man in a lab coat and protective goggles had apparently heard her and was coming her way.

Could it be Luke?

Last time she'd seen him, he was fourteen. A skinny kid with wild hair, acne, and thick glasses.

The man coming toward her was tall with broad shoulders and a narrow waist. If he wasn't six feet tall, he was close to it.

He had thick and wavy brown hair and a weary frown on his face.

Could it be him?

When he reached the doors, she saw intense blue eyes behind his protective eyewear, and she knew.

"Luko!" she exclaimed, feeling an unstoppable smile dawning on her face.

The man's expression went from annoyed to surprised, and a big, crooked smile appeared on his lips. She'd forgotten how the left side of his mouth always went much higher than the right. She'd teased him about it as a kid. He unlocked the doors and awkwardly stood in the entryway, one hand on the closed door and the other on the one he'd pushed open, holding it just wide enough for his shoulders to get through.

"Katie? Katie Murphy?"

Kate smiled. "Yeah! It's me."

"What..." He shook his head and blinked three times. "It's b-b-been fifteen, twenty years? I never thought I'd see you again."

Kate moved forward, wanting to hug her old friend, but he retreated behind the doors, and then popped his head and right index finger out. "Wait here."

"Okay," Kate said, stepping back.

He hadn't changed much after all. Sure, he was taller, bigger, and, she assumed, smarter than he'd been as a kid. He used to read his parents' encyclopedias from cover to cover just for fun. She couldn't believe he still stuttered a little, but the thought of it made her smile even more.

His stutter was why she'd nicknamed him Luko. When they'd first met, he was eight years old, rolling down the street on a cool blue BMX. She was seven, riding on her brand-new yellow bike. She could still remember the day vividly. It was one of only two days she ever looked back on from her childhood.

Her family had just moved into town. It was her birthday, and her parents had gotten her a new bike. It was the exact one she had always wanted. The yellow frame came with a red banana seat, a blue basket, a pink bell, and red streamers hanging off the handlebars. Kate didn't know any other kids in town, and this boy was the first one she'd seen in her new neighborhood. Both of them were riding their bikes on the street. When you're seven, that's reason enough to make friends with someone.

She'd dashed up to him and dared him to compete with her. "First one to the end of the street wins!"

She could still remember the surprised look on his face and the stupefaction moving to his body, making him waver a little. To this day, she still didn't know if he'd fallen over or just lost his balance for a second, but Kate had taken advantage of her head start. She knew she wasn't the fastest girl on a bike, and he'd almost caught up with her, but she managed to reach the stop sign first, ringing her bell to celebrate.

Then she'd parked her bike on the sidewalk, using her fancy retractable kickstand, and walked over to the boy she'd just beat by a hair.

"I'm Kate Murphy."

"I'm Luke O... O..."

"Nice to meet you, Luko," she'd said, extending her hand like she'd seen her parents do when meeting new people.

He'd pushed her hand away and shaken his head.

"No, Luke O... O... O'Brien. O'Brien."

She'd raised her shoulders.

"Nah... I prefer Luko. I knew some Lukes at my other school, and I didn't like them. I don't know any other Lukos. I'll see you around," she'd said before getting back on her bike and returning home.

And that was how their friendship had begun: two awkward, geeky kids who hung out before and after school, read Choose-Your-Own-Adventure books, explored caves, climbed trees, and ran around town.

Kate stopped her reverie when Luke exited the laboratory a few minutes later. He'd traded his lab coat for a plain beige jacket, and his protective eyewear for a regular pair of glasses.

"Oh... Almost forgot," he said before going back in. He pressed a few buttons on an alarm panel, then closed and locked the glass doors behind him.

He stood in front of her, put both hands in his pockets, and then shook his head. "Katie Murphy. God. I can't believe you're here right now."

Kate couldn't help but wrap her arms around her old friend, although she cut the hug short. His strong arms felt right and reassuring around her, but who was he? She didn't know him anymore. He was no longer a kid; he was a grown man.

When she pulled away, she peered up at him and said, "I heard your name today, and I had to find out if you were the Luke O'Brien I knew."

"The one and only," he said with his crooked smile.

She'd found his smile different and cool as a teen, but now there was also something sexy about it, especially when combined with what appeared to be a two-day beard. Very attractive... but the rest was all nerdy: invisible-frame glasses, outdated clothes, awkward body movements. He kind of looked like Gerard Butler acting as the world's biggest geek.

"Luko..."

He lowered his eyes for a moment. "You're the only one who's ever called me that."

"Too bad, it's a great name, and it suits you," Kate said.

They turned to face the elevator.

"Wanna grab a drink?" Kate asked.

"Sure, but let me make a call first."

He reached for his phone. Kate summoned the elevator, and it only took a few seconds for it to arrive. When the elevator opened, he walked a few steps away from her, his index finger motioning "one minute."

"Hey... it's me. I'll be home late, okay?" He glanced at Kate for a second, and then lowered his voice as if trying to hide the rest of his conversation from her. "No, everything's fine. Don't wait for me for dinner. Okay... Later. Love you."

He put his phone back in his pocket. Kate wondered who he'd been talking to, but then again, it was none of her business.

Luke extended his arm to the edge of the elevator door to keep it open. "Let's go. Beer? Coffee? Dinner?"

"How about beers and nachos?" Kate asked, stepping into the elevator.

"Is this what you traded your ice cream floats and fries for?"

They walked a few blocks in a mix of awkward silence and the two of them talking at once, reliving old memories, but only the happy ones. By the time they reached the nearest pub, Kate felt much more comfortable, and Luke appeared less awkward.

"Your stutter is gone," she said.

"I have it under control most of the time."

"That's good. I remember how much kids used to tease you about it."

They took a seat at a table, and Kate ordered two pints of Guinness for them.

"My favorite. How did you know?" he asked.

"I still remember your dad drinking it all afternoon. I just thought you'd follow in his footsteps." She paused for a moment, and then added, "How are your parents?"

Luke let out a long sigh and then said, "Dad passed a few years ago. Bad heart. Mom's doing all right."

"I'm so sorry to hear."

A lull followed, and Kate broke it off, knowing Luke couldn't inquire about her parents. At least she could tell him about her adoptive parents.

"After that day..." she began, but the lump in her throat threatened to choke her. She stopped to gather her breath and then continued. "My uncle took me in and adopted me. I moved to Douglas. I'm sorry I didn't stay in touch. It was too hard."

His eyes softened, and he tilted his head. "I knew you had to leave. I'm sorry I didn't attend the funeral. I tried, but I was too angry... and sad... and confused. My parents forced me to go, but I only got as far as the back of the room, then I ran out. That was the last time I saw you."

Kate forced a smile to help push down the tears that were threatening to come up. "I know... I saw you run out of the funeral parlor." Trying to avoid the nightmares that would inevitably follow, as they often did whenever she talked or otherwise revisited that time in her life, she changed topics. "So, how did you end up working in the crime lab? Give me the

CliffsNotes version of your life. What happened to you during the past twenty years?"

He snickered a bit. "Well, after you left and broke my heart—"

Kate kicked him under the table, interrupting a sentence that didn't make any sense. Had he developed a sense of humor?

He smiled. "Okay, okay. Finished high school, then went to college, studied biology and got a degree in genetics. Now I'm working on my doctoral thesis. Hoping to finish it this year."

"What's it about?"

"I won't bore you with the long title. It's about genes, chromosomes, and DNA. I spend most of my free time staring at blood samples in the microscope and comparing DNA strips."

"Married, children?" Kate asked.

"No, not for me. Unlucky in love. How about you? How did you spend the past twenty years?"

"Graduated with a degree in criminal justice, then went to the police academy. When Aunt Lucy's health started to decline, we moved closer to Boston so she could have access to better healthcare. I like being a BPD cop, but I'm hoping to become a detective someday. Hopefully, sooner rather than later."

"Interesting. How's your aunt doing?"

Kate's smile disappeared; she still missed her. "She passed ten years ago."

Luke paused and placed his hand on her arm. "Sorry..." Then, he promptly yanked back, almost as if he'd touched a hot iron. "Married?"

Kate forced a grin back onto her face. "Divorced, but no kids, so that made things easier."

"Recently?"

She nodded. "Almost a year ago."

The waitress arrived with their beers. After clinking glasses and toasting to their unexpected reunion, Luke resumed the conversation. "So, you said you heard my name today?"

"Yes. Capt. Cranston has allowed me to sit in with the detectives that are on my uncle's case. They mentioned your name, and given how much you liked to dissect frogs and such, I thought it could be you."

"Your uncle? What case?" he asked, then his eyebrows moved up, and he gasped. "Wait... Murphy?"

"Yes, my uncle's been accused of murder."

He shook his head, and the expression in his eyes became that of a doctor about to announce the worst of news. "Sorry... the match is almost certain."

"Yeah, I heard," Kate said before letting out a long sigh. "But I know he didn't do it, so I want to discover how his blood made it to the crime scene."

"Blood *and* hair samples were a match," Luko said. He placed his hand on Kate's and squeezed.

She looked into his eyes. "Kenny is all I have left."

Luke clasped a little harder. "No, you've got me back now, so you've just doubled your support team," he said, smiling.

She placed her other hand on his and clutched it, avoiding his gaze as she felt tears trying to escape. She closed her eyes and took a deep breath, pushing the tears back. She appreciated his comment.

No. Appreciation wasn't it.

She'd desperately needed to hear those words. From anyone. It was good to have a friend again. She re-opened her eyes and shot him a big grin. "How about we get some food? I'm starving."

A couple of beers and a large plate of nachos later, they were back to their old selves, the two kids who could tease each other about everything and laugh it out. Well, almost everything. They were adults after all, so they probably held back on some aspects of their lives. At least Kate did.

Doesn't everyone do that?

They exchanged phone numbers and a long hug before parting ways.

This time, the hug felt good, like a warm blanket on a chilly night, and there was something else there.

∿

KATE WAS ABOUT to set her alarm on her phone when she saw she'd received two new text messages while in the shower.

Tonight was fun.
Glad you tracked me down :P
Your Luko

Talked to Smitty. We're good.
I'll take your shift tomorrow.
Enjoy my evening shift.
PLEASE be nice to my partner.

Great!

She wasn't sure which of the two messages excited her more. But Kate was in a good mood, so she sent them both a smiley face.

CHAPTER FOUR

Kate Murphy
Roxbury Police Station, Boston

THIS TIME, Kate was present when the detectives started their review of the case. They began with how the murderer could have reached the crime scene.

Detective Rosebud pointed to the city map first. "Murphy could have taken the number 14 bus, with two transfers, to make it to the victim's house. Here's the most probable course of action: he left home at 6:20 p.m. and got to the victim's house around 8 p.m., depending on how fast he walked."

Rosebud moved on to the pictures of the victim's house.

"He snuck around the bush to avoid being seen and stuck to the asphalt walkway or adjacent gravel, which didn't leave much in terms of footprints. He entered the house through the bathroom window, which is accessible by first climbing on low storage bins, then the shed. He waited somewhere in the house, maybe the closet or the guest bedroom, until the victim went to bed, at which point he attacked him with a pillow and suffocated him."

Rosebud went to the crime scene pictures.

"The accused's hair was found on the pillowcase, along with

a single drop of blood. Maybe his nose bled from the excitement, or he could have had a small knick in his finger or something. He's diabetic and has many puncture points on his fingers from taking his blood sugar, so that's highly possible."

He then pointed back to the city map.

"The murder would have occurred before 10:30 p.m., which gave the killer enough time to catch his bus and the two transfers required to make it back to his house. He would have been back home by midnight. He left the TV on before leaving the house and turned it off when he returned, so his neighbors would assume he was home all night watching TV, as usual."

"Autopsy says the death occurred between 9:00 and 11:00 p.m., so that works," Wang said, looking at a printed copy of a report that had been left open on the table.

"Anyone come up with a motive?" Fuller asked.

The detectives all shook their head.

"I found one, but it's far-fetched," Fuller continued, taking out his notepad. "The victim and accused attended the same school back in 1952. The victim may have said something to the accused or bullied him throughout his school years. Nobody took notice of that stuff back then. No way there would be records to prove or disprove it. The accused may have wanted to take revenge for past behavior. Considering his previous arrest for attacking a stranger in a bar, it's plausible."

"What?" Kate exploded. She'd listened to them quietly until now, without butting in, although none of it made sense to her. "The accused is old and frail. You'll have a hard time convincing a jury that he's fit enough to walk between that bus stop and the victim's house, let alone climb up to that window. It takes strength to choke someone to death with a pillow. And revenge for being bullied as a kid? Why now? I don't buy it at all."

Chainey rolled his eyes and shook his head. "Here we go. Crazy train arriving at the station."

Rosebud and Wang stayed silent, expressionless as poker players before turning their attention to Fuller.

"Maybe, after many years of looking for him and planning his revenge, he finally discovered where he lived," Fuller said, obviously annoyed. "Wallflower, can you explain the presence of his DNA at the crime scene?"

"How about someone placed that pillow there? Could someone have planted the accused's pillow at the crime scene?" Kate asked.

Wang replied before Fuller could, with a voice much calmer than both Kate's and Fuller's. "It matches the other pillow at the victim's house. It's part of a set of new memory foam. The accused's pillows are musty feather-filled ones. Not possible."

"Other than the pillow-planting theory, does our Wallflower have another stupid explanation for Murphy's DNA being at the scene?" Fuller asked, shooting Kate an angry look.

She shook her head.

"Then shut up or get out," Fuller barked.

Kate remained quiet through the rest of the case review. They covered the transcripts of the original interview with Kenny, and the most recent one, where they confronted him with their version of how it happened.

Kate's nails were close to drawing blood from her clenched fists. No matter how hard she flexed her jaw, bit her tongue, or tried to control her breathing, she couldn't ignore the guilt that was overtaking her. She was failing her uncle, but that feeling was nothing compared to how much she wanted to smack Fuller in the face for the way he was treating her.

The detectives tidied up a few more loose ends that seemed inconsequential for Kate, and then they broke for lunch.

Kate remained the outsider. She had to leave the conference room but wasn't invited to join them to eat, so she grabbed an egg-salad sandwich from the machine in the lunchroom and ate it in the hallway, not too far from the conference room. She didn't want to miss them coming back in.

After gulping down her food, she started hating herself for being so naive. She should have followed them out to eat anyway. She was wasting time here, and they were probably finalizing their case in the coffee shop, or wherever they'd gone.

She needed to do something to busy her mind, something to

make her feel better. She took out her cellphone and sent Luke a text message.

> I had fun last night.
> You haven't changed a bit.
> Glad to have my friend back.

It wasn't a minute before her phone vibrated with a reply:

Glad to have you back in my life.
Text me if you want to hang out.

She sent him a reply:

> Will do.
> Have a great day ;)

The detectives came back two hours later, which all but confirmed Kate's suspicions that they had continued their discussion privately. But there wasn't anything she could do about it now. Instead, she had wasted her "free" time playing Candy Crush ad nauseam and reading an e-book she had downloaded to her phone.

By 3:30 p.m., Kate realized she wasn't going to hear anything new from the detectives. Two of them were off to the funeral to make sure there weren't any other possible suspects.

Attending the burial ceremony was just being overly cautious. They were ready to close the case. The detectives had everything they needed to go to court now, even though their motive was flimsy at best.

She left and went to her locker to change into her uniform for her evening shift. It was going to be a long night.

Kate saw Mansbridge going off his shift as she came out of the locker room.

"Thanks, Mansbridge," she said.

"No problem. Do you want to switch shifts tomorrow, as well?"

"No, I don't think I'll have to, but thanks again. I owe you one."

"No worries. Stay safe out there and take care of Smitty. He's a good partner."

~

THE EVENING SHIFT with Smitty was interesting, to say the least.

He was a good-looking man. Tall, tanned, dark-brown hair, blue eyes, and a slight Italian accent. He was a good cop. Followed procedures to the T, even though he was in constant flirt mode with Kate in the car. It felt good to know he was by her side when they answered a call on a suspected drug deal that ended up with the discovery of a small meth lab.

"So, you'll be spending the night with me tomorrow?" he asked with a smile.

"No, you'll have Mansbridge back."

"Too bad, I was starting to like you, Murphy. You're not as grumpy as they say. Quiet? Sure. But I trust you'd have my back. And you're wrapped up in a nice little package."

"Come on..."

"What?"

"Stop it. You've been flirting with me all evening."

"Italian blood. Can't help it. You're a hot little thing. And single, right?"

Kate rolled her eyes. "Single, but not looking."

"Too bad, but if you hang out with me some more, you might change your mind."

The radio crackled, and he went back to police business.

~

KATE'S SLEEP only lasted a couple of hours and was interrupted by nightmares of her and Kenny being out in a snowstorm.

The blizzard was thick. She could hear Kenny a dozen feet away from her, but the winds were too powerful, and his frail body couldn't fight the gusts. She was doing everything she could to reach out and grab him, but the snow was pushing him closer to the cliff.

He fell down, his body plunging two hundred feet toward the sharp rocks where the frigid waves exploded.

She could hear his short cry for help, but there was nothing she could do to save him.

She awakened in a sweat, her heart pounding hard in her chest.

ON FRIDAY MORNING, Kate went about patrolling on her own, her head and heart both miles away from work. After stopping two drivers for traffic violations, she answered a domestic violence call to find a nasty surprise.

She'd parked her patrol car in the street and entered the apartment building. Someone had conveniently left the front door open while their belongings were being moved into the building.

She'd gotten off the elevator on the fifth floor and was approaching apartment 5F, as indicated by the radio dispatcher, when she recognized the voice of the man yelling behind the door. She'd heard it too many times. But for once, it wasn't directed at her.

Matt. Damn Matt.

She didn't want to deal with her ex-husband right now. She listened in for another minute or so, then heard the sound of a woman, another voice she would have gladly forgotten for the rest of her life.

Couldn't he have left town and let her and the rest of womankind be?

She backtracked to the elevator and pressed the button on her radio to request another unit.

Kate walked back outside, and another patrol car arrived within minutes.

A husky red-haired man came out of the driver's side and approached Kate.

"Hey, what's going on?" he asked.

"Apartment 5F. Violent man fighting with his girlfriend."

"What's wrong? Can't handle it, Murphy?" the officer asked, a smirk on his face. He shared a complicit look with the trainee who'd just exited from the passenger side of their police vehicle.

"Believe me, I can handle it," Kate said, then glanced at the name tag on the officer's uniform. "Clancy. Listen, we don't know each other, but here's why I don't want to take this call. This domestic violence case is my ex-husband and the woman he cheated on me with. So, if it's fine by you, I'd rather not see this son of a bitch again in my life. I'm afraid of what I might do to him if I get the chance. So, please. Please. Go ahead and arrest that asshole. Nothing to worry about with the woman. She's a pushover. That's how he likes them."

"You're full of surprises. Explains the bitterness," Clancy said, the smile now gone from his face.

Although Kate wanted to, she refrained from saying anything more. Bad night's sleep or not, people made it clear why she wasn't partner material. It was becoming more and more apparent she needed to work on her people skills. Clancy was still staring at her.

"Are you good? You'll handle it?" she asked, anxious to get away from the situation.

"Of course, Murphy. There's a Starbucks right over there," he said, pointing at the street corner. "It's got a good view of the building entrance, in the event I decide to take him to the station and you want to watch."

"No, thanks, I'd rather try to forget what he looks like."

"As you wish. We'll take care of it," he said, nodding toward his trainee.

"Thanks, Clancy," Kate said, then, with the bitterness comment still hanging in her mind, she took the time to smile at him. She added, "I owe you one."

The rest of her shift went by without a hitch.

By the time she refueled the patrol car, handed in her

paperwork, and tracked down that they'd transferred her uncle to the Nashua Street Jail, Kate was exhausted, and so she headed home.

She had to do something to get that damn Matt out of her head and fast.

CHAPTER FIVE

Kate Murphy
Kate's Apartment, Boston

WHEN SHE GOT home from work, Kate couldn't think of anything better to do than put on her running shoes and go for a ten-mile run.

At mile nine, she spotted a liquor store. She checked her hidden pocket to see if she had brought any money with her. Running had become such an automated process, she couldn't recall if she'd done so. She found her driver's license, a credit card, and a twenty-dollar bill in there.

She stepped into the store and headed toward the vodka shelf. She had never been able to tell the difference between cheap and expensive liquor, so whatever was on sale would be her treat tonight.

Mr. Boston it is.

Running the last mile with the bottle in a brown paper bag felt a little unbalanced, but it wasn't any worse than pursuing a suspect with her gun drawn.

Once home, she drank a large bottle of Gatorade and turned on the shower to allow the water to get hot. She threw her new bottle of vodka in the freezer next to a bag of french fries and a pint of vanilla ice cream. Ready for her shower, she stripped to nothing on her way to the washing machine, where she dumped her sweaty clothes before walking back to her steamy bathroom.

The hot water felt good on her skin. Her day had sucked. Why did she have to run into Matt? And how the fuck was she going to prove that her uncle was innocent?

Did he do it?

She shook her head.

Not a chance.

However, there was no proof that he didn't do it either.

She got out of the shower, patted herself dry, and then put on yoga pants and a spaghetti strap tank top. She didn't do yoga. She'd once thought about learning it, so she'd bought an outfit and discovered that the clothes were comfortable and didn't bunch up as much as real pajamas when she slept. She still hadn't learned yoga, and probably wasn't going to, but that didn't matter.

Nothing matters now.

After all that had happened, Kate had developed thick skin. She had discovered that she didn't mind being alone. In fact, she preferred it on many occasions. But now, without the option to go over to her uncle's house and play a game of cards with him, she felt lonely. Forsaken.

No way she was going to call her ex, Matt. He was a conman, plain and simple. He was someone else's problem now.

She wondered what Luko was doing tonight. After all, it was Friday. He was probably out with friends or on a date. Didn't she overhear him sweet-talk a woman on the phone before leaving the lab the other day?

She was at a loss for what to do or who to call.

She sat down in the middle of her living room, folded her legs, and then leaned her head into her palms, elbows resting on her knees.

Get a grip, Kate!

She took a deep breath, looked up and tried to focus on facts, not the harmful feelings brewing within her.

She glanced around and tried to be grateful for what she had.

She'd rented this loft not too long after her separation. It was small but cozy; perfect for her. The open concept only hid the bathroom. She could reach her bedroom by climbing up a small set of stairs along the wall. The bed rested against the back, and, through the glass balustrade, she could view her fireplace and kitchen below. The living room opened onto a small balcony, which offered a beautiful view of the city at night. It was just big enough to fit a small patio set for two or a barbecue, but Kate had decided to install a full-size hammock instead. It was huge. In fact, two people could probably fit in it, but she liked it because it comforted her. The mesh fabric wrapped itself around her, offering a full-body hug.

She stood up, walked outside to her balcony, and rested in the hammock for a while, closing her eyes, and listening to the sounds of the city on this warm summer evening. A large oak tree was nearby. She could hear its inhabiting birds chirping to one another. After a half hour, she felt the need for a distraction, so she returned inside and closed the patio door.

She turned on the TV and flicked through the channels, hoping to find a funny movie, but it was in vain. She watched the news for a while. They mentioned her uncle's case, but nothing she didn't know already. Once the news anchor moved on to another topic, Kate turned it off and switched on the radio instead, opting for the soft rock station, or whatever they called the one that sounded like elevator music.

Nothing too loud or too upbeat, but nothing that makes me jump off a bridge either.

Kate walked to the kitchen, grabbed a glass, got the chilled vodka and ice tray out of the freezer, and made her first drink of the night. She added a dash of 7UP, drank it on the spot, and then made a second one to take back with her to the living room.

"Aunt Lucy, Mom, Dad, little Bobby," Kate said out loud, staring at the wall in front of her. "If you can hear me, I need your help. Please guide me so I can free Uncle Kenny."

She shook her head.

Am I losing my mind? I'm talking to ghosts. Again. But who knows what happens to us after we pass? It's worth a try.

43

She smiled as she recollected the stuff she'd done after her parents' death. She'd seen psychics, used a Ouija board, and tried everything she could to get in touch with them, but to no avail.

"Sometimes talking out loud can help," the psychotherapist had told her. And sometimes—with increased frequency these days—she did just that.

She grabbed her cellphone to play another round of that stupid, addictive candy game. When she ran out of lives, she got annoyed by the prompt suggesting she ask her friends for more lives.

What friends?

Why didn't she have friends? A friend would be nice right about now. She reached for her phone again. She texted Luke:

Hey, what are you up to?

Not expecting a reply right away, she returned to the kitchen and poured herself another drink. She grabbed the bottle and brought it back with her to the living room.

When she plopped down next to the coffee table, her phone buzzed with a new incoming text:

Nothing interesting, u?

Same. Want to come over?

Sure, what's ur address?

238 Maple Pl. Apt 3B

OK, b there in 15

:)

∾

LUKO ARRIVED with a bag of chips and a four-pack of draft Guinness.

Kate invited him in. He took off his shoes, and she gave him the grand tour, which took a whole fifteen-seconds.

"Nothing much to show," she said. "I don't need much room. Here's the patio." She opened the door to let him out on it.

"I like it," he said after taking a minute to admire the scenery.

She returned to the living room, and he followed.

He pointed at the vodka bottle on the coffee table. "I see you've got a head start on me."

Kate wondered how drunk she looked. "Well, it's not a habit, but I needed to unwind tonight."

She sat on the love seat and tapped on it, inviting him to sit next to her.

A three-person couch would have been too big for the room, so she'd bought a love seat and a single padded chair. Usually, it felt awkward to sit next to someone on this couch, but sharing the love seat with Luko felt right.

"Did you have a good week at work?" she asked.

"Busy, but okay. How's your uncle doing?"

"I haven't had a chance to..." she started, but felt shameful about lying to him. "No, that's not true, I didn't feel brave enough to go see him because I've failed him. There's nothing I can do. I don't want to disappoint him and break his spirit."

Luke stared into her eyes. Kate felt the need to look away. He lifted her chin with his index finger, but Kate kept her gaze down.

"Katie, look at me."

She obeyed, ashamed of exposing her green eyes that were probably turning red. She could feel them filling with tears.

Luke spoke softly to her as he moved his hand to her shoulder and squeezed it gently. "Right now, he doesn't need you to free him. Kenny just needs you, your company, your support. He needs hope right now and for you to visit him, to make him realize that you care. That's what family is for."

Kate turned away again, and a few tears escaped from her eyes, rolling down her cheeks. She knew Luke was right.

"I'll go see him tomorrow."

"Do you want me to go with you?"

Kate blinked, surprised by his offer. "No," she said with a smile. "I'll be okay."

Luke let go of her shoulder, adjusted on the couch, and reached for a beer. As he popped it open, he said, "Now, enough of the pity party. Let me tell you a good story I heard in the lab today." He wrapped his left arm around her shoulders to bring her closer to him. "Do you know the best way to determine the sex of a chromosome?"

"No, I don't know."

"You pull down its genes."

She snickered and shook her head. "Silly."

"Here's another one: a frog sees an ad for a psychic and wants to know his future, so he calls in. The psychic tells him he's going to meet a beautiful young girl who will want to know everything about him. So, the frog asks the psychic, 'Where will I meet her?' The psychic says, 'In biology class.' "

Kate pulled out of his embrace and pushed him on the chest.

"That's horrible," she said, though she laughed even as she reproached him.

"Maybe, but we're all geeks and nerds in the lab. And to be fair, all the samples we're analyzing have a pretty negative backstory attached to them, so we try to keep it light and positive whenever we can." He got up and walked into the kitchen. "Where do you keep your glasses and bowls?"

"On your right, over the sink," she called out. "Bowls are in the next one to the right."

"Thanks."

He came back with two glasses stacked on top of each other, the top one filled with water. He had a bowl in the other hand.

"Here's some water for you," he said before pouring his beer into the empty glass. While the foam settled, he opened the bag of salt and vinegar kettle chips and dumped them into the bowl.

"It's Friday night. I thought you'd be out on a date with a boyfriend or something."

She laughed for a brief second. "Not me. Haven't been on a date in years."

"I don't understand," he said, assessing her. "The little pig-headed, freckled girl I knew, with the big gap between her front teeth, turned into a beautiful woman. You're obviously smart and independent. That major canyon between your teeth has disappeared. I don't see why you'd be here alone on a Friday night if it weren't by choice."

Kate felt her cheeks warm up.

Was it due to his compliment or the vodka?

Maybe a bit of both.

She smiled, sipped the water he'd brought, and then leaned against him. It was odd to have him here. *Odd, but nice.* She rested her head against his chest and listened to his heartbeat. She closed her eyes for a second, contented for the first time today.

When Kate awakened, Luke's face was close to hers, and she could feel his arms moving from underneath her back and knees. She was now in her bedroom. Had he carried her upstairs?

"Hey, Sleeping Beauty," he whispered when their eyes met. "You'll be more comfortable in here."

He pulled the comforter over her and was heading back downstairs when Kate called out to him.

"Luko..."

He returned to her side.

She reached for his hand. "Come here and lie next to me."

"I should really go home now."

"Just for a minute."

He hesitated then lay next to her, on top of the comforter.

She turned to face him. "Thank you," she said.

"For what?"

"For nothing and everything."

She brought her index finger to his jawline and traced it; his beard felt a lot softer than she'd imagined. He closed his eyes, and she outlined his lips, feeling the left corner of his mouth rise

47

into a smile. After letting out a slow breath, he opened his eyes, pushed her hand down to her side, and then gently grabbed the back of her head before leaning closer to kiss her.

His lips were warm and firm; demanding yet kind. She felt her heartbeat increase as her body responded to his kiss. She moved closer to him, but the comforter was in the way. His lips parted, and she let her passion ignite, fueled by long-harbored feelings for him that she didn't realize existed.

One of his hands went down her back and then up, underneath her tank top. She wanted to touch him as well. Needing to feel the warmth of his body against hers, she kicked the covers down to the foot of the bed. Luke lay on top of her. She started tugging at his T-shirt, but he stopped and pulled it over his head, exposing his chest.

She let her hands run along his firm pecks, stumbling across the odd hair here and there, her fingers brushing down his stomach. She wrapped her arms around his back and pulled him closer.

His hands slid up from her hips to get her top off. Kate arched her back slightly to help him but was surprised when his hands flew away from her and gripped his hair instead. He sat up.

He's stopping?

"No, I shouldn't." His voice was rough and laced with passion and confusion.

"What?" Kate asked.

He pushed further away. "Sorry, Katie. I can't."

Luke got up, looked for his T-shirt, and then put it back on, inside out with the label sticking out below his chin.

He knelt beside the bed, next to her. "Good night, Katie." He placed a peck on her forehead, got up, and then said, "I'll let myself out."

Kate lay there unmoving as she heard the door close.

What happened? How did I screw this up?

∽

ON SATURDAY MORNING, Kate awoke to the sound of her alarm ringing in the distance. Her head felt like a nuclear bomb had detonated inside it, but she fumbled her way out of bed and downstairs toward the annoying sound.

She finally found her phone in the living room, turned the alarm off, and then threw it back on the table. It landed next to a half-empty vodka bottle, a bowl of now-stale chips, a glass of water, and a half-pint of Guinness.

Luko came over, she hazily recollected. *We made out, then... What the heck happened?*

While the details didn't quite form a complete picture, she remembered he'd left suddenly. She checked her phone for a possible text message from him.

There was one unread message:

Hey, pretty thing, how's it going? Want some company?

No name. Unknown number.

She had no idea who had sent her that message.

She had Luke's number in her phone, so this message wasn't from him.

She texted back:

Who is this?

Kate grabbed the beer glass and took it to the kitchen to dump it in the sink. She returned to the table, about to fetch a few more items when she realized she was in no mood—and no state—to clean up right now.

Her phone beeped with a reply to her text message:

An Italian-blooded horse. At your service.

Argh, Smitty.

It was too early for this. How did he get her number? Her head rumbled like the Red Line speeding through the tunnels.

She drank the glass of water sitting on the table and then went back to sleep.

Three hours later, she woke up feeling slightly better, although angry with herself for her behavior and annoyed at not knowing what the fuck had happened.

Relationships were too freaking complicated. Wasn't this why she had sworn off men after her divorce? There was no way she would ever understand and be in-sync with another human being.

She showered then popped a couple of acetaminophens to get rid of what was left of her hangover. She picked the first thing from her closet and ended up dressed in capri pants, a light blouse, and flip-flops. She looked in the full-length mirror hung by the door and decided to tie her hair into her standard, low-maintenance ponytail, before wondering if her outfit was appropriate for jail. She Googled the Nashua Street jail visiting policy and found out that rubber bands and flip-flops were not approved.

I'd better adhere to their rules.

She untied her hair, traded her footwear for loafers, grabbed her car keys, and then headed to see her uncle.

Kate went through the visitor-pass process reasonably quickly before sitting down and waiting for Kenny to appear. As soon as she saw him, it dawned on her that Luke had been right. The energy radiating from Kenny's smile could have powered a small village. There was nothing to fear about how he would react to her lack of progress. All he needed was a friendly face.

He sat down and started speaking. She couldn't recall a time when she'd heard him spew so many words in one sitting.

"The lawyer I got, George Hudson, did I tell you his dad was wrongly accused? That's how he became interested in the legal system and why he later became a lawyer."

"Was he responsible for freeing his dad?" Kate asked, trying her best to match her uncle's enthusiasm.

"No, his dad was sentenced to death when George was still young. He hadn't finished law school yet, but the real killer confessed about a year later."

"Later? You mean... after he had already been executed?"

"Yep."

"That's awful." Kate looked down, not wanting to meet her uncle's eyes right now. She was glad the death penalty had been abolished in Massachusetts.

He continued with a level of ardor that surprised her. "Yes, awful indeed. His family received monetary compensation from the government, which paid for George's school loans and allowed him to graduate. Now, he always makes sure that his mother has everything she needs, and the rest of his money goes toward helping other people like his dad... Like me."

Kate could feel the excitement and hope in Kenny's voice. She feared what she was about to say would burst his bubble, though. She hesitated before telling him to not get his hopes up. She took a breath and let Luke's words echo in her mind: "He needs support, he needs hope."

She decided to keep what she knew to herself for now.

"I'm glad he's your lawyer. He sounds great, and it's wonderful that he's so passionate about helping others."

"They've set the court date for next month," Kenny said.

Kate stared into her uncle's eyes, not sure if he was excited or nervous. "That's good, I guess."

He shrugged. "Hey, did I ever tell you about Julie?"

"Julie who?" Kate asked.

"Julie Murphy."

"No, who's she?"

"My cousin," Kenny said. "She came to visit Lucy and me about... I don't know, thirty, forty years ago. You'd like her."

Kate was racking her brain, trying to recall meeting her as a young child, but that would have been impossible. She still lived with her parents back then. "How old is she?"

"A little younger than me, not sure of her exact age," he said.

Kate was confused as to why he was bringing her up, so she didn't say anything and waited for him to continue.

"She's in Ireland, somewhere around Cork, where we're from."

"Okay..."

"When I'm out of here, I'd like us to go visit her. You'd like her," he said again.

Kate swallowed hard and forced a smile. She knew the odds were against him getting out of jail anytime soon.

Better to impart hope, right?

"I'd like that very much," she said.

"Yeah, that's what we'll do. You'll love how green and beautiful it is. The spot you keep going to on the seashore has nothing on the Irish coast, I tell you."

"My spot is pretty darn breathtaking," she said, keeping things light. "Not sure it's possible. You've never seen it."

"No, you're right, but the Irish coast will take your breath away, I guarantee it."

Keeping up the charade was killing Kate, but she carried on smiling nonetheless. "I can't wait for us to go to Ireland together. It will be a great trip."

The conversation reached a natural lull. Kate wanted to hang around and spend more time with him but didn't know what else to talk about. "Is there anything I can do?" she asked, looking around and realizing that there wasn't.

"No, not really. But maybe..."

"What? Tell me," she said.

"Could you check by my house once a week or so? And tell my snoopy neighbor, Maude, to keep her nose out of my stuff while I'm here?"

Kate laughed. She'd always wondered if the hate he had toward his neighbor was just latent passion from both sides. Maybe something was going on between them. She made a mental note to drop by his house on her way back to make sure everything was okay. If she saw Maude, she'd deliver his message. He didn't own any plants that needed watering, but there could be mail to pick up or bills to pay.

"I'll take care of everything. Don't worry," Kate said.

KATE SPENT most of her Sunday on her computer, Googling

things and people related to her uncle's case with a 24-hour news channel airing redundant information concerning the city's upcoming election in the background. The mayoral candidates were constantly being interviewed, discussing everything from public transit to extra incentives for promoting new business and improving the overall economy in the metropolitan area.

She first looked into George Hudson, the lawyer. He'd been in the papers numerous times. He was good, really good. She found his contact information on a website and left him a voicemail, hoping to meet with him this week to discuss her uncle's case.

Then, she Googled Paul McAlester, the deceased, again. There was nothing new concerning him, other than a seventy-six-year-old man had been arrested, and the case was to go in front of a jury in the coming weeks.

After that, she decided to look up Luko. He (or another Luke O'Brien) was a member of a Dungeons and Dragons forum called D&D Madness, and that same avatar was also active on a few video game forums. His profile picture looked like a Simpsons version of him.

Still a geek at heart. But he's grown into a very handsome geek once you take off his thick glasses and outdated clothes.

She could still see his naked chest and strong arms in her mind's eye. She let out a sigh. He'd freaked out either because he was seeing someone else or because he wanted to act like a gentleman... Or maybe something else happened that she couldn't remember. But a gentleman could have stayed the night and simply slept next to her. What was the big rush to get out of her place? The "someone else" option seemed more plausible.

Kate told herself she'd try to swing by the lab this week, in between calls if she had a slow day. She could just ask him if he was seeing anyone, plain and simple. No point in wondering or wasting time and energy on this.

She reached for the remote and was about to turn off the TV when the anchorman announced a breaking news story: "A body has been found in Charlestown. A homeless man who appeared to be in his fifties was found dead under a bridge. This is the thirteenth homeless death to occur in Charlestown this year."

That's weird.

A police spokeswoman appeared next.

"We do not believe this was a homicide. We suspect the death occurred due to natural causes, but an autopsy will be conducted to confirm our findings. The identity of the man is still unknown, and we ask the public to contact us if they know this person."

The screen flashed a picture of a Caucasian man with dirty blond hair and nasty-looking scars on his face.

"An expert on social care and homeless programs in Massachusetts will join me in a few minutes to discuss our current system. Could we be doing more to help the homeless and prevent deaths? Stay tuned, and you'll find out," the anchorman said.

Although her inquisitive mind wanted to ponder these strange deaths, her heart didn't want to right now. What a horrible way to go: penniless, miserable, and alone, possibly found by dogs or runners.

The thought sent a shiver down her spine. Her uncle wouldn't die homeless on the street, but if she didn't get her shit together and prove his innocence soon, Kenny could die in prison, miserable and alone.

Kate turned off the news. She had some serious thinking and problem-solving to do.

CHAPTER SIX

Kate Murphy
George Hudson's Law Office, Boston

"HAVE A SEAT. He'll be right with you," the bleached-blonde twenty-something receptionist told Kate. Her smile was decorated by piercings above and below the center of her lips.

Kate walked to the empty waiting area, which consisted of a large, well-worn brown leather sofa, a matching chair, and a small coffee table littered with a selection of magazines. She decided to ignore them and breathe deeply instead. Classical music was playing in the background.

Bach?

Her excitement was mixed with apprehension. She was grateful her uncle's lawyer was able to fit her in so quickly, just after today's shift, but no matter how good he was, he would have a hard time convincing anyone that the DNA found at the crime scene wasn't related to the murder.

Has this lawyer seen—and successfully fought—similar cases before? What if he can't help Kenny? How many years will Kenny spend in jail?

Before she could go too far down the what-if rabbit hole, a black hand appeared in front of her and brought her back to reality.

"Miss Murphy? I'm George Hudson."

She got up and shook his hand. "Nice to meet you."

"Likewise. Glad you could make time to meet with me today. Please, follow me."

Kate had seen pictures of him online, but his stature was much more impressive in person. The light gray linen suit and matching hat he wore served to make him a little less intimidating, but at around 6'2" and well over two hundred pounds, he could have easily worked as a bouncer in a nightclub or as a goon for the mafia.

Kate counted four other lawyers' offices on the way to his.

As they reached his office door, George waved a hand toward the room, and Kate walked in. George's office, just like his physique, destroyed all preconceived notions she had of lawyers. Instead of being lined with diplomas, photos taken with famous politicians, or even classic paintings, his walls were covered from floor to ceiling with an eclectic mishmash of family pictures. Some photos were mounted in plain black frames, others in colorful ones, a few were set in antique gold frames that would look more at home in the Louvre than in an office, and one was hand-crafted with dried macaroni.

"They're my reason to get up in the morning."

Kate turned to face him. "Who are they?"

"These are the families I've worked with, to help them through hard times. I know what most people think of our profession, and unfortunately, many lawyers prove them right. Some do it for the money, but I'm in it for helping people and for righting wrongs."

Kate returned her attention to the photos on the wall. Some families were small; some were huge. Some pictures showcased over twenty people proudly dressed in their Sunday best, lined up in multiple rows. There were people from all backgrounds: Caucasian, Hispanic, Asian, African-American, Indian, and more. Kate couldn't believe how many pictures were displayed on this wall alone.

"Did you help all of those people?" she asked.

"I did my best for each and every one, so in a way I did." The look in his eyes changed for a split second, as if a vulture had cast its inauspicious shadow over a lonesome trekker.

"Some of them were successfully proven innocent, and others... well, we just didn't have enough to win, no matter how hard we tried. I do my best to keep my batting average as high as possible."

He pointed to one of the chairs in front of his desk and sat in the chair next to it.

Odd. The chair behind the desk looks much more comfortable.

Kate sat next to him, concluding that he probably wanted her to feel more at ease by sitting at her level. She'd read something about that in a psychology book.

"So, Kenny told me you're a police officer," George said.

"Yes, have been for twelve years."

"How are you doing with all of this?"

"You mean personally?" Kate asked.

"Yes, learning of his arrest must have affected you. I'm sorry for having broken that awful news to you on voicemail. I tried to reach you four or five times before resigning myself to leaving you a message. What are you feeling right now, and how are you coping?"

Kate was surprised by his question, but even more surprised by her reaction to it. Usually, she'd keep her emotions to herself, but she felt compelled to open up and share them with him.

"To be honest, he's all I've got, and I feel like shit for not being able to help."

"That's understandable, but you can't take that burden personally. Let's see what we can do about it."

Kate nodded.

"Do you want to know all the details of the case, as they've been filed with the court?"

"I believe I know most of them. My district commander arranged for me to sit in on the detectives' meetings, so I know about the blood and hair DNA. I also heard one possible scenario involving buses, entering the home through a bathroom window..." She paused, trying to remember, "Oh, yes... and a far-fetched motive involving bullying at school."

"That's about it. There are no witnesses. What does your gut tell you?"

"I've known Kenny all my life. He's a decent man. Yes, he drinks more than he should, he swears, and he got arrested once for getting in a fight, but that was just after his wife had passed away. Her death was tough on him. He's not a murderer."

"My gut agrees with you. And, if you ask me, their description of the attack seems hard to believe, especially after meeting your uncle in person. While I don't know what kind of physical condition he used to be in, I doubt he'd be able to pull himself up through an open window and have enough force, physically and emotionally, to murder a person with a pillow. That's what they're going with."

Kate shrugged and shook her head. "And I've never ever heard the victim's name. If he was upset with anyone, he would have gone on and on and on. Believe me."

George let out a light laugh and put on the pair of glasses he had hanging around his neck before flipping through the file folder lying on his crossed legs. "Attended same school in 1952," he read out loud. "Blah blah blah... Sounds like the victim could have been a bit of a bully as a kid; some testimonials taken by the police at the victim's funeral confirm that."

Kate was surprised by that last statement, but then again, two of the detectives were supposed to attend the ceremony, so it made sense.

What kind of person speaks badly about the deceased at his memorial service, though? That was odd.

"I don't think my uncle would hold a grudge against someone for that long without mentioning him once."

George took off his glasses, letting them hang on his chest. "How do you think his DNA got to the crime scene?" he asked.

Kate opened up her palms and shook her head once more. "I have no freaking idea. It seems ridiculous for anyone to frame my uncle. What would be in it for them? Why go through the trouble? He's got no money, nothing that could be used to blackmail him."

"Exactly, unless the framing was done a bit at random, as a way for the real murderer to walk away a free man," George said.

"You mean someone somehow got ahold of a drop of blood and a hair from a stranger that happened to be at the wrong place at the wrong time?"

George nodded. "Perhaps, or someone could have gotten a hold of it from a DNA bank. I know it's far-fetched, but that's just an idea that's been bouncing in my mind, I haven't fully fleshed it out yet."

"You mean someone breaking into a lab and stealing samples?" Kate asked.

She remembered seeing Luko go back in behind the glass doors the other day to set up the alarm at his lab. Of course, Luke worked for the Massachusetts State Police crime lab, so they had to use security measures to ensure the chain of evidence remained intact. However, many other labs would do the same as well, for privacy, legal protection, or different reasons. No matter how much she racked her brain, she couldn't remember hearing anything like that on the news. At least not recently.

"But the police have both a hair and a blood sample," Kate continued. "Wouldn't it be difficult to steal both types of samples from the same donor? I doubt labs would keep both in the same fridge or vault, or wherever they keep samples. The person would then have to match them, so only one DNA signature is left at the crime scene."

"But getting caught would have much more dire consequences."

Kate shook her head. It didn't make sense. As much as she wanted to hang on to any possible hope, George's idea seemed improbable, and as far-fetched as—no, it was farther fetched than—the bully-revenge motive put together by the detectives.

"Don't worry about it," George said, closing the file. "It's part of my process. I think outside the box. I like to bounce ideas off people, especially when facts put us in a very tight corner. My second idea is based on the victim's career path."

Kate tried to remember anything she'd read or heard about it, but could only recall him owning a few collectible cars, as mentioned in some article she'd found on Google.

"What did he do for a living again?" she asked.

"Him, not much. A boring office worker at an accounting firm, but he had recently become a member of a very obscure political party called 'Green God.' Excuse the term, but Paul McAlester was a 'bastard.' His mom knew who the real father was, but the man never publicly acknowledged Paul as his son. I asked around and found out that his mother claimed his biological dad was a well-known state senator. He passed a few controversial bills that infuriated several groups."

"What do you mean?" Kate asked.

"I heard that the victim was planning to follow in his biological dad's footsteps, start a political career, and leave his job as an accountant."

Kate lifted an eyebrow. "Who's the dad? What's his name?" she asked, curious as to why none of this information had appeared when she'd Googled him.

"Senator Dudley. He died in a plane accident two years ago. They never found the wreckage, but they lost signal over the Arctic Circle and abandoned their search effort six weeks into it. Unlikely the passengers and crew would have survived that long, assuming they didn't die on impact."

Kate vaguely remembered hearing about that plane crash in the news but didn't remember what kind of senator he was.

"You said he infuriated a lot of people. How?"

George let out a sigh. "Where should I start?" he asked rhetorically. "He was a strong proponent of taking the theory of evolution out of our school system and teaching creationism as part of the official science curriculum. He was a strong supporter of oil exploration in the Arctic and Antarctic, and he opposed anything to do with research into curing cancer, or any kind of scientific research dealing with genetics. That's just the tip of the iceberg. He was an extremist on many issues. You may be able to find some of his speeches on YouTube."

Kate nodded as she listened to George describe the deceased senator's political agenda. "I get what you mean. Some people would absolutely disagree with him. Do you think both the dad and son could have been murdered?" she asked.

George cleared his throat and nodded his head. "That's the most plausible story to me. I can think of several people who would have loved to see both of them dead. Greenpeace supporters, left-wing terrorists... you name it."

"Wishing McAlester dead and killing him are two different things."

"Indeed."

Kate pondered the idea for a few more seconds.

"Why would my uncle be framed?"

George thought for a moment and then said, "Wrong place at the wrong time, or at least his genes were."

"So, we keep getting back to the idea that somehow someone robbed a lab or another place where DNA is stored," Kate said before leaning back in her chair. "I don't even recall my uncle doing any kind of DNA test. A hair sample? What for?"

"But don't forget that anyone could break into anybody's home, or be invited into it, and get a hair sample from a hairbrush or a comb. No one would ever notice."

"Nah," Kate replied, shaking her head. "Nobody's broken into my uncle's place. The only guests he has are his neighbor and me. The neighbor's an old lady, so I doubt she'd be able to come up with such a diabolical plan. And other than the DNA sample that got him into the system a decade ago, I don't think he's even provided anyone with a sample."

"Lots of people willingly donate 'samples' of themselves," George said, using air quotes. "Blood banks are a perfect example."

Kate thought about it, but nothing came to mind.

George tossed his hands up in the air. "I know, faaar-fetched. Thinking out loud. You seem to have a good investigative mind, so I'm sharing more with you than I normally would. Maybe together we could come up with an alternate scenario that I could present to the court." He grabbed her hands in his and continued. "To be bluntly honest, the facts we have are not enough to save him. But if we both keep our ears and eyes open, who knows?"

~

KATE LEFT George's office feeling a little more hopeful, yet overwhelmed and confused.

She stopped at an ice cream shop on the way home for a minor celebration. She ordered her uncle's favorite: pistachio gelato in a white-chocolate covered waffle cone with white almonds on it.

When she sat at one of the picnic tables outside the shop, she remembered Kenny had once taken her for ice cream after donating blood. But that was a long time ago. Lucy was still alive back then.

He did have blood samples out there, but wouldn't they have been used by now? And what about hair samples? Could he have given hair samples to see if his DNA would have been a match for some sort of cancer treatment for Lucy?

Kate finished her ice cream while watching a couple walk their dogs in the park across the street. She was not sure if it was the ice cream, the view, or just her thoughts that were exerting their comforting effect, but she felt a little better now. She now had leads, or at least the closest thing to one in this situation.

She could look into nosy Maude's past, just in case, and research political murders and reported thefts at labs or blood banks. It would be a lot of work, but one of these unlikely scenarios could lead her somewhere.

It had to.

Kenny's freedom depended on it.

CHAPTER SEVEN

Kate Murphy
Roxbury Police Station, Boston

FOR SOME REASON, Kate's morning on the job was quiet. Bostonians were behaving, or so it seemed.

When lunchtime came around, she stopped by the food court at Quincy Market to grab a lobster roll. Kate tried to go once a week, whenever she had a not-so-busy day that could accommodate it. So far, she'd had about a fifty percent success rate of finishing her lunch there without being interrupted by a call.

She paid for her meal and asked the young man working the counter if he could give her a few extra napkins and packets of pepper. While waiting, she turned around and looked for a table where she could sit.

The market was busy, which was no surprise since it was just past noon. Very few seats were available; most were occupied by mothers with screaming kids or office workers enjoying their lunch breaks.

Kate was still looking for an empty table when her eyes landed on a couple holding hands. But it wasn't just any couple.

It was Luke, her Luko, with an elegant brunette. He had on the same beige jacket and Dockers pants she'd seen him wear the other day at the lab. The woman wore a plain, black, tight-knit turtleneck with strings of white pearls hanging on it. Her long dark hair and square bangs framed her ivory face perfectly. She sat there somberly while Luke held her hands tightly, his eyes locked onto hers as he spoke. The sight of them with their hands together in the middle of the table sent a sting to Kate's chest.

"Guess I got my answer," she muttered.

Kate turned around to grab the extra items she'd requested then marched toward the parking lot.

By the time she reached her patrol car, she had calmed down.

Who was she to feel so possessive and so hurt by the sight of Luke with another woman? After all, they'd only shared a kiss, nothing more. Maybe the pang in her chest was merely a sign that she was ready to move on and start dating again.

Whatever.

She had more important things to take care of right now, like freeing her uncle.

She checked her phone and saw a red dot on the call icon. She clicked her way to the voicemail screen: one message, left by Smitty.

"Gorgeous, are you free this weekend?"

Well, if she wasn't Luke's type, at least she was someone else's type. Maybe she'd find another guy someday. Probably not Smitty, but at least not all hope was lost.

Her appetite returned, along with a slightly more positive attitude. She was finishing her sandwich behind the wheel of her parked patrol car when the dispatcher requested her assistance with a traffic accident involving injuries.

She radioed in, "I'm on my way."

ON WEDNESDAY EVENING, while Kate was picking up a few items at the grocery store, her phone vibrated in her pocket.

It was Luke.

She declined the call, not wanting to be "the other woman." She'd already been a victim of that evil species. Not that Matt's other woman had been the main reason for their marriage crumbling apart, but she had played a significant role.

No way, Jose.

She was never going to do that to another human being.

Another beep came in a few seconds later, indicating he'd left a message. Although she was mad at him, curiosity got the best of her.

She hit the play button.

"Katie, Luke here. Not sure what to say. I had fun on Friday. Don't know if you're upset at me for... for what happened... or for what didn't happen. Call me back. Maybe we can grab a cup of coffee or dinner... whatever. Take care."

"What the fuck, Luko?" Kate snapped, making a handful of people from the grocery aisle turn to stare at her, including a woman with a young child, probably around six or seven years old.

"Sorry," Kate said, mostly addressing the woman who was now covering her boy's ears.

I should stop swearing.

She could hear her dearly departed Aunt Lucy disapproving in her head.

Kate returned the phone to her pocket.

She didn't feel like talking to Luke this very minute. She didn't want to get involved with a man who was already spoken for, and she had better—and much more important—things to do with her free time right now.

She headed to the checkout, paid for her items, then returned to her apartment, spending the next three hours on her laptop, combing the web for other politically motivated murders that had recently occurred in the Northeast.

Tough thing to do. Google hasn't mastered that part of its algorithm yet.

Could she run a better search through the databases at work? She checked the clock: 11:48 p.m.

Too late.

She turned off the computer and committed to running the searches tomorrow at the station, after her shift.

CHAPTER EIGHT

Kate Murphy
Roxbury Police Station, Boston

KATE RAN into Smitty as she returned her car keys on her way to query the police databases, a task she'd been looking forward to all day.

"Hey, there! You've been ignoring my calls," he said, catching up to her as she walked away.

"I don't recall ever giving you my number."

"To-may-to, to-mah-to. You gave it to my partner. Whatever he's got, I've got. We're a unit," he said, placing his hand on the small of her back. He leaned toward her and whispered in her ear, "A unit just like you and I could be. We'd make a well-oiled machine, if you catch my drift."

"Come on, man! I told you I wasn't looking," Kate said, rolling her eyes at him.

"Your loss," he said, stepping away from her and grabbing keys to a patrol car. "What are your plans for tonight?"

"I'm staying here, doing some research."

"Studying for the detective's exam again?"

She eyeballed him with disdain. "No, personal research."

"Maybe I'll swing by later if you're bored. Could bring you

dinner. The two of us could have a picnic, get to know each other a bit." He winked at Kate.

Mansbridge appeared behind Smitty, and, for the first time ever, Kate was happy she'd get a chance to talk to him. At least that would bring an end to the awkward conversation with Smitty.

"Hey, Mansbridge. How are you?"

"Wonderful, Murphy. How nice to see you again. How are things?"

Kate smiled at him. "Great, I was just telling Smitty here that I had to get going. I've got stuff to do," she said, backing away toward the exit.

"Will you need me to switch to a few more day shifts for you?" Mansbridge asked, just as she was turning around to head out.

"Don't think so," she said, then stopped, turned to face him and smiled. "Nice catching up with you. You both have a great shift."

Both disgusted at herself for taking part in non-productive small talk and pleased she had managed to pull it off, she hurried away to the elevators, shaking her head as if that movement alone could erase Smitty's sleazy lines from her memory.

Now, alone at the computer, a large cup of black coffee and a yellow pad of paper in hand, she logged into the police database and began her search. She drew a table with the accused's name, the victim's name, the connection between them, the motive, murder date, the DNA type that was used to prosecute the accused, and the police case number. She noted any and all murder cases with a not-guilty plea that occurred in New England and other neighboring states over the past five years, with incriminating DNA where the victim and accused weren't related, part of a lover's triangle, or involved with gangs.

A couple of hours and three cups of coffee later, she realized that even with the information she had access to in the database, her search was a nightmare in and of itself.

How can I tell if there is a political angle in a murder if it isn't noted in the database summary file?

She'd have to consult the detailed police files. Hopefully, they were saved electronically. She kept all of these uncertain cases for now; she could try to Google the victim's names later and eliminate the irrelevant ones.

She had a long list of murders. Most of the convicted killers were now behind bars in various state prisons. But maybe some of these crimes had been "solved" by accusing and framing the wrong person.

Hard to tell.

She counted sixty-seven cases on her list, but some of them may not have had a political angle at all. She flipped her pad back to the first page and queried the detailed police case file for the top entry on her list. Just as the information popped up on the screen, her phone beeped with a message from Smitty.

Still at the station?

Yep

Hungry?

As much as Kate wanted to get rid of him again, she couldn't ignore her rumbling stomach. She knew the vending machine had nothing that would satisfy her hunger, and she didn't really have time to head out to grab anything.

What the heck. Why not take him up on his offer?

She sent him a reply:

Starving

We're at Quiznos. I'll get you a sub and swing by in 15?

Awesome :)

Well, he's nice, after all.

By the time his Italian accent greeted her, she'd filled out all of the cases from the first page on her notepad.

"How you doing?" he asked, sitting down on the corner of her desk.

"Exhausted. Thanks so much," she said, extending her hand to grab the sandwich he was offering, but he didn't let go.

"This delicious meatball sub can be yours under one condition."

"What?" she asked, a little annoyed, but her empty stomach was willing to agree to anything right now.

"Tell me what that personal research is all about. You're running background checks on possible dates? Planning a crime of your own?" He smiled and winked.

"Nothing like that," Kate said, pulling the sandwich, but all she could do was squish it. He wasn't letting go.

He smirked. "Tell me, and it's yours."

"Okay, I'm trying to find cases similar to my uncle's."

He retracted the sandwich for a second before saying, "What's up with your uncle?"

"He's accused of murder," Kate said flatly.

With his eyes now the size of two quarters, the smirk disappeared, and he let go of the sandwich.

"Thanks, how much do I owe you?" she asked, unwrapping the food whose aroma had triggered so much saliva she was almost drooling.

"What? Um? What?"

"For the sandwich," she said, after swallowing the first bite.

"Forget about the sandwich. What's going on? What murder?"

Kate gave him the CliffsNotes version in between bites.

When his radio crackled for his unit to answer a call, he stood up. "I gotta go. Mansbridge's in the car waiting for me, but," he said, shaking his head on his way out of the room, "let me know if I can help, okay?"

"Thanks, Smitty."

She devoured the rest of the sub within a minute then was back to work.

By midnight, her eyes were dry from staring at the screen. She logged out of the system and turned off the computer. She sat back and took account of where she stood. She had a dozen pages' worth of data, but some cases were still mostly blank. They'd only been archived in paper form. That meant she'd have to go through a lot of red tape to get Detective Fuller's permission to access those files.

The thought of begging him for authorization made her skin crawl.

CHAPTER NINE

Kate Murphy
Roxbury Police Station, Boston

INDEPENDENCE DAY MEANT lots of celebrations in and around Boston.

Today was Saturday, and all available police officers had been dispatched to ensure Bostonians were safe and well-behaved. With an understaffed department, that meant weird schedules and weekend overtime for most cops, including Kate. She didn't mind, though. She could use the extra money, and she'd reached a dead-end in her research yesterday. She couldn't gain anything else from querying the police database. Sure, she could spend a few more hours Googling things, but, to make real progress, she'd have to talk to Fuller and request access to the paper archives.

He'll probably say no.

The long day turned out uneventful—no riots, no terrorist attacks, and nothing that would make headlines—but Kate was exhausted by the time she returned to the station. She was so drained that she didn't even realize the annoying yells and whistles when she walked into the precinct were directed at her.

"Hey! Blondie!"

She still didn't register that a man was shouting at her until a hand grabbed her right shoulder.

"Hey! Are you all right?"

Kate turned around to see who the hand belonged to. "Oh... Smitty. Yeah, I'm good," Kate said, refraining a yawn.

"How's it going with your research?" he grinned conspiratorially and winked.

Kate took a deep breath then yawned, no longer able to hold it in. "It's been a long day. I'm done now."

"You're done with your research?"

"No, I'm off. My research has taken me to a dead end. I've got to beg Detective Lt. Fuller to let me access the archives. I just don't see how it's going to happen. The guy hates me."

"Archives, you say?"

"Yeah. Fun times."

Smitty raised his eyebrows twice rapidly, grinning. "I may be able to help."

"What do you mean?"

He leaned in as if he had a secret to share. "I've got a way to access those files."

"What? How?" Kate asked, all ears and excited for the first time today.

"Let's just say that Sandy, the girl in charge, she, um, she likes me," he said, winking and moving his hips forward and back in a suggestive motion.

Kate faked a puking sound and shook her head. "Man, do you ever stop?"

"Women like me, and I like to please them," he said with, Kate had to admit, a charming smile. "Hear me out. I've got a proposition for you."

"What?"

"How about I grant you access to some of the files you need from the archives?"

"Why? How?"

Smitty had Kate's full attention, but he wasn't spilling the beans. She slapped her hand against his breast pocket.

"Come on, man. You can't tease me like this. How?" Kate asked.

He flashed his charming smile once more, exposing pearly whites that matched the spark in his eyes. "In exchange for a date next Friday night, I've got that evening off."

"What?"

"Are you also going to ask me 'who' and 'where?' " Smitty asked, teasing her.

Kate squinted while trying to process the offer he'd made. "Wha—"

"Listen, it's your call," Smitty said. "You have my number. If you're interested, send me the case numbers, and I'll work my magic with Sandy."

He left before Kate could respond.

CHAPTER TEN

Kate Murphy
Kate's Apartment, Boston

KATE WOKE up late on Sunday, exhausted from the previous day's overtime.

She had only two things to do today: visit her uncle and decide if she was going to take up Smitty on his offer—as gross as it seemed.

This date could be the gateway to a lucky break in some old file. Although Smitty was a good cop, he apparently had no morals when it came to women or...

Is there truth to what people say about Italian men?

Who cares? How bad can a date with him really be?

A police officer wouldn't spike her drink, right? But that one date could lead to nasty rumors at work if anyone saw the two of them together.

She decided to first work her magic with Google and see if she still needed those archives once she was done. No point wasting any more time imagining Smitty hitting on her during an entire evening.

By lunch, she'd successfully eliminated five cases from her list, thanks to the gossip columns and juicy pictures she'd found online. In each situation, the victim and the accused had clearly known each other. But the rest of the items on her list still lacked too much information for Kate to determine if they could be similar to her uncle's case.

She turned off her computer and grabbed her car keys.

Time to go see my uncle.

The entire drive to jail was done on autopilot. She removed the keys from the ignition but couldn't remember driving there. She recalled starting the car and turning onto the street but had no memory of the route she'd taken. She didn't remember parallel parking her car either.

Shit, I have to get my head on straight. Lack of sleep?

No.

She'd been visualizing the possible outcome that Kenny faced if he was convicted. A lifetime in jail for a murder he didn't commit. He was so frail and weak now. He'd surely become some bigger guy's bitch. That thought sent a shiver down her spine.

No, she had to remain positive. She'd find something—whatever it was going to be—and it would lead to proving his innocence.

It had to.

After going through the visitor registration process, she sat down and inhaled deeply, hoping to clear her anxiety before seeing Kenny. Less than three breaths later, there he was with a wide smile on his ashen face.

"Kenny! I'm so happy to see you. How are you?"

His grin looked strained, and his eyes echoed a deeper, more tragic story as he swallowed and winced.

This isn't good.

"I'm okay," he said, his voice sounding coarser than usual.

"No, you're not. What's wrong?" Kate asked.

He closed his eyes and lowered his head before shaking it slightly. His shoulders rose from his strenuous breathing. Then he cleared his throat and looked up at her again.

"No, I'm good. Went to the doctor this morning." He wiggled

his fingers at his throat. "The end of a bad flu. He gave me medicine. I'll be all right."

As much as Kate wanted to believe him, a part of her didn't. His eyes told a different story. But then again, maybe the medicine he was taking clouded his mind, or perhaps he had finally come to terms with the dreadful situation he was in. George Hudson may have told him that his salvation vehicle was running on the world's thinnest fumes.

"Did you check up on the house?" he asked.

Kate felt guilty. "Oh, I've meant to, but other things came up. I promise I'll go tomorrow. Guaranteed."

"Okay, that'd be good. Could you bring me my rosary?"

Kate frowned. "Your rosary? I didn't know you had one."

Kenny nodded. "It was Lucy's, really. It's in her nightstand. Would you be able to retrieve it from the house and bring it to me?"

She didn't know if the authorities would let her bring anything in here, but that was something for her to worry about later. "Sure thing."

Kenny wiped the sweat pearling on his forehead, and in doing so, exposed the bruised forearm he'd kept behind his back until now.

"What's that?" Kate asked.

"Nothing," he shook his head and backed up on his chair.

Kate wasn't having any of this. "Is someone beating you up in here?"

"No, no, no," he said, shaking his head really fast. "I fell."

"What? Don't give me that bull crap."

"I'm serious. I'm safe. No one is bothering me."

Kate stared at him, and for the first time during this conversation, his eyes seemed to agree with the words that were coming out of his mouth.

Kenny's eyes remained locked on Kate's. "Listen, I'm grateful you came to visit, but I think I need to go and lie down. The medicine is kicking in and making me very sleepy."

"Okay, you take care," she said, still not believing him fully. "I'll grab the rosary from your house this afternoon, and I'll arrange for it to be delivered to you, alright? I can't visit you twice in one day."

"Thank you." He called up a guard to help him stand up.

Strange. But then again, he's as pale as a ghost.

Kate watched him walk away. As he reached the door, he turned around and smiled at her, then he mouthed, "I love you."

Kate's eyes filled with tears and she remained seated for a few minutes, trying to make sense of it all. Her uncle wasn't well. She needed to get him out, and fast.

That meant she needed Smitty's help. Who cared if she had to suffer through an entire evening of flirting with him, or, more accurately, being hit on. At least he was easy on the eyes. And that date would definitely be easier than begging Fuller to grant her access to the archives.

As soon as she reached her car, she got her phone out of her pocket and texted Smitty:

Friday night works for me if you could get me access to a dozen files.

She started the car, and before she could put it into first gear, her phone vibrated with a reply:

Great

Three little dots indicated he was still typing, so she waited.

Send me the case numbers
I'll pick you up next Friday at 7

She took her list out of her purse, unfolded the yellow sheets, and sent him what he'd requested.

She let out a long sigh as she drove off.

This had better be worth it.

≈

WHEN SHE ARRIVED at her uncle's house, she found the front door unlocked. Closed, but unlocked.

Strange.

She quietly pushed the door open and tiptoed her way into the living room before closing it again. She stood still, listening for any sounds. The TV was still there, turned off.

Not many thieves would bother stealing a thirty-year-old set.

But Kenny had a collection of VCR tapes he liked to watch over and over again, and his TV was already paid for, so he'd never upgraded it. In a way, the digital age had saved him money. He'd canceled his cable subscription when they'd called to force him to buy a new TV, or at least the digital adaptor that would allow his rabbit-eared set to continue working.

A sound brought her back.

A drawer being closed?

It came from the bedroom. She quietly exited the house and walked along the outside wall, hoping to catch a glimpse of the intruder. As she approached her uncle's bedroom window, Kate realized she was too short to see above the windowsill. She took a few steps back and spotted a piece of maroon and burgundy flowery fabric. A sleeve. The person moved to the right and walked back toward the dresser, never once turning to face the window, but Kate recognized her large-breasted profile. She looked like Mrs. Potato Head with a triple-D bra attachment.

It was Maude.

Kenny was right. Nosy Maude, indeed!

Kate realized she shouldn't have discarded Maude so quickly as a possible suspect for framing her uncle.

Kate returned to the front of the house and let herself in again, but this time, she didn't bother doing it quietly.

"Hello?" Kate called out, moving toward her uncle's bedroom.

"Hello? Who's there?" Maude asked.

"It's Kate."

"Oh, just a second, dear."

Kate didn't bother to wait just a second. She walked into the room and saw Maude closing a drawer in her uncle's dresser.

"What are you doing here?" Kate asked.

"Well," she started, fidgeting. "It's not what it looks like."

Kate put her hand on her hip. "What is it then, Maude?"

"I know Kenny thinks I'm just a thorn in his side, but I wanted to help."

"Help how?"

"I know where he hides his house key. The fake rock in the empty flowerpot isn't the most original idea. And, with him being in jail and all..."

Maude glanced up at Kate, a puppy look on her face, but Kate didn't cave. She let the silence stretch on uncomfortably until Maude continued.

"I miss him, that's all. I came in here and thought I'd busy myself by cleaning this place up a bit, you know? I did the dishes and, just now, I was putting away the clothes I cleaned."

"What? Why?"

"It's not as if I have many ways to help him."

Kate shook her head. If the woman wasn't in love with her uncle, she had no clue what else it could be. But she'd still examine her past, just in case.

"Do they accept cookies in jail?" Maude asked.

"I have no idea," Kate replied.

"Worth a try, though, right?"

Kate shrugged. "Sure, why not?"

"Will you go visit him again soon?"

"Yeah, I have to pick something up for him. That's why I'm here."

"Oh, perfect. As you know, I don't have a car, so I can't go visit him." Kate, who'd helped Maude deliver the car to the buyer, nodded for Maude to continue. "Could you please wait here a few minutes? I'll pack some I made this morning."

"Sure, I'll wait."

"Wonderful," Maude replied, a large smile on her wrinkled, overly tanned face.

Kate walked to her aunt's side of the bed and opened the nightstand. It contained only a bible and a rosary.

Easy enough to find.

As she held the rosary, she wondered if the item would be allowed in jail.

Could someone deem it to be a dangerous item that could be used as a weapon or as a tool to commit suicide?

She felt the waxy string and plastic beads, realizing the whole thing was cheaply made and would most likely break within a second of being stretched. She could only hope the person in charge would agree with her and let Kenny have it, so she placed it in her pocket and slid the drawer closed.

Out of curiosity, she checked her uncle's dresser. Not that she knew what he usually kept in there. But Maude hadn't lied: some of the neatly piled T-shirts were still warm to the touch.

Fresh out of the dryer.

Kate did a quick walk-through, ensuring the house was safe. No leaks. All was good. She realized Maude had cleaned up quite a bit. Even the toilet had lost the usual yellow ring Kate saw whenever she visited Kenny.

Maude's hurried steps hit the front porch, and Kate went to meet her.

"Here," Maude said, handing her two Tupperware containers and a stack of mail. "I didn't want to open these just yet, but maybe you should. There are a couple of overdue bills from the power company."

"Why two containers?"

"One for him, and one for you. You need to put some meat on your bones if you want to find yourself a new husband before it's too late."

Is this an insult or a compliment?

Kate wasn't that old. She was athletic, fit, and comfortable in her skin.

Whatever.

She smiled, thanked Maude as the nosy neighbor stepped out of the house, and then locked the door on her way out.

Kate got in her car and dropped her new cargo on the passenger seat. Before starting the engine, she opened up one of the containers, grabbed a cookie—which she had to admit was pretty darn moist and tasty—and then headed to jail for the second time today.

She wouldn't be allowed to see her uncle, but being a police officer had to count for something, right?

Somehow, she knew she'd find a way to talk the supervisor into delivering the goods to Kenny.

~

AFTER ENTRUSTING the cookies and rosary with the guard in charge of evening rounds, Kate returned home at 5:45 p.m.

While her phone was on "do not disturb," she'd gotten two missed calls from Luke. No voicemail.

Good thing he didn't bother leaving me a message.

She hit the pavement to clear her head, listening to Bon Jovi's greatest hits as a way to, at least momentarily, forget about her problems and zone out. Music had always helped her think out of the box, especially when paired with a good run. It also acted as an excellent catalyst for problem-solving, but, unfortunately, it didn't spark any new ideas on how to save her uncle.

Sweaty but glad to have gotten her weekly long run out of the way, she rewarded herself by making an energizing smoothie. She turned the TV on to the local news channel and grabbed protein powder along with ice and blueberries from the freezer.

"Coming up, the results of the latest poll for the mayoral election," the anchor said.

Kate normally enjoyed watching the news and staying up-to-date with whatever was happening in and around Boston, but with her uncle's case weighing heavily on her shoulders, she had become sick and tired of hearing about this election. She grabbed the remote and switched to CNN, hoping that some nationally trending news would help her connect her uncle's unfortunate situation to the other cases she'd found.

CNN, too, was currently covering the upcoming Boston election.

Seriously?

She made her smoothie then returned her attention to the

television and saw video footage of the homeless. She turned up the volume.

"This brings the total of non-drug-related homeless deaths on the East Coast to two hundred and fifty-three so far this year. This number isn't unusual, but what is odd is the timing of the deaths. Based on the historical morgue records for the past ten years, homeless deaths normally occur on days with extreme temperatures, whether they'd be frigid winter nights or unbearable heat waves. So far this year, only two deaths occurred when the weather could have played a part. Of course, this number is nothing compared to the number of homeless deaths caused by drug overdoses. These overdoses remain by far the leading cause of homeless deaths in urban America."

For a second, Kate wondered how many homeless people died every year in America. And how many in the world? Could these deaths be prevented?

But her uncle wasn't homeless, and she couldn't think of a way this news could help her solve his case.

She turned off the TV then took a sip. Her smoothie was refreshing, but not as much as her upcoming shower would be.

CHAPTER ELEVEN

Kate Murphy
Roxbury Police Station, Boston

ON MONDAY, glad to be done with her shift, Kate closed her locker door and was taken by surprise when someone tapped her on the shoulder.

"Got your files, Blondie," Smitty said.

"Great! That was fast."

"I worked my magic, as always." His thick black eyebrows bounced up and down rapidly, reminding her of a character from Sesame Street. "They're in my car out back. Four boxes' worth."

"Whoa, that's going to be fun."

"I can think of a lot of other things that would be more fun if you're up for it."

He paused, probably waiting for Kate's reaction, but she didn't know how else to make it clear she wasn't interested. He was helping her out, and she was grateful for that. She didn't want to alienate him, but she didn't want to encourage him either.

"Could I grab them now?" she asked.

"Sure, although I'm technically on duty. But I guess it'll only take a few minutes. I told Mansbridge I was coming in here to use the washroom, and I'd be right back."

He headed out to the parking lot, Kate in tow.

"So, what kind of food do you like?" he asked.

"Pretty much everything."

"Is pizza good for Friday?"

She nodded, anxious to get to the files. "Of course."

"Want to try my homemade pizza?" he asked, holding the building door open for her.

Kate racked her brain, once again not sure how to deal with his question—going to his apartment for a "date" would send the wrong signal—then she remembered seeing a new pizzeria last week.

"Maybe one day, but there's this new place I saw that I want to try. Up on Salem Street. You know it?"

"I think I know which place you're talking about. Never tried it either. Sounds good. Although, I'm sure it won't be as good as mine."

"Should we meet there at seven then?" Kate asked.

"Don't you want me to pick you up?"

"I like to drive."

Kate was happy they'd reached his car.

A Mustang?

That didn't surprise her in the least. He opened his trunk, and Kate walked past two more vehicles before reaching her Subaru and doing the same.

She then returned to grab the first box.

Heavy.

A minute later, the documents now transferred, Kate wished him a safe shift and headed home, stopping at a Dunkin' Donuts on the way to pick up a large coffee and a box of donuts. This was going to be a long—and boring—evening, but the key to freeing Kenny could be in one of those boxes.

Sugar and caffeine will help.

∽

ON TUESDAY, after finishing her shift, Kate ran a background check on Nosy Maude. Nothing came up.

Nosy is all.

Maude cared for her uncle, and, as Kate initially thought, she had no sort of criminal associations or previous history that would suggest she'd want to steal his DNA and frame him.

Kate dug out her hand-written notes from her breast pocket. Last night, she'd highlighted a few people she needed to learn more about, so she ran additional searches and managed to eliminate a few more cases.

On her way out, she saw Reynolds working the reception desk. The last time she'd seen him was when he'd let her in to see her uncle while Kenny was detained at the precinct. Reynolds made eye contact, so she nodded and wished him a good evening.

"Hey, Murphy! How are things?" he called out to her.

"Good, you?"

"Well, working evenings, but someone's got to do it, right? Why are you still here? Didn't you finish a few hours ago?"

"Just doing some research."

"Trying to help that old man you came to visit the other day?"

"My uncle? Yeah."

"Well, good luck."

Kate headed out, feeling a smile drawing on her face.

First Smitty, now Reynolds. It was odd to have people asking about her life, let alone remembering what was going on with her. Maybe "having friends" was a possibility in this district.

Friends aren't like husbands who can cheat on you and turn your life upside down in the process, right?

Then again, there's Luke. Once a great friend, now an asshole who forgot to mention he was seeing someone else.

She had to forget about him.

When she arrived home, Kate ordered some Chinese food and got started with the third box of archived papers. She was flipping through the second file folder when her phone buzzed. Caller ID read "Luke." She ignored it once more.

He'll get the hint one day.

She returned to the next file and found a videotape where the accused had been caught on camera, so he was obviously guilty. She crossed that one off of her list.

By midnight, she'd learned more about seven other victims who could have been murdered for some sort of political or religious reason. For each victim, she Googled and printed everything she could on their extremist views, hoping to find a common thread, some mutual motive to all of them. But none of them appeared to be related. At least, not in an obvious way. The victims' political views were different. She couldn't have seen them voting for the same party, but she had to say that all of them were fairly extreme in their actions or choice of words from what she found on YouTube and various personal blogs.

By 2:15 a.m., she'd gone through the last box and put the cover back on.

She had narrowed down her list to thirty-two people. Kate hoped to find some connection to her uncle's case. Some tiny detail that may have been overlooked, something that was comparable to his case that she could then use to model her argument off of in an effort to help exonerate Kenny.

BY 9:15 A.M. on Wednesday, she'd already caught her fifth speeder in a school zone. After issuing the man's ticket, she returned to her parked patrol car and called George Hudson. She was surprised when the receptionist put her on hold and said he'd take her call in a minute.

Lucky timing.

"Hi, Miss Murphy! Good to hear from you. How are you doing?" his deep voice asked without a pause. "May I call you Kate?"

"Sure. I'm good." Kate was a bit taken aback by his enthusiasm. "And how are you?"

"Fantastic, as usual. You caught me just at the right time. I'm heading to court in about ten minutes. Did you make any progress?"

"Yes and no. I found some archived cases that could be comparable to Kenny's situation. Similar in the sense that DNA was used to incriminate them, they pleaded not guilty, the accused wasn't connected to the victim, and the victim had extreme political or religious views."

"Wow, that's good. There might be a link. Would you be able to drop by the office today? You're working day shifts, right?"

"Not sure if I can swing by during work hours, but I could go after 4 p.m."

"Great, I should be back in my office around 4:30. If you could bring your results, that would be awesome."

"Wonderful. I'll see you later."

Kate hung up and returned to her duties.

AT 4:35 P.M., she walked into George's office with two copies of her results, which she'd transferred into an Excel spreadsheet so her notes would be more legible. Filing so many police reports over the years had made her a fast typist. Ten minutes after work was all it took for her to have that document ready and printed.

"That's great," George said, glancing at the list of victims, names of the accused, dates, locations, DNA, and the other details she'd included. He leaned back in his chair, then grabbed a pencil and circled a few cases on the list.

"A couple of these ring a bell," he said. "Our office represented them, but I think they were incarcerated for life, unfortunately. I didn't represent them personally, but I'm familiar with their cases."

"Do you think we could talk to them?" Kate asked.

"The accused?"

"Yeah, or do you think I would gain more from talking to their lawyers?"

"Their lawyers would have already used all of the information they had to defend them. The accused wouldn't offer any new information either, but tiny details that seemed irrelevant at the time could resurface if they were to recount their stories. One of those could help with Kenny's case." He flipped open a brown leather book that looked like a daily journal. "I'm fully booked with court dates until the end of next week, but let me touch base with their lawyers. I'm pretty sure their clients would be interested in exploring a possible way to prove their innocence."

"Sounds good. I can go by myself if you or the other lawyers can't make it."

His eyes opened wider, seemingly surprised by Kate's offer. "You'd be fine with that?"

"Hey, I want to get Kenny out of this mess. I'll do whatever it takes."

"If I recall correctly, they're not incarcerated in Massachusetts. Would you be fine flying out-of-state to meet them?"

Kate thought for a second. She didn't have a lot of extra cash in her bank account. However, her credit cards had room for a flight or two. "Sure, but I don't think I'll be able to get days off. Could they request visits for me this weekend?"

"They normally require forty-eight hours' notice. Today's Wednesday." He looked up as if figuring out if the timing would work. "Maybe. We'll see, I'll have to talk to them tonight so they can put in the request before 8 a.m. tomorrow morning."

"Sounds good. Keep me posted," Kate said, standing up and getting ready to leave.

"I'll call or leave you a voicemail if I can't reach you." George escorted her to the elevator and shook her hand. "Great work, Kate. I imagine you've spent a lot of hours reading case files to come up with this list."

"It's not like there were many other leads."

"I hope we can get you a couple of visits that will help us come up with a credible story before next Friday."

"Next Friday? Why? Is this his court date?"

"Yes. Not much time, but you've made great progress. I'm sure I'll be able to incorporate some of this information into my existing defense. I'll go through these cases, as well, to see if I can find something else."

"That would be good, thanks."

"Have a great evening, Kate. Do take some time to relax a little bit, okay? You've done good."

"I will. Have a great evening, too."

Kate smiled, hoping her research and upcoming prison visits could prove helpful in court next Friday.

CHAPTER TWELVE

Kate Murphy
Kate's Apartment, Boston

EARLY FRIDAY EVENING, George called Kate to report he had arranged two visits for her: one on Saturday afternoon at the Lewisburg Penitentiary in Pennsylvania and the other on Sunday afternoon at the Elkton Federal Correctional Institution in Ohio.

"Because you're not a lawyer or a relative, we had to twist the truth a little bit so they could let you visit the first one on Saturday. If anyone asks, you're a former colleague of Mr. Forrester."

Kate listened to his tips and made notes of the dress code and documents she'd need to take with her before thanking George and hanging up.

It didn't sound like a fun weekend, but she could learn something new, something that could free Kenny. One step closer was all she could hope for right now.

One tiny step closer.

She dug out her computer to book flights and a rental car. She was busy entering her credit card information when the phone rang. Excited about what the upcoming weekend could reveal, she forgot to check caller ID before answering.

"Hello?"

"Hi, Katie. You're a hard woman to get a hold of."

She recognized that voice.

"Luko... Sorry, I've been busy."

"Listen, I know it was weird. I want to apologize for how I left things... how I left that evening."

"Don't worry about it. I know how things are. I'm an adult. You have other irons in the fire."

"Other irons in the fire?"

"You know..." Kate said, not wanting to spell it out.

"What? You mean other women?"

Kate was annoyed at his question.

He's smart enough to know. Why is he doing this?

"Whatever," she said, raising her brow even though he couldn't see her over the phone.

"Katie. I'm not seeing anybody. Is that what you're saying?"

"I saw you last week with a brunette at Quincy Market. No point in lying to me. I'm a grown-up, I can take it."

"What? Quincy Market?"

Kate couldn't think of anything else she could say to clarify what she meant without feeling a deep pang in her chest.

"Last time I went there, I was with my cousin Sharon," Luke continued. "Her husband has cancer. She'd just found out and didn't know what to do. She needed to talk to someone, so I met with her."

"Oh." Kate felt like an idiot, a total jerk. Then, she remembered the phone conversation from that first night at the lab. "But... what about when we met. Didn't you call some woman to make an excuse for being late for dinner or something?"

"Katie. You're busting my balls here. You've been ignoring me because you saw me sitting with someone and because of something you overheard me say on the freaking phone? What's wrong with you? I told you, I'm not seeing anyone," he spoke so loudly that Kate had to move her phone away from her ear.

Had she heard him right the other day? She wasn't so sure anymore.

"I'm sorry. I've got trust issues," she said. "Divorce has a way of messing with your head."

"That won't work with me. I... I can't do this. You need to sort out your shit, Kate. I can't deal with this right now. Sorry."

A dial tone followed.

Oh shit.

Again, she'd pushed away someone she cared about. Her childhood friend, the one and only real buddy she ever had in her life, the one person who knew her before the incident. If she couldn't believe him or count on him to tell her the truth, would she ever be able to do that with any man? Or anyone, for that matter?

It wasn't like she had any girlfriends to hang out with either.

Yeah. I have trust issues indeed.

She put her phone on the charger and headed to the kitchen to grab a beer... then another. Then another.

A FEW HOURS LATER, her phone started ringing again, waking her up from a nap she didn't know she was taking.

"Where are you? We had a deal," a man's voice said.

"What? Who is this?"

"Smitty. I'm at the pizza place. Been here for thirty minutes already."

"Oh shit. Um... I must have fallen asleep. I'm so sorry." Kate sat up on her love seat. "Give me ten." Kate stood up and sat right down again. "Whoa... Dizzy.... How about take-out?"

"What's wrong with you?"

"Don't ask. Probably a few too many, too quickly."

"We. Had. A. Deal," Smitty said in a slow and quiet staccato. He then continued a little louder, no longer hiding his resentment. "I did my half. What's your half going to be?"

"I'm so sorry, Smitty. Why don't you pick up your favorite pizza, then come over, and I'll brew some fresh coffee for us. How does that sound?"

"Sure. Now you're talking. You want me to *come over*?" he said, his voice overly optimistic with the last two words.

"That's *not* what I mean. I don't think I should drive right now, and I know we had a deal. So unless you have a better idea, I'm inviting you over *as a friend*, okay? No funny business."

"Whatever you say. Anchovies?"

Kate couldn't wrap her head around his ability to change emotions as suddenly as a weather vane could spin. "Sure, why not?"

She gave him her address and walked into the bathroom to splash cold water on her face before starting the coffee machine.

I'm so stupid. Way to go, Kate! Now Smitty will spread rumors that I'm an alcoholic. Shit…

What the heck was I doing before Luke called?

After racking her brain, she finally saw her wallet open next to her laptop, with the screensaver bouncing around.

The flights! I have to book those now.

Of course, her reservation had expired, but she only had herself—and her stupid lack of trust in others—to blame. She could no longer book the flights she wanted, but she nonetheless managed to find a flight from Boston to Harrisburg, Pennsylvania, early Saturday morning and another flight from Pittsburgh to Boston on Sunday evening. She also reserved a one-way rental car from Avis in the Harrisburg Airport with a drop off at the Pittsburgh airport.

She was putting her wallet back in her purse when the door buzzed.

"Pizza delivery," Smitty said over the intercom.

"Come on up. Third floor, apartment B."

Kate headed to the bathroom, glanced at herself in the mirror, redid her ponytail, and then added a touch of lip gloss before returning to the living room to greet Smitty.

A quick double knock preceded his entrance. He wore jeans with a beige suede sport coat and a navy blue silk shirt; his top two buttons were undone, exposing a large golden chain and a dense mat of chest hair. He looked good in a police uniform, but he cranked it up to handsome in his civilian clothes. Add a mustache to this guy, and he could seriously compete with a young Tom Selleck.

Kate grabbed the pizza box from him. "Smells good!"

"Hope you don't mind, I grabbed a slice on the way here."

Kate shook her head and smiled. "That's fine. Once again, I'm so sorry. I fell asleep."

Smitty shrugged, and they headed toward the kitchen.

"Oh, before I forget," Kate said, turning around to face him, "I'm done with the files." Her head pointed to the boxes piled by the door. "I'll help you bring them down to your car later."

She brought the pizza box to the kitchen and placed it on the island, and then grabbed a couple of plates and forks.

"Nah, we don't need those," Smitty said, opening the box, grabbing a piece, and folding it in two.

Kate returned the plates to the cupboard and followed his lead when she realized there were already four pieces missing. She looked at Smitty, and he answered before she even asked.

"I was starving."

Kate laughed as she grabbed a slice.

"Delicious!" she exclaimed after the first bite.

"Duh," he said, raising his eyebrows. "That's why I couldn't stop after just one."

Once the pizza was gone, they switched to coffee and serious conversation.

"So, were the archives useful?" he asked.

"Yes, I guess. I'm going to meet a couple of convicts this weekend to follow up. I want to see if there's a connection between them and my uncle."

"That's good." He tilted his head and raised his brows. "Is that why you drank a little too much?"

"Actually, no. Not at all."

A minute elapsed before Smitty broke the silence. "I guess you're not going to fill me in on that. I get it."

Kate could feel tears coming up just thinking about how stupid she'd been toward Luke.

"Let's just say I have trust issues. I got what I deserved."

"Ex-husband?" Smitty asked.

"What? No." Kate shook her head. "How do you know about him?"

"People talk. Clancy's my buddy. You may have come up in a conversation or two."

"What?" Kate didn't know what to think of his comment.

People are already spreading rumors about me in this new district?

"Nothing bad," Smitty said, shrugging. "He made sense of some stuff for me. You know we're all broken in some way, right?"

She glared at him. "Broken?"

"You know what I mean. We all put on a show. Sometimes we're so involved in maintaining our façade that we forget who we are deep down."

Kate was wondering if he was talking about her or making reference to his non-stop Italian-stallion, womanizer personality. No matter which he meant, she didn't like where this was going. She could feel emotions bubbling just below the surface. She looked at her lap and took a deep breath to push down her imminent tears. No way she'd let him think she was an alcoholic *and* an emotional basket case.

Kate busied herself with the empty coffee mugs, placing them in the sink before heading back to the living room, hoping to give Smitty a subtle sign that it was time for him to go.

"Did you hear about my shift last night?" he asked, following her to the door.

"No, what happened?" Kate asked, her curiosity piqued.

"We found a John Doe in a cardboard box behind a rundown building."

Kate suddenly forgot about her issues and took an interest in what Smitty was saying. "What happened?"

"Dead. Homeless. Maybe a bad heart. Maybe drugs, don't know yet. Makes you re-think your life, doesn't it?" he asked.

"Life is short indeed." Kate didn't know what else to say. She felt bad for the homeless man and still felt guilty for standing Smitty up. "Once again, I'm sorry for not meeting you at the restaurant. Thanks for the pizza and the company. You're a nice guy, Smitty."

He wrapped his arms around her and patted her on the back.

"You're a nice girl too, Blondie. You should let people in once in a while. You may be surprised."

Kate pulled out of his embrace.

"Listen, Smitty. I've got to get up early tomorrow. Long day. I'm going to visit a prisoner in Pennsylvania. Can I help you take those boxes to your car?"

"Sure, or you can help me bring them to the elevator. That would be awesome."

As they carried the final boxes to the elevator, Smitty asked, "Traveling to help with your uncle's case?"

"Yeah," Kate said, nodding as she dropped the last box by his feet. "I hope I'll find a golden nugget we can use in court. His trial starts on Friday and his defense is pretty thin right now."

She stood in front of the elevator and watched him lean sideways to press a button.

"Good luck with that," he said as the doors closed on him.

"Thanks and good night, Smitty," she said, a genuine smile on her face.

CHAPTER THIRTEEN

Kate Murphy
Lewisburg Penitentiary, PA

AFTER GOING through the imposed visitor procedure, Kate was escorted to one of the prison phone booths. She was instructed to sit at the third one and wait. Samuel Forrester would be sitting across the corresponding window in a few minutes.

She didn't know what to expect.

Is this guy guilty? Is he a creep?

I hope he's just an innocent man like my uncle.

This high-security prison held cold-blooded murderers that came in all shapes and sizes. From her training, Kate knew that physical appearances were not always indicative of a person's temperament, but when a tall and slender elderly man sat across from her, her apprehension began melting. A vertical line appeared on Forrester's forehead when he saw Kate. She reached for the phone receiver, and he followed suit.

"Hi, Mr. Forrester, my name's Kate Murphy."

"What do you want? I don't know you. You're not a former colleague."

"I know, but that was the only way I would be allowed to visit you. I'll do my best to be brief. My uncle is accused of murder. I'm trying to prove his innocence, and your case sounds similar to his. I'm hoping to connect some dots and find a pattern that could prove that my uncle, you, and other people like you, were framed for murders you didn't commit."

"Are you a lawyer?"

"No, I'm not. I'm running my own investigation, as the niece of a wrongly-accused man." Kate hoped he wasn't going to ask if she was a cop. He probably didn't like cops.

He stayed silent, his gaze sizing her up. She could tell he needed more convincing.

"I'm only interested in hearing what you have to say, and maybe asking a few questions. I'm doing the same tomorrow with another man who may have also been wrongly accused."

"Could this get me out of here?"

"No," Kate said, not wanting to lie to the man.

He stood up, and Kate knew she had to say something—anything—to keep him on the phone for a second longer.

"Maybe!" she yelped as Forrester moved the receiver away from his ear.

He brought it back, but Kate knew she only had this one shot to get him to stick around.

"I mean your talking to me won't free you this instant, but I may learn something that could force the state to reopen your case, and then... Maybe."

He squinted, staring at her.

"Nothing to lose, and maybe you could gain your freedom back," Kate said after a few seconds of uncomfortable silence.

He twisted his mouth then finally spoke again. "What do you want to know?"

"Tell me about you, what you do... um... what you did for a living and what your life was like until the day they accused you."

"Married, wife, two kids, three grandkids. Happy most days. Typical life. Suburbs. Mortgage. Car loans. What else do you want to know?" he asked as he scratched his head.

"When did they arrest you?"

"They showed up at my home one Monday afternoon. Totally

freaked my wife out. Arrested me right there and then, and then searched my home."

"Can you describe the murder, as you understand it, based on what they said in court?" Kate didn't want to push his buttons, so she clarified that she didn't think he was guilty. "What kind of story did the lawyers invent to make the jury believe you did it?"

"I've heard it so many times, and I've repeated it in my dreams. I can almost picture it as if it happened for real now," he paused, then leaned forward before continuing. "I've never been to the guy's home, but from the trial photos, he looked super wealthy. Nice foreign artifacts. Almost like what Indiana Jones would have in his office. The murderer used one of the heavy statues and smacked the guy on the back of the head, and he fell on his Persian rug. Then, the murderer used a small blade to slit his neck. They never found the blade. That's what they were searching for at my house."

"What evidence did they have against you?" Kate pressed, even though she already knew the answer. She hoped he'd mention a tiny detail that could prove helpful.

"Somehow my blood ended up at the crime scene."

His phrasing caught her interest. "What do you mean? Where was it?"

"I'll never forget the attorney demonstrating it on a dummy in court. It was ridiculous."

Kate waited.

"Imagine I'm holding a knife and sitting on top of the knocked out guy," he started, his fist demonstrating the position. "I dig the blade into his neck. I cut between him and the rug, so I don't get splashed with the blood. You know, blood pressure in a major artery, and all of that. So, blood starts pouring out. There must be a lot of it oozing out, and it's probably starting to pool around the dead guy. The killer freaks out a little, probably wanting to get his feet out of there without stepping into the blood, so he gets up, forgetting that his blade was still in the victim's neck, or maybe he loses his balance a little, and he cuts himself with his own blade, leaving a bloody fingerprint on the back of the dead guy's neck."

He shook his head.

Kate let the silence hang, hoping he'd have more information to give her, and she was rewarded after thirty seconds or so.

"How the fuck did my blood get there? No idea."

"Did the fingerprints match?"

He shook his head once more. "No, but DNA from the blood was a perfect match."

"Same thing as Kenny," Kate said, nodding.

"Who?"

"My uncle. I guess that's a good sign. There could be a larger thing at play here. What do you know about the victim?"

"From personal experience, nothing," he said. "I've never met the guy, but some witnesses say he was involved in community events. I attended one of his charity golf tournaments, but I didn't know it at the time. Who cares who organizes those? I just like to play golf. I was retired, see? Golfing was my one activity that got me out of the house. I signed up for all sorts of tournaments. Anything within fifty miles, I'd be there. I'd join threesomes who needed a fourth. I liked talking with strangers back then."

"Do you know if he had political connections?"

"They said something about him running for office, but I forget. He didn't win, though. Organizing events was one way for him to mingle and become known so he'd get more votes, or raise money for stuff he was into."

Kate kept him talking. "What did they say was your motive for killing him?"

"Something about me being angry at him."

"Were you?"

"No, but I did get upset during that tournament. At the seventh hole, on a par three, we had to sit there and wait because a freaking Canadian goose had decided to take the hole hostage. They had one of the stewards at the tee with us, with a walkie-talkie, and another guy near the green, relaying the goose's movements. She had her goslings with her, see? These birds are protective as hell and fucking dangerous, so the stewards couldn't just shoo them away, and they wouldn't let us play, just in case we hit one of them and killed it with a ball. You know, I told 'em one ball should scare them, and they'd take off without getting anyone hurt. But no. We had to wait there for fifty minutes. Fifty goddamn minutes! Needless to say, a line started to form behind us at that point. No matter how scattered the tee-off times had been, we now had three groups breathing down our necks for the rest of the game. The remaining eleven holes sucked! My worst game ever."

"Did you blame the victim?" Kate asked.

"I blamed the fucking geese! They're freaking everywhere. I don't understand why the golf course owner didn't let us scare off the damn birds. A few dead ones would have been a good thing, if you ask me. They shit all over the place, too."

"Thanks, Mr. Forrester, I get the picture. Is there anything else you could tell me? Anything that seemed odd or out of place to you?"

"You mean other than my blood being there in the first place?" he asked with a blank stare.

"Yeah."

"The freaking fingerprint. Whose was it? They never found out."

She made a note of this. "Did this come up in court?"

"Sure, but they dismissed it, saying DNA from blood was stronger evidence. First, they thought I had an accomplice, then they stuck to the print belonging to a stranger or maybe an off-the-record employee of the guy who checked his pulse then freaked out and left town. Don't know many people who'd bother to check the pulse of a man sitting in a pool of blood, but whatever. I'm the one rotting here, and the owner of that fingerprint got away with murder."

Kate thanked him for his time and promised to be in touch should she discover anything helpful.

He nodded, stood up, and then left the visiting area without saying another word.

Once out of the penitentiary and back into the comforts of

her economy rental car, Kate went over Forrester's words in her head.

No matter how much she tried, she couldn't find a stronger connection than the weird DNA match with an unmatched fingerprint. Maybe the fingerprint from Forrester's case would match one of the unknown prints from her uncle's case?

No. She knew the detectives would have run the print against all those that were already in the system. But then again, people had ten fingers.

Could it have been the same guy, but a different hand or a different finger?

She took out her phone and Googled the victim again. He was pro-life and anti-genome projects, but he was more into creating a greener world, so he was not an oil supporter.

If the two cases were related, she had to eliminate environmentalism as a possible motive.

She'd seen several pictures of the victim with US senators, the New York City mayor, and many actors, singers, and other celebrities. Sure, he had been involved in some minor controversial topics, and he had friends in high places, but was that reason enough to kill someone? Maybe he was just a brown-noser who had offended the wrong person?

She put her notepad down on the passenger seat and turned on the radio. The clock read 3:12 p.m. She knew she had four hours of driving between here and her next visit tomorrow, so she looked at the map on her GPS and decided to drive to Youngstown, Ohio.

She hoped the town would have a cheap but comfortable hotel where she could relax and prepare for tomorrow's visit.

KATE AWOKE in her motel room on Sunday morning, her mind lingering on the remnants of the previous night's dreams, something that involved Luko.

Her alarm clock hadn't gone off yet. The light peeking through the sides of the plastic shades suggested it was around seven or eight o'clock. She reached for the phone she'd left on her nightstand: 7:35 a.m. She opened up the messaging app and started to type a note for Luke:

Sorry

However, she couldn't find the courage to send it. She deleted it and played a few rounds of Candy Crush. When she ran out of lives, she got out of bed and hopped in the shower.

She had a few hours to kill, so she turned on the television and watched sitcom re-runs before checking out and grabbing an unhealthy breakfast in town.

Coffee in hand, she drove to meet Timothy Swanson. She got there an hour before the official start of visiting hours, with plenty of time to review her notes.

The murder he'd been charged with involved a gun, which was never found. The accused's hair had been recovered at the crime scene. They'd also discovered a footprint that matched his shoe size but never found the matching boots. This particular victim was a religious figure, not a political one, but then again, those two groups were a lot more intertwined than most would acknowledge. He was a pastor in a small parish, but quite outspoken on the Internet. She'd found his blog last week, and the pastor had strong views on homosexuality, abortion, and other subjects.

The visit turned out to be uneventful. Swanson confirmed one detail: no fingerprint this time. Just the shoe print.

Similar lines, but no real connection. Swanson didn't offer anything else she didn't already know. She ran out of questions, and he couldn't think of anything else to say, so she thanked him for his time and left the penitentiary.

Kate had to catch her return flight from Pittsburg, so she hit the road.

Along the way, before crossing the Ohio-Pennsylvania border, she spotted a gas station and stopped to fill her tank and grab a snack. She filled up, locked her car, and opened the door to the convenience store, which triggered a small chime.

"Hi there," the middle-aged woman behind the cash register said.

"Hi," Kate replied. "I'm just going to use your bathroom and pick up a few things before paying for my gas."

"Sure thing, dear. In the back," she said, pointing toward a sign across the store.

Her bladder relieved of all the caffeine she'd ingested, Kate took her time and wandered the three aisles, looking for something a little healthier than chips, candy, or chocolate, but the selection was slim.

The doorbell chimed again.

"Hi there, Sonia. A pack of Marlboros, please," a man's voice said.

"Here you go, Sheriff. That'll be $8.95. How's your day going?"

"Well, you know. Typical, but we found a dead John Doe a few hours ago."

Kate grabbed a 7UP, a bag of white cheese popcorn, and a pepperoni stick before heading toward the cash register.

The sheriff was still standing there, putting the change the cashier had given him back into his pocket. He then pulled a picture out of his notebook.

"Do you know this man?" he asked the clerk.

"No, never saw him in my life."

Kate stayed back by a couple of feet. She didn't want to interrupt him; she was in no hurry. But the sheriff turned around and addressed her.

"Ma'am, don't believe you're from around here."

"No, sir. I'm not."

He approached her anyway. "Could you tell me if you've seen this man before?"

Kate grabbed the picture to have a closer look. The man on the photograph had his eyes closed and was resting on a horizontal stainless steel surface.

The picture must have been taken at the morgue.

He had dark blond hair, a scruffy beard, and a pointed nose.

Probably Caucasian, but his skin looked leathered by too much sun.

"Sorry. I don't think so," Kate said, shaking her head before handing back the photo.

He returned it to his notebook and grabbed something else from his breast pocket. "Here's my card if you remember seeing him somewhere. Thanks for your help."

The sheriff then turned to the clerk and waved her a two-finger salute. "Have a great afternoon, Sonia. Stay safe." Then he left.

Kate paid for her gas and her snacks, tucked the sheriff's card in her wallet and headed to the Pittsburgh International airport to drop off her rental vehicle and catch her flight back to Boston.

WHEN KATE FINALLY GOT HOME, after sitting on the tarmac for two hours and being in the air for nearly two more, she felt exhausted and deflated.

She grabbed a pint of ice cream and a can of 7UP and made herself an ice cream float. She sat at her kitchen island and played with her spoon, pushing the ice cream ball down into the liquid and twirling it around. It reminded her of the floats her dad would order at the diner in her hometown.

Simpler days. Where have they gone?

She tried to remember the last time she'd had such a treat.

It was a *long* time ago.

Her parents were still alive. Her dad used to take her to the diner on Sundays, and he'd have coffee and get her a float, but not with root beer like the menu offered. Kate had never liked root beer, so the waitress had tried various soda and ice cream combinations to please her, and they'd finally settled on the plainest of the plain: vanilla ice cream with 7UP.

She couldn't remember her dad's voice anymore. But she remembered that he always made time for her every Sunday.

It was their precious daddy-daughter time. Never missed it once... until she turned thirteen and everything changed.

Her mind flashed to that fateful day.

She and Luko had spent the whole afternoon in nearby caves, pretending to be explorers from centuries ago, discovering new life forms in small ponds and sometimes just playing with their flashlights, making finger shadows and telling each other scary stories.

She didn't know she was about to walk onto the scariest scene of her life a few hours later.

Luko's calculator watch had warned them that they were running late for supper. They'd both be in trouble if they didn't return home right away, so they had run back to their respective houses. They lived a few hundred feet down the road from each other. They had raced back. They were both excellent runners. They'd normally call the other to determine who got to their house first.

But the winner never got to brag on the phone that day.

Kate had opened the front door of her house, out of breath, and shouted, "Sorry, I'm late," before taking off her muddied shoes by the entrance.

She'd instantly realized something was wrong: The house was trashed. Her mom's records were scattered on the living room floor, lamps on their side, broken glass everywhere. Stuff was missing from the mantel.

"Mom?"

No reply.

"Dad? Bobby?"

Still nothing.

Kate had never been so scared.

She hadn't known what to do or where to look for them.

Her instinct had led her upstairs, to see if Bobby was still in his crib. After running up two steps at a time and pushing his bedroom door open, she found her baby brother, but he'd never been that quiet before. The silence was nothing short of terrifying.

"Bobby?"

Kate carefully turned him around in his crib and found him

with his eyes wide open, his neck bruised. She grabbed him, a cold and lifeless lump of flesh in baby clothes.

"Bobby!" she cried out, hugging the baby and running down the stairs with him.

She went to the kitchen, her brother pressed against her chest, but she stopped in her tracks when she stepped into the room.

Maybe the phone rang at that point. She wasn't sure. She wasn't able to move.

All she was able to focus on was her mom and dad sitting on their kitchen chairs with silver duct tape tying their ankles and arms to their seats. Her dad's favorite blue tie was wrapped around his face, covering his mouth. His head was hanging backward, way too backward. His neck displayed a big gap in it, and his suit was covered in blood.

The whole kitchen was covered in blood. The wall behind him, the table in front of him, the tiled floor.

Kate's mom was looking down, her long blonde hair falling and hiding her face, but the bottom six inches of it were matted and dark red.

There was blood everywhere.

Her mom's dress was ripped open.

Blood everywhere.

Kate didn't remember what had happened next. She didn't even remember her own actions, but she knew her childhood innocence had ended right there and then.

KATE SAT QUIETLY and closed her eyes as tears rolled down her cheeks.

She focused on her breathing.

1-2-3-4-5-6 in, hold it; 1-2-3-4-5-6 out.

1-2-3-4-5-6 in, hold it; 1-2-3-4-5-6 out.

"I'm okay. I'm safe. Things will be all right," she told herself out loud.

She took out her phone, and without taking a second to reconsider, she sent Luke a text message:

I'm stupid. I'm sorry. Please forgive me.

She turned her phone off, not wanting to deal with his reply or get anxious over the lack of one. She'd said what needed to be said and now she just wanted to escape and forget. Make the images of her past disappear, at least for now.

She went to her medicine cabinet and grabbed two Clonazepam tablets. Her prescription was running low, so she made a mental note to get a refill. She swallowed them, followed by a tall glass of water.

As she waited for the meds to kick in, she thought of Kenny and how she'd failed him this weekend.

There were only four days to go before his trial on Friday. Could she uncover something to prove his innocence before then?

It no longer seemed possible.

CHAPTER FOURTEEN

Kate Murphy
Kate's Apartment, Boston

ON WEDNESDAY EVENING, with a cup of herbal tea in hand, Kate turned on the TV to wind down and get ready for bed. She couldn't stop thinking about her uncle. She hoped the TV would distract her.

He was due to appear in court in two days, and she hadn't managed to find anything solid that would help with his defense. Of course, George would do the best he could to prove he was innocent, but deep down, she knew Kenny was going to be sentenced to decades in prison.

Her lack of investigative skills could be to blame. Maybe that was why she never passed the interview to become a detective. She didn't know how to dig deep enough, what questions to ask or where to look.

She took deep breaths and continued sipping her tea when the anchor suddenly stopped reading the teleprompter and brought his index finger to his right ear.

"We interrupt this newscast for a breaking news story: Clark Ferguson, one of Boston's leading mayoral candidates has been found dead in his downtown apartment. His body was discovered tonight by his wife Tracy Ferguson, a well-known prosecutor, when she returned home from a business trip. So far, police officers on site have only stated that the suspicious death occurred several days ago and is being investigated."

Whoa. This is a political victim for sure.

Kate couldn't help but wonder if it could be connected to her own investigation. Now, she regretted not having followed the city's election more closely.

What kind of person was he? Was he extremist in his views?

Would Fuller let me in on the case?

She stopped her hopes from escalating. She knew he wouldn't want her there, and this time, Capt. Cranston wouldn't overrun his decision.

ON THURSDAY MORNING, after going for a short run, Kate stretched her muscles with the news playing in the background. The police had released a tape showing a man heading to the victim's apartment. The tape didn't incriminate the man, but the police needed the public's help in locating him for questioning.

There was something about the man's face that rang a bell in Kate's mind.

They paused on the best angle they had of his face. The video was black and white, but the man's hair wasn't really dark. His eyes were probably blue or green; he had a fairly large, pointed nose. Kate took out her phone and snapped a photo of the image on TV. Maybe she'd remember where she'd seen that man before.

Speeding ticket? Domestic disturbance? Out around town?

The newscaster said that he was Caucasian, probably in his forties, about 6'2" and 180 pounds.

Tall and skinny, Kate thought to herself... where had she seen that blond man?

Didn't matter right now, she had to get ready for work. Maybe more information would become available later.

Kate busied herself with work: answering calls, filing reports, and running plates. But she kept her eyes and ears open for anything having to do with Ferguson's murder.

Once she got home, there was much more information to read. The media was all over it. She went through every blog post and article—even those printed in newspapers—and watched each of the major news channels to make sure she knew everything.

They covered Ferguson's electoral platform: better roads, more frequent and less expensive public transport. Fewer "Happy Holidays" and more "Merry Christmas" greetings was one of the things that had gotten him some media coverage, but Kate didn't think people would kill over that. There was nothing offensive or extreme enough to warrant killing him, but he could have had connections, and once in power, could have made things happen for them.

Kate focused her search on who he knew and hung out with. Being in politics, Ferguson was often photographed with people, so all she had to do was find some extremist friends of his.

Easier said than done.

It wasn't like they'd write that in the caption.

After a couple of hours, she called it quits. There wasn't any dirt on him or the people he associated with.

Not a *single* thing, which was a little weird.

What skeletons were in his closet?

Nobody was perfect in this world, and whatever dirt existed on politicians usually came out during their campaigns. He must have done something illicit at least once in his life, right? His electoral support team had done an excellent job hiding it, whatever it was.

Then again, he also had lots of family money and connections. Enough to buy anyone and everyone's silence.

ON FRIDAY MORNING, Kate still hadn't remembered where she'd seen the blond man, but it didn't matter anyway. The TV anchor reported that the mysterious man had stepped forward and volunteered to answer the detective's questions.

At 9:55 a.m., Kate walked into the courthouse in her police uniform, after having locked her weapon and radio in her patrol car. She'd been granted a couple of hours off to attend her uncle's trial and wanted to be there for him.

Luke was slotted to testify that day, along with one of the detectives. She searched the room, hoping to find Luke and apologize in person, but there was no sign of him. His testimony would probably be heard later on.

She made eye contact with her uncle, though. He had on his best smile, but he looked pale. She wondered if he'd gotten over the flu or if he was still fighting it.

Before she could make her way to the front to talk to him, the court was called to order for the arrival of the judge. She took the first available seat once the judge and everyone else sat down.

George and the opposing lawyer voiced their opening statements, and the prosecution carried on with presenting evidence to the court. Kate didn't like the facts that were being introduced, but she knew that somehow the evidence never lied. It didn't look good for her uncle.

At 11:55 a.m., the alarm on her phone vibrated to remind her that she had to leave and get back to work. She'd have to call George later to learn how the rest of it went.

She walked out of the courthouse and headed to the nearest coffee shop to refuel her mind before returning to her patrol car, and sensed that something was odd: people were acting strangely on the streets. They weren't behaving in a dangerous or suspicious way, but the men and women she encountered were way too agitated and talkative.

She walked into a coffee shop and stopped in her tracks. Everyone, including the barista, was gathered around tables, watching videos on people's phones and tablets. Based on the screams and cries heard coming from the devices, along with the dropped jaws, covered mouths, and wide eyes on people's faces, Kate concluded they were all watching the same awful video.

She walked to the closest group and poked her head in so she could glance at the screen. A naked, prepubescent girl, probably seven or eight years old, was lying on a large bed, with her wrists and ankles tied to the corners. She was screaming and crying for her mom. A naked man then approached and placed a piece of duct tape on her mouth. His face never appeared in front of the camera—probably on purpose—but he had a pale complexion and short, wavy brown hair.

Caucasian or a light-skinned Hispanic man, perhaps?

His body was toned but not bulky. After disappearing from the shot, he reappeared again, blocking the girl from view as he stepped between her and the camera.

"Oh no!" Kate couldn't help but say aloud.

The young girl was wiggling her legs and arms, at least as much as the restraints would allow her to, and her muffled sounds made everyone in the group gasp, swear, or turn away from the screen. Kate didn't want to look, yet at the same time, she couldn't stop. She had too many questions running through her mind.

Who's this creep? Why is everyone looking at this video, right here, right now? Did the world go mad while I was sitting in court?

"I can't believe he was capable of such things," a lady in front of Kate said before walking away.

Kate turned around and touched the lady's arm to get her attention. "Who's in this video?" Kate asked.

"You haven't heard?"

"Heard what?"

"That's Ferguson," the woman said. "I can't believe I was going to vote for him."

Holy shit. He had it coming.

AS SOON AS her shift ended, Kate rushed home to scour the Internet. Nobody was talking about her uncle's trial. All the buzz was about Ferguson's pedophile rape tape.

No one seemed to know how it had leaked, or if it was

indeed Ferguson in the video, but photographs of him at the beach with his wife suddenly appeared, and made it clear to most—or at least to Kate—that he was the man in the video.

She was closing her browser window when her phone rang. Caller ID read "George Hudson."

Finally! Some news. Let it be good.

"Hi, George."

"Kate, how are you?"

"Fine." Kate's mind was spinning fast. No time for small talk. "How did it go? I left at noon. What happened after?"

"Well," George said then exhaled into the phone.

That's not good.

Her mind slowed. "Is it over already?"

"No, it'll resume on Monday, but it's not looking good. They'll probably wrap up the case on Wednesday or Thursday next week," George relayed.

Kate let his words hang, hoping that silence would somehow change them.

"We both knew that going in," George continued. "I'm sorry."

"Any chance they'll go easy on him because he's old and frail?"

George sighed again. "In their eyes, he's a killer, so no."

"Well, thank you, George," Kate said. "I know you're doing your best in an impossible situation. How's Kenny holding up?"

"He's tired. I told him to catch some sleep and to rest as much as he can. He needs it."

"Please call me when you get the verdict. I'll try to pop in, but I don't know if I'll be able to."

"Okay, Kate. Try to have a good weekend anyway."

Kate wished him the same and hung up. She needed a friend right about now. A friend like Luke.

She grabbed her phone again and pressed the home button.

"Siri, call Luke O'Brien," Kate said.

Her phone answered in the semi-automatic voice she'd grown accustomed to. "Calling Luke O'Brien, mobile."

She brought the phone to her ear.

"Hello?" his voice made her heart skip a beat.

"Hi Luko, it's Kate."

"Hi," he said like a flatlining heart monitor.

An awkward pause ensued.

"Did you get my text message last week?"

"No. What text message?"

"Oh... I wanted to apologize for... my trust issues."

"No, didn't get any message from you."

Kate frowned. "Weird. I don't know why it didn't go through. I'm really sorry for how I treated you. You deserve better. How can I make it up to you?"

It took him a moment to respond. "I don't know."

"Let me buy you dinner. I could really use some company right now."

He once again remained silent, bringing Kate's anguish up a notch.

"Luko?"

"I'm thinking. Can I call you back with my answer?"

"Sure, I guess," Kate said. "Talk to you later, then?"

"Later, Kate."

After he hung up, she tossed her phone onto the coffee table.

Did he mean later today or later never?

Before she met her ex-husband, Matt, she'd had her fair share of the latter. She had an assortment of male first names on her phone to prove it. Kate made a mental note to delete them one day. They certainly weren't going to call her back now, years later.

At 10 p.m., after spending four hours checking her phone for a potentially missed call, Kate gave up.

Guess he meant later never. Fucktard.

She didn't know if her inner insult was directed at him or herself. How could she keep being fooled by men?

Kate didn't feel like cooking, but she was hungry. She opened the drawer of her coffee table, looked through the assortment of take-out menus, and then settled on pizza and beer.

~

KATE SHOT up in bed as though her brain had been struck by lightning.

"I know where I saw him!"

She ran down the stairs, found her wallet, and then emptied it on the kitchen island. Receipts, loose change, and cards spread across the counter.

She found the business card that Sheriff Wallace, the officer at the gas station in Ohio, had given her then grabbed the phone and looked at the time on the microwave: 4:04 a.m.

Shit. Way too early.

She put down the phone and headed back to bed, but her mind wouldn't fall back to sleep.

Can't be the same guy, though... First, one died more than a week ago, the other is alive and talked to the police yesterday. But they look so similar. They have to be close relatives. Brothers? If the body still hasn't been identified, the sheriff may care about talking to one of the dead man's relatives.

Her tip could be useful. But then again...

Kate realized she didn't even know the name of the person of interest who had talked to the police yesterday, so she got out of bed to see if his identity had been released to the press.

By 6 a.m., she had given up, gotten dressed in jeans and a T-shirt, and headed to the station. She could ask around and find out the identity of that man.

By the time 9 a.m. rolled around, Kate had figured out a bunch of things. She'd gotten the identity of the man: Cliff Montague. He wasn't currently held in custody, but he'd been asked to stay in town, just in case the police had more questions for him. She'd read through his file, and she'd also looked up Luke's home address. She wasn't going to be strung along by another man, forever waiting for him to call her back *later*.

Kate glanced at the clock on the wall and figured it would be fine to call the sheriff now.

"Deputy," a man answered.

"Hi, my name is Kate Murphy. I met the sheriff about a week ago."

"What are you calling about?"

"Last weekend he was asking around about the identity of a man. Did you figure out who he was?" she asked.

"Don't believe so. Still a John Doe."

"I think I can help you identify him. Is the sheriff available?"

"I can patch you over. Who did you say you were?"

"Kate Murphy."

"Hold on..."

A muted click, a short pause, and then another click.

"Hello?"

"Hi, Sheriff Wallace. I met you last weekend at a gas station. You had a picture of a man and were asking about his identity."

"Ah... yes, I remember, the blonde lady with a rental car?" the sheriff asked.

"Yes, that's me. I'm with the Boston PD," Kate said. "Long story short, we've had a murder here recently, and a man came forward for further questioning. That man looks just like your guy."

"But my guy's dead. Can't be the same person."

"Of course not, but maybe they're twins or at least brothers," she suggested.

"Did you ask him if he has a brother?"

"I couldn't, he's been released already, but I thought I'd pass along his contact information, and you could follow up if you wanted to."

"Sure, let me grab a piece of paper. Boston PD, you say?" the sheriff asked.

"Yep. Do you have an email address? I can take a screenshot of the information I have, including his picture, and send it to you."

"That'd be great."

Kate cradled the phone between her shoulder and ear and then proceeded to type the sheriff's email address in Outlook.

"Got it," she said, before repeating it to be sure she'd entered it correctly. "I'll attach his information, and it should be in your inbox in a few minutes."

"Do you have a phone number I could reach you at, in case I need to talk to you again?" the sheriff asked.

"Sure," she said before providing it and hanging up.

Kate felt good about herself. She hadn't been able to help her uncle—at least not yet—but maybe this poor man from Ohio would be identified, his family notified, and a proper funeral could be held for him.

CHAPTER FIFTEEN

Kate Murphy
Roxbury Police Station, Boston

ROLL CALL on Monday morning was different, as though someone had put something in the city's water supply. Everyone was more talkative, more anxious, more driven to find the murderer, although most were happy that Ferguson could no longer hurt little girls.

With no proof of who'd killed him yet, all patrol officers were told to keep their eyes peeled for any suspicious activity.

At noon, Kate knew she wouldn't have enough time to make it to court, but she managed to get five minutes at a coffee shop to grab a sandwich while catching up on the news. The anchorman reported that a letter to the editor had been published in the *Boston Globe*.

The screen changed to a light blue background with black lettering on it:

Our society is headed in the wrong direction, and those in power are responsible. They get involved where they shouldn't, and they abandon those who need their help. They take advantage of powerless children, destroying their lives forever. They take bribes from large corporations that don't have the world's best interests at heart.

Money and power isn't the end goal, life is.

But not everything is as gloomy as it seems. We are here to help, ready to right their wrongs, by any means necessary.

That's *any* means necessary.

Sleep tight. The Lord's servants are watching.
-SJC

The camera returned to the anchorman.

"Who do you think wrote this letter?" he asked the first guest sitting next to him, an Indian woman wearing a business suit.

"By the tone of the letter, I'd say it's a religious organization, albeit a very extremist one," she replied.

Kate had missed the guests' titles, so she didn't know the woman's area of expertise or why she was taking part in this interview.

Anyone who can read would conclude the same thing.

The anchor turned to his other guest. "Dr. Fischer, any thoughts on that?"

A gray-haired man wearing a bow tie and a plaid jacket answered slowly as if he was carefully selecting each and every one of his words. He reminded Kate of those college professors who enjoyed hearing themselves talk. "The terminology reflects a certain level of passion and initiative. Not many people go through the trouble of writing a letter to the editor these days, with Twitter and other social media being much faster avenues for getting the word out—"

"But sending a Tweet would require an audience, a large group of followers in the first place," the Indian woman interrupted.

"Of course," the man continued. "But from my

understanding, this letter was hand-written and addressed to Mr. Edward Fitzgerald, not just to 'Dear Editor.' Once again, who goes to the trouble? The postmark indicated it was mailed in Boston, and the police did not find any trace of DNA, fingerprints, or anything that could point them to the identity of this mysterious person. The writer is meticulous, well-organized, passionate, religious, and angry. If you ask me, that's an explosive mix. I wouldn't want to be a crooked politician right about now."

The television now displayed the guests' titles. The man was a sociology professor at Harvard, and the woman was a social media expert associated with MIT.

"Thank you, Dr. Fischer. Stay tuned. After these messages, we'll share some of our viewers' opinions. Send us your thoughts and comments at @BOSnewstweets."

The dispatcher reported a nearby accident on her radio, so Kate left the coffee shop and returned to her patrol car.

AT 5:30 P.M., Kate was unpacking a few grocery items she'd picked up on the way back to her apartment when her phone rang. The call was from area code 234.

"Hello?" Kate answered, wondering who it could be.

"Miss Murphy, this is Sheriff Wallace."

"Hi, sheriff. How are you?" she asked.

"Good. I'm calling to follow up on what you sent me. You were right about the resemblance between these two people. Look like twins to me."

"Are they?"

"That's what I'm calling about. You said you were a cop?"

"Yes," she said. "I mostly do patrol."

"I'd like a favor, from one law enforcement officer to another."

Kate was puzzled. "What's that?"

"I called up the guy, and he has no interest in talking to me, or providing me with a sample of his DNA so I could test it against my John Doe's DNA here. Thing is, I can't justify issuing a warrant, and even if I could convince our judge, it'd be a nightmare dealing with two different state jurisdictions. You know how that goes?"

Kate wondered where this was headed. "Yeah..."

"Well, at least Montague did say something useful. He told me he'd already provided a DNA sample to you guys when he walked himself in. He had nothing to hide from the police or the public back then, so he willingly gave you his DNA. Now, with your creepy electoral candidate's pedophile tape out there, Montague doesn't want to be involved anymore. Can't blame the guy. That thing's gone viral here as well."

"Okay," she said flatly.

"So... I was wondering if you could help me close my John Doe case without ruffling any more feathers and without complicating things for anyone."

"How? I can't send you his DNA. I don't have access to it."

"I figured as much, but how about I send you a sample of my John Doe, and you request a DNA comparison on your end? I don't care about sticking to protocol. I just want to give this guy a name before we bury him. If the DNA shows some genetic relations, at least I'll have a starting point, and I can trace birth records. Maybe there won't be anything, but at least it won't keep me up at night."

"I'll see what I can do," Kate said. "Ship your sample directly to the DNA section of the Massachusetts State Police Lab, care of Luke O'Brien. He's the lab supervisor. I'll talk to him about it."

Kate gave him the address and hung up.

How would she ask Luke for that favor? Would he even listen to her? Heck, he was a professional. If he wasn't willing to do it, she could go through the trouble of filling out the required paperwork. All human beings deserved to be identified when they died, right? She hoped someone would do the same for her if their roles were reversed.

However, she had to present that idea to Luke. She already had his address, and now she had a reason to go see him, so

Kate grabbed her car keys and purse, and then headed to his house.

A block away from his home, as indicated by her GPS, she stopped at a Chinese restaurant. After parking, she walked in and realized she had no idea what kind of dishes he liked. Figuring a variety would be good—better odds of her buying at least one that he'd eat—she ordered the standard meal for four before heading to the liquor store next door. She got a bottle of chilled white wine, paid, and then returned to the restaurant to wait for her order.

Fifteen minutes later, she got back into her car, meal in hand, and then she made her way to Luke's. She found a parking spot just a few houses down from the address she'd seen in the police records. Her heartbeat increased with every footstep she took toward his house.

Will he be angry at me?

What will he think of me showing up unannounced?

Will he even be home?

The bag of food and her bottle of wine gave her added courage. At least she came bearing gifts.

Luke lived in an old brick building with metal railings and huge bay windows. She walked up the seven concrete steps and then rang the doorbell next to the azure door.

A silver-haired woman answered, wearing a bright yellow dress with little red flowers. Not a particularly flattering fabric, but the pink plastic rollers in her hair and the thick layer of green mud slathered on her face took Kate's attention away from the dress.

"Hi," Kate started, regretting her decision. "I'm looking for Luke O'Brien. Is this where he lives?"

"Yes, and who would you…" the lady said when her eyes suddenly widened. A broad smile appeared on her face, cracking her facial mask, and the woman's arms wrapped themselves around Kate.

Kate's confusion came to an end when the lady pulled back and spoke again.

"Katie, love! I'm so glad you're all right!"

Kate scrunched her face up at the woman standing before her. "Mrs. O'Brien?"

"Who did you think I was?" Mrs. O'Brien brought her hand to her green cheek. "Never mind. I probably look ridiculous like this in broad daylight."

"No." Kate shook her head. "It's just that... I didn't expect to see you here. How are you?"

"Come in, love, come in! I have to take off this mask then we'll talk. It's been so long," she said, pulling Kate by the arm. "Luuuke... Luuuke," she yelled toward the stairs, "We've got company."

He lived with his mom? That explained a lot.

Kate suddenly remembered she was holding bags.

"Oh, I brought dinner."

She'd never been more pleased with her silly habit of buying way too much food.

"You didn't have to do that, girl, but thank you. We'll catch up over dinner. What did you bring?" she asked, tearing away at the bags now sitting on the table.

Luke entered the kitchen behind her, directing a confused look at Kate.

"I needed to talk to you, so I thought I would just pop by," she started. Then she leaned closer to Luke and lowered her voice. "I didn't know you lived with your mom."

"No, she lives with me. There's a difference."

Kate smiled, but he didn't smile back.

A minute later, Mrs. O'Brien wiped away her mask and finished unpacking the meal. Then she requested that Luke and Kate both sit down before prompting them to hold hands to say grace.

"Thank you, Lord, for bringing little Katie back into our lives," Mrs. O'Brien said. "I'm glad you've taken good care of her and looked after her. Thank you for the food, and bless those who've cooked it, and brought it to our table. Amen."

Based on how fast the containers were emptied, everyone was enjoying the food as much as Kate. But halfway through the meal, Mrs. O'Brien's expression changed.

"I still remember the day you came back from your house... Running, in tears, with your dead baby brother in your arms," she said with her voice shaking. "You couldn't speak to tell us what had happened. Poor thing. It was good that Luke and you were playing in these darn caves; otherwise, you'd have been killed, too. I often wondered what had happened to you. If you ever got over it or if it had made you crazy."

Luke slammed his hands on the table. "Mom!"

"I'm serious. I worried a lot about you," his mother continued. "I kept telling Luke to talk to you. He was supposed to ask you for your new address at the funeral, but he never gave it to me. I doubt he even asked you."

Kate stared at what was left of her Kung Pao chicken. "That was a long time ago, Mrs. O'Brien. I'm good now. My uncle took good care of me."

Saying these words aloud brought a sharp pang to her heart. She hadn't helped him a bit. She hadn't even touched base with George today.

"I testified," Luke said.

"And how did it go?" Kate asked.

"Not looking too good for him."

Mrs. O'Brien seemed confused for a second, taking her eyes off Katie and bringing them to Luke. "What's going on. What are you two talking about?"

Luke's face reddened. Kate couldn't tell if it was shame, embarrassment, anger, or a mix of all of these, so she decided to change topics.

"This was a meal for four people, so that means one of us will get an extra fortune cookie," Kate said.

"I love those! I always play the lotto with the numbers on the back," Mrs. O'Brien said.

Luke shook his head. "Lottery is a tax on the poor, Mom."

"It may very well be, but it brings thrills and excitement into my life. What if we won? What would you do, Luke, if you became a millionaire?"

"Not sure. I'd probably build myself a small but comfy house on the coast. And I'd get you your own little condo in town, with a butler."

Mrs. O'Brien frowned at Luke. "Ah... you wouldn't keep your dear old mum in your house?"

"I say you deserve the extra cookie, Mrs. O'Brien," Kate said. "That way you can decide what you'll do with your money when you win."

After dinner ended, Mrs. O'Brien left them alone in the kitchen and headed to the living room to watch her favorite TV show, which was about to start.

Luke adjusted his sitting position, crossed his arms over his chest, and glared at Kate. "Why are you here?"

"I said I was sorry," she started, her hand on her heart, tilting her head. "You didn't call me back, and I need your help with something."

His eyes softened a little, but abrupt words kept coming out of his mouth. "What? What do you need my help with?"

Kate told him of her progress in trying to figure out another motive for the murder, then continued with the story of the sheriff she met after visiting the Ohio penitentiary.

"I was hoping you could help us identify that Ohio man. Sheriff Wallace will be sending you a DNA sample from his John Doe. Could you compare it to Montague's sample?"

Luke shook his head, pushed his chair back from the kitchen table, and then got up. His hands were now braced on his hips. "I'm a 'by-the-book' guy. You know that, Kate. This isn't proper."

She got up as well and reached for his right arm. "No one will get hurt," she said, nearly begging. Kate knew she couldn't do this without him. "It isn't being used in a criminal investigation. Best scenario is you tell the sheriff the two samples are related, and then he's got a starting point to trace the identity of the unknown victim. Worst scenario is there isn't anything in common between the two, and you wasted a few minutes running the test."

Luke waved his arms to the sky, his soft blue eyes locked on Kate. "I've got better things to do with my time."

"If something happened to you or your mom, or if you died without any documents on you, wouldn't you want your family to be notified of your death? There could be a wife, a kid, a mother out there, worried about this man."

"Katie," he said, shaking his head. He stared at her with an intensity she'd never seen in his eyes before. "Fine, but just this once."

Kate hugged him.

"Thank you," she whispered. The hug felt good, like an electromagnetic field recharging her emotional battery. "I've missed you."

"Me too," he said. "Let's grab a drink sometime this week or next, okay?"

"It's a date," Kate said.

CHAPTER SIXTEEN

Kate Murphy
Near Roxbury Police Station, Boston

"THEY'RE IDENTICAL," said Luke over the phone while Kate manned a speed trap in a school zone.

"Are you kidding me?"

"No, Montague's sample and the one your sheriff sent me share the same DNA."

Her hunch had been right, but this made no sense. "How can that be? The first guy's dead."

"They're identical twins."

"Really? Twins have the exact same DNA?" she pressed.

"Identical twins do," Luke said.

Kate's mind raced, trying to make connections with all of the cases she'd read. "Do identical twins have the same fingerprints?"

"No, fingerprints are set in the womb. They change when fetuses touch the amniotic sac. Impossible to have identical fingerprints."

Kate nodded although Luke couldn't see her over the phone. "I didn't know how fingerprints were created. Thanks, Luke. I really appreciate you checking the DNA for me."

She hung up and dialed the sheriff's number. He would now have everything he needed to trace back birth records to determine the identity of his John Doe.

After a brief phone conversation with a very grateful sheriff, Kate wondered about her uncle's DNA. Did he have a twin he didn't know about?

She needed to know. It could affect his case.

Kate looked at the time: 11:15 a.m. If she left her speed trap now, she may be able to talk to him and George when the court broke for lunch.

As luck would have it, she managed to get a short audience with George and her uncle, but under the watchful eye of a security guard.

"Kenny, what I'm about to ask you will seem out of the blue, but something happened that got me thinking."

Her uncle lifted sad eyes to her. "You know you can ask me anything."

"Do you have a twin brother?"

"Of course not," he said, frowning.

"Maybe the two of you were separated at birth, and one of you was adopted by a different family?"

Kenny shook his head vehemently. "No way. Mom and Dad told me the story of my birth so many times, along with seeing the black-and-white pictures of her being pregnant, of me in the nursery at the hospital, of us coming home together. I was the only baby in those pictures and Mom was one of those tiny pregnant women. No way she had two babies in there."

Kate let out a sigh.

"Why do you look so disappointed?" he asked.

"I was just hoping you had one."

"Why?" he said, then laughed.

Kate relayed what she'd just learned about identical twins and the shared DNA.

"Too bad," he said with a strange expression on his face. He was still so very pale. Was it because he'd already accepted the inevitable verdict that was coming his way?

But before she could ask her uncle more questions or try to

reassure him somehow, a call came in for her over the radio, which forced Kate to return to her patrol car, her proverbial tail hanging between her legs.

THE FOLLOWING DAY, just after Kate finished her patrol shift, she got another call from Sheriff Wallace.

"Montague does *not* have a twin," he started, obviously irritated. "I traced his birth records: he's an only child."

Kate was not sure what to say to diffuse his anger. "Maybe they gave up the twin to another family, anonymously?"

"I checked the adoption records for the same day, for all of Massachusetts, and no newborn baby boys were adopted. Unless the parents owed their first born to a mafia goon, there was no identical twin."

Kate could picture the sheriff ready to throw his fist into the wall. "I don't know what to say. Maybe check the hospital records?" she replied.

"Not your fault," he said, moderating his voice this time. "Well, this John Doe is a real admin nightmare. Why did he have to die in my county?" he asked rhetorically before hanging up, leaving Kate clueless as to why he'd called her in the first place.

But the odd call made Kate think about something else. With all of the homeless deaths lately, she wondered if many of them had since been identified. She finished her end-of-shift tasks and headed to the morgue to ask.

A SHORT WOMAN was busy cleaning something over the sink at the morgue, so Kate knocked and walked in through the open door. A dead body was lying on the nearest autopsy table, chest cut open with skin flaps resting on both sides of its torso. Decomposition had obviously affected that poor victim. The internal organs had been taken out and placed on a nearby tray. The smells of rotting flesh and antiseptic products merged into a weird and unpleasant odor. Kate was relieved that her stomach didn't want to purge itself.

She walked over and introduced herself. "Hi, I'm Officer Kate Murphy."

"Dr. Lisa Davis," the brown-haired woman said with a smile. "How can I help you?"

Kate was taken aback by the doctor's warm welcome.

Not many visitors?

Dr. Davis motioned for Kate to come closer.

"I know you're busy," Kate started, "but I was wondering if you have a lot of John Does down here."

The doctor nodded. "We always have a few, but I'd say that number has increased over the past years." She returned her attention to the shears, scissors, and saw as she rinsed them over the sink.

"What about the homeless deaths they talk about on the news?" Kate asked.

"That's the bulk of our John Does."

Kate scratched her chin. "Do you check their DNA?"

"We take samples, have them analyzed, and most of them come back without matches."

The doctor wiped her hands and walked over to a computer monitor in the corner of the room.

Kate followed her. "Do these samples stay in the system to be compared against future matches?"

"No," Lisa said, shaking her head. "The system only contains the DNA of those who were charged with a crime. Plus, they're dead, so they'd just clog the system."

"Do you keep the samples you take?" Kate asked, looking around for a storage area.

The doctor nodded. "Some morgues don't, but here we do. The state lets each county regulate how they operate, but it's prevented us from digging up a few graves in the past, so we find it useful to keep them, just in case."

"Any chance I could have the homeless samples re-analyzed?"

"Sure, but you'll need the required paperwork," the doctor

said before pointing at an overflowing inbox on a desk in the corner.

"Thanks, doc. Have a great day."

Kate left the morgue and headed to Fuller's office.

SHE KNOCKED on the ajar door, and the detective told her to come in. But once she stepped into his office and he saw who had knocked, he added, "Wallflower, what a surprise." As expected, his voice was flat and his glance unfriendly.

"Hi, Detective," Kate said, forcing a smile.

"What's going on in your pretty little head?" he asked patronizingly. "Your uncle's verdict should be out tomorrow. You can't change anything about it."

"I'm not here for that," she said firmly.

"What are you here for?" he asked with an equally abrupt tone and a look of disdain.

"Homeless deaths. Who's on them?"

Fuller let out a sigh. "Wang had the last couple of cases. Why do you care?"

"I have a theory, and I'd like to have their DNA re-analyzed."

Fuller rolled his eyes. "What for? If they didn't commit a crime before they died, believe me, they won't commit one after they're buried." He laughed at his own joke, melting the tension a little.

"Listen, I get that," Kate started before taking a seat in front of him without his invitation to do so. "You remember Cliff Montague? The man who came forward and answered questions about the Ferguson murder?" Kate saw Fuller nod, so she continued. "There's an unidentified corpse in Ohio whose DNA matches Montague's. The tricky part? Birth records prove that Montague doesn't have a twin brother. How do you explain that?"

Fuller leaned back in his chair and flicked his hand in the air. "Birth records are probably wrong. But where does this information come from?"

Kate recounted her visit to Ohio, her bumping into the sheriff, and the events that had followed. "So, what if," she continued tentatively, "with these unexplained homeless deaths on the rise... What if somehow, someone had figured out how to clone people?"

"You mean like that sheep from years ago?" Fuller asked.

She nodded. "Yep. I know crazy, but that's what I'm thinking."

He harrumphed at her. "No way, human cloning is illegal and so is researching it."

Kate shook her head. "Since when do people stop when laws tell them to?"

Fuller slapped his hand on the desk then got up. "You're wasting your time on this."

"But what if?" She lifted a brow to accentuate her question.

"What do you want? What do you expect to prove?"

"I just want to re-analyze all unidentified homeless samples from the past couple of years and compare them to the open and closed case files we have. Best outcome, I might help solve a few cold cases; worst outcome, I've wasted my own time."

"Hmmm... a waste of time and resources for sure," he said, sitting back down, then rocking back and forth a few times before moving his lower jaw sideways and staring at Kate. "Wallflower, your Ohio corpse story makes me curious. And the number of homeless deaths has really jumped up in recent years. I don't believe your theory's anywhere near plausible, but my gut tells me you may be onto something."

Really?

Kate did her best to hide her excitement. She hadn't expected anything from him at all. Finding evidence of cloning—as far-fetched as the idea seemed to Kate right now—could help her prove Kenny's innocence and force them to re-open his case or at least send it to the Court of Appeals.

Fuller contemplated the idea more then added, "Here's the deal: go talk to Wang. Tell her what you told me, and she'll show you the paperwork you'll need to prepare for each of the corpses. I want to be clear, other than the time it takes for her to listen to this, you will not waste any of my detectives' time," he said with emphasis. "Any paperwork that results from that is yours to handle. The crime lab is already back-logged with hot cases. This will have to be their lowest priority. It may take weeks before they get around to these samples. Understood?"

Kate let a smile slip through. "Thanks, Detective."

"Whatever."

Kate got up, left Fuller's office, and then caught up with Wang in the lunchroom.

"Detective Wang," Kate said as she recognized the black-haired woman standing in front of the vending machine.

Wang turned around and snickered. "Wallflower." She shook her head. "What a ridiculous name he gave you."

Kate tilted her head, surprised at her comment. "Why's that?"

"When I first got here, I was 'Tiny Flower,' " Wang said. "Fuller gives everyone nicknames that aren't particularly original."

"I just thought he hated me."

"These two things aren't mutually exclusive," Wang said before pushing a button on the coffee dispenser. "So how can I help you?"

"I just talked to Fuller and ran a theory by him. He gave me permission to request a DNA analysis on the John Does resting in the morgue as well as those from the past couple of years. He said you'd tell me what paperwork I needed to fill out."

"Sounds like fun," she said and then rolled her eyes. "Come on, follow me."

She took Kate to a larger room. Eight desks occupied the bulk of the space, with a few plastic plants, a water cooler, and wall partitions filling the rest. Kate recognized another detective who'd worked her uncle's case; he sat a couple of desks away. He looked up when they walked by and nodded at Wang.

"Sit here," Wang said, pointing to a chair placed alongside the edge of her desk. Wang then opened a tall filing cabinet and flicked through files before retrieving one. After heading to the copier, she pressed a button, waited for the machine to spit out paper, and then handed Kate a duplicated document before returning the original to the filing cabinet.

"Treat this information as confidential," Wang explained. "Shred this copy when you're done, so I don't get in trouble. This is just an example for you to use." She grabbed a pen from her desk and circled a number in the lower left corner. "That's the form number. You can request hard copies of this, but I recommend you look for the online version in the system. You'll need to print three copies for each sample: one for the morgue, one for the lab, and one for you. You fill out as much information as you can, and if you don't want these to come back to you for incompleteness, take this seriously. Did Fuller assign a case ID?"

"No," Kate said, shaking her head.

"Shit. Why do you need these done?"

Kate regurgitated her story about the Ohio body and Montague sharing identical DNA.

"That's not related to Ferguson's murder though. Just use one of my John Doe cases... hold on..." She flipped through another file on her desk and wrote down "195205315" on the photocopy she'd handed Kate.

"Okay, you'll want to have the results compared to our state-wide DNA bank. Heck, you'll want to know if it matches anything nationwide. Ohio isn't exactly next door."

Wang finished going through the four-page form before standing up. She reached for one of her business cards. "Call me if you run into problems or if the morgue or crime lab gives you the run-around. Good luck!"

"Thanks, Detective Wang."

"Call me Jenny."

Kate smiled at Jenny before standing up and walking away from her desk, document in hand. For once in a very long time, she felt like she'd finally made some headway.

CHAPTER SEVENTEEN

Kate Murphy
Roxbury Police Station, Boston

A FEW DAYS after her uncle's guilty verdict. Kate had come to accept his fate and did her best to pretend that nothing had happened.

"There's no point in crying over spilled beer," her uncle had said too many times to count. She smiled now, thinking about her aunt's usual reply: "But clean it now or sleep on the couch for a year."

Kate was taken out of the past by her ringtone. She picked up her cell without looking at caller ID.

"Hi, Kate."

She recognized the rugged voice. "Hi, Luke! How are you?"

"I'm freaking swamped," he started. "Just wanted to thank you for sending all of these samples to our team. Saw your name on the forms. Is Miss Katie afraid I'll forget about her?" he said, teasing.

She laughed. "I didn't want you guys to slack off and enjoy any kind of free time."

"We ran five of these samples today and found matches for two of them. I thought you'd want to know."

Kate sat straight up at this news. "Really? That's great. Which ones?"

"I'm too hungry to discuss that right now," Luke said. "Want to grab a bite?"

"Always! You need to ask?" Kate looked at her watch: 4 p.m.

"Can you meet me in the lab in about an hour? I'll order some pizza."

"Sure," she said. "How about ninety minutes? Traffic may be bad."

"Sounds good. See you then."

"Can't wait." Kate hung up, walked to her locker to change, and then joined other commuters on the busy streets.

The security guard at the crime lab had already received notification that she was coming, so she only had to sign the register and go up to the second floor. When she arrived at the DNA lab, she found the glass doors locked. She knocked.

Luke came out of the back office wearing his regular Dockers and a gray polo shirt. His hair was slicked back. He had removed his goggles, but his regular glasses were still on. Seeing him made her heart skip a beat. She'd missed him. A crooked smile appeared on his lips when their eyes met.

He let her in and hugged her.

Kate felt an unstoppable grin appear on her face. "How have you been?" she asked.

"I've been feeling awful. I acted like an ass," he confessed.

"No, it was all my fault," she said. "I'm sorry, I should've trusted you, and I really shouldn't have shown up unexpectedly at your house the other day."

He nodded at her. "Now you know my dirty little secret. Mom lives with me. It's a little embarrassing." He paused and then added, "I meant to call you and ask you out for a drink, but I figured you'd want to be alone to deal with your uncle's verdict."

"You know me," she said with a half-hearted smile. "I'm fine now. I can talk about it."

He motioned for her to follow him. "Come on. Pizza's sitting in my office."

They chatted some more over their first slices, then got down to business.

Kate wiped her mouth with a napkin before speaking up. "I can't believe you found two matches. These were John Does when they died. They couldn't find a match back then, so what did you find?"

Luke pushed the pizza back a bit to get to his paperwork. "We haven't done all of them yet. They're on the back burner. Most of them are not in the system, but we found a couple that are." He grabbed the file folder sitting on top of his inbox. "This first one," he said as he flipped the folder open, "came back as a match to a Thorpe Pledger in California."

Kate furrowed her brows at this news. "Then why wouldn't they have discovered this when the body came in?"

Luke shrugged. "My guess? Takes a while for paperwork to get processed and entered into the database. The body must have come in first. And we're talking about a different state here."

Kate took the file from him. "I guess Wang will be happy that we've solved one of her John Does."

He continued. "That's not the weird part. Another sample came back as a match, but this time it was to an Owen Westbrook in Texas."

"Good."

"This got me thinking. One case of paperwork filed late is one thing, but two? So, I looked up both of these people in a different database."

Kate was beyond intrigued. "And?"

Luke cocked his head. "Both Thorpe Pledger and Owen Westbrook are rotting in a high-security prison as we speak."

Kate sat immobile for a minute or so, her mouth agape with incredulity. "You mean we have someone serving time, possibly based on DNA evidence, and the same DNA belongs to dead guys? Fuck!"

"Yeah. Double fuck," Luke said, nodding his head.

A few more minutes passed in complete silence, the two of them staring at each other, exchanging confused looks.

Kate was still wrapping her head around what Luke had said when he reached down to open the bottom drawer of his desk. He pulled out a bottle of whiskey and a tumbler then poured himself about an ounce, downed it, then refilled the glass before offering it to Kate.

"Shit!" She tossed it back then asked, "My uncle?"

"That's what I thought about, as well. His DNA could be in the pile of samples we've got to analyze."

"Can you get to it?"

"I really want to, but my team can't take two days off from the priority tasks to finish going through your samples. The DNA analysis doesn't take long, but running the results against all of the databases does," he said. Then, he added, "Delaying hot cases would get me in deep trouble."

Kate leaned forward and took hold of his wrist. "But this is huge. Do you realize what we've stumbled upon? Those samples... We're talking about... clones. Human freaking clones!"

"Or a freak coincidence in the number of identical twins who don't know they have twins out there," Luke added.

"Hold on," Kate said, fumbling through her purse to find her wallet. She dug out Wang's business card and hurriedly dialed the detective's number. When Kate heard the ringtone, she tapped the speaker icon on her phone.

"Detective Wang?" Kate asked, to be sure.

"Speaking"

"It's Officer Kate Murphy. I'm in the DNA lab with O'Brien. He's found two matches. I think you need to come in to hear the results in person."

Wang let out a sigh. "It's 6 p.m. I'm off duty right now."

"I get that," Kate said. "But it's freaking unbelievable. It's huge! We'll have to call in the FBI on this."

"What? Hold your horses, Murphy. Fine. I'll be there in about forty minutes," Wang said before hanging up.

Kate glanced at Luke as they waited impatiently. Luke called the security desk to let the guard know he was expecting another visitor, then they each drank another whiskey in silence before he returned the bottle to its drawer. They had time to finish off the pizza before Wang knocked on the glass door.

Luke unlocked the lab and led her to his office to join Kate.

"This better be good," Wang said when she met Kate's eyes.

Luke filled her in, and then, probably out of disbelief, Wang asked him to log out of his computer so she could log into her account and access other databases.

With Wang's fingers flying across the keyboard—and Luke and Kate lurking over her shoulder—Wang pulled up the case file for Thorpe Pledger. "What the..."

She repeated the process and pulled up a picture of Owen Westbrook. She turned around, her face paler than usual. "I've seen the dead bodies. These are the same people... other than a few scars on our corpses and a missing heartbeat." Her eyebrows hovered close to her hairline. "How? Did they escape from prison?"

Wang checked their police records and then Googled each victim's name, but came back empty. No recent escapes, as far as Google and the databases she could access were concerned. These people were alive and secured behind bars.

She called Detective Fuller, who rushed into the lab thirty minutes later.

Kate couldn't believe that a quiet discussion between two people over pizza had somehow turned into a police frenzy. They even had to leave Luke's desk and move to the main lab area to accommodate the growing crowd, which ultimately saw the arrival of the district commander himself.

"Okay," Capt. Cranston started. "We've got a situation here, and I don't want it to turn into a circus."

Everybody quieted down and waited for him to continue.

"First, O'Brien, I want your team to prioritize the other samples first thing in the morning. I don't want them double-checked, I want the information triple-fucking-checked. And, Fuller," the district commander said, turning to him, "I want your men to request faxed copies of the actual police files from these other states. I also want confirmation that the folks with the matching DNA are still in prison. Call each penitentiary and confirm it. I want it written down and dated."

"Yes, sir," Fuller said. Luke nodded, as well.

"Then, check with birth records," the district commander continued. "Don't want to risk identical twin issues. Confirm that every fucking 'I' is dotted and every 'T' crossed on this one. This is huge, but I don't want our department to become the laughing stock of the force. If we're going to report that fucking human cloning is happening, I want it bullet-proofed. I'll call the judge and make sure we can expedite whatever warrant you need to help you prove this. Fuck." He moved his right hand back through his thinning gray hair.

All ears were on the district commander, but Kate could feel the disbelief in the room. Capt. Cranston was the only one voicing it aloud at that very second, but they all seemed to agree.

"Once confirmed, this will get pulled out of our hands real fast," he said. "This goes well beyond our scope. Fuller, as soon as we've got three confirmed cases, call me. I'll have to report it to the FBI." He let out a long sigh and checked the clock before continuing. "Great job, everyone. Go home. It's past ten. Sleep on it. Maybe you'll come up with another theory that would be more believable. I know I'll be racking my brain tonight before we get into crazy overtime with this. We'll have a shitload on our plate tomorrow."

As the other detectives left, Kate overheard the district commander ask Fuller, "So, how did this come to be?"

"Your Wallflower, sir," he said as he looked at Kate. Their eyes met, and Kate returned to Luke's office to fetch her purse.

"Wow," Luke said.

Kate nodded at him, her heartbeat nearly triple its usual rate. "Yeah. I can't believe this. I won't be able to sleep tonight."

"Hold on," Luke said to her. "I'll lock up as soon as they leave and then we'll walk around for a bit. Maybe some fresh air will help."

Within a few minutes, everyone was gone, leaving Luke and Kate alone for the first time in four hours.

After exiting the building, they walked around the nearly empty parking lot in silence for the first five minutes.

"Do you think innocent people died?" she asked. "I mean, some states still have the death penalty. Do you think innocent people got executed for crimes they didn't commit?"

Luke's eyes darkened at the thought. "Katie, you can't think about that. If, and only if that happened, there's nothing that can be done."

A few more minutes elapsed before Luke continued.

"There's no way this human cloning thing has been going on for years. Dolly the sheep was cloned in 1996, I think? That's almost twenty years ago, and she was the only one that survived out of two hundred twenty-eight cloned sheep attempts. Whoever went to the extreme of successfully cloning humans had to do it after that."

"But that clone is more than twenty years old. How do you explain that?" Kate asked.

Luke shook his head, his eyes wide. "I don't know. It doesn't make any sense to me. His age simply doesn't add up, at least not based on what the rest of the scientific population has been up to. Last year, China made the news with their mass application of pig-cloning technology with a reported success rate of around seventy or eighty percent. And that's with pigs, not humans! I'm sure whoever's managed to clone humans has wasted precious years in trial and error, and their success rate probably isn't that high. It's very unlikely that someone would have been accused and executed already."

Luke always had a way of making her feel better. And he knew so much about so many topics. She smiled at him, and he grabbed her hand before squeezing it lightly.

After circling the building and parking lot a few times, they stopped by Kate's Subaru. Luke's car was just a few spots away.

"Want to come home with me?" she asked.

He cocked his head and put his hands in his pockets. "I'm not sure it's a good idea."

"Not this again, Luko," she said with a long sigh. "I promise nothing will happen. I just want to be held and hugged."

"Fine, I'll follow you home in my car, but I'll have to leave early tomorrow, so I can go home and change."

"Deal."

⏤

LUKE SET his alarm for 5 a.m., and they spooned; Kate wearing her yoga pajamas and Luke in his underwear. Kate's mind kept spinning with *what ifs*...

For the first time in a few months, there was a glimmer of hope: maybe she could free Kenny if his DNA matched one of the corpses'. With this thought, and with Luke's quiet rhythmic breathing behind her, she finally fell asleep.

She woke up a few hours later to a strange sound. She opened her eyes and saw Luke's phone buzzing on the nightstand, next to her clock that read 5:00 a.m.

Where is he?

She turned around: the other side of the bed was empty but still warm.

A few seconds later, Luke walked back into her bedroom, still in his underwear. He looked good in the morning, with his hair a mess and without his glasses. He had muscular legs, with well-formed calves. Those strong arms, and that chest...

Hmmm. Must be hitting the gym a few times a week.

"Up already?" she asked.

"Yes," he said before hitting the snooze icon on his phone and sitting down on the bed. "I don't know how my head does it, but I always get up just before the alarm goes off. Sorry, I forgot to turn it off. I had to use the bathroom."

Kate smiled again. "Thank you for your company last night. I needed it."

"No problem, but I should get going now," he said.

"Stay for just a minute longer. One more hug," she said, but he was walking away already. "Pleeease?"

"Oh, all right, Katie. Just a minute."

She was happy with him next to her. Comfortable. At peace with the world in this very instance. She closed her eyes and fell back to sleep, imagining what she'd like to do to him. The alarm sounded again on Luke's phone and reminded her to put aside her lust, at least for now.

He chuckled as he turned off his alarm once more. "Okay, really gotta go now."

"Fine."

She removed her arm from around him, and he got up before putting on his clothes, and returning to his geeky look.

"Have you ever considered contact lenses?" she asked.

"Nah. Don't really like putting fingers in my eyes."

"You look sexy without glasses."

His cheeks reddened, and he fumbled to put his right foot into his pants leg while maintaining his balance. Kate kept her giggle silent; she'd already embarrassed him enough, so she got out of bed.

"Do you want me to make you coffee for the road?" she offered.

"Would you?"

"Sure, give me a couple of minutes."

She walked downstairs, inserted a pod in the machine, added water, and placed her regular cup underneath it while she opened her cupboard to find a travel mug.

Luke joined her in the kitchen a minute later, with his hair neatly slicked back to his geeky style.

"Do you take sugar, milk?"

"Just black."

She poured the coffee into the travel mug, screwed the top, and then handed it to him. "Here you go, Luko."

"Thanks."

"And this," she said before getting up on her toes and jumbling his hair. "Much better like that."

Luke shook his head and grinned at her. "What is it with women? Men don't want to be changed."

"But this looks really good on you."

He went toward the mirror near the entrance door to see. "Really?"

"Really. I dare you to keep it like that at work today and see what reactions you get."

"Dare me? If I do it, will you hang out with me on Saturday?" he asked with a smile.

Kate thought for a second. "I have a visit booked with Kenny at Cedar Junction in the morning."

"That's fine. You can hang out with me in the afternoon and evening."

"Sure, that should work," she said as she nodded.

"Deal. See ya!"

And just like that, he left, like they used to do when they were kids.

No hugs, no kisses, just, "See ya."

They had made many dares as kids. Come to think of it, most, if not all, of the things she'd dared him to do dealt with frogs, crabs, and fish. Maybe that was how he found his passion for biology.

Who knows? she thought before heading to the shower.

What a day this was going to be.

CHAPTER EIGHTEEN

Kate Murphy
Roxbury Police Station, Boston

KATE HADN'T HAD a chance to clean and iron her uniform the night before—human cloning had pushed aside her regular laundry schedule—so she showed up at the station wearing capri pants and a plain white shirt. She was heading to the locker room, ready to put on the spare uniform she kept there when she saw a note in her pigeonhole:

Murphy,
Go see Capt. Cranston ASAP.
Sgt. Anderson

She hesitated for a second. Should she get dressed first? ASAP coming from the district commander probably meant *now*. No time to change.

Kate anxiously walked up to the third floor and greeted Susan.

"Hi, love. Just knock and let yourself in," she said. "He's expecting you."

"Thanks, Susan."

As soon as she entered his office, he barked out, "Murphy, sit down."

"Yes, sir," she said, trying to discern the expression on his tired face.

"I didn't sleep much last night," he began. "I still can't believe what your rogue investigation uncovered."

Kate had no idea where he was going with this, but the little voice in her head told her she was in trouble.

He slanted his eyes at her. "I get upset when people waste precious time and resources to pursue their own personal quests. I had given you permission to follow-up on your own time, and look into your uncle's case, but you started a much bigger process, involving other people, and their time."

Shit, I am in trouble.

Kate swallowed hard and kept quiet to avoid making things worse.

"However, as much as I despise Fuller for his attitude most days, I gotta admit his investigative gut is right far more often than it's wrong. And both you and Fuller had the right feeling on this. I spoke to Sgt. Anderson this morning, and I'm pulling you off patrol until further notice. The detectives could certainly use another man on this, at least until we have to hand it over to the Feds. Since you're already up to speed, even more than I am, you make the most sense. That way we can keep things tight and quiet for as long as possible. Understood?"

Wow. I get a chance to play in the big league?

She did her best to keep a poker face, but her lips moved into a smile. "Yes, sir."

"But don't get your hopes up, this is only a temporary thing. It's only a matter of days before you resume your patrolling duties."

Fair enough, but at least I'll have a chance to prove myself.

"Understood," Kate said, butterflies in her stomach.

"Go and report to Fuller. He knows already, and he's expecting you."

"Thank you, sir."

Kate left the district commander's office with a lighter heart and a grin like a Cheshire cat. She was going to work toward freeing her uncle. Well, not directly, but her efforts could have an impact on his life. Hopefully.

First, she had to report to Fuller, though.

Fun times ahead.

KATE WALKED to Fuller's office and saw a sticky note on his door:

Wallflower,
Conference room three

Fuller was already addressing everyone when she walked into the room.

"Okay, team. We've got birth records to trace, prison records to confirm, DNA samples to review, and if we can, we need to try to figure out how the fuck these people were cloned. Maybe we've all got a doppelgänger out there roaming the streets, committing crimes, and soiling our identity. This is going to be a nightmare. Capt. Cranston's already arranged for warrants to be issued. Anything that requires one, we've got a guy waiting to issue it for us, at least for Massachusetts, and other people are working on Texas and California as we speak."

He turned around to point to the pictures that Wang finished pinning on the board behind him.

"Wang, fill us in on the two matches the lab has already found."

She turned to face everyone. "As we all heard yesterday, the bodies of these two John Does were found in our jurisdiction, but could not be identified at the time. On the left, we have Thorpe Pledger's doppelgänger, and here we have the real Thorpe Pledger, who looks a tad younger. DOB March 27, 1972. Currently incarcerated at Victorville high-security Penitentiary in California, serving a life-sentence for murder. And on the right, we have Owen Westbrook's doppelgänger and Owen Westbrook himself, who looks older. DOB April 7, 1968. Also incarcerated, but at Beaumont Penitentiary in Texas. Found guilty of first-degree murder."

The room was abuzz with the incredible information.

Fuller nodded at Wang, then said, "O'Brien will call me as soon as they match a third case. Hopefully today. Their team has already gone through five of the twenty-six samples, so we'll see. With any luck..." Fuller surveyed the room. "Rosebud and Chainey, pair up and split the tasks for Westbrook. Wang and Wallflower, dig up everything you can on Pledger."

Kate and the detectives nodded at his order.

Fuller continued with his task delegation. "Dr. Davis, I need you to perform a more detailed autopsy on everything weird about these guys. Fuck, anything that could show they are not the 'originals,' but rather 'copies.' I'm not even sure what you'd look for. Whatever looks suspicious."

"Sure. Will do, Detective," Dr. Davis said before leaving the room.

Being on the East Coast, Kate knew that calling California at this hour would be futile. They tried nonetheless, and all they got was voicemail everywhere. So Kate and Detective Wang used their time to dig up a list of people, offices, and organizations they could contact in a couple of hours to help build their case.

By the time noon rolled around, everyone was on the phone or busy writing notes. The fax machine and printer were spitting out sheets of paper as fast as they could. A timeline had been created for both accused, with documents pinned along it and flashcards with locations and dates: birthdate, school records, change of addresses on file, crime date, incarceration date, current location. Parallel to each accused's timeline ran a second line, with very few items on it. Date and place the body was discovered as well as its current—and final—location.

At this point, it was impossible to determine where the two lines had intersected.

With birth records, they pinpointed the start of the two original lines, with branches going to people and organizations who could confirm there were no identical twins: parents, birth records, and hospital records.

They had checked every box that could be ticked, but they only had two cases.

Fuller walked around, his confidence rising with every note he read, but it was already five o'clock, and there was still no third case.

"O'Brien," he said on speakerphone, "Where do you stand with the samples?"

Luke's voice echoed out in the room. "We've gone through all of them, but only the initial two came back as a match. We've triple-checked those. We're double-checking all of the unmatched samples just to be safe, but it doesn't look good."

Fuller hung up without thanking Luke or saying goodbye. "Shit."

After about twenty seconds, Fuller scanned the now silent room. "Any thoughts? Anyone?"

Chainey spoke up. "We've only tried to match *our* John Does. Maybe we'll find matches with other districts. New York would probably have a shitload of John Does sitting there."

"That would take forever, and it would definitely take the secrecy out of this situation," Fuller said. "Anything else? Fuck, we need something fast. The district commander is breathing down my neck."

Kate raised her hand.

"It's not third grade here, speak up," Fuller said.

"What about Montague?" she asked.

"What about him?" asked Rosebud.

Kate sat tall as she spoke confidently. "This whole thing started because of him. Sure, he's not in jail, he's not accused of murder, but he's got a dead doppelgänger in Ohio. The sheriff couldn't find any birth or adoption records, but he only checked Massachusetts. Not sure if they've buried the body already."

"Can you call that sheriff?" Fuller asked, hope in his eyes.

"Yes, I have his number." Kate took out her phone, scrolled down through her call history, and found the Ohio area code.

She hit the dial button and waited with the phone against her ear.

"Speakerphone," Fuller ordered.

Kate nodded.

"Hi, Sheriff? It's Officer Kate Murphy in Boston. I'm putting you on speakerphone, hold on," she placed her phone on the table in front of everyone and hit the button.

"Can you hear me?" Kate asked.

"Yes, what's going on?" asked Sheriff Wallace.

"Your John Doe. Could you share every little detail you found out about Montague's birth records and hospital records? Everything you know?" Kate asked.

"Sure. As I already told you, birth and adoption records led me nowhere. No sign of a twin brother. Then I tried to get a copy of the hospital records, and I reached another dead end," the sheriff said. "He was born in a small town called Flagstone, and half the town burned to the ground in 1973. The fire unfortunately included the hospital and all of their records. As far as I can tell, that was before they could transfer the records to microfiche or anything, so I got nothing. I tried calling Montague again, but he hasn't returned any of my calls. Other things have come up, so I haven't gotten around to closing that case."

"Sheriff, Detective Lieutenant Fuller here. Your John Doe could be an important part of our investigation. We'll follow up with Montague here, in person, but could you initiate a transfer and send the body to our morgue here in Boston?"

There was a momentary pause before the sheriff answered. "I'm afraid he's been buried already."

"What?" Fuller exclaimed.

Kate was surprised as well, but not angry like Fuller seemed to be.

"Little room here, and we got another body. Some old lady took pity on the man when she saw him on the evening news. No relations or anything. Just filthy rich and felt it was wrong for anyone to not get a proper burial, so she forked out the money, organized it all, and it freed our morgue."

Fuller growled. "Dig him up."

"No can do, I'm afraid."

"We'll fill out the required paperwork, just send it to us."

Fuller proceeded to give the sheriff his fax number and said he'd be in touch. Kate pressed the icon to end the call and returned the phone to her pocket.

"Montague. Okay, let's make this our third official case. Rosebud and Chainey, track him down. Wang, go upstairs to get a warrant and meet up with them. Take him in for questioning again, get his birth certificate if he has a copy of it. Get his parents' address and phone number."

"And me?" Kate asked.

"Man the phones," Fuller ordered, smirking.

Although the task itself was demeaning, Kate beamed with pride. After all, it was *her* idea that had unblocked the real detectives.

BETWEEN CALLS, Kate refilled the paper tray and sorted the pages coming out of the fax machine. She finally received the form the sheriff had sent for exhuming the body. She also found the one they'd need to transfer the exhumed body to their jurisdiction.

She photocopied both, in case she made a mistake, then proceeded to fill them out the best she could. The sheriff had already entered some information, so she added the rest. She was about to send it when the other detectives came back.

"No twin brother," Wang said, hand raised, ready to be high-fived.

Kate's palm met hers. "Good! Could you look at this before I send it out?" Kate handed Wang the paperwork she'd just filled out.

"Looks good, Kate." She added a small note and passed it back. "Fax it to them right away."

Kate looked at the clock: 6:30 p.m. Sheriff Wallace had probably already left his office. She fed the machine, entered the fax number, and sent it. Then she called him and left a voicemail, just to make sure he'd check his machine.

By the time 7 p.m. rolled around, Fuller called a meeting for everyone. Even Capt. Cranston was in attendance. Although Dr. Davis had yet to find abnormalities with the two cloned bodies she had in her morgue, and the third body had yet to arrive, they had everything they needed to support their claim about cloning.

"Okay, folks," the district commander started, a large smile on his tired face. "Excellent work. Expect all hell to break loose now. I'll go and call in the Feds. As discussed yesterday, this case is on a strict 'need-to-know' basis. Keep it under wraps. I expect they'll just take over, but they may want to interview each one of us tomorrow morning, so meet up here at 8 a.m."

Kate was exhausted but had never experienced such a high in her work life. Is this what real detective work felt like? If so, she had an insatiable craving for more.

AT LEAST TWENTY FBI agents were dispatched to their station, and from what Kate could see, all of them were men. So much for the equality ratio. The district commander hadn't lied about what to expect. It felt like chaos had taken over their case.

When Kate arrived in the conference room, Luke was talking with an old man in a white lab coat. He had a gray beard and wore tiny round glasses. The older man even had a pocket protector to hold his pens. Kate smiled and wondered if that's what Luke would look like thirty years from now.

The two of them walked toward her, likely on their way out of the room. Luke winked at Kate as he passed by and she realized his hair was messy just like she'd dared him to wear it.

"Hey," she said, smiling as they crossed paths.

KATE WAS INTERVIEWED by three different FBI agents at once; each seemed to have a different specialty. Although they were on the same side here, the interview felt like she was being grilled, like she'd been caught doing something wrong.

By the time 5 p.m. rolled around, Kate's head was spinning. She was getting ready to leave and looking forward to going home to her private retreat where nobody would be around. She'd had enough of a "social bath" for today. Too many people. Too many conversations. She was drained.

"Wallflower, before you go," Fuller said, grabbing her by the arm and handing over a file. "Fill these out."

"What is it?"

"Paperwork. You got to play with the big detectives on this one, so here's where you thank us back. Fill these out. I want them completed tonight before you go. Slide the file under my door since I'm leaving; my office will be locked."

Kate kept quiet. She flipped through the file and saw one blank report form with a Post-It Note that read, "Five copies."

"Why five?"

"We need a statement from you and each of us real detectives. Look at the form number online. Make them sound a little different, so they don't look like they were written by the same person. Print them, sign yours and slide all five of them under my door. We'll review and sign them in the morning. Better make them good and complete, or you'll have to redo them tomorrow."

She wanted to tell him to go fuck himself, but who was she? She had enjoyed playing along with them, doing real detective work. So instead, she kept quiet, smiled, then headed to the lunchroom with her laptop. The room was empty, so she could at least concentrate. Next stop: coffee machine. She was going to be here for another three hours, so she'd definitely need the extra mental fuel.

CHAPTER NINETEEN

Christopher Kirk
The Colony

"TURN ON THE TELLY. We may see tonight's kill on the news," Christopher said, popping his head out of the fridge for a second to look at Stéphane, who was sitting crossed-legged at the end of the dining room table, his head tilted to the left as he scribbled something into a notebook.

Christopher grabbed a wedge of Brie and some red grapes then closed the stainless steel door with his foot.

Stéphane put down his book and reached for the remote. "What is your channel of choice?"

"The one with the blonde lassie with the full lips. Don't mind looking at her. She's real fit and gets my imagination going."

Christopher took out the wooden cutting board and placed the cheese on it. He rinsed the grapes and put them on a paper towel in a bowl then brought the snacks to the dining room table. He grabbed the baguette that Stéphane had baked earlier and added it to the selection before kicking his boots off and setting his feet on the table.

Stéphane turned on the TV then rummaged through the bottles in the corner bar. "Beverage?"

"Scotch. Why don't we crack open that thirty-three-year-old GlenDronach?"

"*Excellent choix,*" he said in French, grabbing the unopened bottle, two tumblers, and a glass of water. He poured an inch of Scotch into each then dipped his finger into the water to collect a drop before letting one fall into each glass.

He handed Christopher his drink. "Feet off the table. You know the rules."

"Nothing to get wound up about," Christopher said before obeying.

Stéphane raised his Scotch toward him, "To nearly twenty years of hard work that is starting to pay off, finally."

"Cheers," Christopher said, clinking his drink against Stéphane's. "The best is yet to come. Hope our chap makes us proud tonight," he said, pointing his chin toward the television.

Stéphane grabbed a few grapes and looked around the table, his hand feeling the edge of the cutting board.

"What are you looking for?"

"A knife," Stéphane said.

Christopher reached down his leg and pulled his Busse Combat Battle Mistress knife out of its protective holder, threw it up in the air, and then caught the handle as it came down, blade facing him. He handed the handle to Stéphane across the table. "Here's one."

"Did you wash it?"

"What?"

"I don't want to develop a taste for blood. I know what you do with your knives."

"Of course, I washed it."

The news was almost over, and while the fundraiser their clone attended was mentioned, the senator's death hadn't been.

Stéphane glanced at his watch. "Well, it's 10:25 p.m. The party's just getting started. It may not happen until later. Maybe we'll hear about it on the eleven o'clock news."

The end of his sentence was punctuated with footsteps coming their way.

Both men turned toward the clickety-clack of approaching

heels. Christopher had fallen in love with the long-legged woman who wore them before Stéphane had married her. A "classy closet whore with Einstein's IQ" was how Christopher had first described her, although never to her face.

He enjoyed watching her approach, her magenta dress flowing around her, and her fast pace allowing the fabric to wrap around her curvy figure. She wore a thick black belt around her slim waist, which accentuated her giant knockers. The dress's scoop neckline showed just enough bouncing cleavage to send him back to his university days. Those humongous breasts. They had given him everything a man could ever want. Comfort, beauty, so much to grab, soft and delicate skin, her nipples pointing to the sky when she rode him, arching her back. Fucking her for a six-month stint had been the highlight of his Harvard days. So perverse, yet so kind. She still haunted his wet dreams.

"Evening, Juliet," he said.

"Good evening, Christopher," she replied, smiling as she passed, before kissing her husband on the lips. She grabbed a grape, tossed it upward, and caught it in her mouth.

"I'm heading to bed, honey. I'll check the Colony on my way."

"*Oui, c'est parfait, prends ton temps*," he said, suggesting there was plenty of time. "We hope to watch the live coverage."

"Boys will be boys. Enjoy the limelight."

"Good night," Christopher said, watching her leave the room, her hips swaying, and her long legs conjuring even more flashbacks of the crazy sex they'd had.

CHAPTER TWENTY

Juliet Jackson
The Colony

ONCE SHE REACHED the mud room, Juliet took the elevator to the underground level. The doors opened to a small control room that led to an area expansive enough to play football, if it hadn't been for all the pods that occupied the space, along with the wires and tubes that connected them to the floor and ceiling.

She traded her shoes for the smallest pair of rubber boots that rested on the shoe rack. The open-grid flooring was no place to wear heels, especially not stilettos.

She stepped into the Incubator. At first, the endless rows of experimental wombs had freaked her out, their transparent membranes showing the development of the fetuses inside them, with blood vessels working their way around the artificial wombs. The pods worked like the real human parts. Clean blood fed them from the tube connections above, and, after flowing through each pod, the same blood got flushed down through the attachment at the bottom. There were other tubes, as well. One served to regulate the temperature, others were connected to sensors to keep track of vitals.

Because there was no body responsible for carrying these

fetuses, she and Stéphane had managed to keep them in their artificial wombs for two years.

The birth was always messy. She'd only attended one and hadn't managed to stand the sight of it. It had become the guys' job to birth their babies and dispose of those who died before term. A foot below the grid flooring, whatever liquids were discharged during these events merged and followed a slanted subfloor that drained into a large tank. The guys had never told her what they did with the dark brown sludge. A river ran a couple of miles south of the Colony, and the water was always clear whenever she went swimming in it, so she doubted they'd routed it there. She'd never seen a dump truck or any vehicle come to empty the tank, but that was probably good. How would they have explained the contents anyway? Juliet suspected their bloodthirsty guard dogs drank it. There were things she was happy not to know.

She placed her hand on the womb to her left. She had grown accustomed to the sack's rubbery feel and its pulsating rhythm that synced with the Mother's heartbeat. She took out her phone and connected to their music system wirelessly to play a tranquil Chopin nocturne.

She returned her hand to the womb and spoke to it softly. "Hi, little one. There's a big world out there, waiting for you to shine. You'll soon be out, and you'll join our family. We're all very excited."

She looked at the small terminal that relayed the pod's important statistics: the clone's ID number, its full name, its heartbeat, the number of days left in the womb.

"Ethan, my dear, you'll grow up to be a fine young man. I can't wait to meet you in less than a month."

The heartbeat increased, a little out of sync with the swooshing sound that filled the room whenever the Mother's heart would beat.

These artificial wombs made her feel like a real mother, and if it hadn't been for her encounter with Stéphane at a conference twenty years ago, she wouldn't be standing here tonight, surrounded by their babies.

Juliet spent another hour going from pod to pod in one of the dozens of rows. Each night, she picked a different row. There were just too many to do in one night, so she did her best and tried to make time for them before Christopher would take over and turn them into soldiers that would fight to make the world a better place.

About ninety minutes later, she reached the other end of the Incubator and took the elevator up to her and Stéphane's bedroom. She walked into their luxurious bathroom and poured herself a lavender-scented bubble bath in the four-person Jacuzzi, and then walked into her closet.

She untied the belt of her dress. Reaching behind her neck, she awkwardly found the zipper from the middle of her back and then undid it before letting the dress fall to the floor, around her legs. After rolling down her black stockings, careful not to catch her nails on them, she hung her dress up on an empty hanger and walked back to the bathroom in her underwear. She undid her bra and removed her panties, leaving them on the side of the sink to hand wash later.

After testing the water with her right foot, she slid her body into the tub. As she did every night, she took a deep breath, held it, and then let her entire body sink under the water in the deep tub. She could hear her heartbeat, but otherwise, it was silent. The warmth of the water around her body hugged her and comforted her. She felt safe. She stayed submerged until she couldn't hold her breath any longer.

With her head out of the water, Juliet opened her eyes and pulled her hands through her wet hair, pushing down the bubbles and foam to her shoulders. She imagined their babies felt something similar when they were born. Too bad she couldn't remember her own birth.

The music that played on their bathroom's built-in stereo system was the same that aired in the Incubator. While Stéphane and Christopher never understood why it was important to her, she had insisted during the construction of the house, and she had gotten her way, as usual. Juliet liked controlling what their babies would listen to in their artificial wombs. Classical music was pure heaven to her, and she thought it would be good for them, as well. After Chopin ended, Beethoven automatically took over.

Once the water became noticeably cooler, she got out of the tub, dried herself, and then put on a see-through nightgown, the one Stéphane had bought her last Christmas that he loved so much. She returned to the bedroom, kneeled at the foot of the bed, put her hands together, closed her eyes, and began to speak softly.

"Dear God, thank you for another good day. You've been very kind to my husband and me. While you took away my ability to have children of my own, I now understand that you did it because you had bigger plans for me. You knew I would somehow find a way to raise many, many more babies, and I wouldn't have been able to follow this path if it hadn't been for you. Please protect Robbie, wherever he is. Bless Christopher and my Stéphane, and I promise to make this world a better place with the powers you've granted us, thanks to your infinite wisdom. We will make you proud. We will fight to give power back to the good people, taking it from the crooked, power-hungry leaders who are destroying our planet and those who rob children of their innocence in the most awful way. And, as always, we'll do our best to right as many injustices as we can." She crossed herself then said, "Amen."

Stéphane came into the room just as she got up.

"*Ah... que tu es belle, mon amour*," he said.

He walked toward her, wrapped his arms around her, and then kissed her.

CHAPTER TWENTY-ONE

Robert Robertson
The Hampshire House, Boston

EVERYTHING in this room seemed over-the-top: caviar and foie gras hors-d'oeuvres, four-tiered champagne fountains, birds carved out of ice, and shrimp the size of a baby's arm.

Robert crossed the room as if it were his own, nodding and smiling at unknown men and women in their fanciest outfits. He grabbed a martini from the tray a penguin-looking waitress offered. Sipping his drink, he scanned the room once more. The senator had yet to arrive. No way he'd miss his entrance. After all, the senator was the guest of honor. Based on Robert's mission brief, the senator would show up here tonight to help support Freedom and Glory, his charitable organization that sent money to US troops *and* also funded their enemies, although that last part was not known by the public. With his shares in the weapons sector, it made financial sense.

He put his hand in his right pants pocket, feeling the sharp and sturdy plastic blade resting against his hip. Of course, the metal detector hadn't spotted it at the event's security check, but it would work just fine to cut the senator's throat or knife him in the heart. It worked just as well as the metal version; no doubt about it. He'd stabbed many pigs with a replica of that blade. Sure, it was mostly a one-time use weapon, as bones had a way of damaging its sharp plastic edge, but one time was all he needed tonight. He'd rehearsed this kill many times in his head. In fact, that was the sole mission the Colony had trained him to do.

Robert had been raised as a premium soldier. He knew he was part of a breed of extraordinary people with laser-sharp focus who received instructions telepathically, or at least as close to that as technology currently allowed. Since he'd left the Colony, eighteen months ago, his primary task had been to set up roots and fit into society. The rules were simple:

1. He was not allowed to mingle with other people from the Colony unless specifically ordered to.
2. He was to live a quiet life and obey every societal rule until he received his official mission.
3. He was to keep his past private and not discuss the Colony with anyone.
4. He was to remain unattached because relationships were too complicated and would take his focus away from making this world a better place.
5. Each morning, he was to ensure his Colony app was up-to-date on his phone, so new instructions could be downloaded and synced to the chip implanted in his brain.

He wasn't quite sure of the chip's exact location. He couldn't feel it, but because he was instructed to always bring the phone to his left ear, and never to use the speakerphone feature, he figured the device had to have been implanted around his left temple.

A little girl in a ball gown ran past him, hitting his elbow with her head.

"Sorry, mister," she said.

Robert faked a smile. "No harm done."

He watched her try to catch up with a short boy in a tuxedo

and wondered how old they were. Children outside the Colony seemed to drag their feet into adulthood. His childhood had gone by quickly. Everyone at the Colony was on the fast track.

He had no real recollection of his early years. His oldest memories always involved training of some sort, with immersive education sessions held alone in a ten-foot-by-ten-foot room, with TV screens covering three of the four walls from floor to ceiling. Immobilized in a chair in the middle of the room, he had to sit still with his eyelids kept open by a helmet contraption that was attached to the back of his seat, almost like a salon hair dryer he had seen in movies, but with more mechanical clamps.

Education sessions always lasted two hours and included an audio recording with several layered voices. He had never been able to focus on any one of the voices. Each time he was being secured to the training chair, the supervisor had told him, "It will be much more pleasant if you just let it happen, if you let the information reach your subconscious without fighting it." And it had been. He'd learned to breathe his way through each session and found that he could absorb the information much more efficiently. In six years, with two hours each day, he had learned much about the world, its history, and what was wrong and right about it.

In addition to education sessions, each day involved group training led by Mr. C or by senior supervisors. Mr. C was an expert in firearms, knives, and martial arts. These sessions also lasted two hours and were essential components of their training at the Colony. Those who didn't learn fast enough and those who finished last in the group were never seen again. Expelled out of the Colony, or, as Robert had come to realize, used as live bait for final exams.

To graduate from the Colony, each person had to prove his or her ability to follow orders downloaded to their chips, even if, and especially if, it involved killing a specific person. No one had told him that, but he'd reached that conclusion during his final manhunt. His instructions had been to kill the man hiding in the forest. The two-square-mile perimeter was limited by a three-story fence topped with electrical and barbed wire. The prey couldn't escape.

The prey had entered the perimeter a day before him. At the beginning of the final exam, Mr. C had unlocked the small door in the fence and started a twenty-four-hour timer on his watch. Robert had been given a nine-millimeter gun, a knife, and a small flask of fresh water. The rest he'd figured out on his own, using the education and skills he'd learned during his six years at the Colony.

His manhunt had gone well. After seven hours, he had caught the prey, removed his mask, and recognized No. 201, a fellow student who had been expelled. The decision had been simple: kill and live, or fail and die as the next prey. He'd given 201 a quick death before boasting in the glory, pride, and accomplishment that filled his heart.

Upon graduating and being let into the world, they were reminded of how special they were. They'd soon realize there was something different about them and their fast physical and mental development. They had been lucky to be raised at the Colony, for they learned and grew to become adults in just six years after birth.

They were growing so fast that the only clothes trainees could wear were robes and flip-flops. Once they outgrew those items, they would go to the Supply Building and trade them for the next size up.

They were fed well, with food they grew and butchered themselves. They spent a few hours each day tending the fields, working in the gardens or caring for the animals. Robert had enjoyed gardening the most. He could see JJ there, and she often smiled at him from across the garden. He didn't quite understand why he felt a special bond with her. He didn't know who his father or mother was, but JJ was the closest thing he'd had to a mother.

A voice on a microphone brought him back to reality.

"And now, ladies and gentleman, here's Senator Aaron Russell."

The room broke into applause.

Robert knew what to do. He walked to the back, took out his phone, hit his mission app icon, and listened to his final instructions. He waited patiently until the senator had to use the facilities or go to a private room.

~

THREE HOURS ELAPSED with Robert's mind clear and focused, awaiting the perfect opportunity. He wandered the room and ignored anyone who approached him to chitchat. He had a job to do, and he was the right man for it. The senator had to die, and tonight was the night.

Finally, at 1 a.m., he got his opening.

The senator appeared to have found a woman who piqued his interest. Robert had been informed that his target was a philanderer, so there was no surprise there. As the guests started to leave, he managed to get close enough to overhear their conversation. She gave him her address. He mentioned that he wouldn't be able to follow her out publicly, but would meet her there within an hour.

The woman left a few minutes later, but not before turning around to make last-minute eye contact with the senator, who winked at her.

The senator returned to his tall brunette wife, who looked darn good in a white silk dress. He brought with him two flutes of champagne. Robert giggled on the inside. As if champagne would make up for his cheating. The senator's security detail wouldn't leave him alone here; he'd already seen a guard escort him to the bathroom earlier this evening, so following the woman and completing his mission at her house was preferable.

Fewer witnesses, fewer side kills.

He didn't have another plastic blade with him. He only had one shot at this.

He grabbed his jacket from the coat check and marched two blocks east to the now near-empty parking lot where he'd left his 2012 Toyota Corolla.

Twenty minutes later, the GPS on his car indicated he was a

hundred feet from the woman's house. He parked and walked the rest of the way there. Once he located her home, he went around the block once to get a feel for his surroundings and possible escape routes. There was a small alley out back, parallel to the main street. He repeated the same path once more, this time counting how many houses he passed by. Finally, he went into the alley to figure out which back entry was hers.

The alley offered a better way in. Dark, with lots of cedar bushes to hide in. He checked the house. One light was on upstairs. He could see a door on a deck but was not sure if there were motion-activated lights nearby. He bent down and grabbed a few pebbles and dropped them in his pocket.

After creeping his way closer to the door using the bushes for cover, he spotted a patch of grass surrounding the deck. He threw his small rocks past the back door, and most of them landed quietly on the grass, but a few bounced on the wooden terrace. A light turned on. He retreated into the bushes some more, keeping an eye on the window where there was light. He was well hidden by the bushes but realized the back door wouldn't work as a point of discreet entry. A woman's figure came to the window, looked out for a few seconds, and then disappeared out of sight.

He waited for the light to turn off, and continued his way along the bushes, letting his eyes adjust to the darkness again.

He saw a window on the side of the house, but it was too high to reach, without anything to climb on. He continued toward the front of the house, and, instead of the cedar edge he'd been feeling for the past five minutes, he sensed a large tree trunk behind his back. An extensive branch hung just over his head, about six feet from the ground. His eyes followed it to see that it almost touched the roof. Maybe he could climb on it, then jump to whatever they called those fake balconies with a sliding patio door and no room to stand.

The door could be locked, and she could be in that room and see me approach. Not ideal.

He retreated to the alley and went along the opposite side of the house.

A few minutes later, he found a basement window.

Much better.

He pulled out the screen from one side and attempted to slide the outside window panel open. It worked. Repeating the same action with the inner window panel, he was surprised to see it glide smoothly as well. The opening wasn't overly big, but it was wide enough for him to slip into the room.

He crawled into the gap headfirst and cautiously felt the wall as far down as he could to see if there was any furniture below the window. Pleased to find nothing, he retreated, turned around and gently lowered his body until he landed softly on the floor. He tried to decipher the size of the room and where he stood in relation to the house.

Too dark.

His eyes needed to adjust.

The doorbell rang. A second later, footsteps echoed from somewhere above.

Perfect distraction to look for the door now.

He moved with his arms in front of him and one of his legs a foot above the ground, feeling nothing but air, then a wall a few seconds later. He let his fingers run along it, trying to find a doorframe. Keeping his body as far out as possible to avoid a potential collision with furniture, he finally recognized the shape of a knob and then opened the door.

Robert stepped into what appeared to be a hallway, with faint light coming in from his right.

Stairs leading up.

He made his way toward the light and hit the first step with his foot, inadvertently creating a soft creak. He waited.

Did they hear me?

Thirty seconds later, assured they hadn't, he inched his way up the stairs, hoping they wouldn't creak too much, but the fourth step did.

He paused and listened.

Glasses were clinking over jazz and happy chatter.

Still undetected. Lucky me.

One step at a time, he made his way up, timing his

movements to the rhythm of the music to hide the noises. He felt the doorknob in front of him but waited before turning it, still not sure if the people above were aware of his presence. The voices had stopped. Robert hadn't been paying attention to what they were saying before.

Did they hear something?

He remained quiet and listened. The song was ending and, in the short pause before the next one started, he overheard faint moaning.

Good. They got busy.

The next song came on, and the level of their excitement went up a notch. Now was his chance. He had no idea how long the old fart would last.

It's now or never.

He turned the knob, pushed the door open, popped his head out, and looked toward where the music and moans came from.

The senator was kneeling. His wrinkly butt cheeks clenched to the rhythm of her moans as he fucked her. Her bare legs were spread around him, her heels resting on the floor. She was lying flat on her back on what appeared to be a coffee table, but then raised one of her red-soled heels to rest on his shoulder.

Robert inched his way closer, matching his pace with their loud moans, which more than covered the sounds of the creaky hardwood floors. He was ten steps away from the senator, his blade out and ready, when the CD player switched to a different disc.

Beethoven's Fifth Symphony started playing, snapping Robert right out of his trance.

CHAPTER TWENTY-TWO

Robbie Robertson
Agatha Lindsey's House, East Boston

BEETHOVEN'S FIFTH reminded Robbie of his youth.

JJ used to play it for him when he was sick. She'd let him build castles with Legos, and they'd talk to each other. He loved JJ and often wondered what had happened to her.

Was she still at the Colony?

But more important matters were at play.

Why am I standing in a tuxedo behind a naked couple? Why do I have a sharp plastic blade in my hand?

Robbie could taste something fishy and rich in his mouth. His throat was parched. His heart was beating fast.

Where am I?

But before he could remember how he got there, the naked woman saw him and screamed.

He lowered his blade, glanced around for a way out, saw the entrance hall on his left, and then ran toward it.

What now?

He ran to the street, placed the knife in his right jacket pocket, where he found a set of Toyota keys. He walked a few houses down before finding a gray Toyota that reacted when he pressed the unlock button. He sat still in the driver's seat while realizing what had just happened.

He had nearly murdered a man. He had to prevent that from happening again. The music must have made him come to his senses.

Beethoven.

He turned on the radio, scrambled for a minute, and then found the classical music station. He turned off his phone. But what about the rest?

Could some other sound or visual clue trigger the killer in me again? Better not risk it.

Robbie had no idea where he was. He programmed "police" into the car's GPS and followed the directions to the nearest station. Once there, he opened up the glove compartment and found a pad of paper and a pen.

He wrote:

Lock me up, I need to talk to a detective about a murder, play Beethoven if I don't cooperate.

He left his knife in the glove compartment and placed his phone in his jacket pocket before walking to the front desk and showing his note to the officer on duty.

After waiting for a few minutes, another police officer took his jacket and escorted him to an interrogation room on the second floor. The man left Robbie alone with his thoughts.

The longer he waited, the fuzzier things got. He could hear a clock ticking on the wall. He tried to remain calm, to stay out of his trance, but pain began pulsating in the back of his head.

He closed his eyes, but all he could hear was his heartbeat and the ticking clock.

CHAPTER TWENTY-THREE

Robert Robertson
Roxbury Police Station, Boston

THE DOOR OPENED, and Robert lifted his eyes.

A fat man in a brown suit offered him a glass of water. "You wrote this note?" he asked, pushing a piece of paper toward Robert.

Robert stared at it, then at the man.

What had happened? The last thing he remembered was the senator's wrinkly ass and the red-soled heels.

Now, he was in what seemed to be an interrogation room. Did he get caught? Did he kill the senator? And what was this stupid note about?

He didn't remember.

"Hey, I'm talking to you," the fat man said. "What's your name?"

Robert looked up, annoyed and wanting to crush the man's blond-haired head against the stainless steel table, but the fatso got up and left.

A minute later, Robert got up as well and tried to open the door. It was locked.

Of course.

He returned to his seat and took notice of his environment to come up with an escape plan. One table and two chairs, each bolted to the floor. One television monitor attached to a corner of the ceiling, out of reach. Two solid walls, one with a locked door, and the other with a large mirror, probably two-way.

How many people are on the other side?

Nothing to grab, and nothing to throw at the mirror either. Placing his hands in his pants pockets, he tried to feel for his plastic blade. Gone. What did he do with it? Did he throw it out? Did he give it to the police? What about his cellphone? It wasn't in his pockets either.

The door re-opened, and this time the fat man had brought in reinforcement: a tall brown-haired man, an iPod, and mini speakers. Fatso pressed play, and Beethoven's notes filled the small room.

"So, what's your name?" the thinner, taller man asked.

Robert was confused. Having trouble focusing, he looked at the fat man, the other man, the door, the mirror, the speakers... The room wasn't spinning, but he felt dizzy nonetheless.

What's going on?

The fat man nodded at the other, then they left, along with their music.

Letting out a sigh of relief, Robert calmed down. He could feel his shoulders lowering, his breath decelerating. Then, the annoying music filled the air through the built-in speakers in the ceiling.

Why the fuck are they playing shitty music in here?

It felt like his mind was being crushed. He couldn't formulate his own thoughts, only notice his memories fade and dissolve away.

A short pause between songs gave him a small reprieve, and then the first few notes took him out of his trance.

Ta-ta-ta-taaaa, ta-ta-ta-taaaaa...

CHAPTER TWENTY-FOUR

Robbie Robertson
Roxbury Police Station, Boston

BEETHOVEN'S FIFTH had brought him back. His note had worked.

Robbie stood up, looked straight into the mirror, then waved at whoever was watching him from the other side.

A minute later, a chubby, curly-haired man in plain clothes entered and sat down before taking a deep breath. The door reopened a few seconds later, and a taller, brown-haired man came in.

"Ready to talk?" the chubby man asked.

"Yes," Robbie said.

"I'm Detective Rosebud," he said, "and this is Detective Chainey." He pointed at the taller man. "Who are you?"

"I'm Robbie Robertson."

"Mr. Robertson, why are you here?" Rosebud asked.

"I have information you need to know."

The tall man remained standing, not saying a word but staring at Robbie with a blank expression.

Rosebud rested his elbows on the table and joined his hands together in a fist. "About what?" he asked.

"A murder."

"Finally," Rosebud said before sighing. "Did you kill anyone?"

Robbie felt his left eye twitch. "Tonight? No."

"And in your lifetime?" Rosebud asked.

Robbie nodded. "Probably."

"Okay, we'll talk about that in a second, but first, what's going on here? Why didn't you want to talk to us a few minutes ago?" Rosebud inquired.

Robbie looked down at the table, the twitch in his left eye becoming stronger. He had no idea what had happened in the past few minutes. "I don't know."

"Hey," Rosebud said, snapping his fingers to get Robbie's attention again. "Are you on drugs, Mr. Robertson?"

Robbie shook his head. "No."

"Do you suffer from a mental disorder?" Rosebud asked.

Robbie looked up, annoyed. "No!"

Rosebud waved his hands at him. "Fine, that's just fine. I need to check something, and I'll be right back. Would you like something to eat? A sandwich? Cookies?"

Robbie shook his head then changed his mind just as the men were leaving the room. "Cookies would be great."

CHAPTER TWENTY-FIVE

Detective Malvin Rosebud
Roxbury Police Station, Boston

ROSEBUD AND CHAINEY headed to the interrogation room's observation area to join Joseph Morven, a BPD criminal profiler, and Cameron Lack, the FBI agent in charge of the cloning case. Rosebud still had no idea why the FBI agent had wanted to snoop around this weird walk-in situation, but if Lack wanted to waste his own time, Rosebud couldn't care less. He had nothing to hide. He just wanted to get this over with and head home.

"Well, he seems freaking nuts to me," Rosebud said. "Chainey, can we run a check on him: background, previous record, et cetera? See if any nutjobs have escaped from hospitals, jails, or rehab centers recently?"

Chainey chuckled. "I'm on it," he said before leaving the room.

Rosebud looked at Morven. "What do you think?"

The profiler had volunteered to sit in on this one as a way to take a break from the cloning circus that had started earlier today with the arrival of the FBI. Rosebud didn't expect a detailed analysis from him. Morven's brain was probably as drained as his was.

"When the Fifth Symphony started, within a second of hearing the first few notes, the man's facial expression changed," Morven said then paused. "This particular song acts as a trigger. The previous few tracks confused him, but nothing like that one. It flipped a switch. I've set your iPod to repeat this single song in a loop, so be ready for it."

"Really? First I have to download this crap, just in case it matters. Now I have to listen to it, over and over, and over? Will this day ever end?" Rosebud scratched his head and looked at Morven again. "So, you think he's a psycho?"

"Absolutely *not* what I said," Morven replied, his face stern. "He might be schizophrenic or could suffer from another mental disorder. My background in psychiatry isn't strong enough for me to diagnose him." He turned toward Agent Lack. "Is your psychiatrist still here?"

"He's gone home. So far, there's no indication we should be involved. Unless he says something that links him to this cloning-murder case, I'm leaving, and I won't involve any of my guys."

Chainey came back just as the FBI agent was finishing his sentence. He waved two sheets of paper in the air.

"Well, you may want to stick around," Chainey told Agent Lack. "His name and DOB came back with two matches. And have a look at these driver's license pictures," he said, handing them over.

Agent Lack nodded as he examined the sheets. "Same name, same DOB. They look like twins, but different addresses. Unless the mother wanted to call both her twins the same, it sounds to me like this guy is living a double life. Well, up until yesterday, the double life would have been the only plausible option to me. But with your latest discovery, I guess we *could* have another clone on our hands. I'll send a couple of my agents to the other address to check it out."

Lack turned to Morven before continuing. "I'm calling in Dr. Dobbins, just in case." He took out his cellphone.

"I need a drink," said Rosebud before exiting and heading to the lunchroom. He walked swiftly while massaging his temples.

A headache was building up. This day didn't look like it would end anytime soon.

A minute later, he was surprised to see the lunchroom occupied. "Murphy?" he called out. The clock on the wall read 11:04 p.m. "What are you still doing here?"

"Putting the finishing touches on your reports. Yours, Fuller's, Wang's, Chainey's, and mine. Fuller needs them first thing in the morning," she told him.

Rosebud couldn't help but giggle. "Yeah, I bet he does."

He reached for a paper cup and selected the Dark Ethiopian blend on the machine, then pressed for one sugar to be added.

"Whatever, I wasn't in a position to say no."

"It's part of making it," he said. "We've all done something like that at some point. Some suck dicks; some fill out paperwork. Part of earning your stripes."

"Why are you still here? Fuller left hours ago."

Rosebud shook his head. "Chainey's still here, too. You wouldn't believe the wacko who just walked in. We may actually have a live clone on our hands. Oh, almost forgot," he said, walking over to the vending machine. "Cookies. Might as well get some for me, too."

He purchased two packages of Oreos. The coffee machine spat out the last few drips, and then he took his cup out of the dispenser.

"A live clone. Really?" Murphy looked like someone had injected her with caffeine. "Can I go and sit in?"

"Nah. Don't think Fuller would approve," he said as he shook his head and watched disappointment creep on her face. "The weirdo may not be a clone anyway. He's probably just crazy and running a double life." He stirred his coffee. "Hope you finish those soon so you can get a few hours of sleep before tomorrow."

Rosebud chucked his stir stick into the garbage and started walking out of the lunchroom.

"Should be done in about thirty minutes," Murphy said as she looked at the clock.

Just after turning the corner out of the lunchroom, he

stopped and backtracked. He peeked his head in the room to look at Murphy. "Thanks for filling out my report. I appreciate it."

She smiled. "No problem."

CHAPTER TWENTY-SIX

Dr. Everett Dobbins
Roxbury Police Station, Boston

"SO, WHAT HAVE WE GOT HERE?" Dr. Dobbins asked the group in the observation room as he walked in.

"Dr. Dobbins," Agent Lack started with a faint smile. "Thanks for coming. This is Robert Robertson. He seems to have a mental block or some personality split that gets triggered when he hears Beethoven."

"Would it be all right if I go in?" Dobbins asked while looking at Lack.

"Of course," Lack replied.

"Dr. Dobbins, here are some cookies," Rosebud said, handing over one of the packages he'd just purchased. "Robertson said he wanted some earlier."

Dr. Dobbins took the cookies and entered the interrogation room. He walked to the chair and sat opposite Robertson with his legs crossed, examining the man's flat expression before resting a pen and pad of paper on his lap. Robertson's sleek brown hair appeared to have gel in it, and his tuxedo clashed with the interrogation room's decor.

"Robert, how do you do?"

"Hi."

"I'm Dr. Dobbins. Would it be all right if I asked you a few questions?"

"Whatever," Robertson replied.

Dr. Dobbins slid the package across the table. "Here's a snack for you."

Robertson snatched the Oreo wrapper from his hand before Dr. Dobbins had fully released his grip.

"Hungry, I see. I was told your name is Robert Robertson. Is this correct?"

"I like Robbie better."

"Okay, Robbie. What's your middle name?"

Robertson glanced up as he chewed on a cookie. "Middle name?"

"You know, on your birth certificate. Do you have an extra name that appears on there? Most Americans have a middle name."

Robertson raised his shoulders as he swallowed.

Dr. Dobbins continued. "Tell me about you."

"What?" Robertson asked before reaching for the last cookie.

"For example, what do you do for work? Or what do you enjoy doing in your free time? What are your favorite television programs?"

Robertson stared at him impassively then raised his shoulders again.

"How about your parents?" the doctor asked.

Robertson looked down and shook his head without saying a word.

"Are they dead?"

"Don't know," Robertson replied, his eyes still aimed at the table.

"Who's your best friend?"

"JJ."

Dr. Dobbins made a note on his pad. "Who's that?"

"Juliet."

"Where is she?"

"Don't know," he said, fingering the packaging, his bright blue eyes showing a hint of sadness.

"Do you miss her?"

He nodded profusely. "Yes."

"Do you have other friends?"

"No."

"Well, I'm sure that's not entirely true," Dr. Dobbins said. "What about old friends from school?"

Robertson remained silent, but his eyelids drooped.

Dobbins noted the change in him, so he said, "Tell you what. I'm thirsty. I'm going to get myself a cup of tea. Do you want anything to drink?"

"No."

The doctor stood up, left, and then returned to the observation room.

Agent Lack was waiting for him. "So, what do you think?"

Dr. Dobbins scratched his head. "Not the most talkative person. You said he walked himself in? His answers were short. He doesn't trust me. That 'Juliet' he mentioned... Do we have a female agent who could come in for a few minutes? I reckon he might trust a woman more than he does men."

Lack looked at Rosebud and Chainey. "I've got an all-male crew this time," Lack said.

Rosebud snapped his fingers. "Hold on. I saw Murphy a few minutes ago in the lunchroom. I'll see if she can come in."

CHAPTER TWENTY-SEVEN

Kate Murphy
Roxbury Police Station, Boston

KATE WAS TURNING off her laptop when Rosebud rushed back into the lunchroom, out of breath.

"Great, you're still here," he said.

"What?" Kate asked, a little annoyed. She looked at the clock on the wall: 11:30 p.m. It was late, and she was exhausted.

Better not be about more paperwork that needs to be filled out tonight. I need sleep.

"The FBI's psychiatrist wants a woman to interview the wacko, and they don't have one on staff. Follow me."

"Really?" Kate exclaimed, her heart jumping in her chest.

A chance to do more detective work. Real detective work this time, not just filling out reports, and with the FBI? I'll be interviewing a clone! This could even help me free Kenny. Well, maybe.

She stood up quickly, fueled by adrenaline, but the long day and lack of sleep from the previous night made her dizzy. "Let me grab a coffee first, though. I need one," Kate said.

"Of course."

A few minutes later, her computer packed, a small coffee and the completed reports in hand, she followed Rosebud to the interrogation room. As they passed Detective Fuller's office, she slid the paperwork underneath his door.

"Let's hope you won't have to redo those," he said, grinning wide.

Rosebud filled Kate in about Robertson, his note, Beethoven, and Dr. Dobbins before they reached the door to the observation room, so she was caught up to speed.

"Let's drop your stuff here and meet the doc," he said, letting her into the room before him. "This is Officer Kate Murphy," Rosebud said. "Patrol cop undergoing detective training." He nodded toward the thin, gray-haired man wearing tortoiseshell glasses. "This is Dr. Dobbins, with the FBI."

Kate couldn't believe what was happening right now. Did Rosebud think she was *undergoing detective training* for real? *Nah.* Maybe it was just the simplest way to explain why she was involved with the case. *Whatever.* She was playing in the big leagues, about to interview a clone! Now, *that* was something.

"Pleased to meet you, Officer Murphy. Thanks for joining us on such short notice. I'll be going in with you. I think he may trust women more than men." Dr. Dobbins paused, examining her. "Would you mind letting your hair down?"

"Why?" Kate asked, taken by surprise by his request.

"You look a little stern with the way it's coiffed right now. Don't get me wrong. Perfectly suitable for work, but I'd like him to bond with you, not be intimidated by you. Maybe we can let go of the professional police officer image and go with a more feminine, nurturing look? In fact, we don't even have to mention you're a police officer unless he asks."

Kate nodded in agreement, anxious to help in any way she could. "Fine by me."

She took out her bobby pins and the elastic band of her ponytail. She ruffled her hair to style it the best she could, considering it'd been up all day.

"Splendid," Dr. Dobbins said before pointing toward the door. "Let's go."

Kate followed him into the interrogation room, butterflies in her stomach.

"Robbie, I'd like you to meet Kate."

"Hi, Robbie," she said with a bright smile.

"Hi, Kate."

"Kate, please sit down. Why don't the two of you chitchat and get to know each other? I'll be back later," Dr. Dobbins said before leaving her alone with the brown-haired man. Although he was dressed in a tuxedo, he had a boyish charm to him. Maybe it was the wave of his hair or the sadness in his bright blue eyes.

My first official detective interview alone!

But Kate knew she wasn't really alone. A small crowd was observing her at this very instant.

I have to show them I can bond with a suspect.

She listened to the music for a moment, and then said, "I like Beethoven, especially this piece. It's so... majestic, don't you agree?"

Robbie stared at her silently, but his expression wasn't angry or annoyed. His traits were soft and he had a certain light in his eyes, as though he was reminiscing about his life.

Kate pressed on. "Beethoven must remind you of someone or something in your past, right?"

"JJ. We listened to this song all the time when we were together."

Past wife or girlfriend?

"Tell me about JJ."

"You look a little like her," he said. He reached out and touched her hair. Although startled, Kate did her best not to let it show.

Play along, if anything starts going wrong, one of the observers will surely step in.

Robbie smiled. "Your hair is silky and blonde like hers."

Softly, Kate led him on. "Tell me more about her."

"She read to me and made Lego castles with me."

"Ah," Kate said, realizing Juliet wasn't a girlfriend, but probably his mother, sister, or babysitter. "That must have been a long time ago?"

He shook his head. "No, not really."

Kate lifted a brow at him. "What do you mean?"

"It was at the beginning of the Colony training, so maybe eight years ago," Robbie said, so matter-of-fact.

Kate did some mental math. He appeared to be in his thirties. *What kind of man plays with Legos in his twenties?*

"Tell me more," she said.

"About JJ?"

Although more intrigued by the Colony training, Kate didn't want to risk losing the trust they were establishing. "Sure, I'd love to learn more about her."

"She was so beautiful. So kind. She used to rock me to sleep. She took me away from the others when I was sick. She cared about me. I miss her."

Something doesn't add up. He must have problems remembering things or dates.

"Do you know where JJ is now?"

"No, not really." He stared down at the table, his right hand doodling imaginary graffiti on the stainless steel table.

"Robbie, is JJ still alive?"

He looked right back up, an anxious flame in his eyes. "I hope she's still alive! I don't want her to be dead."

Kate continued her line of questioning while trying to keep him at ease. "Robbie, do you know where she is?"

He appeared calmer now. "Probably at the Colony."

She was intrigued. "And what is that?"

"What?"

"The Colony. What's that?"

His eyes widened. "Oh. I'm not supposed to tell anyone about it."

"Who says you're not supposed to?"

"Mr. C."

"Who's he?" she asked.

A vertical line formed between his brows. He tightened his jaw. "Mr. C is evil."

Kate kept silent, hoping Robbie would expand on the mysterious Mr. C.

"Violent. Dangerous. That's what he is."

"Is Mr. C at the Colony, as well?"

"Probably. He has to train new people."

"What new people?"

"The new generation."

What the heck is he talking about? A new generation of clones? How many are there?

"Where do they come from, these new people?"

"What do you mean?"

"Do they arrive by bus? Where were those people before showing up at the Colony?"

Robbie seemed confused. "Nowhere. We appear there."

"Appear? Like magic?" Kate asked with a slight laugh.

"No, like children."

"You mean the new people were born there?"

"Yes."

Before continuing, Kate let his reply sink in, trying to understand how that was even feasible. "How many children are born there?"

"A lot."

The door opened behind her. Kate turned around and saw Agent Lack come in and point her toward the door. "I'll take over," he said.

Although annoyed, Kate knew she wasn't a detective and understood her place. She smiled and nodded at Robbie before leaving the room. "I enjoyed talking with you, Robbie."

"Me too, Kate," he said, a faint smile on his lips.

She returned to the observation room, curious to see how Agent Lack would carry on, so she could improve her interviewing skills. She thought she had done pretty well.

Dr. Dobbins nodded at her. "Good work in there, dear." Then, he returned his attention to the window.

Agent Lack spoke up, his voice authoritative and loud. "Tell me more about the Colony."

Robbie seemed angry and upset. His face reddened.

Lack pushed on, though. "Robert, I want to help you, but you need to tell me more about the Colony."

Robbie shook his head, staring at the table.

"How about Juliet? JJ? Can you tell me more about her?" Lack asked, softening his voice a little.

Robbie looked up and crossed his arms over his chest like a kid about to throw a temper tantrum. "No."

Agent Lack stood up, his index and middle finger waving toward the one-sided mirror.

Kate felt a nudge on her side and turned to the doctor.

"Kate, go back in. See if you can regain his trust," Dr. Dobbins ordered.

"Yes, of course," Kate said before doing just that, smiling broadly.

"Sorry about that, Robbie," she started after taking a seat in front of him again. Lack left the room.

"I don't want to talk to other people," he said firmly.

"Why is that?"

"I don't trust them."

"Who?"

"Men."

"You prefer women?" she asked.

"Nah... not really."

She was confused. "Why do you talk to me?"

He shook his head. "I don't know. You look like JJ."

That had to work to her advantage. "So, Robbie, you came here tonight to talk to a detective about a murder. Can you tell me more about the note you gave them?"

"Yeah... that. It's complicated. I'm not sure I understand it all."

"Go ahead, give it a try. Maybe I'll help you make sense of it."

"Okay. So..." Robbie let out a long sigh. "I don't know where to start."

Kate spoke clearly and slowly. "Start with tonight. Where were you just before you got here?"

"I was in a woman's house."

She nodded. "Okay, who was she?"

"Don't know."

"How did you get there?"

"I think I followed the address in my GPS."

Kate repeated what she'd heard. "So, you don't know the woman's name, but you know her address?"

"That's right."

"Where did you get her address?"

"I'm not sure about that. It's fuzzy."

"What were you doing in the woman's house?" Kate asked.

Robbie thought for a moment and then said, "I don't think I was there for the woman. Maybe just for the man who came to *visit* her."

"So she had a guest in her house, a man, and you were there, as well."

"Yes, but they didn't know I was there."

"Who was the man? Do you know?"

"Senator Russell."

Kate looked in the mirror even though she knew she couldn't see people's reaction. She asked, "Are you sure?"

"Yes, I've seen him on TV before. I'm certain it was him," Robbie said confidently.

"Could you tell me what the senator and the woman were doing at her house?"

Robbie giggled. "Making strange noises," he said.

"What?"

He blushed and then lowered his voice to a whisper as though he had the world's biggest secret to share. "They were having sex."

Kate tried not to laugh, but she couldn't help it. Why was this grown man unable to talk about sex openly?

"Why were you in the woman's house?"

Robbie shook his head again. "When I came to, I had a knife in my right hand, and I was about to kill him."

"Did you?"

"No."

"What did you do?" she asked.

"I froze for a second. The naked woman screamed, and the senator turned around, so I ran out the door."

"Then what?" Kate asked.

"I walked around the neighborhood for a while, then found a

car that worked with the keys I had, just down the road. I came here right away and wrote the note before I could tune out again."

She wasn't sure what he was talking about. "What do you mean by 'tune out'?"

"I don't know."

Kate paused, giving him a chance to figure things out.

"It's like... Sometimes I don't know where I am or how I got there. It's like, I get dressed and appear someplace without remembering how it happened. Sometimes I recall a few things right after, but most times, I don't remember anything."

Kate pointed up, indicating to the music. "And Beethoven? Why did you ask us to play it?"

"That's what I heard on the stereo at the woman's house. I don't know. I just thought if it worked once, maybe it would again."

"So, you came here because...?"

Robbie's lips quivered. "I didn't want to kill anyone. I figured it would be much safer for everyone, including the senator, if I got myself locked up in here."

"Fair enough," Kate said, and a knock on the mirror interrupted her. "Excuse me, Robbie, I'll be right back."

Kate stood up and walked into the observation room.

"Let's wrap this up for tonight," Agent Lack said. "We're going to follow up with the senator and see if he can corroborate Robertson's story. We'll check his car's GPS to get the woman's address. We'll see what we get. Tomorrow morning, we hope he'll be his 'other self' since we won't play Beethoven in his jail cell."

Kate nodded firmly but was not sure if she was supposed to await further instructions.

"Wrap this up, Murphy," he continued. "Tell him he's got his wish, he'll spend the night in jail, but you'll talk to him again tomorrow."

"Yes, sir." Kate returned to the interrogation room, sat with Robbie for a few more minutes, and then relayed what would happen to him.

"So things will be good?" Robbie asked.

"At least the senator will be safe tonight," she said. "Thanks to you."

"What will happen to me?" he asked, a hint of fear illuminating his bright blue eyes.

"Hard to say. We can talk more tomorrow. You can tell me more about JJ, Mr. C, and the Colony, and we'll see what we can do, all right?"

"Good." He reached for her hands across the table and clutched them. "Thank you, Kate."

"I'll see you tomorrow, Robbie. Get some rest."

The door opened, and two uniforms came in to escort him away.

Rosebud and Dr. Dobbins came in right after.

"Good work, dear," the doctor said. "We've got a lot to cover tomorrow. Why don't we meet first, discuss the points I'd like you to interrogate him on, and then you'll keep building that trust with him."

She nodded, knowing how exhausted she'd be in the morning but she was charged up for being so involved. "Sure, 8 a.m.?"

Rosebud looked at his watch. "Shit, man. It's 1:15 a.m. now. Hope you catch some Zs. I'll talk to Fuller to fill him in."

Kate walked out and turned around. "Did they find the real Robert Robertson?" she asked Rosebud.

"Yeah. The FBI agents said he looked identical to this guy, and he doesn't have a twin. We're going back with a warrant to request a blood sample, and we'll compare both tomorrow."

"Good," Kate said.

She grabbed her things from the observation room then headed out to the elevator.

What a day!

CHAPTER TWENTY-EIGHT

Kate Murphy
Roxbury Police Station, Boston

AT EIGHT O'CLOCK SHARP, Agent Lack began his brief in conference room three.

"Okay, guys. We've got a live one, and it's looking like he's got a split personality. Murphy will continue interrogating him until further notice. I've requested a female agent join our team. She's on her way as we speak. Braidy and Lewin, you'll be observing and recording the interview, so go and get comfortable in there."

He turned toward Dr. Dobbins and Kate. "Doc, any thoughts or recommendations for Murphy on how to approach this morning's session?"

"I reckon we'll see the other side of his persona. Beethoven triggered his latent personality, but I don't know how long it takes for him to return to his more violent side, who had no issue stalking and killing a man. I don't know if the other persona will respond to Officer Murphy or not."

"So, what are you suggesting?"

"We should see if he expresses any recollection about who she is and what happened yesterday. That would be interesting to note. Make sure we're recording his facial expression. Perhaps the dominant personality has new information that could be useful to us, details that the latent side wouldn't know about."

Lack took the lead again. "We're starting off without Beethoven, and see what we'll get." Turning to Kate, he continued, "The overall goal of this interview will be to determine the identity of Juliet and Mr. C, as well as finding the location of this Colony."

"Sounds good," Kate said.

They headed down the hall to the observation room. As they entered, Braidy announced that their recording equipment was all set up and ready to go. Beethoven's Fifth was queued, but they would wait until they got Lack's signal to play it.

"We're good to go," Lack said to Kate.

She let herself out and joined Robbie on the other side of the mirror. She tried to make eye contact with him, but he was staring down at the table.

Odd. Maybe he didn't see me come in.

"Good morning, Robbie."

Nothing.

She sat in front of him, tilting her head to try to see his face. "Did you have a good night's sleep?" she asked.

He lifted his head, looked toward the door for a second, then looked at her straight in the face.

"LET MEEE OOUUT," he yelled, steel in his eyes.

A shiver sprinted down her spine.

This wasn't the same man—or at least the same persona—as yesterday. His body was hunched over the table, his elbows parallel to the edge, his fists pressed against each other. Ligaments and muscles twitched in his arms.

"Robbie, it's me, Kate," she said, reaching her hand out and placing it on his forearm.

Before she could blink, he grabbed her wrist and pushed it back away from him, his fingers so tightly wrapped that she thought he was going to break her arm.

"Ow!" she yelped. "Stop it!"

His eyes locked onto hers. Kate had never been on the

receiving end of such an angry look; even her violent ex-husband had never mustered that much hatred into one stare.

And then, the first notes of Beethoven's Fifth echoed loudly in the room.

He seemed confused, then looked down at his hand, and immediately released the pressure of his grasp. He brought his hand up in the air like he was waving a white flag of surrender.

"Sorry, Kate! Did I hurt you?" Robbie asked.

Kate brought her wrist up and massaged it with her other hand.

"I'll be okay," she said with a forced smile.

I'm sure I'll have a nasty bruise, though.

She had no doubt his angry alter ego would have broken it without hesitation.

"What happened just now?" she asked.

"I don't know. You were suddenly sitting in front of me. I don't remember getting here."

"What do you remember? What happened since you last saw me?"

"You left the room. Then I was escorted to a jail cell, then..."

"Then?" she pressed.

"Nothing. I'm here again, talking to you." His shoulders drooped.

With her sore wrist resting on her lap, she reached out with her other hand and patted his hands.

"There, there. That's all right. We don't need to worry about the stuff in between right now."

He lifted his head, a faint smile on his lips.

Kate started her interrogation again, gently. "Yesterday you were telling me about JJ and Mr. C. How about you tell me more about them?"

Robbie took a deep breath and then said, "JJ is beautiful and smart. She gets her way with Mr. C and Mr. S."

"Who's Mr. S?" Kate asked.

"Her husband."

"Are there other people that run the Colony?"

"There are supervisors, but JJ, Mr. C, and Mr. S are the only ones in charge. Every supervisor answers to one of them. The rest of the people are all pupils like I was."

Kate didn't understand the reference. "Pupils?"

Robbie nodded. "That's how JJ referred to us. Mr. C used a meaner word. He doesn't like us like JJ does."

"How about Mr. S?"

"We didn't see him much. He's a very smart man. He taught a few classes, and he was called whenever one of us got sick."

Kate took note. "He's a doctor?"

"I guess."

"You're not sure?"

"From what I see on TV, doctors save lives."

"And?"

"When pupils got sick enough to see Mr. S, we never saw them again," Robbie said.

If Kate weren't conducting the interview herself and seeing the innocence and honesty in Robbie's eyes, she'd have a hard time believing everything he was saying. She pressed on, genuinely curious to learn everything she could about the strange people and things that happened at the Colony. "What do you mean?"

His voice became solemn. "I think they died."

"Do you think Mr. S killed them?"

Robbie lifted his shoulders. "I don't know. Some of us got really, really sick, real fast. Maybe Mr. S couldn't help them."

"Could you describe these three people to a sketch artist?" Kate asked before seeing hesitation in his eyes.

I have to sweeten the deal.

"The artist could make a copy of JJ's drawing for you to keep. Would you like that?"

Robbie beamed with joy. "That would be awesome!"

Bingo.

"Okay, hang tight, and I'll be right back. Do you want something to drink or eat?"

"Tea and biscuits would be good."

"Sure." Kate left and went into the observation room.

THE LAST HOPE

"How British of him to ask for tea and biscuits. How's your wrist, dear?" Dr. Dobbins asked as Kate entered the room.

She glanced down at her wrist that had darkened already. "Just a bruise, nothing broken."

"It's interesting. He definitely has a split personality disorder, and Robbie is the latent one. I reckon that he rarely comes out. Robert is the dominant one. If this man has killed before, Robert would have done it, not Robbie. I don't know if Robbie would know about Robert's murders."

Agent Lack got off the phone. "Our sketch artist will be down here in a few minutes. Murphy, you'll go back in there with him. Start off with Juliet."

"How about the tea and biscuits?" Kate asked.

"I'll go get him his snack," Lewin said. "I need to stretch my legs."

CHAPTER TWENTY-NINE

Kate Murphy
Roxbury Police Station, Boston

THE SKETCH ARTIST and Kate entered the interrogation room, and Robbie gradually began to describe JJ:

"Her blonde hair is long and really wavy on warm sunny days... She has small eyes and a narrow and pointy nose. Her lips are big, sometimes red hot, sometimes light pink. Her skin is soft, and she smells of jasmine," he said wistfully.

"Is she tall?" Kate asked.

"She often wears high heels, and with them, she's really tall, taller than you."

"I'm five-foot-eight," Kate told the artist. "Much taller than me?"

He spaced his fingers by about four inches. "Maybe this much taller?"

Kate nodded and made note of it. "How about her figure? Would you say Juliet and I have a similar body shape?"

"No. You're much too... sporty," he said.

Kate smiled. "You mean she has nice curves?"

"I guess."

"Large breasts?"

He blushed. "Yes."

"Is she skinny, average weight, or chubby?"

"Pretty thin, other than her boobies."

Kate chuckled, realizing it was almost as if she was speaking with a pubescent boy instead of a grown man. "Does she speak with an accent, or does she sound like you and me?"

"Like us," Robbie said. "But the men speak funny."

Kate cocked her head. "Funny how? Can you tell what accents they have?"

Robbie seemed frustrated momentarily. "I don't know. They often used words I didn't understand."

"That's okay."

The sketch artist continued his work for a few more minutes. After some fixes based on Robbie's feedback, they had a decent portrait of Juliet.

"I will get a copy of this?" Robbie asked, his eyes bursting with hope.

Kate nodded. "Yes, I'll make sure you get a copy, but first we also need you to describe Mr. C and Mr. S the same way."

NINETY MINUTES LATER, they had all three portraits done.

Mr. C looked like a walking military stereotype. Scar on his right cheek, brown hair, crew cut, tall, and muscular.

Mr. S seemed a bit older, balding, gray hair, closely set eyes, crooked nose, and a small potbelly. But the feature that made Kate smile was his gunslinger mustache. He had long sideburns that turned into a beard along a few inches of his jaw, combined with a horseshoe 'stache. That left him with three big gaps in an otherwise full beard.

The sketch artist left and promised to bring back a copy of Juliet's drawing.

"That was very helpful. Thank you, Robbie," Kate said. "Would you like more tea?"

"No, thank you, but I'm hungry."

"Let me see what I can do. I'll be back."

Kate once again returned to the observation room.

"We're running the sketches against our databases to see if we can find a match," Lewin said.

"Can we get him something to eat?" Kate asked.

"We'll order pizza for all of us in about an hour," Lack said. "He can have a few slices then. Get him to describe that place he called the Colony. He might remember some landmarks we could pinpoint on our end."

"Sure. I'll quickly run and get snacks first. I'll be right back," she said.

Kate stopped by the lunchroom, grabbed a couple of Pepsis and two bags of Doritos from the vending machines, then she went back to Robbie.

Beethoven's Fifth was still playing on repeat. She sat down and handed him one of the bags of chips. "We'll get pizza for lunch in a little bit, but here's something to tide us over."

"Thanks," Robbie said as he tore into the snack.

"So, what can you tell me about the Colony? Is it close to here?"

Robbie looked up as if trying to locate a loose piece of memory floating in his brain. "I'm not sure."

"Would you take a plane to get there?" Kate pressed.

"No, I've never been on a plane."

She scrunched her face up. "Are you sure?"

"Well... I don't recall ever being on a plane," he said. "But I guess that doesn't mean I haven't been."

"Fair enough. How about trains?"

He nodded profusely. "Oh, we could hear trains in the distance at the Colony."

"How far out?"

"Really, really far, but some nights, we'd hear their whistles."

"That's good," Kate said, feeling like she was getting somewhere. "Would you say the trains came by a lot?"

"Hard to tell. We spent a few hours outside when we had to tend the gardens or slaughter animals. The rest of the time, we were underground, learning and improving our skills."

Kate sat forward. She really wanted to learn more about their activities, but she had to follow Lack's orders and focus on locating the Colony. "Do you think you could recognize a satellite picture of the place?"

"I don't know. There isn't much to see from above."

"What could we see?"

"Large fields, a garden behind the main house, another building with the entrance to our training facility, a fenced-off area, but you wouldn't see that from above. It would look like any farm from the sky."

"What about the terrain around it?" she asked. "Are there mountains, hills, rivers, lakes?"

Robbie thought for a moment. "A few hills, but nothing like the mountains out west. There's a river a few miles down. Juliet took me fishing there once. It also runs through the perimeter for the final exam."

Final exam?

Kate made a note to return to that topic later on.

"Is it a big river? Would you be able to cross it without a boat?"

"Not too big, but there are some deeper parts, where the trout hang out."

"Trout? Do you remember other types of fish? Bass? Catfish?"

"No, just trout, I think."

Maybe it was close to one of the popular trout fishing areas in the Northeast. "That's good. Did you catch any?"

"No, they weren't hungry that day. That's what Juliet said."

Kate smiled at his reply. *How nice of Juliet to explain it to him that way.*

She certainly didn't sound like an evil person, but that wasn't what Kate needed to focus on right now. She returned to her line of questioning. "Is the Colony close to the ocean?"

"No, no ocean."

"How about the weather?" Kate asked. "Did you go outside during the winter?"

"Yes, sometimes, for training exercises."

"Was it cold?"

Robbie's head bobbed. "Of course, and there was lots of snow."

Kate was hoping his answers would narrow down the search zone, but it felt like she was questioning a child. "Did you get a lot of snow storms?" she continued.

"A few each year."

"How about tornados, hurricanes, that type of stuff?"

Robbie tilted his head. "No, some windy days, but nothing too bad."

"And during the fall, what colors were the trees in the hills?"

Robbie smiled, and his eyes widened. "All sorts. They're beautiful in the fall: red, orange, and yellow. Real pretty out there."

Kate had exhausted the list of weather questions that had come to mind, so she moved on to some of her notes that could help pinpoint the Colony's location. "What kind of animals lived in the Colony?"

This seemed to excite Robbie. "Chickens, pigs, cows... a few goats. We had lots of fresh eggs and milk, and we made our own butter. These were our duties. I much preferred gardening or making butter over slaughtering the cows and pigs."

The door to the interrogation room opened, and Lack came in, accompanied by a redheaded woman holding a pizza box topped with three soda cans.

"Hey, Robbie," Agent Lack started. "I'm Cameron, and this is Stephany," he said, pointing to the woman next to him. "We thought we'd all eat together while you keep telling your story to Kate here."

Lack removed the cans from the top of the pizza box, which Stephany then slid onto the table before opening and letting out a delicious aroma of pepperoni and cheese.

Robbie reached for a slice, folded it in half, and swallowed a third of it in one bite.

"Man, you're hungry," Stephany said. "They tell me this is the best pizza in town. What d'you think?"

Robbie kept quiet, seemingly enthralled by eating.

"Kate," Agent Lack said. "Come with me."

Robbie glanced up at Kate like a child looking at his mother about to abandon him on the side of a highway.

"Don't go!" he yelled.

"I'll be right back, Robbie. You'll be in good hands with Stephany," Kate assured him.

Kate followed Lack out of the room. "I'd like to let Agent Turner—Stephany—bond with the suspect and get you off the case."

A pang resonated in Kate's chest. She was the one who had discovered the first clones. She'd worked her butt off on the case and had barely slept during the past week. She was the only one who had managed to bond with Robbie. But Kate's rational side understood Lack's point of view. It made sense to keep things internal. The bureau had taken over the case, plus Kate wasn't even a detective, after all.

"That's totally fine," she said, lying through her teeth.

Kate's heart was heavy. She didn't know if the sadness originated from losing her case to the Bureau or if it was because she'd started to bond with Robbie and wouldn't be able to see him again.

"Hang around, though," Lack said. "We're not sure if things are going to work out with Agent Turner. He's obviously comfortable with you, so we may need you back."

Kate nodded and smiled. "Of course, sir. I just had the one slice, so could I leave and grab a bit more to eat, then? I could be back in an hour."

"Sure. Go ahead."

Lack returned to the observation room, and Kate stayed in the hallway. Feeling a little distraught, she reached for her phone, turned it back on, and then called Luke.

He picked up after the third ring.

"Hello?"

"Hey, Luko. How are things?"

"Good, quite interesting, actually."

"I'm off for lunch, care to join me?" she asked.

"Um, sure. Give me five minutes to wrap up what I'm working on, and then I'll meet you at the Pleasant Pheasant?"

"Sounds great, I'll get us a table."

Kate popped her head into the observation room to see if Fuller was in there, but he wasn't. She didn't know if she was supposed to report her whereabouts to him, as well, or just Lack. However, since the FBI had taken over the case, she was probably fine leaving.

"I'm off to lunch. I'll be back later," she said to the entire room.

Dr. Dobbins nodded, and the rest ignored her, too busy staring at the new agent's attempt at bonding with Robbie.

"Do you prefer to be called Robbie or Robert?" Kate overheard from the speaker in the observation room as she headed out. The door was about to close when the doctor's nasal voice echoed out in the hallway. "Officer Murphy!"

She stopped and turned. Dr. Dobbins was holding the door ajar, his head in the opening.

"Yes?" Kate said.

"Keep your mobile on, won't you? It's not looking too promising with Agent Turner."

"Sure thing, Doctor. Want anything from the pub?"

He scratched his chin. "If they have fish and chips, that'd be bloody marvelous."

"It's Boston. I'm sure they do. I'll bring some back for you."

She headed out of the building while wondering why she had offered to bring him back lunch. Maybe because he was the only one who'd been giving her positive feedback on her interviewing skills? Then again, perhaps her skills had nothing to do with her successfully eliciting useful information from the clone; she'd just lucked out because of her hair color.

Whatever.

She was on her way to meet Luko for lunch. What else could she ask for?

Well. Kenny was still in jail, but at least they were making real progress toward coming up with a plausible explanation of why his DNA had been at the crime scene.

CHAPTER THIRTY

Kate Murphy
Pleasant Pheasant Pub, Boston

KATE FOUND a small table near the back of the restaurant and
ordered a coffee and two glasses of water. She left her phone on
the table, just in case Agent Lack or Dr. Dobbins called.

She was browsing the menu when Luko sat down.

"Hey there!" he said, smiling. He took off his beige jacket and
laid it next to him on the booth, then placed his briefcase on
the table.

"Good to see you," she said. "You must have been hot in that
jacket."

"It's supposed to rain and cool off later today," he said with a
shrug. "I don't like to be unprepared."

"Sure, I get that," she said, although she had almost broken a
sweat in her short-sleeved white cotton blouse just walking here
because it was so hot and muggy outside. "What's up with the
briefcase?"

"Oh, that's what I'm excited about. I'll show you, but first
I'm starving."

They flagged the waitress over and ordered burgers. Kate

added an order of fish and chips to go before handing back her menu to the waitress.

"Hey! What's that?" He reached for her hand and turned it around. "What happened to your wrist?"

Kate looked down. The bruise had gotten much darker. "Oh... Long story, but I'm okay. So? You've kept your hair the way I suggested," she said, extending her unbruised arm to mess his hair up some more.

"Oh yeah... that. You were right. Women smile at me a lot more now. It's strange."

Kate giggled. Poor Luko. He had no idea how handsome he was underneath his geeky layer.

"So, you owe me Saturday afternoon and evening, right?" Luke said.

"Of course, wherever you need me to go, I'll be there. I'm planning to go visit my uncle in the morning then I'm all yours. A bet's a bet."

He blushed a bit.

"But anyway, here's what I wanted to show you," he said. He grabbed his briefcase, and placed it upright on his lap, between his body and the table, to open the combination lock.

She watched him spin the tiny dials and stop them on 1-2-3 and 3-2-1.

"Really?" she asked with a giggle. "That's your secret combination?"

He rolled his eyes at her. "The important thing is that I remember it, right? The only reason why I keep it locked is so it won't pop open while I'm holding it. That's happened before."

Kate smiled as she imagined Luke fumbling, running around to catch pieces of paper flying in the wind.

"Don't laugh." He brought his case flat on the table, opened it, and took the contents out: pictures of a bunch of red lines with yellow ends.

"What is that?"

"I've been testing and re-testing the blood samples, comparing the two, and I finally found a difference."

"Is that blood? That's not what I remember from high school. Shouldn't it be a bunch of red puffy globules and stuff?"

He shook his head. "Using the blood samples, I ran some tests on the chromosomes."

"That's what those are?" she asked, her eyes on the images scattered on the table.

"Hold on." He flipped through his pile of pictures and found one that had large X shapes on it. "These are chromosomes. See the bits at the end? They're telomeres. I've added fluorescence to show them more clearly."

"Those are telomeres?" she asked, pointing.

Luke nodded.

"What do they do?"

"They're extra bits at the end of our chromatids. They mostly serve to protect our biological information and prevent it from deteriorating or fusing with nearby chromosomes."

Kate didn't understand where he was going with his detailed information. "So...?"

"Here's the thing," he started. "Telomeres can also serve to indicate a person's biological age. The older you get, the shorter these get. But not everyone's telomeres shorten at the same speed. That part is still being studied. Lifestyle and other factors may be at play. So, in a nutshell, a sixty-year-old man with long telomeres would normally be expected to live a longer and healthier life than someone with much shorter telomeres."

She shrugged. "Why are you telling me all of this?"

"Well, that's the difference between the cloned DNA and the original DNA. The cloned DNA has really, I mean, *really* short telomeres. It's as if the clones were much, much older than the originals. Like they've lived the original's entire life and then some."

Kate stared at the images in front of her. She let the consequences of his discovery settle in her mind, her hopes for freeing her uncle quickly escalating to the summit.

"Could you check a blood sample taken at a crime scene and compare its telomere length against the length of someone else's sample and present both versions to court?" she asked. "Kenny's telomeres should be much longer than those on the blood sample retrieved at the murder scene, right?"

Kate's heartbeat sped up.

Had Luke found the evidence she needed to reverse Kenny's guilty verdict?

"Well..." Luke's expression turned somber, and he reached for Kate's hand. "Sorry, Katie, but no. Unfortunately, telomere testing is not definitive. While I'm confident that the samples are different, our current legal system isn't ready for that. First, we'd have to prove the whole cloning thing in court." Luke let out a long sigh. "But, by the time the FBI's done with their investigation, we should have plenty to go on, and if Kenny's telomeres don't match the crime scene sample, who knows?"

The waitress arrived with their order, and Kate allowed herself to hope for a second.

Maybe...

"Could you test Kenny's sample again, just so we know?"

Luke shook his head. "I don't have it anymore."

Kate's phone started vibrating.

"Hello?" she answered.

"Hi, it's Agent Lack. We need you back here ASAP."

"I'll be there in fifteen." She hung up and got to her feet. "Sorry, I gotta go." She waved the waitress over, got her food wrapped up to go, along with the fish and chips, and then left cash on the table.

Luko wolfed down his burger before the waitress came back with her doggy bags. "I'll go back with you. I need to show this discovery to the FBI biologist."

They walked back together. Kate held her purse in one hand, and two doggy bags in the other. She was starving, and it would take her a few minutes to walk to the station. Hopefully, that was enough time to gulp down her burger on the go. "Do you mind holding my stuff?"

Luke looked at her with horror. "Your purse? No way! But I'll hold the other doggy bag."

She shook her head. "What is it with men and holding women's bags?" She squeezed her purse between her arm and her body, like she imagined the French carried their baguettes, and then peered into the first doggy bag.

"Fish." She closed it again and handed it over to Luke.

She opened the other bag, grabbed the burger out of it, and then handed the bag to Luke. "Do you mind?"

"No problem. As long as it's not a purse."

Keeping her handbag clutched under her left arm, she managed to flatten and squeeze the burger enough to take her first bite while walking.

"Ah, fuck!" A drop of ketchup had landed on her white shirt.

Luke snickered. She turned to sneer at him, annoyed that he took fun in her bad luck, and realized he was busy digging into her bag.

"Hey," she yelped. "Those are my fries!"

"I'm carrying lots, see. I have to lighten the load." Kate sent an infuriated look his way. "Okay, I'll stop. Hey," he said, nodding at a park bench. "Just sit for a minute, and eat your burger."

Kate agreed, realizing that it was probably the best way to avoid getting yet another stain on her shirt, and it would just take a minute. They sat. Luke left her fries and the other doggy bag next to her then walked toward a food vendor.

He's still hungry?

She swallowed the rest of her burger before Luke returned with a water bottle and a few paper napkins. Kate was now eating her fries, gulping them down a handful at a time.

He unscrewed the bottle cap and took a big sip of water. "Ah... Refreshing. Now, let's see what we can do about that stain."

He tilted the bottle a little to moisten a napkin and handed it over to Kate. "Probably best if you did it considering where the stain is," he said, pointing toward her left breast.

Kate tried to rub it out, but the napkin turned to mush and fell apart in seconds.

"Hold on, I'll pour a little water, then you can use those to absorb it," he said, handing over the rest of the napkins he'd brought back with him.

Kate was taken aback by the frigid water and let out a yelp, which surprised Luke and made him spill more than he was supposed to. At least that was what she assumed.

"Shit! That's cold."

"I know. Refreshing, isn't it?" he teased.

Kate had used up all of the napkins, and her shirt was now dripping wet.

"Hold on. I'll get more."

When he returned, he had a dozen napkins in each hand. He proceeded to pat her shirt dry.

"Hey, do you mind?" she said, feeling awkward for the spectacle they were putting on. A few people strolling through the area had stopped in their tracks and begun to stare at them. Men wore big grins, and some women also smiled, while others seemed to share Kate's embarrassment.

"Sorry," Luke said, taking his hands away from her shirt, now aware of the commotion he had caused.

Kate could feel her cheeks warm, but she kept patting her breast with the napkins to dry it. The bulk of the stain was now gone, but the shirt was still wet enough to show her lacy red bra underneath it.

Luke took off his jacket and placed it on her shoulders. Suddenly, the geeky style didn't seem like such a bad idea after all.

"Thanks, let's go. I'm really running late now."

CHAPTER THIRTY-ONE

Kate Murphy
Roxbury Police Station, Boston

KATE RETURNED to the observation room and handed Dr. Dobbins his lunch.

"Ta, love," he said, presenting her with a twenty-dollar bill.

"I've got it," she said, pushing his money away.

"No, no, I insist. I had a craving for it, and you went through the trouble. It's still warm! Dear lord, take my money. I won't take no for an answer."

Kate shook her head and grabbed his cash. Probably impossible to win an argument with a psychiatrist. And there was no such thing as extra money in her world.

Lack tugged her by the elbow.

"Murphy, he's not responding to Agent Turner, so we're gonna stick with you, but we're gonna do it our way."

"What do you mean?"

Haven't I been doing it their way all along?

"Follow me," Lack said, but then he turned around. "What's up with the ugly-ass jacket?"

"Long story. Any chance I could quickly go and change shirts?"

Lack looked her up. "You got something here, in this building?"

"Yes, I just have to go to my locker."

"Okay then. Be quick. Meet me in conference room two."

Kate hurried downstairs, changed into a fitted long-sleeve T-shirt, and headed back to meet Lack. Five minutes later, they were back on track.

"So, this is where we stand now," he said, pointing at the wall.

Kate was looking at a US map. Several states had been blacked out, but most of the northeastern states were unmarked. "We've eliminated quite a few, but we'll need specific information to narrow down our search, and I don't know the exact questions we need to ask just yet, but I've got people working on it. We've got biologists, geologists, you name it," Lack said.

He walked to the next wall, where Juliet's, Mr. C's, and Mr. S's sketches were displayed. "We've got profilers and agents digging through all sorts of data, trying to narrow down their search and find a match for each of these."

As they were heading out, Kate noticed two pictures posted by the door on another section of the wall: the driver's license of the real Robert Robertson and the mug shot of the clone. They looked like identical twins. Some information was listed under each picture: vital stats, DOB, etc. A copy of their fingerprints was also included. She approached the wall to look at the thumbprints. They were definitely different.

Just like Kenny's case: different fingerprints.

"Don't worry too much about the timeline. We'll bulk this up later. We've got agents interviewing the real Robertson to figure out when and where his DNA could have gotten harvested, but right now you need to get as much information out of the clone as possible," Lack instructed her.

He exited the room, and Kate followed him back to the observation area. On their way there, he continued briefing her:

"We'll need to feed you precise questions as our specialists come up with them. Dr. Dobbins can also help you phrase your questions better if you face resistance from Robbie." He stopped in his tracks and dug a hand into his jacket pocket. "Here's an earpiece," he said, handing it over to Kate. "Go ahead, put it in."

Kate was amazed at the size of the object. No wires or anything. It looked like a tiny and mostly transparent earplug except that it was made of a more robust material.

"Let's test this out," he said entering the observation room. Kate followed him and watched him head to the far corner. He took a small piece of black plastic, no bigger than a USB stick, brought it to his lips then pressed a button on it.

"Can you hear me?"

Kate stepped back and brought her right hand to her ear, surprised by the sound.

"Too loud?" he asked.

"Yes."

Lack turned toward another agent, sitting in the corner, who adjusted something on a laptop.

"How's this now?"

Kate nodded. "Good."

"Perfect," he said, stepping toward her. He moved a strand of hair she had tucked behind her ear, so it now covered the earpiece. "Best to leave it hidden."

"I should just relay your questions then?"

"Yes, and come up with your own if you don't hear anything from us. We're going to lower Beethoven's volume a bit. Can't stand this fucking song anymore," he said. "But anyway, go back in. Bond again. Ask questions like you were doing. However, when I talk to you, you need to ask that question ASAP. You'll end up getting unrelated questions, but do your best to make them sound conversational. Connect them somehow."

"All right, I'm going back," Kate said, returning to the interrogation room.

Robbie made eye contact with her as soon as she entered the room.

"Hi, Robbie." She smiled.

"Where did you go?" he asked, pouting.

"I'm sorry, Robbie. I got called out."

It seemed as if he might cry. "You promised you were going to be right back."

"I'm sorry."

"You're not like Juliet. I don't know if I can trust you." His arms were once again crossed on his chest, his stare locked on the table in front of him.

"You can, Robbie," she said before she walked behind him and placed her hand on his shoulder. "I'm here to help you."

"But you keep going away."

"I know, I know. I'm sorry," she squeezed his shoulder a bit, then walked back to the opposite side of the table and sat down. She got a hold of her notepad and pen.

"How about this," she said before writing down her phone number. She handed it to him and explained, "If you ever need to talk to me, and I'm not here, ask someone to get ahold of me, okay? You'll be able to talk to me anytime you want."

Robbie took the piece of paper and placed it in his pants pocket. He examined Kate some more, a hint of insecurity showing in his eyes. "Why did you change shirts?"

"Oh... that?" she said, looking down at her new top. "I'm clumsy. I spilled ketchup on my other shirt, so I changed."

"Why didn't you eat with me? You said we were going to have pizza together, and then you left me alone with the other woman. I don't like her."

"I'm so sorry, Robbie. I promise I'll stay here with you all afternoon."

"Okay."

"Good recovery, Murphy," Lack said into her ear, causing her to jump just a bit. "Now, get him to tell you more about the Colony."

Kate adjusted in her chair and then asked, "So, why don't you tell me more about you and what you did while you were growing up at the Colony?"

"I already told you," Robbie said. "I was training, gardening, and slaughtering."

"But what about when you were younger? Do you remember riding a bike?"

He shook his head. "No."

"Playing board games like Monopoly?"

"No, but I played with Legos."

"Tell me about that."

Robbie readjusted in his chair, his body seemingly more relaxed now. "Most of the time, we played with Legos during training. We were given a drawing of a building, and then we had to build it with our blocks. We had to make them fast, and be pretty accurate."

"What do you mean *accurate*? With colors?"

"No, colors weren't important, but we needed to get the walls, windows, and doors right. After the pictures, we advanced to watching a short movie showing the building, and then we'd have to build it from memory."

"Wow. That sounds like fun. Did you enjoy that?"

"It was okay, but that's not what I wanted to do with the blocks."

"What did you want to do?"

"When Juliet played with me, she let me do my own thing. I could build anything I imagined. I made garages where I parked the toy cars she had bought for me. I made the tallest towers I could build with all of the blocks, and she would play with me."

"What would she do?" Kate asked.

"I would make up stories, and she'd go along with me."

Lack's voice sounded in her ear. "Ask him about cars. Maybe we can trace their vehicles."

"When you played garage Lego, did you pretend to have a real car sometimes? You know, make the noise and everything?"

"Yes, that was fun. I would switch gears, like race cars."

"Where did you learn about switching gears?"

"On TV and during training."

"What about real life?" Kate asked. "Did you drive a car at the Colony or were you taken places in a vehicle?"

"We never went anywhere. But I did drive a truck. It had two steering wheels: one for the instructor and one for me. We drove it around dirt roads on the farm."

"Do you remember what color it was?"

Robbie nodded. "Blue with a white stripe."

"Do you know the make? Was it Ford, Chevrolet?"

"It was a Ford F-150."

Kate smiled, imagining what it would be like. "Really? You learned to drive in an F-150 with two steering wheels in it?"

"Yes, it was older than what people drive now. There was not even a seatbelt in it."

"Really? Were you scared?"

Robbie shook his head and grinned. "No, it was fun."

"Who was sitting next to you?"

"Mr. S."

"And was he a nice instructor?" she asked.

"I guess, but he always sounded funny when he said things."

"Like what? Can you remember something he said?"

Robbie made a funny face, rounding his lips and furrowing his brow. He lowered his voice and said, *"Poot your foot on ze clutch."*

Kate laughed at his imitation. "Do you think he was from Europe?"

He shrugged. "Maybe. He said words I didn't understand."

"Like what?"

Dr. Dobbins spoke into Kate's ear, "Repeat this to him: *'Bonjour, au revoir, je te reverrai ce soir.'* "

"What about things like *'bonjour, au revoir...'* " Kate had forgotten the rest of the sounds and Dr. Dobbins repeated the last part in her ear. "Or, *'je te reverrai ce soir.'* " ·

"Yeah, that sounds familiar," Robbie said, nodding.

Dr. Dobbins chimed again, "Try this: *Buenos días, adios, por favor.*"

Kate repeated.

"No, no Spanish."

She smiled. "You speak Spanish?"

"No," Robbie said, "but sometimes I hear it on TV, so I've picked up a few words."

Dr. Dobbins chimed in yet again, and Kate tried to repeat the sounds he'd made. "How about *'Gooten Morgen. Vee gait es deer'*?"

"No, I don't know."

The doctor's voice spoke one more time, "That's all I've got. Sounds like Mr. S is French."

"Did Mr. S speak in the other language with Juliet or Mr. C?"

Robbie pondered before answering. "Sometimes. When he was angry or happy, but not for very long."

"Did you ever hear Juliet or Mr. C speak in that same language back to him?"

Robbie tilted his head and thought for a second. "No, I don't think so, but Mr. C. often spoke fast, and said words I didn't know. One of the men who was here yesterday spoke a little like him."

"Maybe Dr. Dobbins? He's British. Is Mr. C British?"

"I don't know. He just speaks differently."

Dr. Dobbins interrupted. "Hold on. I've got mock-up accents on my computer. Maybe he can recognize one of them. If we can narrow it down, it would help."

Kate smiled across the table. "Robbie, if I played some voices, would you be able to tell me if it sounds close to his accent or not?"

He lifted his shoulders. "Maybe. I don't know."

"I'll run out and grab a computer."

"Will you really be back this time?" Robbie asked desperately.

"Yes, I swear," Kate promised. "I just need to get a computer. I'll be right back."

Kate locked eyes with him, smiled again, and then went into the observation room.

Dr. Dobbins called her over to his laptop. "I'll show you how this works." He opened up a browser window to the bl.uk website, then navigated to the sound directory for the United Kingdom. A map of the UK with tiny people appeared. "You can click on it, and it will play some audio recording of what people sound like."

A new FBI agent Kate didn't know interjected, "You got an iPhone?"

Kate nodded.

"Use Siri to demo some of the other accents he may have

confused with the British accent, just to make sure the guy isn't Australian before you waste your time narrowing down which UK accent he may have."

"How do I do that?" Kate asked.

He pulled out his phone, went to the Settings screen, then General, then Siri.

"See," the agent said, pointing at the screen. "You've got English (Australia), English (Canada), English (United Kingdom), and English (United States). Test out the Australian English. Once you've set up Siri's language, ask your phone questions or ask Siri to tell you a joke, and you'll hear the voice in a decent-enough accent."

She turned on her iPhone and took the doctor's laptop with her back in the interrogation room.

"Hey, Robbie. We're gonna play a little game," she said, placing the laptop on the table, and taking out her phone.

"My phone!" Robbie got up and reached across the table.

"No, that's *my* phone," Kate said, clenching it.

"Oh..." Robbie sat back down, disappointment painted on his face. "Where's my phone then?"

"It's probably in a bin with the rest of your belongings that they wouldn't allow in your jail cell. Why?" she asked.

"There's something about my phone."

This piqued her interest. "What?"

"I don't know, but they use it to send me messages."

"They call you?"

"No. I don't know how they tell me stuff. Maybe you can figure it out."

Kate hoped the agents behind the glass were already on this, getting Robbie's phone to examine it. "Do they track your whereabouts using your phone?"

"Maybe, but they can do more than that without the phone."

"What do you mean?"

"I think they placed something inside my head."

Dr. Dobbins chimed in her ear, "Does he mean *brainwashing* by placing *thoughts* in his head?"

Kate paraphrased the doctor's question aloud for Robbie to answer.

He shrugged. "Yes, but they also placed a real thingy in my head."

"A thingy?"

"I don't know what it is, but it hurts sometimes."

"Where is it?"

Robbie pointed to the back of his head, behind his left ear, but a little more toward the center of his head.

"What kind of ache is it?" Kate asked him.

"Sometimes it feels like a little 'whoosh—whoosh—whoosh,' " he said, closing his fist, then spreading his fingers outward, and repeating the motion a few times.

"A throbbing pain?"

Robbie shrugged his shoulders again. "Maybe, if that's what 'throbbing' means."

"Does it last long?"

"It depends," he said.

Agent Lack spoke in her ear again, "We'll X-ray a dead clone and extract the device; we may have more questions later. His cellphone is on its way up. Maybe he can unlock it and show you how he uses it."

Kate went with his lead. "Robbie, if I go and get your cellphone, will you show me how you use it?"

"Sure."

Figuring out Mr. C's dialect seemed less important now.

They used iPhones to control their clones? Maybe the app could be traced back to the makers and to the Colony. Then again, no way Apple would allow a dangerous app to be sold through the App Store. His phone was probably jail-broken so whoever was in charge of setting up their phones could install their own unapproved programs.

Kate grabbed the doctor's laptop and her cellphone before going back into the observation room, where she overheard Lack on his phone, "Yes, email Mr. S's sketch to the French's *Département de la sécurité territoriale*. Use our contact there. Let me know as soon as you hear."

Someone knocked on the door just as Lack hung up. He opened the door, took the bin of items an agent handed him, and then placed it on the table near the one-sided window, so everyone could see its contents: a jacket, a pen, some pocket change, a set of keys, a cellphone, a small crucifix medallion on a thin silver chain, and a wallet. Lack opened up the wallet and counted the money aloud. "Twenty, forty, sixty, eighty, one hundred, one twenty, forty, five, six, seven. One hundred and forty-seven dollars plus a driver's license." Lack opened up a small zipped pocket and tilted the wallet on its side. "And seventy-five cents. No credit cards, no bank cards. No rewards or points cards of any sort. Where does he get his money from? Under his bed?"

"I'll ask him. Can I get the phone?" Kate asked.

Lack picked it up and pressed the home screen button, but nothing happened. He pushed and held the power button to turn it on. An icon appeared, indicating the bootup process was underway. Then, an empty battery symbol appeared, and the phone went back to a black screen.

"Ah shit. Anyone have a charger for this phone?" Lack asked.

The new agent inspected the charging slot below the phone. "My charger should work. I'll go and get it from my car."

"Technology," Lack said, shaking his head. He looked at Kate. "Go ahead and ask him about the money in the meantime. I'll bring the phone in once we've got it charged up a bit."

"Yes, sir."

She went back to the interrogation room and apologized to Robbie for not having his phone with her just yet.

"We're finding a charger right now. I'll be able to give it back to you soon." Kate paused for a second, trying to come up with a way to ask about money. "Robbie, you must buy food or eat in restaurants sometimes, right?"

He nodded.

"How do you make money to pay for things?"

He cocked his head at her. "I use the money in my wallet."

"I realize that, but when it runs out, where do you go to get more money?"

"I don't know," he said. "From what I see, there's always money in my wallet. I don't know who refills it or how."

Kate wanted to snicker at that comment, wishing she had that same problem. However, she stayed on course. "Do you always pay cash for things? Or do you have a credit card?"

"Always cash."

Dr. Dobbins clicked in. "Ask him if he believes he has an alter-ego that takes over his body during the days when he doesn't remember anything?"

Kate relayed the question.

"What do you mean?" Robbie asked her.

"Do you think there are two people inside of you, and only one gets to speak at a time?" she asked more clearly.

"Maybe."

"Do you think the other person would know where you get your money?"

Robbie nodded while frowning. "Probably."

"Could you make him talk to me?"

This time, Robbie shook his head. "You wouldn't like him."

"Why not?" she asked.

"He's evil. He's no good. He's like Mr. C."

"And you?"

"I just want to help. I didn't want to kill that senator. I want this to stop." His bottom lip began to quiver. "I want to see Juliet, and I want to be hugged. I miss her." Robbie's voice had cracked a little on his last few words; his eyes were now watery.

Kate walked around the table, lowered herself to his seated height, and hugged him. "It's going to be all right, Robbie. It's normal to miss the ones we love."

Her therapist had used those same words to her many times, many years ago. Now she repeated them in hopes of helping someone else. "Cry if you want, it's allowed."

Robbie cocked his head toward Kate and stayed quiet in her embrace. His breathing went from a light staccato to a more relaxed and steadier flow. She knew that pattern well. She had cried silently so many times before.

Robbie pulled out of the hug and looked up at her, his eyes

red, their faces just a few inches apart. "Do you think I'll see Juliet again?"

"We'll do our best to find her," she said.

Kate's legs were starting to go numb from the quasi-kneeling position she'd been holding. She stood up and returned to her chair. "When was the last time you saw her?"

"I don't know. Maybe two years ago? Time goes by so fast."

"Yes, it does," she replied without thinking. Kate still couldn't believe she'd just turned thirty-three or that she'd lost her parents and brother two decades ago already.

Lack popped his head through the door and called out to her. "Here's the phone, it's got forty percent power. That should be enough for him to show you how he uses it."

"Thanks."

Kate returned to her seat, beaming. "Hey, look at what I've got!" she said, bringing the device to Robbie.

"My phone!"

Kate stayed by him and watched as he touched the code to unlock the screen: 9-9-9-1.

A collection of apps appeared. Nothing too strange at first glance: weather, alarm, calendar, web browser, etc. Similar stuff to what she had on her own home screen.

"Are there apps you really like? Some that you use all the time?" she asked, trying to prompt him.

Kate listened to Robbie talk about the photos he took of squirrels in the park as well as the weather app. This side of his persona was so innocent. His dominant ego would probably have much different taste and use for the phone.

"May I see your phone for a second?" Kate asked.

"Sure, you want to look at my pictures?"

"I'd love to."

Robbie handed her the phone, and Kate started the photo app. She scrolled through the pictures he had taken. He indeed liked squirrels in the park. And birds on branches, ducks on ponds, and other animals and plants. His photos were pretty good, too. After going back through dozens of wildlife pictures, an unflattering image of Senator Russell eating ribs with sauce dripping down his chin appeared. It wasn't something that anyone could have grabbed from a press release or media kit. It was as though a paparazzo had taken it without permission. She flipped to the next picture and saw the Senator casually coming out of a small deli.

"What about this one, did you take it?"

Robbie glanced at the phone. "No, I don't remember that."

Kate left the photo app and returned to the main screen. She flipped through the rest of the phone, trying to see if anything stood out as abnormal.

"You don't use social media?"

"No," he said, shaking his head.

"Why not?" she asked.

"I don't know who I would connect with."

"What about schoolmates?" she asked.

"I don't know their names," he said flatly.

"What do you mean? Didn't you have a best friend at school?"

"Juliet was my best friend."

"What about the other kids?"

"We don't know anybody's name. We're given numbers. I was 212."

Kate sat back in her seat for a second. "So you'd talk to 156 and say, 'Hey 156, can you help me in the garden?' "

His face grew quite serious. "No, we weren't allowed to talk to each other."

Kate was confused. "Didn't you say you had group training sessions?"

"Yes, but the only person talking would be Mr. C. All we did was listen and obey."

"How did the instructors know which numbers you were?"

"Our robes. We used a marker and a stencil to write it on the front and back of our clothes."

"Didn't you say that you changed robes a lot? The robes must be covered with numbers?"

"No, the ink goes away when we wash them. We had to write our number on them all the time," he explained.

"So does 212 mean that you were the 212th student at school?"

"Maybe. The younger ones had high numbers, in the thousands."

"How young were they?"

"Well, it depends."

"Roughly. How old did most of them look?" Kate asked.

"Time doesn't work the same there as it does here," Robbie explained as he laced his fingers together.

"What do you mean?"

"Children. Here, where we are now, they take a long time to grow up."

"Of course, they don't become adults until they turn eighteen, and that's pretty much the same everywhere."

"No," he said, shaking his head. "Not there."

Kate's confusion and disbelief escalated fast. She kept quiet while trying to make sense of it all.

Robbie continued. "We become adults before leaving the Colony."

"You said training lasted six years," Kate added.

"Yes."

"And Juliet played Legos with you as a kid. Were you a twelve-year-old kid then?"

Robbie's own frustration was apparently mounting. "No... Maybe... No."

Kate leaned toward him over the table. "And you also said you met Juliet eight years ago... At the beginning of your training. You look like you're in your thirties. I'm really confused, Robbie."

He banged his head on the table a couple of times, then returned to his previous position, a frown on his face. "I know. People's ages confuse me a lot."

"Tell me what you remember," Kate said softly.

He let out a long sigh. "When Juliet rocked me in her arms, I was probably about this high," he said, his hand lower than the table. "We spent six years, so six summers, falls, winters, and springs at the Colony, training. When I did my final test, two years ago, I pretty much looked the way I look now, but with fewer lines on my face and a little more hair."

Kate nodded again. "You aged faster than normal?"

"I think so."

She let that new detail sink in before continuing.

That explains why the clones can catch up to the originals in age and appearance.

"Is everyone at the Colony the same?"

"Yes, all pupils grow up really fast there. But not Juliet, Mr. S, or Mr. C. They didn't change quickly like we did."

Kate sat back in her chair and stared at Robbie for a few seconds. He did have some graying hair around his temples. Tiny crow's feet adorned the outside of his eyes. *Was that all there yesterday?*

No one prompted her to ask this, but she felt it was necessary to say, "Would you let us run a full medical test on you? Maybe we could figure out why you're aging so fast?"

Robbie's head bobbed up and down. "Sure, but I think we're running out of time."

"Out of time for what?"

He lowered his voice to a whisper. "I think they know."

She leaned in some more. "Who are they?"

"Mr. C and Mr. S."

"They know you're here?"

"Yeah."

"How would they know?"

Before Robbie replied, Kate realized the tracking device could be in her hands. She checked the phone settings: the device location feature was enabled. She disabled it. She looked at the list of apps he had installed once more, and most of them were pretty standard, except for one called "C.O.M."

"What does that one do?" she asked, moving the screen so he could see the icon.

"Don't know."

Kate started the app. Black screen. No sound. Nothing.

"Maybe there's a bug or compatibility issue. It doesn't seem to work," Kate said out loud, mostly for the people in the observation room.

She went through the rest of the apps again, but couldn't find anything out of the ordinary, except for the C.O.M. app. Then, a thought occurred to her: maybe he had a time zone set for where the Colony was. She turned on the clock app and checked. *No.* Eastern Time showed, but this didn't mean anything.

While in the clock app, she checked if he had alarms set up. He did: 6:00 a.m. daily. Because she was struggling with finding a decent alarm sound to wake up to, she pressed the sound name associated with his daily alarm, and a short clip started playing, way louder than the Beethoven piece they'd been listening to for hours. Some heavy metal/punk sound.

"That's what gets you out of bed?" she asked, looking up, a smile on her face. "That's a bit rough."

Right before her, Robbie morphed into his other persona. His brow locked into a frown, and his gaze turned icy. Even the color of his eyes grew darker, as though a steely shade of metal was added to his irises. His jaw clenched as he reached across the table, snatched the phone out of Kate's hands, and then smashed it against the edge of the table twice before hurling it at the one-sided mirror.

He growled at her. "I want out of here. You've got no right to keep me locked up."

Agent Lack's voice sounded in her ear again. "I'm coming in to retrieve the phone pieces before he destroys them even more. Try to calm him down."

"Robbie—" she began.

"I'm not that fucking limp dick. He's gone." The man who'd just voiced those words wasn't Robbie.

She swallowed hard, trying to remain in control. "And who are you?"

"Robert," he said.

She held her hands up. "Calm down, Robert. We don't want to hold you against your will. You're here because you walked yourself in."

He stood up and slammed his fists on the table. "Not me. The fucking wimp did. I want out. Now."

"I understand," Kate said, doing her best to stay composed. Her heart pounded hard against her chest. This man scared her to death. He could break her neck in a second if he wanted to.

Beethoven's Fifth roared louder in the background. The door popped open, and Lack came in with two agents who, after being on the receiving—then giving—end of a few well-placed punches, got Robert into handcuffs.

"Stop wasting your time," Robert said, his chest bloated and his eyes twitching with anger. "I've figured out your trick. Limp Dick doesn't know what I'm up to, but I can recall most of what he says or does. I've been waiting for him to give me a chance to take over again, and I'm not going to let this stupid music take me away this time."

"Murphy," Lack said, taking her attention from Robert. Lack's hands were filled with tiny pieces of plastic from the cellphone. He nodded toward the door.

"Time to go," she mumbled before opening the door and leading the way out.

"And that's the end of that," Dr. Dobbins said when Kate and Lack walked in the observation room.

"Give me a container," Lack ordered the agent in the corner.

The agent looked around and settled on his Tupperware bowl. He emptied out a half-eaten sandwich, wiped the bottom with a napkin, and placed it on the table, below Lack's hands. The remnants of the phone fell in with a clatter. Lack brought his hand through his hair, shaking his head.

Pretty sure AppleCare won't be able to help with that one.

"So, what have we got to keep him here now?" Kate asked.

"Senator Russell and the woman won't press charges because they don't want this story to leak to the press," Lack replied. "We need something else. We've already had him for nearly twenty-four hours. Be original, folks. Anything."

"False ID?" the agent in the corner suggested.

"As far as we know the ID is legit, but good thinking. Track it down. Track this guy's official birth certificate. Someone must have falsified documents to get another copy of his birth documents, a driver's license, and whatever else they got for each clone. Maybe that will lead us to the Colony," Lack said.

Kate stared at her bruised wrist. "Violence against an officer?" she suggested.

"Sure," Lack replied, tilting his head. "That should stick for a few hours. We'll find other stuff to keep him in for as long as possible."

Kate looked at the Tupperware bowl and the phone remnants it contained. "If your IT guy manages to get anything out of this junk, his code was 9-9-9-1. Doubt it'll be useful, but who knows. That weird app didn't do anything. At least I don't think it did."

"Let's try to get a warrant to do a full physical exam on him," Lack said. "And, guys, let's not let this incident bring us down. At least we're done with fucking Beethoven."

"Yay, worsh shelebrating," the agent in the corner said, his mouth full of food.

"Go and read him his rights. We'll likely have to get him a lawyer," Lack continued, talking to the agent in the corner. He then turned to the doctor. "Doc, do you still need Murphy here for anything?"

"Not at this moment," he said. "She may come in handy again. The dominant persona probably won't let Robbie out anytime soon, but maybe later, if he calms down."

"Okay, Murphy. You're off for now. I'll talk to Fuller and your district commander. I'll request to have you around tomorrow or... Fuck, today's Friday, isn't it?"

Kate checked her watch. "Yup."

Four thirty, Friday afternoon.

She hadn't seen the week go by at all.

"Go home," Lack said. "We know how to get ahold of you."

"Have a good weekend," she said.

"You as well, dear. Cheerio," Dr. Dobbins said.

Kate headed to the elevator, mixed emotions stirring inside of her. So much had happened this past week. So much new and unbelievable information had come out. Was Robbie yanking her chain with the fast-aging process? Would this information be helpful in freeing Kenny?

If courts were to publicly acknowledge that blood samples were no longer sufficient without telomere testing, how messed up would the system get? How many people were currently jailed based on DNA samples? How many of those people were innocent? And, how many were guilty but would use this loophole to get out of jail?

There was a reason why this was going to be a long process.

At least she'd be able to see Kenny tomorrow. She missed him. She was looking forward to telling him all of the stuff she'd learned this week and how much closer she was to proving his innocence.

But then again, she wouldn't be able to share any of this with him. She'd signed that nondisclosure agreement. She'd risk going to jail herself if she spoke of her new-found knowledge.

CHAPTER THIRTY-TWO

Kate Murphy
Kate's Apartment, Boston

KATE COULDN'T GET her mind out of overdrive. She knew what she needed to do to clear her head: go for a run, a long run.

She laced up, grabbed her water belt, money, ID, phone, and then headed out. Where? It didn't matter. As long as she kept moving, as long as her feet were hitting the pavement, her mind would eventually wind down.

She ran. Whenever she hit a red light, she jogged around the block and crossed whatever road had a green light. She didn't care where she ended up. With the GPS on her phone, she'd be able to find her way home.

When her running playlist came to an end, she took a break. The heat was unbearable; hard to believe it was past 7 p.m. She spotted a 7-Eleven just a few buildings down. A Mr. Freeze or something like that would cool her down and give her more energy for the run home.

Once in the store, she looked at the selection of treats in the freezer and grabbed an ice cream bar.

Who cares if it gives me cramps or makes me want to puke? I could just walk home.

Back on the street, she discarded the wrapper in the garbage can next to a bus stop before looking for a place to relax and enjoy her treat. An old man was sitting at one end of the bench; she sat at the other.

The first bite of the ice cream was all that she had hoped for: creamy, cold, chocolate-covered goodness. Within seconds, Kate had gulped down the entire thing. She nabbed her water bottle and leaned back, taking in her surroundings. She had no idea where she was, but the neighborhood didn't feel unsafe. She took out her phone and looked at the map. Most street names didn't ring a bell, except one: Beacon Street. Wasn't it where Luke and his mom lived? She could recognize the blue door if she ran by it. Better yet, she could look him up in her contacts to get his address.

Not a minute went by before she determined Luke lived just a couple of blocks away.

Why not pop by and say hi?

She returned the water bottle to her belt, got rid of the wooden stick she'd unknowingly been chewing on for the last minute, then headed toward Luke's house.

A few minutes later, she walked up the steps, rang the bell, and Mrs. O'Brien answered the door.

"Katie! How nice to see you!" She hugged her before continuing. "Would you like to come in?"

"I'd love to. How are you?"

Mrs. O'Brien led Kate to the living room and apologized for its state of disarray. "I haven't had time to clean up." She moved a pink piece of crocheting work in progress to allow Kate to sit on the couch.

"I really shouldn't sit down," Kate said. "I'm all sweaty."

"No need to worry. This couch's seen much worse."

Kate sat on the edge of the cushion, not wanting to lean her sweaty back against the hideous tapestry that covered the sofa. It wasn't flowery, but it still didn't qualify as acceptable living room furniture to Kate and her younger taste in home decor. It was an embroidered landscape featuring little cats and dogs running on a farm with tall mountains in the background.

"Is Luke around?" Kate asked.

"Not yet. I haven't seen much of him lately. He's been spending his evenings at work. He told me he discovered something amazing, something that could help him with his doctorate. When I asked, he shooed me away, said it was about things I wouldn't understand. He's probably right. My boy's got quite a brain. I don't have his smarts. Never liked school much, but at least I still got my head. I'm grateful for that. The lady next door keeps trying to come in here; she's lost it. She doesn't know where she lives anymore. Hope I won't turn out that way. So, where were you running to?"

"Here and there. I just needed to clear my head. When I realized I was in your neck of the woods, I thought I'd drop by and talk to Luke. But seeing as he's not around..."

"He shouldn't be too long. He knows I make meatloaf for dinner on Fridays, and he never misses that." She paused and looked at the time on the VCR. "He should be home shortly. Would you like to join us for dinner?"

While the idea sounded good, Kate felt the chills coming on, like they always did when she stayed in her sweaty clothes too long after a run. The cold air conditioning blowing on her right now didn't help.

"I need to head back. I still have another hour or so of running before I get home."

"That's a shame. Would you like to take some meatloaf with you? I made lots of it."

Kate wanted to, as she could smell it, and her stomach growled for it. Memories of her visiting Luke's house as a kid flashed through her mind. She'd had Mrs. O'Brien's meatloaf many times before, and it *was* delicious. "I'd really like to take you up on that, but I don't want to run with it. It'd be awkward, and it'd end up a big pile of mush by the time I got home."

"You're probably right."

Kate stood. "Well, I guess I should get going if I want to make it home before dark."

"You take care and keep in touch, dear," Mrs. O'Brien said, escorting Kate to the door.

"Will do. Take care, and please say hi to Luke for me."

Kate headed back home. She knew she had to go southeast from here, so she did. She ran on unknown streets for a while, the setting sun guiding her like a compass until she reached a part of town she recognized. It was easy to make her way home from there.

All she needed now was a bubble bath. Hiking out on her secret trail by the ocean was her favorite thing to do in the whole world, but taking a bubble bath came a close second.

Once home, after rehydrating with a tall glass of water while pouring her bath, she stripped down to nothing, and then let her exhausted body sink into the vanilla-scented bubbles.

Now, this is a peaceful evening at home!

She grabbed a small hand towel, folded it in half, soaked it in the warm water, and then placed it behind her neck. She closed her eyes and tried to keep her mind still by focusing on her breath. Of course, thoughts came and went, like they always did, but she relaxed for a few minutes until her buzzer echoed in the living room.

Someone's at the door.

She ignored it.

Whoever this is will go away.

She closed her eyes again, but her phone rang within seconds. She'd left it in the kitchen, so she couldn't see who it was.

Fuck.

This person knew her cell number, too? Relaxation time was officially over. She stepped out of the tub and wrapped herself in an oversized bath towel.

Better not be Smitty.

She didn't want to fight his advances tonight.

She walked to the intercom by the door, and answered, "Who is it?"

"Meatloaf delivery man."

She couldn't help but laugh when she realized it was Luke. "Come on up, and let yourself in, I have to get dressed."

Kate buzzed him in, removed the deadbolt, and then cracked

the door open before heading upstairs to dry off and find something to wear. She'd only had time to put on her panties when Luke knocked on the door below her.

"Hey, Katie!" he called out.

Hearing his voice without the intercom's distortion made her smile. She liked how hunky he sounded.

"Hey, Luko. I'll be just a minute. Make yourself at home."

She heard him close the door and move into the kitchen. She didn't know what to put on and now wasn't the time to change her mind twenty times. If Luke hadn't already seen her, he would any second. No time to put on a bra and find the perfect clothes. She grabbed a baby blue dress with spaghetti straps, slid it over her head and headed downstairs.

She heard the microwave's hum when she reached the main floor.

"Special delivery from Mom," he said with a smile when she walked into the kitchen.

"That's so nice! Please thank her for me. And thank you for the home delivery. How much do I owe you?" she asked, teasing him.

"Oh, I don't know. I had to drive out of my way to make it here," he said, flashing her a grin. He opened his arms. "A hug should do."

"Of course!"

She walked into his open embrace and wrapped her arms around his waist. He smelled nice. She tried to pull away, but he kept her close. "I'm taking my fifteen-percent tip."

She laughed, and he let her go, then the microwave beeped, and he took out the warm plate.

"Here you go, Katie. Where would you like to eat?"

"Will you have some with me?"

"I've already had three servings."

She laughed at him. "Who says you can't have a fourth?"

"No, I'm full," he said, his arm drawing a flat line. "Want to eat here? Living room?"

"Let's go to the living room," Kate said, before turning

around to grab a drink. "You'll at least have something to drink with me, right? Beer, water, coffee, wine?"

"What beer do you have?" he asked.

Kate opened the fridge. "Guinness or Sam Adams."

"Guinness, please."

Kate grabbed two cans and glasses, then brought them to the coffee table. Luke had already sat himself down.

He opened and poured the drinks, and Kate joined him on the love seat.

"Thank you again. This is really nice," Kate said.

"No problem."

Kate closed her eyes while savoring the first bite. Just as good as she remembered it.

"So, are you ready for tomorrow?" he asked as she continued to eat.

"What do you mean?"

His eyes widened. "Tomorrow's *my* Saturday, remember?"

"Oh yeah! How could I forget?" she said, realizing she had indeed forgotten all about it. The cloning situation had been the only thing on her mind, but now that she was officially off the case until Monday, she was curious about Luke's plans for tomorrow. "What is the mystery thing I have to do?"

"Finish eating, and I'll show you."

"Show me?"

"Yes, I brought something," he said, pointing to a duffle bag sitting by the door.

Kate's curiosity was piqued. "Are we going to a paintball place?"

Luke laughed. "No."

"What is it, then?"

"I'll give you two more guesses."

"The stuff in there, is it for me, you, or both of us?"

"It's for both of us."

"Will it be just the two of us there, or will there be more people?"

"More people. *Lots* more people."

Kate tried to figure this out in between bites. *Weddings have lots of people, and they happen on Saturdays, but wouldn't make sense for him to bring a duffel bag full of stuff for it. Some sort of outdoor stuff? Like fishing? Collapsible fishing rods and fishing gear... Maybe?*

"Are you taking me fishing?" she asked.

He screwed his face up at her. "Hell no. One last guess."

"Some sort of class? Cooking lessons?"

Luke shook his head. "What kind of guy would want to do that?"

"Lots of guys take cooking classes," Kate snapped at him.

"Probably 'cause their woman forced them to."

"That's just silly. There are lots of male chefs, famous ones."

"Whatever. Not my thing. We're not going to a cooking class. Besides, what would I have in the bag for cooking classes?"

Yeah, doesn't make sense.

She threw her hands up. "Well? What is it then?"

"Done eating?" he asked before standing up.

Kate nodded and stood up as well.

"I'll go and get rid of this," Kate said, taking her empty plate and dirty fork to the dishwasher.

Luke picked up his bag and brought it to the coffee table. "A bet is a bet, right?" he asked.

"Yes," she said with some reservation. "Although, you're starting to scare me a little."

"Don't worry. It'll be a lot of fun, at least for me. Not sure if it's up your alley."

"Show me already," Kate demanded, her anticipation mixing with annoyance.

"Ready?"

Kate punched him. "Open your damn bag and show me."

Luke inched open the bag, staring at her. He was doing it on purpose. She'd never been patient, and he knew it.

"How long does it fucking take to unzip something? Shit or get off the pot!" She seized the bag from him and unzipped it in a split second.

It contained colorful fabric, plastic pieces, and two see-through plastic sleeves with long straps, like those pass holders people sometimes wore at conferences.

"What is all of this?" she asked.

"We're going to Comic Con."

"What?"

"A comic book convention."

"You're shitting me."

"No, I even got you a costume."

Kate rolled her eyes. "Do I *have* to wear it?"

"Yes, everyone who goes wears a costume, and I doubted you had one, so I picked one up for you."

"It may not fit..." Kate said, not super excited at the idea.

"I asked Mom to help me with the size. She's pretty sure it'll fit."

Kate looked at Luko's eager eyes and couldn't turn him down. She smiled before asking, "So what are we going as?"

"You'll be Wonder Woman."

Kate didn't know if she was annoyed, angry, or just plain surprised.

"Really?" she asked.

"Yeah, you'll like it, I swear. Don't you remember how much we enjoyed watching Wonder Woman on TV on Saturday mornings?" he asked with a cheeky grin.

"We were kids..."

"Yeah, and deep down, you're still a little girl, Katie. Don't kid yourself."

She wasn't convinced she wanted to go, but a bet was a bet. She shook her head. "Whatever. You kept your hair the way I asked, so I have to do whatever I agreed to do."

"That's the attitude. Let's drink to that," he said, clinking his glass against hers. "Cheers!"

"I still have to go see my uncle in the morning, though," she added.

"Of course," he said. "We'll go right after that. I've already got the tickets. It'll be crowded, but we'll get in."

Kate found it difficult to imagine why people would dress up as superheroes and cram themselves into a conference hall with other strangers in costumes.

"What do people do there? I mean, what is there to see and do?"

Luke adjusted on the couch. "We'll see some famous actors, comic book writers... We'll do lots of people-watching. You'll enjoy it, but I'm not doing it justice. It's much better when you experience it in person. You'll see soon enough."

"And what will you dress up as?"

"Dr. Who."

"Who?"

"Dr. Who, you know? British? Phone booth?"

Kate shook her head. "What?"

"You don't know? Katie, you're in for a treat, I'll show you." He took out his phone and started the Netflix app. "What's your Wi-Fi network here?"

Kate gave him her password and walked to the kitchen to grab a couple more beers.

She returned and handed him one.

"Great, thanks," he said. He tapped the cushion on his left. "Come, sit down and watch this. You'll love it. I know."

Kate plopped back down and refilled her empty glass.

Luke pressed play on his phone, and then rested it on the coffee table, close enough for both of them to watch despite the tiny screen.

After viewing the first episode, Kate had to admit it was interesting, and she was curious about seeing more, but on a bigger screen. "Let me get my laptop. We'll see better."

Kate came back, entered her password to unlock the screen, and handed Luke her laptop.

After watching the second episode, Kate wanted to see yet another one, but the battery only had ten percent left. As much as she loved her apartment, it lacked one thing: an extra power outlet in the living room. There was one behind the wall-mounted TV, and she'd once tried to plug something else in there. She almost broke her flat screen in the process, so Kate swore she wouldn't do that again.

"Wanna come upstairs? I need to charge my laptop, and we

can either sit upright on the kitchen bar stools or make ourselves comfortable on a bunch of fluffy pillows."

Luke lifted his eyebrows. "Fluffy pillows it is."

He shook his can, the widget making its distinctive sound against the empty aluminum shell. "Do you have any more of these?"

"No more Guinness, but I have other beer in the fridge," she said, already upstairs. "Do you want more? I can run to the store."

"Nah. I'm fine with whatever you've got," he said.

"Come and join me when you're ready. Could you grab me a glass of water as well, please?" Kate asked.

"Sure."

Kate fluffed up the pillows and placed her extra comforter against the wall. It was always handy in her bed frame drawer. She loved it on those rare cold nights when a second layer of feathers made a difference, but she mostly used it when reading in bed. She'd wrap herself in a comfortable little cocoon.

"Here you go," he said, placing a glass of water on an empty coaster on the nightstand next to her. "Do you have other coasters?"

"Nah, don't worry about it. They're cheap IKEA tables. Not sure why I use this coaster sometimes."

Luke joined Kate on the bed.

"Oh, I forgot," she said.

She hopped off and plugged the power cord into the wall. "We should be good now. Lights on or off?"

"What do you think?"

"Off?"

"Sure," he said.

They watched their third and fourth episodes cuddled in bed, Kate resting her head against Luke's chest, the computer supported by their laps. While the show was entertaining, Kate's energy was just about depleted.

"Katie?" Luke's voice woke her up. "Enough for tonight?"

She couldn't stop herself from yawning. "I think so. It's been a long week."

Luke closed the laptop, placed it on the nightstand next to him, and then got up. Kate buried her body farther under the comforter and rested her head on the pillow.

"Please stay," she said as she fought to keep her eyes open. "Stay with me, okay?"

But staying awake was a losing game.

CHAPTER THIRTY-THREE

Kate Murphy
Kate's Apartment, Boston

PALE MOONLIGHT SLIPPED through the window and shone on Luke's exposed back and jumbled hair.

Kate smiled. He'd stayed.

She leaned in closer and spooned him, wrapping her right arm around his waist and placing her hand on his chest, her head pressed against his back. From his skin emanated something musky yet clean. She moved her fingers up and down his chest, following imaginary lines until she fell asleep once more.

A few hours later, she awoke in the little spoon position. They'd somehow moved, and Luke now had his arm around her, his warm breath bouncing on her hair. She closed her eyes again and tried to absorb the comfort of this fleeting moment, but her dress had bunched up around her waist, creating a lump. She couldn't get rid of it without obliterating the safety of his embrace. His arm rested just below the lumped fabric, on the small of her waist.

She listened to the cadence of his breath. His soft, rhythmic heartbeat had almost hypnotized her back to sleep when his arm moved. He tightened his grip and moved his body closer to hers while his hand lingered on her hip and then slid down the outside of her thigh, caressing her leg. After pushing her hair away to expose her neck, he brushed it with a kiss.

Kate felt him harden behind her, which nudged her out of her sleepy state. He returned his hand to her waist before pulling her closer. His soft lips made their way to her back, then her shoulder, moving the dress's spaghetti strap out of the way as he brushed her skin with soft kisses.

He pulled away and rolled Kate onto her back, then lay over her, one leg between hers and the other still at her side. His blue eyes locked onto Kate's, but no words were spoken.

For half a second, Kate wondered how bad her morning breath was, but the thought escaped her mind when their lips merged into a passionate, demanding kiss. Her lust for him could no longer be restrained. Her body wanted his. Her mind and heart did, too.

He kissed her neck, inching his way down in a lascivious feast. His hands explored her hips and her waist before grabbing her bunched up dress and moving it upward. She lifted her back and raised her arms, clearing the way. His hands cupped her breasts, and he straddled her, eyes still locked onto hers.

Lowering his torso against hers, he then swallowed Kate's lips in another kiss. She ran her fingers down his back, pressing him against her. His erect member extended an open invitation to satisfy her hunger for him, but fabric stood in the way. She reached down into his briefs. She squeezed his buttocks with one hand, and explored his warm skin with the other. Her fingers reached between his legs, gently cupping his balls, and then glided upward, along his shaft, until she reached the underwear's elastic band. She stretched it to clear his cock and then used both hands to push his briefs down as far as she could.

He took care of the rest. His hand moved to her inner thighs. For a minute, he teased her through the fabric of her panties. He sat up, resting on bent knees, and pulled down her underwear. She watched him finish undressing her. She liked the sight of his large cock pointing to the ceiling. He pulled her panties all the way down to her ankles.

Kate broke the silence. "Hold on," she said, then she rolled over to her nightstand and opened it.

Luke grabbed her ass while she fumbled in the drawer.

"Here," she said, turning around to face him, handing over a condom.

"In a minute," he said, leaving the untouched wrapper on the sheet next to him.

He kissed her stomach and caressed the inside of her legs with his fingers. He teased her, moved both his lips and hands closer and closer to her sweet spot but never reached it. By the time he finally kissed her nether lips, she was warm, wet, and ready. She wanted him. She wanted him inside of her now.

But Luke appeared to have other plans.

She closed her eyes and relaxed, enjoying what his tongue and fingers were doing, letting a few moans escape. Her body had begun quivering. She reached down and tugged on his hair to get his attention.

"Now. I want you in me, now," she ordered.

Luke sat up, reached for the condom, unwrapped it, and put it on. Kate grabbed his cock and guided him.

"Slowly," she said.

She closed her eyes and let out a deep sigh, enjoying how her insides parted to make room for his shaft. Once he was fully in, she reopened her eyes and smiled. His gaze was locked on her, his lips barely crooked into a smile. He increased his cadence, and it didn't take long for Kate to start quivering again. She dug her fingers into his back.

"Faster! No, let me," she said, forcing him to roll over while managing to stay inside her.

Kate took over, straddling him, arching her back, and moving her hips up and down as she rode his cock. He grabbed her pelvis and held her steady, taking over the tempo, faster and faster. Their moans grew louder.

Kate came, then Luke.

She leaned onto his chest, keeping him inside of her. Her

heartbeat boomed in her core, pulsating against his cock that had yet to deflate. She pressed her upper body against his, closing her eyes and resting her face against his chest. She didn't want to move because, for the first time in a very long time, she felt at home in this very instant. If perfection existed, this was it.

The moment ended when Luke tapped his fingers on her back. "I gotta go," he said.

"What? Already?" Kate asked, not wanting to believe he was a fuck-then-dash guy.

"I mean... to the bathroom." He nodded his head in that direction.

"Oh. Of course," she said as she rolled off of him, careful not to spill the condom's contents. Luke beat her to it. His hand was holding the condom's base against his deflated shaft.

"Here," she said, handing the box of tissues she'd grabbed from her nightstand.

He cleaned himself up, then walked butt naked to the bathroom.

Kate realized how much she'd missed having a naked man in her place... It was even better when it was this hot guy who cared about her and knew her well.

Still in bliss, she glanced at the clock: 8:18 a.m. She'd have to get ready soon. The visit with her uncle was scheduled for 11 a.m., and it would take her at least thirty minutes to get there, plus the processing time at the facility, another hour or so. She should probably head out of the house around 9 a.m.

Cupboard doors clunked in the kitchen, and Kate realized Luke was done with the bathroom. She headed downstairs and joined him in the kitchen.

"Good morning," she said, wrapping her arms around him and kissing his back.

He turned around. "Good morning, indeed," he said, and then kissed the top of her head. "If your neighbors have binoculars, we must be giving them a great show. Two naked people in the kitchen."

"Nah... They'd have to be perched up in a tree somewhere to see in here. I walk around naked all the time."

"Really?" Luke had a strange smile on his face. "A little nudist streak in you?"

"On my way to the shower, silly. Not while lounging around. *That* would be weird. Coffee?" she asked.

"Yes, black, please, but I'd like to quickly hop in the shower first, if you don't mind."

"May I join you?" Kate asked with a wink.

He smiled and cocked his head. "Sure."

Their quick shower turned into another lovemaking session.

An hour later, Kate and Luke finally began sipping their coffee in the kitchen. Luke wore the same jeans and plaid shirt he'd worn the evening before, and Kate wore capri pants and, despite the heat, a long-sleeved shirt that covered her bruised wrist. She didn't want Kenny to see it and worry about her.

"What time are you going to see your uncle?"

Kate looked at the clock on the stove. "I should get going now. Wanna come with?"

Luke shook his head. "I don't know your uncle."

Kate drained her coffee and set the mug down. "He's a friendly guy, most days. I'm sure he'd like an extra visitor. Plus, if you come along, we could take your bag of costumes and go directly to Comic Con from there."

"Yeah, that's true."

He seemed to ponder his options for a second. Kate watched the time. She'd have to get going very soon.

"What do you say?"

"Sure, why not," he finally said.

"I just want to brush my teeth, put on some make-up, and I'll be ready in a few minutes."

Luke rolled his eyes. "I've heard this before. I'll pour myself another cup of coffee."

"If you want, but I'm serious, I'll be five minutes max."

"Sure," he said, a skeptical look on his face.

"I'll prove it. It's 9:32 a.m.," she nodded toward the stove.

Two minutes later, her teeth were cleaned, and she was admiring herself in the mirror. Their lovemaking had added a healthy rosy glow to her cheeks. She put on a little eyeliner and pink lip gloss. She ran a comb through her wet hair before returning to the kitchen.

"It's 9:36 a.m. Told you!"

"You've restored my faith in women. I'm ready to go," he said. He headed toward the door then stopped in his tracks. "No wait, you'll need a pair of high-heeled shoes or boots for your costume."

"What color?" she asked.

"Doesn't really matter, they'll be covered by the costume, but you may want to pick a comfortable pair. You'll be walking around lots."

Kate returned to her bedroom and fumbled through the boxes stored in her closet. She picked a pair of sandals with a two-inch heel. They were the most comfortable ones she had.

Shoes in hand, Kate snatched her purse and car keys while Luke unzipped the costume bag. She dropped her shoes in it before exiting the apartment and locking up.

KATE DROVE to MCI Cedar Junction high on post-orgasmic vibes, enjoying the magical bliss of their budding relationship.

She and Luke exchanged smiles and hardly kept their hands off of each other. As though she were a rabbit in heat, Kate knew that if it hadn't been for the jail visit and Comic Con, they would have probably spent the entire day naked in her apartment.

She could hardly believe what had happened. They'd bumped their old relationship to a new status. It had a solid foundation based on childhood memories, with a fresh dose of adult lust thrown into the mix.

Will this turn into something serious?

If things sour, will it end my freshly re-kindled friendship with Luke?

She didn't want to think about these questions right now. All she wanted was to feel the excitement and joy that this morning had brought and to savor every minute of it.

I'll be spending the whole day with Luke, which is gonna be nice.

After parking her car, they walked hand in hand to the

visitors' registration area, unaware that their idyllic day was just about to encounter its first hiccup.

Although the prison had okayed Kate's visit for this morning, Luke wasn't on Kenny's approved guest list. Therefore, he would not be allowed in. The overweight and disgruntled female corrections officer who stood behind the desk was adamant about it. Luke presented his Massachusetts State Police Crime lab ID along with a sparkling smile, but that didn't sway the woman in making an exception. Not even this once.

"I'm so sorry, Luke. Do you mind waiting here?" Kate asked.

The corrections officer interrupted their conversation again with more bad news.

"No can do," she said. "You can't stay here. Only approved visitors are allowed and only for a specific time."

"I'll just wait in the car," Luke said. "Do you have the keys?"

She handed them to him and kissed him goodbye before returning her attention to the overbearing officer.

Thirty minutes later, Kate was finally escorted to a meeting room where she waited for Kenny to show up.

When he walked in, she couldn't help but notice how skinny and frail he seemed compared to the other prisoners.

He smiled at Kate. She wanted to hug him, but she knew the rules. The officer had been clear during her pre-visit brief: no touching. Kenny sat on his side of the table and greeted Kate.

"Hi, Kenny! I'm so happy to see you. How are you doing?"

"I'm fine. You look different. Is it your hair?"

"No, nothing's different with my hair," she said. Kate was ecstatic they were making progress with the cloning theory but couldn't share that with him. She was not sure if she should tell him about Luke. Then, she couldn't stop herself and decided to spill the beans, at least those that pertained to her romantic life.

"I've met someone."

Her uncle brightened up. "Ah, the glow of love. That's what's different about you," he said. "Hope this one's not a scumbag like the previous one."

"No, definitely not. He's an old friend from... before."

"Before?" Kenny asked, squinting a little.

"My best friend when we were kids."

"Ah. What's his name?"

"Luke O'Brien," she said.

"O'Brien, you say?" Kenny thought for a moment and then nodded. "Irish. I like that. Good choice. Do you know where his family's from?"

"I have no clue where they're from originally."

"A man's roots are what makes him who he is. If you find out where he's from, you'll know where he's headed."

That's deep of him to say. He probably has a lot of free time on his hands to analyze things.

"Find out," Kenny insisted. "Maybe we'll go visit his roots in Ireland if I ever get out of here." He scratched his neck and smiled.

"Speaking of which, I think you should rephrase that to be 'when' you get out of here," Kate said, grinning.

Kenny sat straighter, his eyes connecting with hers. "What do you mean? Have you talked with George lately? Did something new come up?" His voice rose an octave in pitch.

"Something's come up all right, and I think it will help, but I can't talk about it right now," she told him. "I think we'll be able to reopen your case. You just have to sit tight and be patient for a little while longer. I really think we're onto something big. We should be able to prove your innocence."

"Sit tight and wait. That's all I can do I guess," he said and then once again scratched his neck and smiled.

Kate wondered what terrified her uncle this time. "So, how are they treating you here?" she asked.

"Oh, it's not as bad as you'd think. I'm an old man. I keep to myself cause I don't want any trouble. I got nothing they want. Three meals a day and a roof over my head is all I need. And no grumpy Maude that won't get off my back."

Kate smiled. "Yes, I saw her the other day when I picked up your rosary. She misses you badly. I took care of your bills. Everything's good with the house."

"Tell that old bag I'm glad to be locked up here; for once she can't bother me."

Kate laughed. "Sure, will do," she said, and then improvised a little. "She also told me to give you a kiss on her behalf."

Kenny snarled. "You can tell that woman to keep her filthy lips away from me! At least these walls protect me from her."

"You love hating her," Kate said with a laugh. "Think you may hate loving her, too?" She observed Kenny's reaction, but it was what she'd expected from him. He mumbled something to himself, and all she got were the last few words, something that ended with "...stupid Maude."

Kenny asked about what was happening at work, but Kate couldn't really go into too many details.

"I got to hang out with detectives this week," she said. "I really enjoyed it."

"Good, I'm sure you did great. You'll make detective in no time now. You deserve it."

Kate smiled. If only it were that easy to make detective. But at least she was playing with the big boys, and loving every minute of it.

They chatted about other things (weather, sports, and the food he was eating) until the security guard announced that her visit was over.

After saying goodbye, Kate returned her visitor's pass and headed back to the car, excited to see Luke again.

He was sitting on the hood, streaming a video on his phone when she got there.

"Did you miss me?" she asked, catching him off guard.

"Tremendously." He flashed her his crooked smile, slid off the car, wrapped his arms around her, and whispered in her ear, "You don't want to know what I've been thinking about while you were in there."

"Tell me, please," she said, letting him feel his way under her shirt.

"I kept undressing you in my mind, letting my fingers reach—"

A woman cleared her throat behind them.

Kate turned and saw the cranky corrections officer

approaching a nearby car. "Are you fucking kidding me?" she mumbled.

"Let's get going to Comic Con," Luke said. "Should we change here first and then head there directly?"

"I don't really want to use their bathroom and come out dressed as Wonder Woman. I may get more than a throat clearing from her or whoever took the next shift."

"Why don't I drive and you can change in the car?" Luke suggested.

"And you?"

"I'll just change in the parking lot once we get there. Let me open the trunk to grab the costume bag." He looked at the key ring and found the right button. "How was your uncle?"

"Okay, I guess. Each time I see him, he seems weaker and paler. He's lost weight, but he says he eats plenty and he's treated well."

"Prison is probably tougher on him than he lets on, but he seems to be all right? Well, considering..."

Kate nodded. "Considering he shouldn't be there in the first place?"

"Yeah... that, too."

Too?

Kate wondered what else he was referring to, but Luke had already changed topics.

"Are you excited? Your first Comic Con ever," he said, enthusiasm spewing out of his mouth.

Kate flashed him her biggest smile. She was thrilled, all right, but not about Comic Con.

The high she was on came from playing detective for a few days and having made progress on proving Kenny's innocence, at least potentially. Comic Con was just a distraction to her. The case was now in the FBI's hands. Spending the day with Luko was just the cherry on top of the sundae, Comic Con or not.

CHAPTER THIRTY-FOUR

Kate Murphy
Downtown Boston

FORTY-FIVE MINUTES LATER, they drove into the Seaport parking garage, but it was full. They roamed for another twenty minutes until they noticed a minivan pull out of a spot on a side street.

After parallel parking, Luke switched off the engine and faced her. "You make an awesome Wonder Woman, Katie," he said before kissing her. "Hope you're ready for a wonderful first-time experience."

After Luke got out of the car, he grabbed the costume bag, traded his plaid shirt for a white one, and then layered a brown blazer on top. Since his costume was far less intricate than Kate's he was nearly done. He stretched the rubber band from his bow tie, slid his head through it, and then tucked it under his shirt collar before reaching into the bag one last time for the two plastic pass holders and ribbons.

"Dr. Who's good to go," he said.

"Did you buy this costume or were these things already in your closet?" she asked teasingly.

"The bow tie and jacket? They were in my closet, but I don't normally wear them at the same time."

Kate let out a light laugh. "Not normally? You sometimes do?"

"I don't have many blazers or ties."

Kate kissed him. "You're a geek."

"But I'm not like the other geeks you'll see today, I'm *your* geek," he replied, kissing her back.

He placed her pass around her neck then did the same for himself before opening the trunk. Kate took her phone out of her purse and then dropped the costume bag in the trunk.

They had already taken a few steps toward their destination when Luke stopped. "Your cape!" he said.

"Oh. I must have left it by the windshield."

"I'll get it."

Luke ran back to the car and returned with the red piece of fabric. He tied the cape around Kate's neck and closed the Velcro strap.

"You look great, Katie."

"Thanks! You too, Doctor." She looked at her phone and her outfit for a few seconds. She didn't have any pockets, and it wasn't as if she could just hide it in there. But she didn't want to leave it behind either since she felt a little naked without it.

"Would you mind keeping it in your pocket?"

"Sure, I've got lots of them." He dropped Kate's phone in his left breast pocket. "Let's go and meet some superheroes."

They arrived at the Seaport World Trade Center just after 2 p.m. The streets were filled with people in costumes, so Kate didn't feel so out of place anymore, although she was a little self-conscious with her outfit, which basically consisted of a one-piece swimsuit with a built-in, padded, underwire push-up bra. She also wore wrist covers, a golden headband with a star on it, and leg warmers.

Luke pulled out his phone and showed the EventBrite codes for their single day admissions, and they were allowed inside. Kate wondered how much these tickets had cost him. Based on the number of people in the conference center, Comic Con organizers probably made a fortune. Enough to pay celebrities to come in. She recognized a *Lord of the Rings* hobbit walking among the crowd near them.

"So, what do you think?" Luke asked.

"There's a lot of people here," she said.

"Lots of *awesome* people. Would you like to have your picture taken with one of them?"

"I don't know. No, that'd be silly," she said, shaking her head.

"Hey, there's nothing silly about this. There's lots to do here," he said before pulling out a folded sheet from his back pocket and handing it to Kate. "Here are our options for this afternoon."

Kate had a look. There were several discussion panels and Q & As being held in the amphitheater, a list of photo ops with celebrities, and other game-type events planned for the ballroom.

"I don't know," she said. "So much stuff, so many people."

He nodded enthusiastically. "I should have warned you about this. I freaked out the first year I came. But the inner geek in me was so excited that I stayed, and I loved it. Why don't we just walk around for now?"

"Sure, sounds good." Kate squeezed his hand, happy to have him with her. It wasn't that she hated people; it was just that being surrounded by so many at once was a bit dizzying. Plus, she knew how dangerous crowds could be.

Luke led her down a row of booths, slowing down to peek at some of the displays. She saw several comic book series she'd never heard of. Many of the artists were there, sketching and showing their work to whoever would stop and talk to them. The talent these guys displayed was surreal. The man in front of her was drawing an underwater scene in charcoal with a character that looked like Poseidon.

Kate had never been able to draw anything better than a stick figure. Although her imagination was fruitful, she had never managed to give form to the images she saw in her head. How wonderful it would have been to simply take a picture of what she saw in her mind's eye. It would have made her teenage years' psychotherapy sessions much easier on her.

"What are you thinking about?" the therapist would have asked, and she'd have pressed a button on a remote. Her mental images would have been spit out on photo paper, in all of their dark and bloody goriness. But Kate suspected that having articulated and described what she saw in her nightmares or whenever she closed her eyes had played an important part in her therapy.

Although the bloody visions were few and far between now, Kate still woke up in a sweat from time to time. She kept dreaming of drowning in a pool surrounded by people. No matter how loudly she yelled, no matter how much she waved her arms in the air, nobody saw her. She could always recognize a few faces in the crowd: her mom, her dad, her uncle, her ex-husband, some people from work. She'd watch them walk away, one at a time. The crowd around her would dissipate until no one was left, and then she'd lose all of her strength and sink to the bottom of the pool.

But Kate wasn't afraid of water. In fact, when she first explained this regular nightmare to her therapist, he'd suggested she take swimming lessons. So, Kenny had paid to enroll her in classes at a nearby YMCA where she learned to swim. She wasn't the most graceful swimmer, but she could remain afloat and go from point A to point B and wasn't afraid of drowning. Even after successfully passing her swimming lessons, she kept having that dream.

The therapist had said something about abandonment issues, but who could blame her for that? She'd lost everything as a child. The love of her parents, her baby brother, her innocence. And now, even Kenny had been taken away from her. She knew she couldn't rely on anyone. Anyone but herself. If anything happened, then she'd blame herself for it. There was no point in blaming the universe or anyone else.

We are who we choose to be. We are responsible for our own lives.

Kate felt Luke's hand pulling her aside.

"What's wrong? You've been staring at this guy for a few minutes. You haven't even answered his question."

Kate gazed at Luke, puzzled. "Sorry." She then turned to the artist. "I like your art. You're very gifted. Beautiful."

Kate walked away from the artist, embarrassed. Luke followed her.

"Are you all right?" he asked again.

She tried to shake herself out of it. "Yes, my mind was somewhere else."

"Oh, look at him!" Luke pulled her toward a man dressed as Wolverine from the X-Men movies.

Luke nearly bounced in excitement. "He looks just like the original comic book version. Can you take a picture of me next to him?" he asked, handing her his phone.

Kate nodded and took a couple of shots. Luke seemed like a kid again.

"Thanks," Luke said to the Wolverine man and again to Kate when she returned his phone. He looked at the pictures she took then kissed her.

They walked by a few more booths, then one drawing caught her gaze: A bunch of men were running, seemingly scared and angry, and large letters spelled out the word "CLONE" across the cover. She stared at it, and the man behind the table started speaking to her.

"This is a sci-fi story, completely original. It'll soon be turned into a TV show, as well."

Cloning, a sci-fi concept? If only that were the case.

"What is it about? The storyline?" Kate asked.

"It's about Dr. Taylor. He's enjoying his life just fine until an identical, bloodied version of himself arrives at his front door and tells him that he's one of his many clones and that all of them are after his pregnant wife and unborn child."

Kate nodded without thinking. "Pretty neat," she said, walking away as her thoughts started on a downward spiral.

What would be worse? Knowing that you have clones or having them and not knowing? Having an army of them, or just the one? Having your clones wanting to kill those you love, or having them commit crimes on your behalf and ruining your life? How does the Colony work anyway? Do they make multiple clones of a person or just the one?

She thought about calling Agent Lack or Dr. Dobbins to find out if they'd gotten more out of Robert, but realized this was not the place or time. They'd told her they'd call her if they needed her.

She saw Luke across the aisle. She went back to him and circled his waist with her arms. He turned to face her, wrapped his arm around her shoulders, and then kissed the top of her head. She wondered if he'd be in her drowning dream one day. If he'd reach down to help her, or if he'd ignore her like the rest and walk away.

Who knows?

But right now, she didn't feel lonely with Luke at her side.

After two hours of wandering around, Kate was genuinely enjoying herself. Comic Con was a good distraction and an excellent place for people-watching and celebrity-spotting.

Kate and Luke turned into the next aisle, and they both gawked when they saw the naked blue woman from X-Men, wearing nothing but blue paint. Kate remembered she changed shape in the movie, but she didn't recall her character's name, let alone her actress's name.

"Mystique!" Luke exclaimed.

"Wanna take a picture?" Kate asked him.

"No need. I've got much better mental images in my head." He kissed Kate, and they headed away from the crowd, toward food vendors and small tables near the back of the room.

"If we weren't here right now..." Luke started, letting the words hang.

"If we weren't here what? What would you rather be doing?" she asked, teasing him.

She leaned against the empty table behind her, knowing very well what he was referring to, but she wanted to hear him say it.

"You know what I'd want to do." He lifted her up and sat her on the table. He stood between her legs and wrapped his arms around her, underneath the cape. He kissed her on the neck and whispered, "I would start by—"

A ring and vibration originated from his jacket, interrupting him.

"My phone," Kate said, exacerbated.

Luke pulled back, got it out of his pocket, and handed it over.

"Unknown number," she said aloud. "Hello?"

"Kate?"

"Who is this?" she asked.

The person caught his breath. "It's me, Robbie."

Kate jumped off the table and walked away, a finger in her other ear in an effort to block the background noise. "Robbie? What's wrong? Where are you?"

Shouldn't he be at the station? Why is he calling me instead of Dr. Dobbins or Agent Lack?

"I'm at a park somewhere. I don't know how I got here."

"Are you at The Common?"

"No, I don't think so."

"Are you alone?"

"Yes, I found your number in my pocket."

"Tell me what you see around you. Anything special? An odd building? Flowers? Statues?"

He paused before answering. "Not much, but I can see the harbor."

Kate spun around as if trying to see for herself. "What part of the harbor? What can you see?"

"Boats."

"What kind of boats, Robbie? Tankers?"

"Some, in the distance, but lots of sailboats."

"How big is the park?"

"Lots of benches along the waterfront."

Kate was mentally running through a list of parks she'd gone through in and around Boston. "Can you see a building with a clock on the tower?"

"Yes, in the distance," Robbie answered after a few seconds.

"Children's park?"

"Yeah, I can see lots of kids playing around metal bars and such."

"Do you see a gazebo with a funny looking pointy top?" Kate asked.

"Yeah."

"I know where you are. Stay there. I'm coming."

Kate sprinted back over to Luke. "I have to go."

"Why?" he asked with confusion. "Who's Robbie?"

"Long story. I can tell you on the way," Kate said, pulling his arm, but Luke had planted his feet on the floor.

"Tell me who he is," he ordered her.

It appeared as though Luke wouldn't move until she explained herself.

What is going on with him? Is he jealous?

She moved closer and said, "It's the thing I *can't* talk about here, you know?" She took a step back to make eye contact with Luke who had a confused look. She shook her head. "I gotta go. Now. Give me the car keys or come with me," she said firmly.

He dug the keys out of his pocket but kept them in his closed fist. "Kate, if you're seeing someone else, you *can* talk about it here. Tell me now. Who is the other guy?"

She approached close enough to whisper. "It's the fucking clone. I *have* to go talk to him."

Luke's face changed. "Jesus! Coming with you." He gave her the keys, and Kate ran out as fast as she could, but the flock of superheroes was thick. She could barely walk at a brisk pace until she finally left the crowded building, at which point she began to run to the street where they'd parked.

Kate got to the car and had already taken off her cape and leg warmers then put on her jeans and shirt on top of the rest of her costume by the time Luke arrived. Thirty seconds more and she would have left without him.

"What took you so long?" she asked, fury making her blood boil.

"I saw Stan Lee and had to take his picture. What's the matter, why is this so urgent? Can't the FBI handle him?" he asked as he pulled open the passenger door.

Kate got in, moved the driver's seat forward, and then started her car as he sat and buckled his seatbelt. She'd already merged back into traffic before she began explaining herself.

"The FBI let him go. Not sure why, but I guess the agents didn't have enough to hold him any longer. This clone has some sort of split personality. Robert, the dominant side, doesn't let Robbie, the weak side, surface very often. Robbie's the one I've been talking to these past few days, trying to get information out of him. Robbie could turn into Robert any second, Luke. Robert's the killer side. Only the Robbie side talks to me."

"And why aren't you calling the cops?" he asked.

"I *am* a freaking cop!" she growled out as she gripped the wheel.

"And what if he's trying to trick you?"

"Robbie? No."

Luke begged of her. "What about Robert?"

"He'd just run away. He doesn't want to talk to me."

"What do you hope to gain from this?"

"Can we stop with the questioning? I'm trying to get us there as fast as possible." She floored it as she steered the car into the exit lane for the Ted Williams tunnel that would take them over to East Boston.

"Where are we going?" he asked.

"Piers Park."

SHE PARKED the car and looked at Luke. "Stay here. He won't talk to me if there's someone around."

"I don't like it, Katie," he said protectively.

"Fuck, Luko," she said, her teeth clenched. "I've been through this over and over these last few days. For some reason, I'm the only one he trusts."

She left Luke in her car and ran to the park. Kate slowed her gait to a walk once she got there, partly because she'd forgotten to change shoes—running in heels was plain dumb and painful—and because she didn't want to attract attention.

She walked around the park twice, looking everywhere for

Robbie, but after twenty minutes, she resigned herself to the fact that he'd left already.

She sat on the steps of the gazebo, facing the harbor.

Fuck!

She'd missed him and couldn't call him back.

Robert was probably back in control.

She was annoyed and upset at herself. Maybe Robbie could have told her something important. Something that could have led them to the Colony, to where they could have proven that her uncle had been cloned. Something that could get him out of jail. If she'd been home, maybe she could have gotten to the park faster. If she hadn't had to change, maybe she could have got to him in time.

A tear rolled down her cheek. She closed her eyes, and a few more tears came, pushed out of place by her eyelids. She curled up and grabbed her ankles, resting her face between her knees.

Breathe in... 1-2-3-4...

"Missed him?" a voice said in front of her.

She looked up. "Luko! You were supposed to wait in the car."

"I know, and to be fair, I checked to make sure you were alone before I approached you. It's been thirty minutes. I was worried, so I walked around the park. I'm sorry. I probably sounded like a jealous jerk earlier."

"You think?" she asked, sending him an icy stare.

"Sorry."

Kate wasn't sure she was ready to accept his apology just yet.

"Can I sit?" he asked.

It's not his fault.

Kate made room for Luko to sit next to her and wiped more tears off of her face.

He moved his thumb under her eye. "Are those directed at me?"

Kate didn't reply. She didn't even know why she was crying.

"I'm sorry," she said.

"Don't be. I'm sorry," Luke said.

Luke sat in silence, but his right leg started fidgeting. She placed her hand on his knee to make him stop.

"Sorry," he repeated.

"Stop being sorry. It's not your fault. It has nothing to do with you."

"Let's walk then. Let's just enjoy the view and breathe," he suggested.

Probably better than wallowing in self-pity.

CHAPTER THIRTY-FIVE

Christopher Kirk
The Colony

TWENTY LARGE MONITORS arranged in four rows occupied the wall in front of them, each displaying a task that had already been assigned to a clone.

Stéphane and Christopher had just finished reviewing all of their current missions. Their plan was unfolding nicely enough, except for one puny detail that was staring at them right in the face.

"Pop open that one, will you?" Christopher requested.

Stéphane pressed a button, and the clone's face expanded to fill two of the high-resolution screens.

"That sissy," Christopher hissed. "I should've slit his throat when I had the chance."

Stéphane pulled up Robert Robertson's vitals on the screen to the right of his profile picture. His heart rate and blood pressure were normal. He hit another button, and the communication screen appeared with a red warning flashing across it:

"Primary phone cannot be pinpointed."

According to the screen, the secondary device had been

activated somewhere in East Boston.

"What the fuck happened to his original phone? Stéphane, check the map, will you?" He read off the coordinates.

"Police station," Stéphane said.

"Fuck. Assign the Delete & Destroy program to run next time the primary mobile gets rebooted. Pull up the tosser's whereabouts since the cocktail party."

Stéphane brought up the tracking screen and double-clicked one of the icons to access the clone's current location, then typed in a prompt to request GPS coordinates for the past three days. On a separate screen, he pulled up a map of Boston, and one-by-one, he entered the latitudes and longitudes that had been recorded by the implanted chip.

"Cocktail party until 11 p.m., some residential street 'til midnight, police station for a couple of days until this afternoon. Roaming through East Boston since," Stéphane reported.

"What did the fucking wanker do?" Christopher asked, ramming his fist into the wall in front of him.

"*Calme-toi!* We can figure this out. It's a residential street. The Senator probably followed some first-class bimbo home, and our clone followed him there. Would it not make sense? Then, he messed up and got arrested?"

Christopher ground his teeth together. "I never fucking trusted this one. Did he become a coppers' nark? I should have killed him when I had the chance."

"You know JJ wouldn't have let you. Not him. And our brainwashing program is good. There's no way he would betray us. They let him go, did they not?" he asked, nodding his head toward his current location on the map.

Christopher walked to the large keyboard area. He hated this thing. Way too many buttons and knobs. The worst part was the touch screen that Stéphane kept using. With so many gestures that did too many different things, he could never remember how many fingers he needed to move—and in what direction—to make the information he wanted appear on the main screen.

He backed away from the console.

"Fuck it. Stéphane, look at the senator's expected

whereabouts for the coming fortnight, and see what dormant clones we've got to finish that nancy boy's job."

Stéphane pulled up the senator's calendar, which JJ had hacked last winter. According to her version of its acquisition, she'd managed to meet him at one of his official public appearances, flirted with him, got to meet him in his room late at night, and worked her magic while he was asleep. Now, they had access to his up-to-date whereabouts anytime he changed his online calendar.

Christopher and Stéphane knew what JJ did for them. Things that would have been impossible for a man to do. Christopher admired how calm Stéphane acted about the whole thing. If he had married JJ, he wouldn't have let her sleep around, even to help them achieve their goals. However, he appreciated their current arrangement. They all did their share of illegal stuff: JJ used her body and seduction skills, Stéphane used his money and his connections to bribe the right officials and ensure the Colony had the technology it needed, and Christopher was the only one of them that ever got his hands bloody.

If it weren't for him, their army of clones would just be a bunch of drones, walking around, doing God knows what. He was the one who'd brainwashed and trained them to become killers. He'd also ensured that those who didn't show enough potential got terminated, all of them, except fucking Robertson, whom JJ had grown attached to.

Fucking motherly instincts.

Now, they had to re-assign the job to another clone. While they hadn't seen any report of an assault on the senator on the news, that didn't mean it hadn't occurred. And with the clone having spent days at a police station, all signs pointed to a failed attempt.

"We have these guys in Boston," Stéphane said, bringing up twenty-nine dormant clone profiles.

"Let's see. I want a solid chap this time. Or even a bird! Actually, yeah. Something with tits would be better since the senator's probably increased his security. Check to see if we've got a pretty one. He's not gonna go for a 'butter face.' "

Stéphane accessed the women clone profiles with a dormant status one at a time, and Christopher vetoed them all out based on their photos, except for the last one. "She'll do."

"I agree," Stéphane said, looking at her detailed profile. "With make-up and a pretty dress, she'll work fine."

The stats on the screen showed her measurements: 5'8", 130 pounds, 26" waist, size 3, 34" length for pants, medium tops, 36D bra.

"Yeah, she'll do just fine. I remember this one. The goods are there. I tested her out myself," Christopher said with a smirk, his mind taking a short trip down memory lane.

He glanced at the rest of the information they had on file. She'd graduated two years earlier, same class as fucking limp-dick Robertson. She'd excelled at knife skills. That was good. Knives were much easier to sneak into a room than a gun.

"Let's get her a plastic knife." Christopher walked over to the wall next to the window that overlooked the Incubator then pressed the intercom button. "JJ, we need you in the Brain." He turned to address Stéphane before continuing, "...unless *you* want to figure out what type of fucking dress we're supposed to get her to wear to that event."

"Not a chance," Stéphane said.

"Thought so." Christopher returned his attention to the calendar. "Boat fucking christening?"

"Sounds good," Stéphane said, nodding.

"We can plant her somewhere nearby, on a boat, in a bikini? Or see if we can add her to the guest list? Upload the Activation Program to her mobile now. It should load tonight when she puts it on charge."

Stéphane typed in a command on the console, and the status on Nicole Lewis changed from "Dormant" to "Activated." Stéphane updated the mission details, as well. He entered the senator's name and the date of the planned killing: four days from now.

"Once JJ figures out the outfit, you'll upload the details of Nicole's mission to her mobile, right?" JJ walked into the room as Christopher finished his question. "Speak of the devil. We'll need your fashion eye on this one."

After relaying their plan and reviewing the profile picture, JJ agreed. "He'll fall for a bimbo, but he needs to know that she's got class. He wouldn't dare attempt anything with someone who'd risk running to the media with dirt on him. Let's dress her up in a classy cocktail dress, introduce her as..." She paused to finish reading her profile. "British nobility," she continued. "It says she can pull off a British accent? You figure this out. Make her far enough from the Queen that we wouldn't know her, but close enough that she'd be very keen on keeping her personal life private." She paused again, this time looking at the calendar. "Looks like he'll be there for a full afternoon and possibly the evening. There's nothing planned that night. That snake is probably hoping to hook up with someone."

She turned to Stéphane.

"You'll find another boat nearby that we can use for a day or two? Plant her there, ready to sail out."

Stéphane nodded.

JJ then faced Christopher again. "How do you plan to dispose of the body? Ocean? Leave it in the boat? We may need to hire a crew if you want her to leave the jetty—"

"Fuck," Christopher interrupted her. "The whole point of these clones was to not worry about getting caught. She can kill him right there on the boat. Stéphane can find the right boat to rent, but we'll give her the money, and she'll pay cash. Double the price wanted by the owner and he won't ask questions. A day will do."

"If she gets caught, we won't be able to use her again," Juliet said.

"These things die way too fast anyway. When have we been able to use one of them more than once?" Christopher asked.

"You're right. She graduated two years ago. She probably only has another six to twelve months before she starts getting sick," Stéphane said.

"Too young, too soon." JJ glanced down.

Christopher snarled at her. "Stop it. It's not a person. Our clones are just things. You can't feel bad for things we created."

Juliet glared harshly at him. "Sometimes I think *you* aren't a person either, Christopher."

"JJ!" Stéphane interjected.

"If it weren't for me, we wouldn't have these trained killers. We wouldn't be on our way to changing this world, getting rid of corrupt politicians, pedophiles, and selfish arseholes who are destroying the earth for more money and more power," Christopher said.

"I'm not saying you're not good at what you do," JJ added in a much softer tone.

"Then what are you saying?" Christopher asked, his blood throbbing in his temples.

She hung her head. "We may need to nurture them a bit more."

Christopher walked toward her.

"Nurture them? Like how you fucking overbearingly fostered Robertson? Look at where it's gotten us. He might have blown our cover. That wanker was at a police station for almost forty-eight fucking hours! Did he say anything? Is our cover blown? Our Appalachian Retreat Rehab Center may no longer be enough of a front to protect our operation. What if he remembered stuff he wasn't supposed to recall? What if you've mothered him too much?"

He pushed her and pinned her against the wall when he finished shouting at her. His large palms were on her shoulders, his fingers digging into her skin and his face inches from hers. He could see her breasts moving up and down with her accelerated breathing. She was scared. He wasn't sure if he wanted to fuck her or kill her right there and then. But Stéphane stepped in before he made up his mind.

"JJ, get back to the floor; Christopher, take a breather. We'll get the senator. Stop thinking about Robertson."

Christopher dropped his hands but kept his eyes locked on JJ's until she glanced away. A second later, she left the room and returned to the Incubator.

"Stop being an ass. She's my wife, and we need her," Stéphane said. "Go relieve some pressure."

"Fuck! Sometimes I just..." Christopher shook his head but kept the rest of his trailing thoughts for himself. As he grabbed the doorknob to exit the Brain, he turned to Stéphane and added, "Finalize the detailed mission and send it off. I'll be in my room for the rest of the evening. Don't bother me."

~

CHRISTOPHER EXITED the room and took the elevator back to the main house. He needed to relieve some pressure indeed, or he'd blow up and kill JJ.

Once he got upstairs to his room, he found No. 4 asleep on his bed, with her long strawberry-blonde hair spread on the pillows. Her cherry-red lips matched the lacy lingerie she wore. She was lying on her side with red high heels on, black stockings attached to a fancy red suspender belt, and the tiniest pair of panties. Other than a puny triangle of fabric, it was really just a bunch of strings.

He undid his belt buckle and pulled it out of its loops, creating a swooshing sound that woke her up.

"Hi, Christopher," she said before sitting up in bed.

From No. 1 to No. 4, they'd all had JJ's velvety voice, and her exact look: her pointy nose, luscious lips, fleshy breasts. They were the only clones he'd treated like real people... kind of. He thought of No. 4 as JJ and fucked her like she was JJ in the good old days, but it stopped there. He probably had another two months to go with this one, but it was all right. No. 5 was growing fast. With each iteration, Stéphane would tweak something here and there, and they lasted a little longer.

A decade or so ago, they'd tried to clone all three of themselves, but only JJ had taken. Once they'd realized how fast the clones were aging, they'd repeated the experiment with JJ's DNA, testing and tweaking to improve the lifespan and slow the aging process. However, the body itself hadn't required any tweaking at all. He was hard just looking at No. 4.

He didn't care that she didn't have JJ's knowledge or conversational prowess. She appeared just the same, and he didn't keep her locked up in here for dumb banter and chitchat anyway.

Christopher was furious at JJ at this very moment, but No. 4 was so darn sexy in front of him that he almost forgot about it. No. 4 brought her ass closer to the edge of the bed and spread her legs open, letting her calves dangle against the mattress. Her knockers held up high as she leaned back on her arms, her back straight.

Just like JJ in her prime, around twenty years old. Great tits. Firm arse. Tight as hell.

She licked one of her fingers and then brought it down to the tiny triangular piece of fabric. She pushed it aside to expose her shaved pussy as she played with her clit. Her other hand pulled down one of the straps from her nightgown, and she revealed one of her giant tits, grabbing it firmly, teasing him with her erect nipple.

"Come here, big boy," she said.

The porn movies he'd made her watch were paying off. The words that came out of her mouth next were filthy, just as he liked them. Oh, how she'd learned how to touch herself to excite him!

He pushed her back on the bed, dropped his pants to his ankles, and took out the small blade he kept in his right combat boot. With the tip of his knife, he traced a line. He started at her chin and went down along the delicate skin of her neck, taking a detour to her exposed breast, outlining the contour of her nipple, and then ended in the middle of her chest. He twisted the tip of the blade and pulled, ripping the underwire support. He drew a diagonal line from there to the side of her waist, applying just enough pressure to pierce the fabric, but not enough to cut through to her skin. He snipped the strings on both the left and right sides of her tiny panties and tossed the knife on the carpet, far away from the bed.

Dick in hand, Christopher stood up again, already priming himself for what was to come. "Rip it off, now!" he ordered.

She obeyed, exposing every inch of skin he was interested in. She was a good bitch.

He yanked the back of her head and pushed her down toward him.

She knew what to do next. No. 4 was there to relieve his pressure, and relieve his pressure she did, again and again.

~

CHRISTOPHER'S ALARM went off at five o'clock. He slapped No. 4's arse and got out of bed. No time for fucking her—or fucking around—this morning. Another long training day lay ahead of him: things to do, arses to kick, and possibly some human or animal necks to slit. He put on his old army-issued cargo pants and a T-shirt, and then picked three blades from his assortment of knives.

Once dressed and shaved, he walked down to the kitchen, poured himself a cup of coffee to-go in a travel mug, laced the spare set of muddy boots he'd left by the patio door a couple of days prior, and then picked up a heavy set of keys.

Heading across the cornfield, he walked past the seed silo before stopping by the small red shed. After unlocking the padlock, he swung the wooden door open and walked in. He climbed onto the tractor and started the engine. The roaring sound didn't last long, though. A few seconds were enough for him to drive it a far enough down the path to uncover the trapdoor leading to the clones' housing. While he could have accessed it by going through the Incubator, he needed to let some of them out today, and they never let clones in the house. That was an unbreakable rule—except for his sex clones.

He unlocked another padlock and swung open the metal trapdoor to land flat on the ground where the tractor had been a minute earlier.

After descending the thirty-eight rungs on the metal ladder, he turned around to unlock yet another deadbolt before opening the door leading to the clones' supervisors' headquarters. He was greeted by C34, his current senior supervisor. After creating the first three generations, Christopher, Stéphane, and JJ had realized that three people training and managing an army of clones wasn't sufficient. But they hadn't wanted to risk hiring real people to do their work, so they'd started using the best clones to supervise training instead. All in all, it had been a great call. It'd finally given them a chance to relax a little and take care of other tasks.

"Nothing to report. All is well, Mr. C," C34 said.

"Good."

A dozen screens covered the wall in front of them. Clone quarters were monitored 24/7: dorms, communal showers, cafeteria, kitchen, hallways, training rooms, etc. Even the fields and gardens above were surveilled by cameras mounted on telephone poles, but these only worked in the daytime since most of their land wasn't lit at night.

Christopher spent a few minutes watching one of the junior supervisors walk a group of recruits from the dorm hallway to the cafeteria. The clones were orderly. The team assigned to the kitchen was busy cooking for their peers. A group of sixth-year recruits had just entered the shower, but now was not the time or place to zoom in on the fully-grown cloned women like he had done a few times before.

On another screen, a troop of about sixty first-year recruits arrived in the playroom; this was one of the newest groups. An outsider would have labeled the assortment of colorful pipes, slides, and boards as a playground, but this one was underground and only awkward clones learning how to move their bodies used that room. Accidents were common there, and the most junior groups had required six supervisors to ensure they didn't inadvertently lose clones due to unfortunate mishaps.

Just as the thought crossed his mind, Christopher saw a small clone fall off the top structure, landing on his arm. A supervisor rushed over and reached for the walkie-talkie he carried on his belt.

"Control Room, this is A23," his voice echoed in the room.

"Go ahead A23," C34 said.

"We have an injury in the play area. Looks like a broken arm. We need Mr. S for medical care."

"Stand by."

C34 reached for the phone and dialed extension 1.

"Mr. S, sorry to wake you, but we have a broken arm in the play area... Yes, sir... Thank you." He hung up the phone and reached for the radio again. "A23, this is Control Room."

"Go ahead, Control Room."

"Mr. S is on his way. Expect arrival in five minutes."

"Thank you."

Christopher returned his attention to the other screens so he could ensure the final exam area was ready to go. He waited the full three minutes to let the cameras rotate through the sixteen angles that covered important sections of the fenced-off area: the entrance, the spots where the stream came into and exited the fenced-in zone, the tall tree that could topple over if it got really windy, etc. Everything seemed fine. No obvious tear in the fence.

He turned his attention to the next screen: the "jail" for lack of a better term. Those who'd failed to master knife or gun skills and those who didn't obey orders due to a brainwashing resistance or other irreparable weaknesses were sent there until they were needed for a final exam. He could only see a few from the camera's current angle.

"How many prey?" he asked C34.

"Thirteen."

"How many left in this month's graduating class?"

"Twenty."

"Does it look like we may be able to get seven more prey in the coming weeks?"

"Possibly. A14 noticed two possible flaws in his group and A19 reported one possible flaw last night," the supervisor said before reaching for one of the note pads hanging on the wall. "Here's last night's report," he said, handing it over to Christopher.

Christopher copied down the IDs of the possible flaws and returned the pad to C34 before directing his attention to the daily schedule posted on the wall. There were twelve groups in each training year. Every group appeared on the large schedule in front of him, with slight variations on the otherwise standard training plan, which allowed Christopher to train each of the twelve groups, one after the other.

First year: play area, school, cleaning, sleep
Second year: kitchen, cleaning, school, knife, survival, play area, sleep
Third year: cleaning, school, knife, survival, garden, gun, sleep
Fourth year: school, knife, survival, garden, gun, cleaning, sleep
Fifth year: knife, survival, slaughter, cleaning, school, hunting, sleep
Sixth year: martial arts, school, cleaning, hunting, driving, sleep

Their clones didn't sleep much, about four hours per night. It wasn't something they had planned, but the clones' accelerated circadian rhythm worked in their favor, giving them more time for training. Most mundane activities were overseen by junior supervisors: cleaning, playing, and training sessions. After all, it was easy enough for anyone to strap a person onto a chair and press a button to select a program.

At some point during the previous year, Christopher had passed on the knife, gun, and animal slaughtering sessions to their best Training Supervisors. He knew they'd soon get sick, die off, and would need replacing, but that was the beauty of their system. There would always be new clones ready to take over, as needed.

Christopher took their daily reports from the wall and flipped through all three sheets.

Everything was going well.

"Radio the sixth-year supervisor," Christopher ordered. "Tell him I'm on my way to martial arts."

"Yes, Mr. C."

Christopher left the room and headed down the hall, passing several brainwashing rooms. He could see lights flickering through the small openings in the doors. Clones were learning languages, math, geography... pretty much anything they needed so they wouldn't stick out like sore thumbs in society's arse. It had taken them a long time to create this curriculum. They had combined various existing footage from real educational tapes and had added subliminal messages and mental triggers to speed up their knowledge acquisition. Of course, they'd incorporated an ethics course that covered their values and explained why some people deserved to die for their sins.

After about twenty doors, he arrived at an intersection, and turned right, heading toward the communal room where the Martial Arts session was to be held. The group supervisor halted his platoon just as they reached the door.

Perfect timing.

Christopher loved the punctuality of clones. They'd never been exposed to lateness. Plus, good ole Mr. C here would have made an example of whatever wanker wanted to start that trend.

The group came into the room, laid down the blue mats to cover the concrete floor, and formed a large circle around Christopher.

He went right to work. "This morning, we'll learn defensive moves. By the end of this session, you'll be able to free yourself from an attacker. This is a pass or fail lesson. I need a volunteer."

All twenty students raised their hand. Christopher picked the first to his right. A fairly tall, medium-built young man with thick brown hair.

He instructed him, "For your own sake, pay attention. You're just a few days from graduating. Don't mess up now."

CHAPTER THIRTY-SIX

Kate Murphy
Kate's Apartment, Boston

KATE PARKED her Subaru in the underground lot and turned off the ignition.

"Do you want me to keep you company?" Luke asked.

"I don't think I'd be any fun to hang around with tonight."

"That's fine. We all have bad days," Luke said, "but they're much easier to handle with friends around."

She hung her head. "I don't know."

"Are you hungry?"

"I don't know," she repeated.

"Let's just go upstairs with the bag. You can grab your clothes and shoes. One thing at a time, okay?"

"Sure." She just wanted to sit in silence, alone.

After getting off the elevator with Luke, Kate unlocked the door.

"Why don't you go and take a shower? Unwind. I'll unpack this and leave your stuff on the coffee table," he offered.

Kate couldn't think, but a shower sounded nice. Water always soothed her. "Yeah, I'll do that."

She cranked the knob to the hottest setting and stripped,

letting her clothes rest on the floor in a jumbled mess. The steam was already fogging up the mirror when she hopped in the shower. The water droplets began massaging the back of her neck as she breathed in the thick vapor, feeling exhaustion overtaking her. Suddenly too tired to keep standing, she sat in the tub, brought her knees to her chest, and then let the water hit her on the head and back. She pressed the drain shut, pulled the shower curtain out and let the water level rise.

Once it reached two inches from the top, she shut it off and sat there in silence, still holding her knees, and now rocking back and forth, creating waves around her. Without realizing it, she'd started to push water out of the tub, splashing mini-tsunamis onto the tiled floor. The sloshing sound took her out of her trance, and she stopped rocking. She let go of her legs. She couldn't lean the way she faced without the faucet stabbing her in the back, so she turned around—splattering the floor once again—then leaned back and closed her eyes.

After a while, her arms floated up next to her. She opened her eyes to notice that her right wrist had taken on more colors, but it only hurt when she touched it. The swelling had gone down. She closed her eyes again, took a deep breath, and imagined being at her secret spot, hearing the ocean, breathing in the salty air. She wondered when she'd have a chance to go there again.

A knock interrupted her thoughts.

"Katie?"

She'd forgotten about Luko.

"Katie?"

"Yeah," she said.

"Dinner's ready."

"I'll be out in a minute."

"Take your time. Can I come in?"

"Sure. It's unlocked."

Luke opened the door and stepped in. "Whoa!" He lifted his foot, his sock dripping wet.

"Sorry," Kate said.

"It's not toilet water, right?" He took off his socks, rolled up the bottom few inches of his jeans, and walked toward the corner rack.

"Can I use a couple of these?" he asked, pointing at her bath towels.

"Be my guest."

Luke threw them flat on the floor, then swooped them over the sink to squeeze all of the water out of them, and repeated for a second, then third time. He left them in the sink, along with the wet bath mat and her wet clothes. After folding another guest towel in half, Luke set it on the floor in lieu of a mat then put down the toilet seat cover and sat on it.

"How are you feeling?"

"Meh," she said, not bothering to make eye contact.

"Are you hungry?"

"Meh."

His hand touched her shoulder. "Come on, Katie. Missing your chance to talk with Robbie today isn't the end of the world. Let's put something in your stomach. It'll do you good."

Kate looked at him, finally understanding what he'd said. *He made dinner?* She couldn't remember what she had in the fridge.

"Did you order in?" she asked.

"No, I cooked."

She smiled at him. "What did you make?"

"Are you curious 'cause you're scared it may be terrible?" he asked, his lips hinting at a smile.

"I don't have that much food left in the house. Are we having s'mores? Or jelly sandwiches?"

He got up, reached for the towel hanging on the rack, and then stood by the tub. "Come out, and you'll see."

Kate pressed the drain open with her foot then got up. She stepped over the tub and onto the makeshift bath mat, walking into the towel he was holding out for her.

"Careful, it may be slippery." Luke wrapped the towel around her and kissed her.

"Dry yourself up, and come join me in the kitchen." He was about to leave the bathroom when he looked at the sink. "I'll put these in your washer. Where is it?"

"Don't worry. I'll take care of it after I get dressed."

He nodded at her. "I'll head out to grab something real quick. Will you buzz me in when I get back in a few minutes?"

"Sure."

Kate's numbness had dissipated, and Luke had been kind enough to clean up her mess... and cook. She wondered if he was any good in the kitchen, especially after what he'd said when she thought they were going to a cooking class. She dried herself up and walked out of the bathroom.

As soon as she opened the door, a pleasant aroma greeted her nostrils.

"Smells good! Tomatoes?" she asked.

Luke didn't answer.

He must have left already.

She walked upstairs to her bedroom to find dry clothes. She looked around and, after spending the day in a slightly uncomfortable outfit, the only appealing option was her yoga clothes, a.k.a. her pajamas. She didn't have to dress up for Luko. If he stayed around, it was because he chose to. She felt no obligation to look pretty right now, so she headed back downstairs in her comfiest clothes, her wet hair held up in a ponytail, bath towel in hand, then started a load of laundry with all of the wet clothes and towels.

The buzzer sounded just after she started the washer. She muffled the male voice by pushing the button to open the front door right away, and then left her apartment door ajar so Luke could let himself in.

The delicious fragrance of the food filled the room, and Kate's curiosity could no longer be held. She saw one pot on the stove. She picked up the lid to have a look: pasta sauce. He must have found some ground beef in her freezer somewhere. Lots of garlic, onions, tomato sauce, and green pepper? There might have been one of those left in her fridge. It smelled amazing... gourmet, even. She saw her colander in the sink, cooked pasta resting in it. She returned her attention to the stove. The heat was off, but the sauce was still piping hot. She took a spoon from the drawer and sampled it.

"You cooked me dinner, Blondie?"

Kate was taken aback.

That isn't Luke's voice.

She spun around.

"Smitty? What are you doing here?"

"Hey, was just in your 'hood, thought I'd check up on you. See how you're doing now that your uncle's trial is over. Haven't seen you much at the station. The sergeant said you were helping the detectives with a case."

While Kate was trying to make sense of his unexpected visit, Smitty made his way to the stove and peeked in the pot.

"Hey! Pasta sauce. My type of girl!"

Kate didn't know what to do, or what to say. The front buzzer gave her an excuse to walk out of the kitchen.

"Expecting company?"

Kate nodded her head. "Yeah, I thought you were someone else, that's why I buzzed you in."

He put on a bad fake frown then lifted one of his eyebrows. "You saying you're not happy to see the Italian Stallion here? On pasta night? Come on!"

"Smitty, listen. I've got company," she moved to her apartment door, opened it, and showed him the way out. "I'm happy that you swung by, but now's not a good time."

"Not a good time for what?" Luko said, appearing in her doorframe, a baguette and wine bottle in hand.

Kate sighed. *Awkward.*

"Hey, lab guy! What are you doing here?" Smitty asked, a confused look on his face.

Smitty had been with the Boston PD for at least a decade. It made sense that he would have encountered Luke a few times throughout the course of his duties.

"Hey," Luke said, nodding his head at Smitty, then sending an inquisitive look at Kate. "Got us some bread and wine. Didn't know there would be three of us for dinner."

"Smitty was just leaving."

"Was I?" he asked, disappointment dripping from his face. "I'd love to stay. Smells good."

"Sorry, Smitty," Kate said. "Now's not a good time at all. I'll call you, okay?"

Smitty looked at Kate then Luke before walking out of her apartment without saying anything else.

Kate closed the door and returned to the kitchen in silence.

Luke didn't say a word either.

Kate had nothing to be ashamed of, but she didn't dare look at Luke right now. She was afraid of how he would react, especially after how he'd behaved after Robbie's call. She busied herself by dishing out the food Luke had cooked.

She finally broke the silence when handing him his plate. "TV?"

"Sure," he said. "Are you going to look me in the eyes and tell me what's going on?"

Fuck, is he really that jealous?

She met his icy stare.

"Smitty's a friend. That's it," Kate said. "He's been helping me out. He dug out some archives for me to help with my uncle's case, so he just popped by to see how I was doing."

"Are you sleeping with him?"

"What?!" Kate couldn't believe he'd just asked her that.

Luke flattened his mouth. "From where I stand, it sounds like you've used him, and me, to get to your means. You begged me to help at the lab. Maybe you begged him to help you, too? I slept with you, who's to know if you've slept with him, as well? Maybe that's how you get your way in this world. Maybe that's how you intend on making detective."

Kate stood still for a minute, her head fighting against her bleeding heart.

What the fuck is wrong with him? How did he reach these conclusions based on what he saw? And he said I had trust issues before? What the heck do you call that, Mr. Jealousy Freak?

"I can't believe you," she finally said. "Don't you know me better than that? Luko, I... I can't even look at you right now."

Kate got up, took a few steps away from him before turning around once more. "That's what you think of me? You think I whore my way around?"

She stormed into the bathroom, tears running down her cheeks, her flesh hot with anger.

A couple of minutes later, a rapping sound echoed from the other side of the door.

"Katie, I'm so sorry. I didn't mean *any* of what I just said." Luke's quiet voice was overflowing with remorse. A silent minute went by before he continued. "I have trust issues. You don't know, but... a few months ago, I ended a relationship with a woman named Jasmina. I was with her for almost five years. Then, one day, at a conference in Philly, I ran into not one, but two of my colleagues who, after a few too many drinks, confessed they'd slept with her during our relationship. You're not her. I have no right to judge or doubt you. I'm so sorry. I'm sorry for earlier at Comic Con, and I'm sorry for just now. You don't deserve this. I can let myself out if you don't want to see my face anymore."

Kate stopped her silent sobbing and glanced around the room. Hard to believe the two of them had made love in this shower this very morning!

How did the day go from blissful to awful?

"Katie, are you okay? Talk to me," Luke begged.

She kept silent, pondering her options. This was her Luko. That Jasmina woman certainly sounded like she'd hurt him bad. That would be enough to turn anyone into a jealous freak. It wasn't like he'd hit her. All he did was spurt out words he didn't mean, probably out of fear of being cheated on again.

"Katie, I'm worried. Could you say something? Anything?"

And it wasn't like it took him days to apologize. He'd made up for his harsh words in just a few minutes.

"I'm fine," she finally said, a bristle in her voice.

She heard him rest against the door. "Do you want me to leave?"

"No, it's all right. I'm coming out."

A puppy-eyed Luko awaited her on the other side of the door. She wrapped her arms around him.

"I'm sorry. I didn't mean any of that," he said.

"I know you didn't. How about some food now?"

"Yeah, I'll reheat your plate."

They sat in front of the TV and Kate flipped through the channels, hoping to find a comedy, but there weren't any good movies on. She settled for a *Friends* rerun.

A few bites into Luke's home-cooked meal, Kate remembered that she had Parmesan cheese in the fridge.

"Parmesan?"

"Sure, if you have some."

"Coming right up," she said, heading back to the kitchen. She opened the fridge to get the plastic cheese dispenser and got the opened wine bottle from the kitchen counter.

"Here you go, Luko," she said, placing the items on the table and stealing a kiss before sitting down again. "I had no idea you could cook."

"You assumed that I couldn't cook because my mother lives in my house?"

She laughed and reached for her wine glass. "Yeah, pretty much. Who would think a grown man who still lives with his mom knows how to cook?"

"Mom moved in with me after Dad died. I lived alone before then but felt I should take care of her. I'm sure you'd do the same for your uncle, right? When he gets out of jail, if you ever feel like he's not doing well on his own, wouldn't you take him in?"

Kate had to think about that.

As much as I love my uncle, as much as I want to do everything I can to free him right now, I'm not sure I'd be able to care for him at home. Sure, for a few days or a few weeks, no problem. I'd love to. But making it a permanent living arrangement? I'd never be alone to reflect on my shit, to process stuff, to let facts sink in.

Am I a bad person? A horribly selfish person?

"I don't know if I could," she said.

"Maybe it's different for you. If your parents... or your baby brother..." Luke let the words trail, never finishing his sentence, and Kate was thankful for that.

"Let's see what else is on TV tonight," he said, changing

topics and taking the remote from her. He cycled through a few channels before settling on the 24-hour news channel.

"Breaking news: human cloning has leaped from science-fiction to reality. Our source confirms that clones are among us, looking identical to their DNA donors. It is unclear at this time how many clones exist, and how they came to be, but we've received reports that at least one human clone has been discovered in the United States."

"Holy shit," Kate said, bolting up. "Someone leaked it out to the media."

Just as she finished speaking, her phone started ringing from somewhere in the kitchen. She got up and followed the sound to find it in her purse.

"Agent Lack here. Did you hear?"

"Yeah, just saw it on TV. Who leaked it?"

"That's what I'm calling about. Was it you?" Lack asked.

She tightened her grip on her phone. "No! Of course not."

"Make sure you don't talk to the media or provide any details to anyone. This goddamn case has gone bonkers on us."

Kate said, "I understand. By the way, Robbie called me today. I'm assuming he was let go?"

"Yes, we had to release him around noon, but we've had a couple of guys doing surveillance on him. When did he call?"

"Late afternoon," she told him. "I think he was at Piers Park. I got there as fast as I could, but he'd already left."

"That explains one of the calls he made. Did he tell you anything more?"

"No. It sounded like he was willing to share more, though."

"Who knows if he'll call again?" Lack said. "I could arrange for you to wear a wire."

"No point. I can relay whatever he tells me if he calls again," she promised.

"We'll touch base tomorrow, or otherwise I'll see you Monday. I'll talk to Fuller and your district commander, make sure you can remain available to us in case he contacts you again. Call me right away if he does."

"Yes, sir. I will."

When Kate hung up, she realized Luke was on his phone, as well. "Of course. I'll see you Monday," she heard him say.

"Work?"

"FBI guy, checking that I wasn't the leak."

Kate returned to the table. "I wonder who it was."

They finished their meal and refilled their glasses. The newscaster didn't have anything to say that they didn't already know, but at least he didn't know as much as they did... at least for now.

She pulled out her phone and dialed George Hudson's number. If the media knew about it, she might as well talk to the lawyer and see if any of that publicly available information could be used to help Kenny. She left him a message, asking if he'd have time to meet with her early this week.

"We live in a messed up world," Luke said.

Kate stared blankly at the TV. "Indeed," she said before letting out a yawn.

"Tired?"

"Exhausted." She stood up, grabbed both of their plates and flatware, and then took them over to the dishwasher. The stove clock indicated it was already 9:30 p.m. She wouldn't be able to stay up for much longer.

"I'm going to bed," Kate said. "Do you want to spend the night?"

"How are you doing?"

"I'm fine."

"I'll head home then," he said. "I need to get a good night's sleep before tomorrow. We're good?"

"Yeah, Luko, we're good. Thanks for dinner and drive safe," she said before kissing him goodnight.

CHAPTER THIRTY-SEVEN

Kate Murphy
Kate's Apartment, Boston

A LARGE BLACK coffee in hand, Kate turned on the TV to see if the source had leaked any more cloning information, but the young blond anchorman was covering a different story this morning.

"Breaking news: Cardinal Francis Daugherty, Archbishop of Boston, was found dead in the Mission Church early this morning."

A headshot of the famed cardinal appeared above the anchorman's left shoulder.

"At 6 a.m., Cardinal Daugherty's lifeless body was found by a member of his parish. Police officials have confirmed that the body was left naked on the church's altar. The official cause of death was stabbing, but our source also reported that the body had been desecrated. No details were released as to the nature of the mutilation. No one has been arrested, but with the numerous accusations of pedophilia and child abuse lodged against the cardinal, the list of suspects could be long. More than four hundred cases have been filed to date since he took office five years ago. The cardinal presided over a diocese of more than

24,000 students, from kindergarten to high school. No official word on whether or not these cases will be dropped."

Shit. What is it with powerful men and kids? Have they all turned into pedophiles?

Kate turned the TV off. Wanting to ignore the atrocities of the world for a while, she grabbed her copy of the latest *People* magazine and headed to her hammock. She'd been reading it for thirty minutes or so when her phone rang. Was Luke missing her already? She reached into her back pocket and saw that it was Kenny's lawyer returning her call.

"Hi, Kate. George Hudson here. How are you?"

"Good, you?"

"Doing much better than half the people in this world. I can't complain. I'm grateful to live another day. I don't know what to think of the cloning stuff they keep talking about in the news. What were you saying in your message yesterday? You think your uncle was cloned?"

She adjusted the phone to her ear. "Yeah, long story. I can't divulge the details, but let's just say I know more than what they're saying on the news, at least more than what they knew last night. I haven't paid attention to what they've been saying about it today."

"It's been a freak show of specialists, theorists, and whoever else can get their fifteen minutes of fame. Folks are panicking."

"Crazy, I know. It's taken me a while to wrap my mind around it, but it's true. It's happening," Kate said.

"Why don't you come over to my house for dinner tonight? Marilou is making her world-famous fried chicken. I'm sure you'll love it. It'll just be the three of us. My kids are out of town this weekend."

Kate was surprised by his offer. He was so *not* the typical lawyer.

"Sure. I'd love to. Let me put you on speakerphone so I can access my contacts and type in your address."

She entered the information into her phone, and then repeated it out loud to make sure she had gotten it right.

"What time should I arrive?" she asked.

"Any time after four o'clock will be good. It looks like it's going to be another hot one. We can relax and chill with some of Marilou's pink lemonade. Also delicious."

"What can I bring?"

"Oh, nothing at all. No need. We'll have everything."

"Sounds good. I look forward to it."

"See you in a few hours."

"Perfect, see you soon," she said before hanging up.

CHAPTER THIRTY-EIGHT

Kate Murphy
George Hudson's House, Boston

WEARING pink slip-on sandals and a light linen dress imprinted with Japanese cherry blossoms, Kate parked in the driveway next to the old home. She grabbed her purse and the small bouquet she'd picked up for her dinner hosts before locking up her car.

George's house was small, with burnt-orange bricks covering its sides and freshly painted white doors and window trims. Kate swung open the white wooden gate and followed the concrete pathway leading to the front porch. Bushes peppered with yellow flowers lined the path on both sides. By the time she reached the top of the stairs, George Hudson was already outside, greeting her.

"Kate!" he said before hugging her. "Nice to see you. Come in. I'll introduce you to Marilou."

Kate stepped into his home. It was cozy and decorated in bright colors and patterns. Just like his office walls, his living room was covered with pictures of people: mostly families, small and large, white, black, and every color in between. The furniture was modest but practical. She saw a larger picture of an older woman in a frame above the fireplace.

"That's my mother, Bertha. A wonderful woman."

"She's beautiful."

"And here are my kids, Sean and Julie," he said, pointing to a picture showing two bright-eyed young adults in graduation gowns.

"Twins? Are they here?"

"No, they're attending a friend's birthday party. They're wonderful. They were eighteen in this picture. Now they're twenty-one years old. Really blessed to have such fantastic kids."

"Ah, there you are," a female voice said behind her.

"Kate, this is my wife, Marilou."

Kate extended her hand toward the petite woman in the red apron. She wore an orange bandana over her hair, and an enormous smile decorated her face. Marilou pushed Kate's hand down. "No handshakes in this home. We hug. It's lovely to meet you, Kate."

The generosity and friendliness of George and his wife kept surprising Kate. She hugged Marilou back.

"Oh, and these are for you," Kate said, handing the small bouquet to Marilou.

"They are lovely. You didn't have to, but I love them. I'll go and put them in a vase right away."

"Your home is beautiful," Kate said.

"Thank you," George said. "Why don't we go and sit in the backyard? It's breezier and cooler in the shade."

They walked through the open patio doors and took their respective seats on white rattan chairs. A small glass table stood between them and on it sat a large pitcher of ice-cold pink lemonade, condensation beading off its side. George poured the drink into two of the three tall, empty glasses that were stacked next to the pitcher.

"Here you go, this will cool us down," he said, handing a glass to Kate. "Hard to believe it can be this hot. But let's enjoy it while it lasts. Winter will be around in no time."

"You know it," said Kate, clinking her glass against his. "Cheers, and thank you again for the dinner invitation."

They sipped their drinks in silence for a few seconds.

Marilou's lemonade was as sweet and delicious as he'd promised it would be.

Kate wondered how different the world as they knew it would be by the time winter started.

"With everything that's going on," she began, "you know, cloning and such, do you think the legal system will re-open closed cases? Could previous evidence be deemed invalid?"

"Well, I've been thinking about this, and I won't lie to you. It's kept me up all night. What if? What if? My mind has been spinning, reviewing one case after the other. Wyatt, Lucas, Leopold, Marcia... and of course, Kenny. So many people may stand a chance. Another chance to restore their freedom."

A moment passed. Kate sat quietly, waiting to hear the rest of his thoughts.

"However, the legal system will have to deal with it differently. We can't risk having the whole system crumble. Cloning could have an impact on so many cases. First, we'll have to know for sure what evidence will be affected. Is the DNA identical, I mean, not just 99.999%, but one hundred percent identical? What about fingerprints? Would they also be identical?"

"Fingerprints are different," Kate said.

"How do you know?"

She turned to face him. "This has to stay between the two of us." George nodded, and Kate continued. "We know that for a fact, and DNA is near identical, but not 100%."

"What do you mean? How?"

"The way I understand it, clones are almost like identical twins, with different fingerprints, but same DNA. However, at the end of the chromosomes, the clones' telomeres are shorter. Samples could be compared to determine if the telomere length matches, but the length keeps changing with time, so..."

"So cases with solid fingerprint evidence couldn't be re-opened, just those with DNA evidence," George said.

Kate nodded. "I guess so. And I'm not sure about really old cases as well. Let's be realistic. I don't think they had the technology to grow clones twenty years ago. At least I hope not."

His eyes grew wide. "When do you think they started cloning people? And who are they?"

"I can't talk about them. Don't know much and I've got absolutely no idea when they would have started, but it couldn't have been before Dolly the Sheep, right? That was 1996."

Kate thought of Robbie, who looked to be in his thirties. How had he aged so fast? He said he'd been through six years of training. And he'd left the Colony a year or two ago? *Eight years ago?* But he couldn't have just appeared out of thin air, he had to have been created, and that probably took time, probably nine months, right?

He was cloned at least nine years ago.

But was he part of the original group?

Were there others before him?

She sipped the rest of her drink and allowed her questions to bounce around in her head, unanswered for now.

George offered her more lemonade and continued speculating aloud. "Sounds like your uncle could be affected, though. It's recent, and only DNA evidence. I wonder if the telomere length would match."

"If it doesn't match, do you think it would be enough to prove his innocence?" she asked.

"If I were on the jury, it would convince me, but our legal system is not ready for all of this to unravel. We could see decades of backlog, re-opening cases..."

Silence filled the air before Kate spoke again.

"The thing I still don't get is the overall motive," she said. "Do the clones have a blacklist of victims or do they just kill at random?"

"You're thinking about the faint political theme you found earlier?" he asked.

"Yeah, as well as Ferguson and the cardinal. No proof yet, but it sure sounds like it could be the work of clones, right? Both men were authority figures, both abused kids. However, McAlester didn't appear to have been a pedophile. Do you think he was?"

George thought for a moment. "People sometimes take awful secrets to their grave."

Kate tried to remember who the victims had been for the two cloned men who were wrongly rotting in jail in California and Texas, but couldn't remember right this second and George stopped her pondering when he snapped his fingers.

"That's it!" he said. "If someone had some sort of records, an official list of identities that had been cloned. That would work for the courts. It wouldn't burden the system. That would force specific cases to be re-opened. That's what you need to get."

"The FBI is trying to track their location down. Maybe they'll find a list once they do."

Marilou opened the patio door and peeked her head to announce that dinner would be ready in about five minutes. Then she added, "Darling, could you help me set the table? I think we should eat outside. It's so hot in the house."

"Sure thing, Marilou." He turned to Kate and said, "If you'll excuse me."

Kate stood up. "Let me help."

A few back-and-forth trips to the kitchen later, they had a feast in front of them: Marilou's famous fried chicken, coleslaw, cornbread, green beans, and homemade pecan pie.

Kate helped herself to however much she wanted, as gently ordered by Marilou.

Fork in hand, she was ready to dig in when Marilou spoke again, "Dear Lord..."

Kate put down her silverware, glanced at Marilou, and then mimicked her posture: head down, hands together.

"... thank you for the food in front of us. Bless the men and women who worked hard to make it happen. I'm grateful for the farmers who seeded it, cared for it, and harvested these delicious and nutritious ingredients. I'm grateful for the chicken that gave its life so we'd have something to eat. I'm grateful for our country, our hard-working people that transported this food and made it available to us, for the electricity that allowed it to be cooked, and, most importantly, for the people who sit here now, ready to enjoy this food together. Without people, we are nothing. Thank you, God."

"Amen," George said, and Kate repeated it.

"Well, let's dig in," Marilou ordered.

"Smells and looks wonderful," Kate said.

Marilou smiled at Kate's compliment. "Let's hope it tastes as good."

George stole a kiss from his wife sitting next to him. "Oh, Marilou. It always does."

Kate wasn't sure of the proper way to eat her fried chicken. She wanted to use her hands instead of the knife and fork that were provided to her but waited to see what her hosts would do. Instead, she started with the beans. Garlic-infused with a bit of a kick.

"Delicious," she couldn't help but say out loud.

"Wait until you try the chicken," George said, holding the drumstick with his left hand, ready to bite.

Kate followed suit, and the moist flesh exploded in a symphony of flavors in her mouth.

How can chicken be this good?

"I gotta have your recipe," Kate exclaimed.

"Sorry, dear. It's a secret, but you're welcome to come over anytime to enjoy it with us," Marilou said.

Kate laughed. Every bite of this meal was out of this world.

Marilou kept the conversation going. "So, George tells me your uncle is in prison?"

Kate nodded as she chewed, then said, "Yeah, I went to visit him yesterday."

"How was he?" George asked.

"Fine, I guess. Morale is pretty high, but he seems weaker, maybe a little sick or something."

George looked at her with inquisitive eyes. "Do you know about..." He stopped the words in their tracks.

Kate stared at him, wide-eyed. "About what?"

He looked down, then up. He pushed his tongue against the side of his mouth. Maybe he was thinking... or removing some food stuck between his teeth. "Nah... nothing."

Kate set her fork down. "No, you were going to say something about my uncle?"

He glanced at her again, this time, he tilted his head. "I wonder if Kenny, if all of them, have heard the news about cloning. I would imagine this would cause quite a riot in the prisons right now."

"Yeah," Kate said. "I didn't even think about that. They have TVs, so they must have heard about it."

"We'll see. I'm sure they'll talk about it again on the evening news. It seems to be the only thing they talk about."

Kate wondered what the FBI had discovered over the weekend. She hoped it was much more than what the news would cover tonight. She couldn't wait until tomorrow to find out.

CHAPTER THIRTY-NINE

Kate Murphy
Kate's Apartment, Boston

KATE'S STOMACH and hopes were still full by the time she returned home from George's house.

She had confirmed that her best course of action would be to follow the FBI's goals, to track down the cloning operation, and hope like hell they would find some records that would once and for all tell the world that her uncle was innocent. She hadn't liked seeing him so frail in prison. He may have put on a show to make her feel better, but he didn't look healthy. He didn't seem fine at all.

She changed into her pajamas, made herself a cup of peppermint tea, and sat in front of the TV, remote in hand.

"Lab-Made Humans on the Loose," was the caption at the bottom of her screen.

"How can people know for sure if they are an original or a clone?" the anchorman asked the guest, Dr. Lewisa Maple. According to the caption, she had a Ph.D. in biology and psychology and was associated with one of the Ivy League universities.

"If I understand your question correctly, you're asking if we can sense or somehow tell if we are a clone?"

"Yes. Is it possible to tell?" the anchorman pressed.

"Needless to say, no studies have ever been done on this subject," Dr. Maple said to the audience. "The original and the clone share the same DNA, so they'd look identical, but I don't think they'd share identical thoughts. Without opening up the 'Nature vs. Nurture' debate, I think it would be fair to assume that, if two identical people were placed on different spots on this earth, grew up in different areas, had different interactions with different people, they'd turn out to have different personalities. Studies have already proven that identical twins who've been separated at birth and brought up in different environments have values that vary. They may look alike, plus or minus a few scars or injuries—lost an arm or an eye in an accident, or something like that—but I'd assume they'd have the same eye color, same hair color, etc."

She paused for a moment, her index finger in the air. Dr. Maple took a sip from her glass of water before continuing. "Getting back to your original question, unless someone told them they were clones, they wouldn't know. If you're not sure if you're an original or a clone, ask your parents. That's the only advice I can offer. If your mother remembers giving birth to you, you're an original."

The anchorman let out a light laugh. "Good one, Doctor. Interesting that you bring up identical twins. Some twins say they sense something about the other. They claim they can tell if the other person is in danger or worried. Do you think it would be similar between an original and a clone?"

Dr. Maple appeared to think carefully before voicing her opinion. "Once again, we're stepping outside my area of expertise. I don't know. What you describe is ESP, and I can't say I'm a believer. Twins who supposedly connect with their sibling know about the existence of the other. In the case of cloned people, the originals don't know, and the clones may not know either."

"Let's look at the only case that's been divulged to the media.

The clone is dead, but the original is alive and well. Mr. Montague refused to be our guest tonight, but from his past comments, he didn't know he had been cloned and had no idea when his DNA would have been harvested—"

"Fuck!" Kate yelled toward the TV. "The sheriff's the leak!" Kate missed the rest of the anchor's questions.

"The DNA could have been harvested anytime," Dr. Maple answered. "Off the top of my head, let's make a list. At birth stem cells are abundant in the umbilical cord. But would someone have done that thirty years ago? Probably not. Nowadays, many people are willing to pay to have their DNA frozen and kept in a safe place, just in case. Donor clinics: from sperm banks to blood banks, many people's DNA is readily available, stored in secured, temperature-controlled environments. But really, your DNA, my DNA, everyone's DNA is all around us. On our hairbrushes, used Band-Aids, nail clippings, you name it."

The anchor seemed pensive for a moment and then said, "So, there is no way to know if and when our DNA could have been harvested?"

"Correct."

"Thank you, Dr. Maple." The anchorman turned toward the camera. "We'll be back in a few minutes with Mr. Edward Fitzgerald, editor at the *Boston Globe*, with an update on the latest letter he's received from SJC. Stay tuned."

Her phone buzzed. Caller ID read "Luke."

"Are you watching the news?" he asked.

"Yeah. Caught it a few minutes ago."

"Did you hear the mayor?"

"No, what did he say?" Kate asked.

"Not much, typical speech. The main message was not to panic and that we were not likely to meet a copy of ourselves out on the street."

"Not my biggest concern."

Luke let out a sigh. "I know. How was your day?"

"Good. Had dinner with my uncle's lawyer—Oh, it's starting

again," she said, returning her attention to the screen but keeping the phone next to her ear.

"Last week, SJC wrote about crooked politicians and the Lord's servants watching us," the anchorman reminded viewers. "It left many of us worried. And this week, another letter will be published in tomorrow's paper. We have the editor here with us tonight. Good evening, Mr. Fitzgerald."

"Good evening."

"Before we divulge the contents of the latest letter, can you tell us if the SJC signature makes any more sense this time?"

"No, we still don't have an identity. Because of the religious tone of the letter, many have speculated. The 'S' could stand for 'Shepherds,' 'Sacred,' 'Saint,' or 'Savior.' 'J' and 'C' could be 'Jesus Christ,' but we don't know. These letters could mean anything."

The interviewer pressed, "Can you tell us how this letter was delivered to you?"

"It was handwritten and mailed in an envelope with a stamp, the traditional way. It was addressed to me, personally, and this time, it was sent to my home address, which is unlisted. SJC has gone out of its way to get this information to me."

"And what did the letter say?"

"I'm afraid you'll have to get tomorrow's paper to read the full letter," the editor said.

The anchor smiled but persisted, "Any chance you can give us an idea of what it talks about?"

"Let's just say it talks about Judgment Day, the Lord Savior, and them having just begun their work."

"And the complete letter will be in tomorrow's *Boston Globe*?" the anchor asked.

Kate muted the TV and returned her attention to Luke on the phone. "Unbelievable," she said.

He sighed again on his end. "The world's officially gone crazy."

"Religious fanatics. Aren't they the most dangerous people on this planet?"

"They're up there on the list, that's for sure," Luko said.

"Anyway, I was just calling to wish you good night. I'll be dreaming of you tonight."

Kate's heart skipped a beat. "Good night, Luko. Sweet dreams."

"Good night, Kate. I... I..." he said, letting a heavy pause fill the airwaves.

Oh, no. What is he about to say? Don't voice it for the first time over the phone.

"What?" she asked, hopeful he wasn't going to say he loved her.

"Want to grab dinner with me some day this week?"

A wave of relief went through Kate's mind. "Sure, we'll play it by ear. I don't know what my schedule will be like. I'm meeting with the FBI tomorrow morning. I don't know if they'll keep me on the case or if I'll go back to patrolling."

"Okay, keep me posted. Good night, Katie."

"Good night, Luko."

She turned the volume back on to see if there was anything else worth listening to, but the channels were all regurgitating the same information.

So Juliet, Mr. C, and Mr. S are religious fanatics? Hard to believe based on how Robbie described Juliet, but he probably didn't get to know her that well.

All Kate needed now was to prove that Kenny was somehow connected to these religious fanatics. She needed records.

CHAPTER FORTY

Kate Murphy
Roxbury Police Station, Boston

"LISTEN UP, FOLKS," Agent Lack said in a booming voice, silencing the thirty or so people that crowded into the conference room.

A table stood in the middle of the space, holding a laptop computer, projector, three donut trays, a box of muffins, and two pump-action coffee dispensers. Most attendees were unknown to Kate, probably all FBI, except for Capt. Cranston, Detective Lt. Fuller, and his team of detectives. Stephany, the brown-haired female agent she'd met a few days ago, Wang, and herself were the only women present. Kate felt a little out of place—and Fuller's current gaze in her direction made it clear she didn't belong here—but Agent Lack had requested for her to be present. The door squeaked, and Kate saw Luke squeeze in just before Lack resumed.

"We've confirmed that the Ohio sheriff is our leak to the press, so we know what the media got. They'll be tracking every little detail, so keep your mouth shut. We can't afford to lose any element of surprise if we manage to pinpoint these peoples' location. And, this also applies to the severed dick in the cardinal's mouth. I've heard the giggles."

More laughs and giggles uttered around Kate.

Is that how the cardinal's body was mutilated?

She smiled. It was hard to feel bad for a pedophile, especially one in a robe.

"This detail hasn't been released to the public, and it needs to stay that way. We still don't know if it was committed by a clone or not, but it fits in nicely with the cloners' latest letter to the editor. Here's where we stand," Lack said then nodded at a short brown-haired man holding a remote.

The PowerPoint slide changed into a map of the Northeastern United States.

"The red areas are pockets that could potentially match the location of the Colony," Lack continued. "We're going through satellite pictures and eliminating as many as we can, but it's tough. We couldn't trace any past locations from Robertson's cellphone. We're going through land title records for anything that could remotely match the clone's description of the place."

He nodded again, and a new slide appeared.

"This is Juliet, or JJ, as described by the clone and rendered by the sketch artist."

Another nod, another slide.

"We had nothing in our database, but it's amazing what you can find nowadays with Google's image search. Meet Juliet Jackson," Lack said, this time showing a real picture of her. She was a beautiful woman. The sketch artist had done a great job capturing her delicate, pointy nose and her full lips. Her close-set, sultry eyes made her appear curious and sensual at the same time. Her strawberry-blonde hair looked similar to Kate's, explaining why Robbie had bonded with her in the first place.

Lack changed slides again, this time showing a picture of Juliet standing up. Their hair was similar, but their bodies were definitely on two opposite ends of the spectrum. Kate was athletic, her hips narrow; she'd never been able to fill more than a B-cup bra, while Juliet was the picture of pure, raw sex-appeal. Sensuality was oozing out of her like honey out of a comb.

Lack switched to another image of her, then another. The last photo was of her standing in a very short dress with a deep neckline. An old brick building was in the back, along with groups of young adults, books in hand.

"Harvard University, 1980," Lack continued. "Once we got her full name, we tracked down her story. A brilliant woman. Well educated, a degree in medicine, with a master's in fertility. Graduated at the top of her class."

Another nod, another slide.

"Here's what she looks like today, or at least that's the most recent picture we found. She's fifty-six years old, married to Stéphane Moissonneau, whom we believe to be Mr. S."

Another nod. This time the slide showed a man who Kate recognized based on what she'd seen the sketch artist draw, but this was a much younger version of him. He looked like a man in his mid-twenties. His hair hadn't started to bald or turn gray.

"Doctor Moissonneau was born in France. His parents immigrated to America when he was eleven. He's now fifty-four. Also a graduate of Harvard Medical. We assume that's where they met. Their marriage certificate was signed in Boston in 1981. Master's in biology and doctorate in genetics. He was involved in helping map the human genome way back in the project's early days. Doctors we spoke to thought very poorly of him. They said he'd published a research paper that discredited him as a scientist, and then he lost his medical license because of some experiment he'd done. Something related to his paper. We got a copy of that research paper, all one hundred and twenty-one pages of it," he said, holding up a thick pile of sheets clipped together by the largest paper clip Kate had ever seen.

"It's filled with gibberish and fancy medical terms I don't understand. I have no intention of reading it." He waved it in the air, then said, "Thompson or Purdy, if you can read this, be my guest."

He threw the thick report onto the table before continuing, "At the time, he was working at a university. When his peers and colleagues turned their backs on him, he disappeared from the map. Left without warning or even picking up his last paycheck.

Hasn't been seen since then. His drivers' license hasn't been renewed in decades. No credit cards in his name, but his family's filthy rich and back in France now. He's got access to plenty of money."

A nod, then the slide changed once more, this one showing the sketch artist's third representation.

"As for Mr. C, no luck so far, but we'll keep looking into the background of both JJ and Mr. S. We're hoping some dots will connect somehow. We believe he's English, but could be Australian, Irish, or god-knows-what."

Lack brought a cup of coffee to his mouth, sipped, smacked his lips, and exhaled loudly before continuing his brief.

He nodded again to request the next slide. "I'm sure all of you have read or heard about the editorial letters in the *Boston Globe*. If you haven't read the latest one yet, here it is."

The PowerPoint slide now displayed the letter:

If you've misused your power, misled others, or accepted bribes to promote a misguided soul's evil plans, it's time to repent of your sins. Judgment Day is coming.

We're among the crowd. We're watching. We're ready to act. We've only just begun. Once we clear out the trash in this part of the country, we'll move on to another part, then another.

We will not harm those who pursue their true path, those who respect and model our Lord Savior. But we are following His orders and have created our army. We're ready to wipe the world clean of all evils.

You know who you are, and we're watching you.

Get ready for Judgment Day.
- SJC

After a minute of silence, Agent Lack continued. "Both letters were signed SJC, and so far the public seems to believe the signature to be religious in some way, but it's pretty clear the initials stand for Stéphane, Juliet, and some male name starting with a C. Makes it freaking difficult to find. Let the crowd believe it's Saint Jesus Christ or whatever. Fine by me. Any questions so far?" Lack asked.

Kate looked around. Most agents were also scanning the room with their eyes and remaining otherwise motionless, except for Luke. He slid between agents, approached the table, then took the thick report. "I'll have a read. I speak genetics."

"And you are?" Lack asked.

Before Luke could even open his mouth, the gray-headed, bearded man she'd seen with Luke before answered. "He's the DNA lab supervisor. I asked him to join us. He knows more about the topic than Purdy and me combined."

"What he said," Luke said, smiling at Lack.

"Fine. This information is on a strict need-to-know basis, but if you can make sense of this crap, give me a summary in plain English."

"Will do," Luke said before retreating to the back of the room with the report.

An agent directed a question at Lack. "How did you get a recent picture of her but not him? Are we sure they're still married?"

Lack responded, "Yes, as far as we know. She seems to be the public one. I suspect that, even at her age, she has her ways of getting information out of men." Muffled giggles rumbled across the room. "She must be the one who travels to and from the Colony to take out money, pick up supplies, whatever they don't have access to there."

"When was she last seen?" another person asked.

"Her most recent picture was from a fundraiser, about six months ago. Waterfront, here in Boston." Lack turned his attention to the man holding the remote. "Lockheart, could you bring that image up? It should be saved in the same folder." He waited for a few seconds, then continued once the fundraiser picture appeared on the wall behind him. "We've put out a

BOLO on her, so we can surveil her and hopefully follow her back to their Colony."

"Do they own any land?" yet another asked.

"We checked. Nothing under these names, but who's to say they don't use other names?" Lack replied. "We're going to send these pictures out to various law enforcement agencies throughout the Northeast to see if anyone recognizes them. One of them has to have seen her. And they'd remember her for sure."

"What about Robertson, the clone? Where is he now?" Kate asked.

"We had to let the fucker go. Nobody pressed charges, and we had no legal grounds to hold him or force him to go through the DNA tests we wanted to run. But we've got two guys surveilling him as we speak, and, Murphy, you'll go and join them as soon as we break here, just in case he goes split-bonkers-latent on us. If he does, he may save us hours'—if not days'—worth of research when he starts talking again."

"Yes, sir." Kate hadn't done much surveilling, but it'd certainly beat patrolling. She was looking forward to hanging out with FBI detectives. "How do I get ahold of your guys?"

"Lamoureux here will fill you in," Lack said, nodding his chin toward a thick-chested, grumpy-looking man across the room from her. Kate's eyes met his for a brief nod.

"How about DNA harvesting. What do we know?" another agent asked.

Lack shook his head. "Nothing."

"How many originals do we have that were cloned for sure?" someone else asked.

"Four. What we know about them is on the wall in the next conference room." He took a deep breath and then continued. "We tried to find a commonality among them, but couldn't. We moved on to pinpoint the location of the Colony instead. Feel free to dig up more dirt. It's worse than the proverbial needle in the haystack."

Another man spoke up: "The picture of her, six months ago,

did we ask the organizer of that fundraiser? He must have her contact info if she was invited."

"We checked and were told she wasn't invited. She crashed the party," Lack said, looking behind him at the picture that was still up.

"Senator Russell is in that picture," Kate said. "I bet he's got Juliet's contact info. Probably not where his secretary or wife could find it, but maybe on his phone?"

Lack nodded thoughtfully. "Worth a shot. Hardwell, follow up on that."

"How about future victims?" Capt. Cranston asked. "Any thoughts on who will be next?"

"Fuck," Lack said with a laugh. "Show me a politician who isn't crooked, and I'll shit my pants right here, right now. Every freaking power-hungry guy in this town is probably on these crazy bastards' list. I don't mean any disrespect, Captain Cranston, but there's no way your team can protect them. The list is just too fucking long: judges, mayors, senators, CEOs, priests... who knows who else? If these people have bloody shit on their shoes, they have to watch their backs."

Agent Lack reached for a donut on the table and bit into it. The room remained quiet for a few seconds longer. Probably sensing everyone's eyes watching him chew, he looked up. "Get to work," he said, his mouth half-full, his hand waving them out of the room.

Kate headed to meet Lamoureux, but he raised his index finger, making her stop a couple of feet away from him. He pulled out his phone, flipped it open, and then dialed a number.

"Where are you? Sending the bait over."

"The bait?" Kate asked, lifting a brow.

"That's your role," Lamoureux said. He pulled out his notepad, scribbled something, then ripped out a page. "They're sitting in a black Ford Taurus, near this intersection."

He handed her the paper.

"What if they move before I get there?"

"Better hurry."

Kate hesitated for a second before asking, "Could you write down the number you just called?"

He shook his head, let out an annoyed breath, then grabbed the piece of paper out of Kate's hand. He added a series of numbers without checking his phone, and then returned the paper to Kate.

"Thanks," she said, hurrying out of the room. She was pretty sure the numbers he wrote were just random ones from the top of his head to appease her.

Jackass.

Luke was waiting for her by the door at the back of the room.

"Gotta run. Talk later," she said, not even feigning a smile. She was still annoyed at Lamoureux and his more-than-likely fake number.

Luke's only reply was, "Okay," with a disappointed look in his eyes.

Fuck.

No time to worry if she had hurt his feelings, somehow, again. He knew how busy she was. He'd heard the same stuff she'd heard. There wasn't a second to waste.

Kate ran downstairs to grab a set of patrol car keys but found that all of them had been checked out. "Where are the other keys?" she asked the shift supervisor.

"They're being maintained."

"I need a ride."

"Capt. Cranston took you off patrols for the week. I don't have an extra car for you."

"Fuck! Can you radio for a pick-up here? Please? I need to get to Winthrop."

"Ooh la la, pretty Murphy is playing detective and needs a ride," a voice said behind her.

Kate spun around and saw Smitty mocking her.

"Smitty, what's wrong with you?" she asked, annoyed. "The FBI asshole is already fucking with me. If I don't get there soon, I'll be led down a rabbit hole. They hate me even more than you could possibly despise me right this second."

The sergeant stared at her for a couple of seconds, looked at

Smitty, then reached down to the radio behind him. "Unit 4, swing by the station for a pick-up. Front door."

A few seconds later, an affirmative response was heard.

"Thanks, Sergeant. I appreciate it," Kate said.

She hurried to the front door. No way she was going to miss this one and have to beg for another pick-up.

CHAPTER FORTY-ONE

Luke O'Brien
DNA Laboratory, Maynard, MA

LUKE RETURNED TO HIS LAB, thick research paper securely locked in his briefcase.

He was annoyed at the way Kate had ignored him earlier this morning. She hadn't even taken the time to smile at him or touch his hand.

Nothing.

Maybe it was the stress of the situation.

Maybe she doesn't like public displays of affection.

Whatever.

One day he'd figure her out. But for now, he had to focus his energy on the paper at hand: *Reproductive cloning in primates: resetting the nucleus without damaging the spindle protein.*

The idea both excited and repulsed him. Through his Ph.D. research, he'd read up on the subject. And now, because of Kate and this cloning case, he had spent even more time investigating where science stood and how it could have leaped from science-fiction into reality.

The spindle protein problem only mattered for primates, so it affected humans. Cloning Dolly in 1996 hadn't involved dealing with this issue, so this 2002 paper was certainly ahead of its time, considering Snuppy the dog was cloned in 2005. A religious sect and Korean scientists had proclaimed they'd successfully cloned humans in the late 1990s and early 2000s, but none of these assertions had been proven. As far as the world knew, human cloning was not an option.

But these three crazy people showed us we were wrong!

He poured himself a strong cup of coffee, got a notepad and a pen, and then closed his office door. This was going to be fascinating, to say the least.

BY 8 P.M., Luke had gone through the entire paper and felt like he needed to take a shower, both physically and mentally.

Dr. S. was a mad scientist, albeit a very clever one.

Luke couldn't help but think of him as Frankenstein. He wondered where he'd conducted all of his experiments. His paper had been thoroughly researched, well-written. Based on the evidence and tests he claimed to have performed, Dr. S had solved the problems dealing with the spindle protein and resetting the DNA in adult primate cells.

While reading the report, Luke had handwritten notes that he could pass on to the FBI. He took out his laptop to type them up, so the agent in charge could understand what he wrote.

Summary of Dr. Moissonneau's paper

- Cells harvested for human cloning are somatic cells (i.e., every cell EXCEPT sperm and eggs) thereby eliminating sperm banks as a possible source of DNA harvesting. Blood, skin tissue, organs, and other sources of DNA are all valid. Dr. Moissonneau mostly used fully-grown adult **blood cells** in his research, although adult **skin cells** were also used.

- Human cloning requires an ovum, so unfertilized female

human eggs are required. Frozen egg clinics may be a target for the cloners as they would need a lot of unfertilized eggs. The DNA from those eggs would NOT match the clone's DNA, so it would be impossible to trace.

- In addition to the donor's DNA and a female egg, a female uterus would also be required, where the fused cell would be implanted until maturity. A large number of women would be needed as surrogate mothers (missing women? volunteers?), or they could have perfected an artificial uterus (technically challenging, but not insurmountable for someone with money and enough intelligence to clone human cells).

- The somatic cell nuclear transfer process discussed in the paper is very detailed, and irrelevant to this case unless you want to replicate it. It involves:

A- Retrieving a somatic cell from the "donor" (male or female).

B- Resetting the genetic information contained in the donor cell to an embryonic state.

C- Removing the nucleus from the egg.

D- Inserting the nucleus from the donor into the egg and fusing the two using electrical current and advanced techniques. This results in a cell very similar to a freshly fertilized egg, except that the DNA only comes from the donor. None of the mother's egg remains.

E- Implanting the fused cell into a surrogate mother and waiting for it to mature, as a normally fertilized egg would.

Dr. Moissonneau's research paper discussed how to enable the fusion of human adult cells, and how he reset their genetic information to return to the embryonic state. The closest proven technique was done in 1997, where another primate, a rhesus monkey, had been cloned but from embryonic cells, not from an adult monkey. If you need more information, I recommend following up with the scientists involved in the 1997 monkey cloning process or the 2014 mass-production of cloned pigs in China.

The following is speculation only: Dr. Moissonneau was likely discredited because he couldn't demonstrate the new type of dye he had supposedly discovered that wouldn't damage the cell and that helped him identify and remove the egg's nucleus without removing the spindle proteins (without these proteins, cells can't divide, so cloning would fail).

LUKE PRINTED a copy of his notes, reread them aloud to make sure they were written in plain English—or at least as plain as he could make them without losing the gist of what the paper was about.

The clock indicated 9:40 p.m. already, so he took out his phone to see if he had missed any calls. Not one. Not even from Kate. He wondered what she was doing right now.

Should I call her?

Nah, she's probably busy or exhausted like I am.

Luke took the FBI biologist's business card out of his wallet and dialed his number.

"Hi, Dr. Purdy?"

"Yes, speaking."

"This is Luke O'Brien from the crime lab."

"Yes, have you found something?"

"I guess. The paper may help narrow down the search as to what type of cells were harvested for cloning. I can fill you in on the technical details tomorrow when we meet, but I thought I'd send you my notes and you can decide if you want to send them to Agent Lack tonight."

"That's wonderful."

"May I email them to you at the address on your card?"

"Yes, please. That'd be perfect."

"Will do. Call me back if you don't get it within five minutes."

Luke hung up, emailed the file, locked up the lab, and then headed home for a well-deserved shower.

CHAPTER FORTY-TWO

Christopher Kirk
The Colony

CHRISTOPHER SLID OPEN the patio door and walked into the farmhouse, his boots plastered with wet mud.

"Smells like freshly brewed coffee," he said.

"Just made it. Take your filthy boots off," Stéphane said from across the room. "Juliet washed the floor this morning, and she won't be pleased."

Stéphane then saw the green camouflage bag Christopher had brought back and walked over to him to get it.

"What do you have in there?" Stéphane asked, smiling.

"Four dead rabbits, skinned, gutted, and quartered." Christopher handed him the bag. "Ready for your magical hands. That should be plenty for our celebratory dinner tonight. I may even get No. 4 to join us."

Stéphane rolled his eyes. "You know that'd be weird."

"Fine, I'll just bring her leftovers once we're done."

Now bootless, Christopher ambled over to the granite counter to pour himself a cup of coffee. He sipped it, and then backtracked on their conversation.

"Weird my arse. It was Juliet's wish to clone ourselves in the first place. Not my fault she can't stand seeing her younger self."

"What about knowing what you do to her younger self? How would you feel seeing yourself at the table?"

"It'd be the dog's bollocks. I'd joke with myself. I'd be my own best mate. Can you imagine? We could split our tasks amongst our twins. I could spend all day hunting, eating, and fucking. My No. 1 could do the weapons and martial arts training. No. 2 could dispose of the corpses. No. 3 could update and supervise training programs. What would No. 4 do...? Let me think..." He let his thoughts trail but remembered it was pointless. "Too bad our genes didn't take. Did you ever figure out why?"

"*Non*," Stéphane said. "Still hovering around a ten percent success rate. Cloning is more complicated than becoming a Master Chef. It's unpredictable. Random errors occur with individual genes, which reminds me: I forgot to drain the dead ones today."

"Nah. Don't worry," Christopher said, standing up and resting his empty coffee mug on the counter. "Cook dinner. I'll take care of those before they contaminate the system. I'll grab wine on my way back. What do you reckon would go nicely with rabbit?"

"See if we have any of the *Château Fond Cyprès* left. It was so delicious last time. Perfect match. If not, go for a Syrah or whatever tickles your fancy."

"Where's JJ?" Christopher asked.

"I don't know. Probably down there, doing whatever she does."

Christopher headed toward the elevator to go to the Incubator.

As Stéphane had suspected, JJ was around, either in there or up in the master bedroom. Her stupid classical music was humming along, resonating through the room. She needed it to ground herself, she'd said.

Fucking crazy is what it was.

Before stepping amongst the plethora of throbbing wombs,

he looked at the display: A dozen or so lights were flashing amber. These were the ones he'd have to drain now. At least they hadn't turned red just yet, so the system was still uncontaminated.

He got dressed in the waterproof overalls hanging by the door, then put on a pair of rubber boots and thick black rubber gloves that covered most of his arms. He hefted the bulky wrench that leaned across the door frame and headed into the Incubator, walking toward the first amber light he saw: the third pod to his left. The display showed the clone's name and age: Frank Saggs, 544 days. Christopher had gotten used to the conversion after all these years: about eighteen months.

The tosser will be heavy, nearly two stones.

He pressed the red stop button on the display, then closed two valves above the pod: the red one to cut off the blood supply, and the yellow one to stop the embryonic fluid intake. He bent down and closed the blue valve to disconnect the blood drainage line from the pod. He grabbed his wrench and loosened the drainage pipe connection, a smelly, slightly yellowish embryonic liquid oozed out, flowing through the metal grid and landing on the subfloor with a loud swooshing sound.

He waited until most of it had drained, then knelt underneath the pod, his shoulders supporting the weight of the dead fetus. He manually unscrewed the rest of the threads, until the nine-inch bolt came loose and landed in his hands. He pulled out the connection and stretched out the rubbery material that made up the artificial uterus wide enough so gravity could do the rest. The kid-sized slimy fetus landed, lifeless, at his feet.

What killed him? Heart defect? I'll never know.

He followed the umbilical cord that still connected the corpse to the pod, and yanked on it, detaching the placenta from the rubbery exterior. A loud sucking sound resonated in the room before a gross pile of membrane joined the dead fetus on the floor next to him. Doing his best to ignore the nasty smell, Christopher bunched the rubbery uterus material again until he could squeeze it back into the connection, and re-screwed the nut back on, then the hose.

Christopher got up and headed to the console, carefully avoiding the dead body and gooey membrane, as these things were slippery as hell. He lifted the safety cover, and then pressed the button that opened up the floor underneath the pod. The body and tissues made a loud thumping noise as they hit the subfloor.

He waited until the surface pneumatically returned to its position and the safety clips re-appeared below the edges before stepping on it and using his wrench to reconnect the bottom. After opening a black valve underneath the pod, then another black valve above it, he allowed the cleaning fluid to work its magic.

After sixty seconds, he closed both valves and opened two white ones to rinse and drain the pod. Another thirty seconds then he was done with this one. He deleted the identity from the database and changed the unit's status to "Empty," which turned off the flashing amber light and lit up a blue one.

Taking his hefty tool with him, he stepped over to the nearest amber light. Juliet Jackson, 350 days.

No. 6. Now, that's a shame!

He repeated the process and, two hours later, all fourteen amber lights had turned to blue. He was glad to be done, his shoulders a little stiff and his gut no longer able to stand the stench.

Christopher headed back out toward the entrance, but took off the rubber boots and gloves and hung them upside down on the rack just by the door. He then removed his overalls and hung them on another rack, and then put on a pair of flip-flops before stepping to the side to turn on the water.

He'd only forgotten to do that once, and the smell from his gear the following morning had been enough to teach him a valuable lesson: that shit stank like hell if he didn't clean it up. So he did. They had a good set up, though. It didn't feel like he was doing a bird's job. It felt closer to cleaning a vehicle in a carwash. All he had to do was flip a switch to change between rinse and soapy water and just aim the pistol at his gear.

Voilà! Done!

It would drain and dry overnight, and then it would be good to go for tomorrow.

Time for a drink.

Wearing his flip-flops, he crossed the Incubator again to reach the other end of the house, where JJ and Stéphane's bedroom was, but also where the wine cellar was located. As he opened the door, the music got louder, JJ was in there, somewhere.

"Hey JJ," he yelled.

The music stopped. He repeated his greeting.

"What do you want?" Juliet's voice asked from above.

"Just picking up wine for tonight."

He heard footsteps above his head, coming toward the staircase.

"Did you catch anything?" she asked, peeking above the rail, her blonde hair hanging down.

"Rabbits. Stéphane's cooking them as we speak."

"Lovely," she said. "Need help with the wine?"

"Should be all right. I'll get a couple of *Château Fond* Something."

Christopher stepped toward the cellar entrance, but he'd only taken two steps before she spoke again.

"No, we're out of that one," she said. "I'll come down and pick one for you."

She started descending the stairs while Christopher savored every second of her saucy approach toward him. First, her bubble-gum colored furry sandals appeared on the top steps, then her long legs descended, followed by some matching silk fabric dragging behind her like a cape. The pink baby-doll gown she wore soon came into view; it was barely long enough to reach her thighs, so he regretted not having stayed by the stairs as he was willing to bet she didn't have panties on. Her waist and huge knockers appeared next, gently bouncing with every step she took. She was already drinking, carrying a glass of red wine with her.

She smiled at him. "I'm sure we'll find something else that will pair just fine."

He let her lead the way and inhaled her jasmine scent as she passed by him.

"Draining?" she asked.

"Yeah, is the stench still on me?"

"A little."

"What were you doing up there?"

She shifted her eyes suggestively. "Reading. You should try that sometimes. It's good for stress relief."

"I've got a more effective remedy for that," he said, grabbing his junk.

She shook her head. "Chris, you've still got one of them?"

"Yeah, No. 4 is young and healthy... for now."

Juliet bent down and pulled one of the wine bottles out of the rack, then pushed it back in.

He knelt next to her and watched her repeat the process for a few more bottles.

"I wonder..." He stared at her, not bothering to finish his sentence.

She turned her attention to him, their faces inches apart. "What?"

He slid his finger along her shoulder underneath the silky robe. "I wonder if you feel it when I touch her, just like I used to touch you." He moved his finger to the light freckles on her cleavage. "When I fuck her, when I make her come—"

"Stop it," she swatted his hand away.

"Don't you miss it?"

"No, I don't miss it, and I don't feel it." She stood up, bottle in hand. "Take this one."

Instead of joining her motion and standing up, he stayed on his knees and placed his hands firmly on her hips, which were now perfectly positioned for him. With his index fingers, he lifted the smooth, silky fabric up to her waist.

No panties. Just as I suspected.

A tiny strip of trimmed strawberry blonde hair greeted him.

"Chris, no."

"For old times' sake."

He clutched a handful of her arse. *Still firm.*

319

"Stéphane could come in any minute," she growled at him.

"Not a chance. He's busy cooking us a nice meal."

He traced the contours of her pussy with his fingers, then began licking her delicate skin. She tasted good, even better than he remembered.

"No, we shouldn't," she said, gently pushing him away from her.

Christopher got up and stood just inches from her before whispering in her ear, "Why the fuck not? It's not like being married to Stéphane has made the two of you exclusive. Intelligence gathering or not. You and I, it's been what... twelve years? Twelve years of build up? You want it, too," he said, his fingers reaching down to touch her pussy again. "You're wet already."

He pushed her against the old wooden table that occupied the cellar.

"You stink," she said half-heartedly.

"Get over it."

Her sultry eyes locked onto his and she reached down to undo his belt, her breathing getting heavier by the second. He unzipped his pants, and she tugged at his engorged dick.

BACK IN HIS ROOM, with No. 4 resting on the bed as she always did, Christopher hopped into his en-suite shower.

He would have liked to have lingered in JJ's scent—it had felt good to get the real thing for once—but he needed to rid himself of the awful embryonic odor. He'd have to instruct No. 4 to update her grooming style to match JJ's latest pubic do. He lathered himself with pine-scented soap and smiled. He'd made her come twice, all the while her stupid husband was cooking them dinner. Christopher would be willing to bet he was a much better lover than Stéphane was. Probably had a bigger knob than the gormless Frenchman, too.

"Bollocks," he said aloud, turning off the water.

"What's up, Christopher?" No. 4 asked.

"Nothing. Go back to sleep. Read a book or something."

He'd forgotten the damn wine down there.

Nah, it'll be okay.

He could go and get it now, on his way to dinner. Stéphane would still be clueless, so Christopher got dressed in a pair of worn-out combat pants and a clean T-shirt. "I'll bring you back a tasty meal later," he told No. 4 before closing the door behind him.

He turned down the hall and headed back to the kitchen.

"What took you so long?" Stéphane asked when he saw him.

"Spilled some of that nasty liquid on myself. Took a shower."

"I mean down there. How many were there?"

"Fourteen total."

Stéphane looked at the clock on the wall. "Still. Three hours? That was slow. Did you have problems with one of the pods?"

"A few tight connections, you know. Typical stuff."

Christopher knew the computer recorded everything for each pod: pressure sensors on each of the supply and drain lines, timestamps on all of his actions. Stéphane could look it all up and figure something went amiss. He'd taken too long down there after the last pod was drained and cleared.

"Spent a while cleaning my gear," Christopher added. "You know how bad and sticky that mess is. A couple of fetuses were almost ready to come out. Some of it got into my overalls. Bloody awful smell."

Stéphane shook his head. "That's a shame, losing them when they're so close to being ready."

"Yeah."

"Where's the wine?"

"Oh, I forgot." Christopher stood up. "I'll go get it now. You said *Château Fond* what?"

"*Château Fond Cyprès.*"

"I'll be back in a minute."

"Tell JJ dinner's ready."

"Will do."

As Christopher walked out toward the elevator, he sensed

Stéphane's gaze on his back. *Nah.* His story held up. He had nothing to worry about.

He headed down the elevator, through the control room and the Incubator and back to where he was a few minutes earlier. Classical music was still playing in the background.

"JJ, dinner's ready."

"What?" The music stopped.

"Dinner's ready. I forgot to grab the wine."

"Okay, I'll be right there," she said.

Christopher walked into the cellar and immediately recognized the smell that lingered in the air.

He'd have to get rid of the odor before Stéphane came in here. He went over to the table and saw a wet spot where she'd sat after both of them came all over the place. Christopher hadn't worried about getting her pregnant. She was in her fifties, after all. Their bodily fluids had mixed and leaked out onto the wooden table, leaving that unmistakable smell in the air.

He removed the blood-stained handkerchief he kept in his pocket, normally used to wipe off his blade. He dabbed all he could, then stuffed it back in his pants. He procured the bottle she'd picked earlier, looked for another one with the same label and walked back across the Incubator.

He checked his gear by the control room entrance; it was mostly dry. He set the bottles aside, hid his handkerchief into one of his boots, and brought his gear back into the room, next to two other sets of overalls, gloves, and boots.

With wine in hand and evidence of his crime tucked away, he returned to the kitchen.

"No more of that Château Fond Cyprès, but this should do," Christopher said.

Stéphane looked at the bottles. "*Ah oui. Très bon choix,*" he said, complimenting his selection.

Christopher opened up the first of the two bottles and poured it into the decanter Stéphane had brought to the table. Stéphane had taken the time to set the table for three and had even placed fresh wildflowers in a vase.

"Looks good," Christopher said.

"Thanks. We've got lots to celebrate tonight," Stéphane said as he brought a bowl of tossed green salad to the middle of the table. "Turn on the TV, will you?" he asked.

Christopher did, then he sat down with the remote in hand. It was exactly 6:00 p.m., and the opening music ended as the camera zoomed onto the anchorwoman with the luscious lips.

"Another day, another murder. Zach Woodhams, former CEO of Mason Communications Inc., a Fortune 500 company, was found dead in his Boston apartment earlier today. Police declared the death suspicious but did not provide any other information. Viewers may recall a previous news story we aired on Mr. Woodhams four months ago when he had fired an employee due to his religious beliefs. Shortly after that, another dozen employees were let go for religious or ethnic reasons, and Mr. Woodhams was then forced to resign, with a hefty departure bonus."

"And now, there's a little less racism and religious discrimination in the world!" Stéphane said, bringing Christopher a flute of chilled Belgian beer. "Something to drink while the wine breathes. Who knows how long Juliet will take."

"I told her dinner was ready."

"Women. You know how they are. She may need another thirty minutes."

Stéphane joined Christopher at the dinner table, waiting for their next minute of fame.

At 6:25 p.m., the news anchor interrupted the sports guy mid-sentence through a listing of baseball scores. The camera zoomed onto her as she brought a finger to her ear.

"And this just in. Another murder in Boston. This time, in the Public Garden. A body was found just minutes ago by an out-of-town tourist. We take you live to the scene, with Alice Hawkridge."

On the screen, a brunette now stood in the park, microphone in hand.

"Alice, tell us what you know."

"Well, Catherine, we don't know the identity of the victim, but I have Mr. Hervé Comptois here with me. He's the French-

Canadian man who discovered the body." She turned to him. "Mr. Comptois, how did you find the victim?" she asked, bringing the oversized microphone close to the bald man's mouth.

"I was lost. I need directions, so I walk to the man I see on the bench. I say 'Mister, Mister,' and he doesn't say anything. His eyes are closed."

"What did you do next?"

"I tap him on his shoulder. I think maybe he's sleeping?"

"And then?" the reported prompted.

"He falls on his side, on the bench, and then I see blood behind him on the bench, and under the bench, in the ground. I yell, 'Police, police,' and lots of people come. One man calls on his cellular phone, and then the police come."

"Thank you, Mr. Comptois." The reporter faced the camera again before summarizing the situation. "This is all we know at the moment, Catherine. As you can see behind me, the police have closed off an area of the park, and they're running their investigation."

"Did the police make an official statement?"

"No, not yet, but I'll be here to report it when they do."

"Thank you, Alice."

"And here's to two!" Christopher said, raising his nearly empty beer glass in the air before gulping down the last swallow.

He poured himself some wine.

"I can't wait to hear how they'll describe this tosser. Once they identify him, they'll find lots of dirt..." Christopher shook his head and exhaled loudly as one of his childhood memories flashed in his mind. The emotional wound that his fat, pale-skinned, ginger-headed, perverted neighbor had inflicted decades ago hadn't healed. Probably never would. "Who knows how many kids' lives we've just changed today. I'll gladly kill each and every child-abusing wanker on this planet with my own hands. If only I..." He filed his negative thoughts away. It was time to celebrate. "Wine?" he asked, looking at his French colleague.

Stéphane brought his glass closer to the decanter, then repeated with JJ's glass just as she entered the dining room.

"What took you so long?" Stéphane asked.

She walked over and kissed him.

"I took a nap, and it messed up my hair, so I showered. Had to blow-dry it and get pretty again, just for you, dear."

She sat down and picked up her wine glass. "What did I miss?"

"Two down, three to go. Yours haven't been announced yet," Christopher said.

Stéphane had gotten up and was now behind the stove, taking the pot out of the oven. The delicious smell of sage, onion, and slow-cooked rabbit intensified. He dished out large servings of the stew and handed out slices of bread to everyone.

"As always, you outdid yourself, *chéri*," JJ said.

"Hard to mess up fresh meat like this," Stéphane replied. "*Merci*, Christopher." He raised his glass toward him before taking another sip of wine.

The weather forecast was next, and Christopher turned his attention to the telly again. *Plenty of sunny days ahead.*

"I'll get the trainees to butcher one of the cows tomorrow, so better get the freezer ready. We could all eat a good steak on the barbecue. Looks like the weather will work for us."

"Who else are we waiting for tonight?" JJ asked, her attention still on the screen.

Christopher wasn't sure if she was avoiding his gaze.

Probably. Hunky-dory.

He felt a little guilty, but below the surface stirred another emotion, which he didn't want to identify just yet. He missed the start of Stéphane's sentence, too absorbed in his thoughts.

"...the judge who granted corporations the right to patent DNA from food and genes, and the top lobbyist for oil exploration in the Arctic."

"Aren't these a little all over the place?" JJ asked.

"That's the idea, sweetie. Isn't it? We want *all* of them to rethink their actions. Not just those who disrespect the environment and give cancer to thousands of innocent people, like your Aunt Anne. We'll start to get national coverage. It's not like there's only one group that's messed up."

Christopher chimed in, "I'm really proud of Gonzo, whatever his name is. That job with the pedophile cardinal yesterday was ace, and he didn't get caught. We'll have to give him another task before it's too late."

"How about the pretty girl with the senator?" JJ asked.

Christopher checked the date on his watch. "That's tomorrow, right?" he asked, looking at Stéphane for confirmation.

"Yeah, the boat christening is tomorrow."

"He'll step up his security after tonight," JJ said.

"Yeah, but he won't be able to resist her fun bags and tight arse. Unless he's interested in a dark three-way with one of his bodyguards, she'll manage. Or maybe he's got a female security detail? That would be something." Christopher smiled, and Stéphane grinned right back.

Stéphane opened up the second bottle of wine, and they moved to the living room. "You want to bring her some rabbit stew?" he asked, his chin pointing up toward Christopher's bedroom.

Christopher had forgotten about No. 4 for a moment. She was probably sleeping or watching porn, as she'd been programmed to do.

"Sure, I'll take some up now."

Stéphane poured a generous serving of stew and grabbed two buttered slices of bread. He also served a small glass of wine and placed everything on a tray before handing it to Christopher.

"Wine?" Christopher asked.

"She has to drink something, doesn't she? Might as well taste good."

Christopher went upstairs and placed the serving tray on the floor to free his hands so he could turn the doorknob. He could hear the television through the door. She was "studying." He smiled.

When he opened the door, she was sitting in bed, butt naked, legs spread wide open toward the door. One hand squeezing her right breast, the other busy fingering herself.

"Looking good," he said.

She took her hands off herself.

"No. Continue. Please," he said, curtsying.

He went to the corner of his room and placed the tray on his "writing desk." *That's a misnomer.* It had been the dining room table for his cloned bitches and a solid sex prop with a suitable height. Maybe twice in ten years had it served its intended purpose.

He sat on the chair, unzipped his pants, and enjoyed seeing No. 4 finish herself off.

CHAPTER FORTY-THREE

Kate Murphy
Somewhere in East Boston, MA

IT WAS Kate's second day in the black Ford Taurus with Agents Palmer and Rodriguez. With yesterday's record five murders, everyone—at both the BPD and FBI levels—desperately needed to catch a break with this case. The mayor was on their asses, the public was on edge, and the FBI agents who were sitting in front of Kate had already voiced their discontentment with surveilling a useless clone when they could be better used doing something else.

Anything else.

"Isn't this the most exciting time of your life? This guy still isn't doing anything," Palmer said. He moved a box toward Kate in the slot between the two front seats. "Donut?"

"Sure," she said, grabbing a honey-covered treat.

Robertson had been having coffee by himself in the café two hundred yards in front of them for ninety minutes now.

"This guy's so freaking boring to watch," Palmer continued.

"Hey," Rodriguez interrupted, peering through binoculars. "He's on the move. He's going to the register... Taking out his wallet... Talking to the waitress... Heading out." He put the binoculars down and started the car.

Kate could see Robertson clearly now: he was coming out of the coffee shop and heading down the sidewalk, away from them.

Is this Robert or Robbie? Probably Robert.

Their target was walking fast and about to disappear from their view. Rodriguez re-entered traffic and turned onto the street where Robertson had vanished.

"Here," Palmer said, pointing to an empty spot reserved for deliveries.

Rodriguez pulled over and turned off his engine.

"Should we follow him on foot?" Kate asked.

"No, two days ago, he left in a vehicle, and we lost him for a little while. We're staying in the car."

"Don't you want to see what he's up to?"

"This is the same as yesterday morning before you joined us. Coffee, then bank," Rodriguez said, pointing to the building Robertson was about to enter. "Don't worry; we'll be back to the coffee shop shortly."

Kate had started to understand how the FBI agents felt.

"I followed him in there yesterday," Palmer said, looking back at Kate. "He accessed a safety box."

"What was in it?" she asked.

"Not sure. He left empty-handed. We got a warrant, but the box was empty when we checked."

Palmer reached for his phone and hit a speed dial button.

"He's back at the bank. We may want someone to surveil the bank 24/7. The deposit box could be a drop-off for money, instructions, weapons, something... Yeah." Palmer hung up.

"Let's just hope he's not going to sit on a bench and feed birds for three hours again," Rodriguez said, still looking through his binoculars.

Twenty minutes later, Robertson exited the bank. Nothing in hand. He headed down the same sidewalk, farther away from them, and continued for a full block before Rodriguez started the car and moved closer.

Robertson kept walking then brought a phone to his ear.

"Murphy! Maybe now's our lucky break," Rodriguez said, excited for the first time today.

Kate took out her phone, hoping it would ring any second now, but it stayed as silent as the latest murder victims. Robertson was calling someone else.

Shit.

CHAPTER FORTY-FOUR

Juliet Jackson
Somewhere in Rural Massachusetts

AFTER STARING at static electricity warning stickers for a couple of minutes, Juliet returned the fuel nozzle to the gas pump holder. Her phone rang in her purse, and she walked away. She didn't believe cellphones posed real explosion risks but didn't want to earn a Darwin Award finding out she was wrong either.

She answered on the fourth ring. "Hello?"

"Juliet?"

"Yes. Robbie?"

"Yes, it's me."

"You found the new phone and my note?" she asked.

"Yes, of course," Robbie said flatly. "How else would I have your number?"

"We know you were at a police station in Boston. Are you still there?"

"No."

"Are they listening to you now?" Juliet asked.

"No. I found this phone and your number yesterday, in my safety deposit box. They can't be tracking it."

"Are you being followed?"

After a short pause, Robbie said, "No, I don't think so."

"Mr. C isn't pleased with you at all. What happened?"

"I... I realized what I was about to do, and I didn't want to. It felt wrong, so I stopped."

Juliet shook her head, mostly annoyed but also understanding. "Are you still taking your meds?"

"No, I stopped. They were making me dizzy and sleepy."

Juliet let out a sigh. "Robbie, you know you need to take those, or your mind goes a little woo-woo. You remember what Mr. S said? 'There's only one of you.' These pills keep it that way."

Juliet paused, but Robbie didn't say anything. "Where are you now? I'll bring you a refill."

"I'm in East Boston," he said.

"I'm about an hour away. Meet me at our regular coffee shop?"

"Yes," he said breathlessly. "I miss you, Juliet. I can't wait to see you."

She hung up.

What did he get himself into this time?

She wasn't even sure why Robbie was still alive. Normally, when clones failed their mission—or when they showed the slightest hint of weakness—that was the end of them. No ifs, ands, or buts. He should have become prey in a final exam or Stéphane should have triggered the self-destruct mechanism.

Maybe her boys had made an exception and protected him because they knew how much she cared for him?

But the police haven't found our operation. At least not yet. Robbie didn't tell them that much, right? Or is it just a matter of time?

Phone back in her purse, she entered the station, and then paid cash for her gas, as usual.

She saw Sheriff Mullinger pulling in as she headed back to her Jeep. He parked his patrol car by the pump, behind her vehicle.

Is this it? Is he going to arrest me?

They made eye contact. Juliet nodded, the sheriff nodded back. He was a nice man; he kept to himself and didn't ask questions. They'd met many times over the past decade. He'd even asked her out once, but she'd turned him down, gently. Toying with the local law enforcement's heart would have been a bad move on her part.

She looked into her rearview mirror as she drove off, making sure nothing had changed. The sheriff didn't pursue her. He was standing by his car, filling up his tank.

Even cops need gas, no way around it.

Robbie hasn't spilled the beans on our identities, at least not yet.

The road bent, and she lost visuals. Worries that Robbie had already said too much evaporated.

She glanced at the clock on her dash. Stéphane and Christopher would wonder what was taking her so long.

Whatever.

They'd chosen to lock themselves onto that acreage and had elected her the sole errand-runner.

Their decision.

But she knew she had to do what needed to be done.

Robbie was like a son to her, but he was also their biggest liability. For the plan to work, and for the greater good, she had to do what needed to be done, even if it would break her heart.

She'd hopefully find out what Robbie had leaked to the cops before taking care of him, for good.

CHAPTER FORTY-FIVE

Christopher Kirk
The Colony

IT WAS LUNCHTIME, and Christopher was hungry. He'd looked left, right, and center, but Stéphane was nowhere to be found. There was no food in the fridge, either. At least nothing Christopher wanted to eat.

Where the fuck is he?

Stéphane normally cooked them lunch at 11:30 a.m., but Christopher hadn't seen him for hours, which was a little odd. However, he could be busy with medical duties. That'd happened before.

It wouldn't hurt to at least go downstairs to check up on things and see how many amber lights were flashing. He could drain a few dead fetuses before they contaminated the system.

Maybe that's where Stéphane is.

He headed down. When the elevator doors opened, he was greeted by silence. No music. JJ wasn't around either. The board was flashing, indicating that eleven pods needed to be drained.

Bollocks. Might as well do it now.

Christopher snatched the set of men's overalls and rubber boots closest to him. Both he and Stéphane wore the same size, and they cleaned it each time, so it didn't matter which gear he wore.

He was dressed and ready to go in the Incubator, wrench in hand, when he remembered the handkerchief he'd left in his boots the evening before. He really should bring it back to his room before Stéphane found it. He backtracked to the shoe rack, then dug down the first of the men's boot. *Nothing.*

The other. *Nothing.*

Weird.

Had he placed it in JJ's smaller boots instead?

He checked those as well. *Empty.*

He took off his boots, pretty sure he'd have felt a lump if the handkerchief was in one of them, but he needed to double-check.

Holy fucking wanker. It's gone.

His primal instincts were telling him that something was wrong. Something was very wrong. And his intuition had *never* misled him. In his army days, it'd pulled him out of explosion range before unknown grenades had blown; it'd made him zigzag for no reason when hidden mines had to be avoided.

And where was JJ right now? He hadn't seen her either since this morning.

Fuck, Stéphane found out.

He'd found the handkerchief, then confronted her, and she spilled the beans.

Fuck. Fuck. Holy fucking wanker.

Stéphane wasn't a blood-thirsty, cold-blooded trained killer like Christopher was, but the Frenchman was surely mad in his own way. Stéphane was in a league of his own when it came to intricate, delicate assassination strategies.

Christopher had stepped over a line he shouldn't have crossed. JJ was more than just pussy to Stéphane. And there was a history there. Had this repeat notch in Christopher's belt been the straw that broke the Frenchman's back?

Stéphane was the cook here; he was also their doctor. Without wasting time planning anything as complicated as he'd seen him conjure up before, he could easily poison both him and JJ. And they wouldn't know it until it was too fucking late.

Did he kill JJ already? Is he out there right now, disposing of her body?

He stood motionless for a minute, trying to make sense of it.

No, that can't be. He loves her. He probably won't forgive her, definitely won't forgive me, but he won't kill her...

But what if...

Christopher ran across the Incubator, reaching the Supervisor's Control Room in record time. A startled C35 greeted him as he stormed into the room.

C34 must be off sleeping.

"Have you seen Mr. S?"

"Today?"

"Yeah, to-fucking-day. When was the last time you saw him?"

"Around eight or nine hours ago, Mr. C. There was an injury at the playground. Then he left. Do you need the exact time?" he asked, taking the logbook in front of him, ready to flip to that entry.

"No."

Christopher moved his attention to the security cameras, hoping to see Stéphane in one of them. He paid particular attention to the fenced-off area.

He could be in there, disposing of her body.

But no. Nothing.

"Is everything all right, Mr. C?" C35 asked.

"Yeah, call me if you see him or JJ."

"Will do, Mr. C."

Christopher ran across the Incubator, took off his cleaning gear and put his combat boots back on. He then walked through the kitchen and up to his bedroom.

"No. 4, wake up," he said, approaching the bed.

No reaction.

He placed his hand on her shoulder, about to shake her awake when the temperature of her skin stopped him. He rolled her over. No. 4's eyes were wide open.

Christopher knew better than to check for a pulse. The only thing he didn't know was if she'd died of natural causes or if

Stéphane had tested out his poison—meant for him and JJ—on his sex clone.

Fuck!

Christopher picked up his gun and his favorite knife then opened the drawer where he kept his fake passports. He hadn't used them in ages. After checking the expiration dates to find one that was still valid, he grabbed it, along with the stash of money he'd hidden in the back of his writing desk and a little black book filled with usernames and passwords.

I'm not sticking around here to find out. Fuck you, Stéphane.

He ran out the patio door, toward the garage. The Jeep was gone, but the old F-150 they used for driving lessons was still there, keys in the ignition.

Is JJ just out running errands? Am I just imagining things?

His gut was broadcasting an alarm signal that he couldn't ignore. Christopher was no longer certain that Stéphane would murder them both, but like an animal sensing the arrival of a hurricane, he knew danger was at his doorstep, and he had to get away. Now.

He put the pedal to the metal and headed the fuck out of the Colony.

CHAPTER FORTY-SIX

Kate Murphy
Somewhere in East Boston, MA

KATE SAW Robert hang up and return the phone to his pocket, feeling useless in the backseat of the FBI's surveillance car.

A few minutes later, the radio screeched.

"...All units. Got a report from a nearby sheriff, JJ's been spotted near Southbridge; she's heading East on Highway 90, driving a silver Jeep. May be headed toward Boston. Two unmarked vehicles have been dispatched to surveil and pursue. Do not attempt arrest. If seen, report her location. We want to follow her back to the Colony. I repeat, do not attempt arrest."

Palmer took out his cellphone and dialed a number. "She may be heading out to meet Robertson. He was on the phone with someone just a few minutes before the dispatch... Sure... We'll keep an eye on him."

After Palmer hung up, Kate returned her attention to Robertson, who sat on a park bench, looking toward a small wooded area away from the street.

"Here you go... feeding fucking squirrels again," Rodriguez said.

After giving food to the local wildlife for forty minutes, Robertson returned to the coffee shop.

That's when Rodriguez spoke up and reported having spotted her. Hard to miss. She wore large sunglasses, but her strawberry-blonde hair and long legs were dead giveaways. She'd parked along the street, a few spots down, and was now heading to the coffee shop where Robertson sat.

Palmer got on the phone. "We have a visual on JJ; she's meeting Robertson as we speak... What about the plate on the Jeep?... Will do." He then turned to Rodriguez and said, "Plate's registered to a man from Chicopee. They're paying him a visit as we speak."

Rodriguez pulled out his binoculars again. "They're in line... Approaching counter... Ordering... He's looking for a table... She's picking up two coffees, heading to the sugar and cream station... Whoa! She's got a small vial... Pouring it into a cup—"

"Alcohol?" Palmer asked.

"No. Powder I think."

Palmer squinted, trying to see without binoculars. "Both cups?" he asked Rodriguez.

"Just one... Stirring, adding milk, sugar... Walking... Sitting down... He gets the spiked coffee."

Palmer took out his phone. "Palmer again. Listen, she sat down with him and looks like she's spiked his coffee. Do we intervene? ... Sure? ... Okay."

He hung up and faced Rodriguez. "We stay put."

Robertson and JJ talked, talked, then talked some more. She finally stood up, hugged him, and then left the coffee shop. He followed her outside, a few steps behind. Kate could only assume that she'd requested it to be that way. She couldn't see his facial expression from afar, but his slumped posture compared to how he'd usually held himself while they'd surveilled him spoke volumes.

JJ returned to her vehicle, and he stood still, staring at the street in front of him, looking right then left. He finally headed back the way he'd arrived, toward the park.

"Are we following him or her?" Rodriguez asked.

Palmer took out his phone yet again. "They're going their separate ways. Which are we following? ... Okay." He hung up and turned to face Kate. "Murphy, get out. Follow Robertson on foot. We'll follow her."

"You got it," Kate said.

She stepped out, closed the door, and then they drove off. The Jeep was already in traffic when Rodriguez slid their car behind JJ's, a dozen vehicles between them.

Kate took a second to stretch her legs, which felt good after spending so many hours crammed in the back seat. She saw Robertson ahead of her by about two blocks. She joined the pedestrian traffic and headed in the same direction. The streetlight changed, and Kate caught up to him while he stood at a corner, waiting for another light to change.

Standing just a short distance behind Robert on the sidewalk, Kate pondered what to do. Should she slow down and walk at an awkward pace? Or should she stop and pretend to look at a store's window to increase the space between them?

Before she could pick an option, Robertson collapsed, so she ran to him and knelt by his side.

"Robbie, can you hear me?"

He's grunting. No, he's trying to breathe, convulsing.

She moved his body onto its side, in case he was going to puke. "Breathe, okay? Concentrate on your breathing. I'll get some help," Kate said.

She picked up her phone and dialed 911 for an ambulance. As she finished giving her location, Robert's eyes met hers.

No, not Robert.

It was Robbie's soft blue eyes that were staring at her.

He squeezed Kate's hand and said, "Help me, JJ..."

The pressure from his fingers dissipated seconds later, his eyes loosely locked onto the far distant sky. He exhaled one last time. Kate placed two fingers on his neck, checking for a pulse, but found nothing.

He was gone.

A light breeze made his hair twitch, but his chest was no longer rising and dropping, his muscles no longer responding.

An autopsy would likely confirm he'd been poisoned. Was there a point in attempting resuscitation? Kate didn't base his right to live on whether he was a clone or an original. She'd learned to care about Robbie, and wanted to help him, but she'd seen how fast the poison had acted. Giving him mouth-to-mouth resuscitation would endanger her. That poison had acted fast as hell. Whatever amount was still on his lips from the coffee could kill her in minutes.

His eyes staring at the sky reminded her of her parents' eyes decades ago, when she'd found them in the bloody kitchen. Painful memories flooded over her. She looked at him one last time. He appeared more peaceful now; the world's worries no longer weighing on his shoulders. Her hand reached toward his face, and she lowered his eyelids.

A small crowd had gathered around the two of them on the sidewalk, but she didn't care. The FBI agents had witnessed the crime being committed at the coffee shop minutes earlier. Trying to rush over there to retrieve a fingerprint from a tiny container in a garbage can no longer felt important. There were three reliable eyewitnesses and the autopsy would determine the chemical composition of the poison JJ had used.

The ambulance arrived, along with a police cruiser. Kate made her statement and then hitched a ride back to the station.

Unable to stop herself, she wiped away a single tear.

KATE RETURNED to the second floor, ready to report to Agent Lack. She found him in conference room three. He and Fuller were staring at the maps she'd seen earlier. Very little was left unmarked. They'd made great progress narrowing down the Colony's location.

"So, Robertson's dead?" Lack asked, even though he already knew the answer.

"Yeah. Are they still on JJ's tail?" Kate asked.

"Heading west on Highway 90. Who knows how far she'll drive. We should be able to pinpoint the Colony's location in an hour or two, assuming she doesn't see us trailing her. But I'm not worried. My guys aren't wet behind the ears. They know how to do their job."

"Is there anything I can do?" Kate asked Fuller, knowing he was technically the one she should be reporting to.

He sneered at her. "There's always paperwork to be done. You can start with these reports." He handed Kate a thick pile of forms.

"Actually, no," Lack said, taking the papers back from her hands. "If you don't mind, Detective, I think it'd be better if she helped us with something else."

Fuller raised his shoulders, and Lack gave her a different pile.

"Those are Robertson's interview transcripts," Lack started. "The contractor flagged a few inaudible parts. You were there for most of it. Listen to the recording again, and fill in the blanks, if you would?"

Kate scanned the conference room, trying to find a spot to sit down.

"Best if you find a quieter room. You won't be able to work in here," Lack said.

"You're right."

Kate left the room with her new assignment. It was going to take hours. Long, boring hours. But she took solace in the fact that she was doing her small part in a federal case that could finally help free her uncle... hopefully.

She went to the lunchroom to grab a coffee, and walked around the floor for a little while, hunting for a quiet spot. FBI agents had taken over the entire floor, except for one of the interview rooms. She let herself into the observation booth. Empty, small, and cozy. Perfect for the task at hand.

Kate started at the beginning of the recording, but then realized she didn't have to listen to the whole thing, just the flagged bits where the transcriber hadn't been able to understand the words. Her additions wouldn't make it into official transcripts but could be handy in court. She flipped through the sheets until she reached the first flag, and then fast-forwarded the recording to reach the appropriate section. She played it once, then again, and again.

After the fourth attempt, she rewound it to get more context, and once she heard it another time, she managed to fill in the first blank. She repeated the process about a dozen times more, until she took care of the last blank.

She collected her things, reordered the pages and stared into the empty interrogation room in front of her, reliving the past few days in her head.

Robbie hadn't been a bad person. Many of the murder victims the Colony had targeted had been much worse human beings. Maybe the Colony had somehow incarnated karma? These pedophiles and corrupt politicians had it coming. However, innocent people like Kenny, Samuel Forrester, and the other wrongly accused had suffered and had seen their reputation destroyed for something they didn't do, and that, Kate could not forgive.

These three mad scientists had granted themselves the power to create life, and to end it, totally disregarding the innocent people they framed in the process.

"Hey, Wallflower. Murphy," a voice took her out of her increasingly angry ponderation.

Kate turned toward the door and saw Rosebud's brown eyes locked on her behind his thick black-framed glasses.

"Hey, what's up?"

"Still helping the Feds?" he asked.

"I guess, but I think I'm done."

"This case has gone fucking crazy. Did you hear the latest?"

"What?" she asked.

"That senator Robertson told us he was about to kill. Remember him?"

"Senator Russell?"

"Yeah," Rosebud said, nodding. "Apparently the job got done this afternoon."

"Robertson couldn't have done it; he's dead."

"Dead? Didn't know. But a woman's our main suspect. How did Robertson die?"

"Poisoned."

"Crazy world. Still can't wrap my mind around this fucking cloning situation. Don't know if I should feel bad for a dead clone or bad for their evil victims with all of the nasty shit they did to others. Anyway, I'm taking off. Going to the pub with Wang and the others. Wanna join us for a beer?"

That idea sounded awesome right about now.

"You guys going to be there long?" she asked.

"Don't know. A few beers, unless all hell breaks loose."

"Sounds good," she said with a smile. "See you there."

FIFTEEN MINUTES LATER, updated transcripts back in Agent Lack's hands, and with her official dismissal off of the FBI case, Kate walked into the Pleasant Pheasant.

She was surprised when Detective Fuller approached her, two beers in hand and a neutral expression on his face. It wasn't a smile, but it was definitely better than his regular look. She took it as a semi-seal of approval or something to that effect.

He handed her one of the beers.

"Listen, good work, Wallflower. The Feds are on their asses. Just a handful of farms to pick from now. They'll find them tonight."

"That's great news."

"Well, I only wish they would have allowed us to stick around to see the resolution of the case, but whatever. Not our jurisdiction. At least—"

Kate heard Rosebud call out her name and she turned around. He was pointing at an empty chair between him and Wang. Kate wanted to hear more from Fuller, learn what the FBI had uncovered since she last spoke to Lack, but Fuller changed topics.

"I'm not much for chitchat," he said. "Go and join them, but I just wanted to say that if you want to apply again to be a detective, I'll write a recommendation letter for you."

Kate was taken aback. Surprise and pride made her heart pound in her chest. "Thank you, Detective," she said.

Fuller walked away, leaving Kate with an irrepressible smile on her face. She took out her phone and texted Luke, inviting him to join them at the pub.

CHAPTER FORTY-SEVEN

Agent Cameron Lack, FBI
Roxbury Police Station, Boston

CAMERON LACK GOT off the phone and addressed the dozen of agents who stood around him in the conference room. "We've got them," he said, allowing himself to smile briefly.

The room filled with claps and loud cheers, which attracted a few straggling FBI agents back into the room. Once the group's excitement receded, Lack turned to the map behind him and circled the Colony's location.

"This is where Juliet turned off," he said. "Rodriguez and Palmer are standing by a few miles down the road. We don't know how many clones they have in there, but it could be in the hundreds, so our two agents will not go in on their own." Lack turned to Peterson. "Can you get a SWAT team organized and deployed in a couple of hours?" he asked him.

"Sure. That shouldn't be a problem," Peterson said.

"Then make it happen," Lack ordered before returning his attention to the map. "We'll need to use the element of surprise, but we don't know how their buildings are set up. Robertson said the clones were kept underground most of the time. Maybe this entire section between the house and the farm buildings is developed underground," he said, once again circling an area in the blowup aerial photograph. "It could even be larger than that. We may have thousands of acres to cover. There could be tunnels or multiple floors. We don't know what security measures they have in place either. Rodriguez said a couple of guard dogs barked at their car when they drove by."

Cameron closed his eyes for a second and brought his hand to his face, moving it down across his cheeks, feeling the strong stubble that had grown out.

"Clark," Lack said. "Now that we know the exact location, see if we have previous aerial views of the site. There could be images of the underground structure being built. Who knows?"

Clark nodded and headed out.

"Lamoureux," Lack said, making eye contact with him. "Go help Peterson and brief the SWAT team leader. Make sure they have tranquilizing darts to take care of those dogs and have a small reconnaissance unit look at those buildings first. Be mindful of security cameras or alarm systems and disable them if possible. We need to cover all potential exits if we want to catch them. Once they report back on the structures, we'll helicopter the team in and raid the place. Our number one priority is to catch JJ, Mr. S, and Mr. C. Number two is to capture all evidence of cloning: computers, blood samples, you name it. The team can't just barge in there and destroy everything. The clones themselves will be our third priority. Any questions?" he asked, addressing the entire room.

Silence was his only answer.

A COUPLE OF HOURS LATER, the SWAT team leader was on his way to the Colony.

Agent Lockheart had hooked up the feed from the SWAT team leader's camera to the television screen in the conference room and had just finished testing the audio, as well. The television wouldn't relay the communication between the SWAT leader and his team, only the private feed between the team leader and the temporary FBI headquarters at the BPD station.

"Agent Croft, this is Agent Lack. Can you hear me?"

"Loud and clear," Croft said.

"What did the reconnaissance unit uncover?"

After a few seconds of static mixed with various sounds one could expect from a flying helicopter, Croft's voice became clear again. "The woman and her husband are in the house. No visible sign of Mr. C. Four dogs have been taken care of. No alarm systems. A few cameras, but none close to the main house. There's a trapdoor hidden underneath a tractor in one of the farm buildings."

"Good," Lack said. "What's your plan of attack?"

"The house will be our initial target," Croft said, his voice once again partly masked by a layer of white noise. "We've located three entrance points. The helicopters will drop us off two miles west of the house. We'll proceed on foot to maintain the element of surprise. We'll explore the underground area once we clear the house."

"Sounds good. We'll be watching you," Lack said before correcting himself. He had no idea what Croft looked like. The screen only showed the inside of the helicopter. "Or at least we'll be watching what you're looking at. Good luck."

AFTER RELAYING BORING images for over an hour, the SWAT team leader's camera finally showed something exciting. The farmhouse was about two hundred feet ahead. The building was lit from the outside with a bright lamppost. It was a two-story structure, recently built or renovated in a modern style.

As the men approached, Lack could see a few silhouettes peeling off from the group.

Probably on their way to surround the building.

A few minutes later, the team leader was close enough for his camera to relay images of JJ and Mr. S. arguing in a kitchen. A large stainless steel fridge was in the background. No curtains protected their privacy. Plates and glasses were being thrown around.

At least they're not paying attention to what's going on outside their house right now.

"Lack," Croft's voice crackled. "We're going in."

"Go ahead," Lack replied, anxious to see if Mr. C was in there as well.

Over the next minute, the leader ran toward the house, making it difficult to focus on the images he was broadcasting without becoming nauseated.

Two minutes later, the team had cuffed the couple and were proceeding to search the rest of the house. Lack wished he could have been there in person to see the expression on their faces or hear what they had to say. He'd have to wait until the team reported back to find out.

About five minutes of a televised house tour later, Croft radioed back in, "A dead woman was found in a bedroom. I'm heading upstairs so you can get a visual."

Twenty seconds later, a half-naked woman akin to a younger JJ appeared on-screen.

Looks like they cloned themselves as well.

"We found expired passports from various countries on the desk here," Croft said, walking toward it.

"Fantastic," Lack said when he realized the photos matched the drawing produced by the sketch artist for Mr. C. "Bag those, please."

Finally making progress on figuring out his identity.

"No sign of Mr. C, but we found the entrance to the underground level. I'm heading there now."

Lack's excitement grew with each step the team leader took, but Lack wasn't prepared for what the camera displayed once Croft exited the elevator.

The control room was impressive. However, it was nothing compared to the extensive space he walked into next. It was filled with semi-transparent blobs with wires and tubes protruding out of them. It was straight out of a science-fiction movie. Lack couldn't even see the walls limiting the room. He had to pinch himself, close his eyes, and reopen them a second later to confirm he wasn't dreaming.

"Are you watching this?" Croft asked in an incredulous voice.

"Yeah," was all Lack could muster. He had no other words.

No noise could be heard in the conference room as Croft explored the rest of the cloning incubation area; his images obviously surprised every one of the FBI agents that stood around with Lack. Other SWAT team members appeared in front of Croft's camera at times, making it a little easier for Lack to believe he was staring at live footage.

Ten minutes later, reality having sunk in a little more, Lack asked Croft, "Where are the clones themselves? Was there another level accessible from the elevator?"

"No, only kitchen and this level, but hold on," Croft said before going silent. "One agent reported seeing a door out of this room. I'm on my way. Maybe that's where the clones are kept."

"Good."

Croft's camera relayed more and more of the growing clones in their semi-transparent blobs.

How many eggs do they have in there?

Man, some of them are huge! They look as big as my nephew, Teddy, and he's two years old!

"I'm at the door," Croft's voice chimed in again. "It's locked from this side; it makes sense that the clones would be on the other side, unable to escape. Just got a report that there's another door as well, unlocked."

"Go to the unlocked one first. Maybe Mr. C is there," Lack ordered.

"Roger that."

A few minutes later, the stream of images from the incubation area was gone. Now, Croft was broadcasting another section of the house. Upstairs was a large bedroom, a luxurious bathroom, and a den. A spacious wine cellar occupied the lower floor.

"Whoa," Lamoureux said out loud, surprising Lack. "Certainly wouldn't mind having *that* in my house."

"Nothing here. Mr. C is not in this part of the house," Croft reported.

"Maybe he's with the clones," Lack suggested. "Get that door unlocked."

"Someone spotted keys in the control room. We'll try them first before breaking the lock."

Five minutes later, Lack and everyone in the conference room finally understood the extent of the cloning situation. After having cuffed the person manning what appeared to be another control room, Croft's camera focused on the dozen of images being relayed via the live security footage airing on the console. Some of the screens were dark, but the majority displayed inconceivable images: several groups of clones were walking down the halls. Others were playing, reading, showering... They appeared to range from three to twenty years of age.

Fuck! How many are there? A thousand?

"Um," Croft started. "Do you want us to arrest them all?"

"Hold on before you storm in," Lack said. "Can you check the camera feeds and see if you can spot Mr. C?"

Ten minutes later, they had gone through three cycles of images from the control room screens. There still wasn't any sign of him.

"Okay. Go ahead. I'm ordering a bunch of buses. We'll..." Lack stopped his sentence in its tracks.

We'll what? Take them to Fenway Park for processing?

There are too many of them.

"No," Lack resumed. "Croft, lock them up in whatever rooms you find. Check every washroom, hallway or whatever space you encounter for any sign of Mr. C. We'll have to keep the clones there for now. I'm on my way."

CHAPTER FORTY-EIGHT

Months Later

Kate Murphy
George Hudson's Law Office, Boston

MINDY, the receptionist, escorted Kate and Luke to George's office. He smiled and greeted them both when they came in.

George pointed to the two chairs in front of his desk. "Please sit down."

"Did you hear anything?" Kate asked, taking a seat.

"Yes. It's looking good for Kenny, all things considered."

He shuffled through the loose pieces of paper lying on his desk and picked up a yellow sticky note.

"November 23rd is Kenny's court date. I believe we've got everything we need to release him. I've got the FBI case number and a copy of the records found on site showing that his DNA was used to create a clone in September 2006. Based on the computer files uncovered by the FBI, Kenny's blood sample was stolen, along with a bunch of others, in June 2003."

George read off of another sheet in Kenny's file. "FBI records indicate that Juliet had volunteered to help collect blood in various clinics in and around Boston. The evidence points to her having stolen small vials of these samples for her personal use."

George looked up, summarizing the rest from memory. "From the sound of it, Juliet did a few of these stints in Massachusetts and in surrounding states, enough to steal over 7,300 samples. We've got everything documented. I'm certain the judge will release him as soon as he hears the new information we have on this case. Kenny's already served almost four months and, by then, he will have served five months. But all things considered..."

What things considered? That's the second time in less than three minutes.

"What else is there to consider?" Kate interjected, annoyed. "He's innocent. He's been cloned. He's stuck in prison."

George looked at Kate, then Luke, then Kate again.

George's inquisitive eyes worried her. He tilted his head, and then finally spoke. "His health."

"What do you mean his health?" she asked.

"You don't know?" Luke asked.

"What don't I know?" Kate asked, her anger now directed at Luko.

He grabbed her hand and squeezed it. "Kenny's sick. Really sick."

"What? How would you know?"

"When I looked at—"

George interrupted Luke. "Maybe we should let Kenny announce it to Kate."

"Announce what? He's not here right now, and both of you obviously know something I don't," Kate said, standing. "Tell me. Now!"

"Your uncle's dying of cancer," George said, solemn as a pope.

"What?" Kate fell back into her seat.

"He has acute myeloid leukemia," George continued. "He found out last year, at least that's what he told me. He decided not to seek treatment. Something about how his wife suffered through chemo, and he didn't want to impose that emotional and financial burden on you. I looked into his disease after he told me, and the odds of survival aren't great, especially for the elderly."

Kate blinked a dozen times, and then finally remembered to breathe. She couldn't believe Kenny had kept this a secret from her.

She turned to Luke. "How did you find out?" she asked him.

"He gave a blood sample when they arrested him. Not sure why he didn't just do the mouth swab like most people."

Kate smiled weakly. "He's got a really bad gag reflex."

"They took a drop of blood—probably off his finger—and, out of habit from my Ph.D. research, I always look at the cells first before doing the DNA sample. Something was wrong with his blood: not enough red cells, lots of blast cells. I didn't know what disease he had exactly, but I knew it was something bad. I just assumed you knew."

She hung her head. "Well, I didn't."

The silence weighed heavily for a minute until Luke broke it.

"How long does he have to live?" he asked George.

"When I met him, after the arrest, he told me he had six to nine months max. The doctors were pretty certain he wouldn't see another winter."

"You're saying that all things—including his health—considered..." Kate prompted.

"I've requested that his case be prioritized, possibly moved to next week," George said. "The judges will consider it, but there's no guarantee they'll approve my request. One could argue that those who've already spent years in prison for a crime we now know they didn't commit could get prioritized over your uncle's case."

"Can't a judge issue a pardon to all of these people right away?"

"Everything has to be documented, and proper procedures still have to be followed."

Kate slammed her hands down. "You're telling me my uncle could die in prison while waiting for his court date? Even though we've got all the evidence needed to free him right now?"

Luke reached over and squeezed her hand. "We can't fight the system," he said. "George and everyone are doing everything they can. Kenny will make it, and he'll clear the Murphy name, just like you told me he wanted to do."

"I hope so."

"Kate, I'm sorry to ask, but there's something that has been bugging me," George started.

"What?"

"You were working on this case. Do you know if they caught the SJC scientists who were responsible?"

"They got the woman and her husband. But the mysterious Mr. C wasn't there when the FBI arrived at the Colony. I don't know if they've managed to track him down since."

"Ah."

"Why did you want to know?" she asked.

"I was hoping it would make me sleep better at night, but now I regret having asked. I don't like knowing that one of them is still out there."

CHAPTER FORTY-NINE

Weeks Later

Kate Murphy
Coastline Near Cork, Ireland

KATE TASTED the salty breeze on her lips. The Atlantic Ocean wore more or less the same shades of gray on this side of the pond, but the Irish sea somehow felt more powerful, wilder yet more mysterious and more hopeful than her secret hiking spot in Maine.

Kenny was right.

The rolling green hills of Ireland were stunning, and so was the Irish coastline. She was glad she'd finally come to see it in person, with Kenny by her side, although he'd traveled here in an ornate silver urn.

Facing the roaring ocean, Kate inhaled deeply. She was far enough so the waves couldn't reach her and drag her in, but close enough to feel the droplets splattering her face when the crashing waves exploded on the polished rocks.

She stared at the ocean for a long time before finally finding the words she'd meant to tell her uncle.

"Kenny, I'm sorry it took me so long to clear your name and

get you out of prison. I'm sorry we never had a chance to try to defeat that cancer together. I could have found the money. We could have kicked that leukemia in the balls, but I can't change the past. I respect your decision."

Kate paused, feeling tears rush to her eyes.

"I know this isn't how our visit to Ireland was supposed to be, but I'll do my best to follow your plan. I'll trace our family roots, so I can better ground myself like you said. I'll track down our extended family, my cousins, however far removed they may be. I don't know if I've ever thanked you enough for taking me in all those years ago. I know I wasn't always fun to be around. I'm sorry for that, and I'm sorry for all the mean things I may have said to you. I know I'm a bit rough around the edges at times. I never meant to hurt you or Aunt Lucy. I miss you both. I hope you're happy, free of pain, and at peace with the world now."

Kate forced a smile on her teary face. "I bet you're smiling your ass off right now. You won't have to deal with Nosy Maude ever again. Please don't go and haunt her just for the fun of it."

Large, cold rain droplets started hitting Kate's face. It was time to bid her final goodbyes.

"Kenny, I miss you. May you forever rest in peace," she said, swallowing the lump in her throat before opening the urn and scattering his ashes into the wind, one handful at a time. Kate then tilted the urn and let the entire contents escape and trail off into the wind, toward the rocks and the roaring ocean.

She closed the empty urn, wiped tears from her cheeks, and turned around to look at the small rental car she'd parked on the side of the country road.

Her veil of sadness lifted when she saw Luko, still leaning against the car door, gazing out over the rolling green fields that went for miles. This Irish excursion was a new experience for Kate: she was ready to open her heart and let new people in. Through the magic of the Internet, she'd managed to trace Julie Murphy, the cousin Kenny had told her about, and she was planning to meet her tonight at a pub an hour's drive from here.

With her boyfriend by her side and her recent promotion to homicide detective, Kate's life was looking up.

TO BE CONTINUED...

...in more police procedural mysteries/thrillers featuring Kate Murphy as she pursues her detective career in Boston.

If you'd like to read more stories from C.C. Jameson, please post a review where you bought this book. The more reviews, the faster C.C. can quit the dreaded day job and write more stories for you to read and enjoy.

Thank you for taking the time to read and review this book.

To receive regular updates and new release notifications, join C.C. Jameson's reader group by visiting this website:
http://ccjameson.com

THANK YOU

I would like to thank my family and friends for believing in me. In particular, I'd like to thank my parents who let me stay at their cottage so I could finish drafting the first published version of this book in a peaceful setting. I'd like to thank Sébastien who helped me navigate through police procedural problems and Marley and Claire, my editors, for making this story reach its full potential. My special thanks also go to Sorriso who provided me with lots of constructive criticism, and to Sara, Stephenie, and Rachael, three fantastic friends who helped me find and fix several typos in this book.

Thank you to my sisters, aunts, uncles, cousins, grandmas, and friends who listened to me going on and on about my writing dream.

And thanks to all my readers, especially those who leave a review. **You are the best!**

AUTHOR'S NOTES

I began writing this story several years ago.

If you'd like to learn more about the origin of this story please join my reader group. It's totally free, and I'll send you around two emails per month that will gradually introduce you to me as a writer and how this specific story came to be.

To thank you for joining my reader group, you'll receive the exclusive character and police files associated with the story you just read:

Join here: http://ccjameson.com

BOOK CLUB

SUGGESTED DISCUSSION TOPICS

If you choose to read this book as part of your book club, the following questions could help trigger some interesting discussions.

The themes and topics hinted at in this book are broad. I don't claim to know the answers to the following questions, but I believe their importance will only increase as technology and new discoveries could one day enable human cloning.

Who should determine someone's right to live or die?

In this book, SJC decides to cull the herd and assassinate certain people based on their own beliefs about rightful and wrongful actions.

Do you think people should decide who lives or dies? If so, who? Judges? Other authority figures? How about a group of people such as a jury?

What qualifications should be required to allow a person (or group of people) to make such decisions?

What crimes (if any) should lead to the death penalty?

Is death penalty legal in your state/province/country?

If so, what methods are used to kill the convicted? Do you

think they are humane? Do you believe wrongly accused people could end up on death row?

If the death penalty is not offered where you live, was it ever used and, if so, when was it abolished?

How do you define "life"?

While the question may seem trivial, it's not. With new medical breakthroughs and scientific discoveries, it's now possible to 3D-print new organs. What's to prevent us from 3D-printing new life one day?

When does life start? At birth? At conception?

Do you think a fetus is the same as a newborn baby in terms of living entity?

Is abortion okay? If so, under what circumstances?

Is it okay to terminate a pregnancy when certain tests are performed and parents discover that their future baby has a serious disease or deformity?

If human cloning, 3D-printing of people, or other breakthroughs happen that enable the creation of "artificially-created life," should these "artificials" have the same rights as us?

Would you fear that "artificials" could overtake the world if their genetic code or intelligence was superior to ours?

Or would you fear "artificials" could become a burden on society instead due to increased costs associated with healthcare, education, population boom, etc.?

Do you believe the current laws, regulations, and systems are sufficient to prevent scientists from exploring human cloning and other research that have ethical implications?

As a society and as an individual, where do you draw the line when playing with genetics? Is it acceptable to try to find a cure for cancer? Is it acceptable to try to extend the average lifespan?

Assuming these two things are now possible, but cost hundreds of thousands of dollars, would it be acceptable for only the wealthy to afford these genetic improvements?

Are the current laws and regulations ready to tackle topics

such as genetic improvements? For example, athletes could potentially receive transplanted organs or enhanced muscles that would improve their performance. Should such genetic improvements be allowed? And if so, do you regulate them?

Legal insemination processes currently allow future mothers to "shop" for their future baby's genetic dad based on his physical, mental, and other attributes. Based on the availability of such service, one could say that the process was deemed "socially and ethically acceptable," but what about genetically creating babies to match a desired genetic profile such as tall, blond-haired, blue-eyed, free of diseases? Is this any different? Is there an ethical dilemma now?

Should parents be allowed to pick the genetic profile of their future children?

And the list of questions doesn't end here...

To learn more or voice your concerns about ethics related to genetics and the human genome, consult these websites:

http://www.ethicsandgenetics.org/
http://www.bioethics.com/
https://www.genome.gov/
http://genetics.thetech.org/about-genetics/ethics

ABOUT THE AUTHOR

C.C. Jameson is an ex-military officer now wanderlust-driven author. Other than politically unstable countries, those with visa restrictions, or where only the wealthy can live, no place is out of bounds for the single, adventurous author.

C.C. loves spending time alone in nature, writing at home, or drinking in pubs or bars. Hobbies include listening to live music, learning new languages, reading tons of books, and making up stories for readers to enjoy.

The name C.C. Jameson was born out of two authors' imaginations while chatting at a bar somewhere in Florida. Drinking was involved, of course, because it's one of C.C.'s favorite activities and a *must* for the introverted author while in social situations. As for the C.C. part, it corresponds to the author's real first initial, but doubled because it sounded better. Plus, that's how many people refer to *Canadian Club*.

So, C.C. Jameson is not just an anonymous author's pen name, it's a drinking name, too.

Learn more at http://ccjameson.com.

facebook.com/ccjamesonauthor
twitter.com/ccjamesonauthor
bookbub.com/authors/c-c-jameson

Made in the USA
San Bernardino, CA
05 December 2019

60907317R00229